Don't Let Them Know

Know

L. K. Lawrence

DEDICATION

TO ALL THE DREAMERS, MY BROTHER NATE,
AND MY COUSIN MARCI

stands still and uses her peripheral vision to see if anyone in her line of sight seems overly interested in her. When that doesn't produce an explanation for how she feels, she slowly looks from side to side for a more expansive view. She is disappointed that no one within the library seems remotely aware she's even there. With a sigh, she shakes her head to rid it of the silly notion and takes 'The Sands of Crime,' the most recent in the cozy mystery series she is reading, back to the cubicle where she left her purse.

The cubicle is one of many that are grouped in a section of the library. Some stalls have computers the public can use, and some are just cubicles where people can sit and work or read, as Lucy chooses to do.

In the dream, still feeling the observer's eyes upon her, Lucy self-consciously—and hopes with grace—sits in the cubicle chair and attempts to read the book's first page. But she feels about as comfortable as Lucy Ricardo did when she was in the Brown Derby and William Holden watched her eat spaghetti. She fights against the feeling of being watched, and after many stops and starts, she finally completes what is usually a simple task. With that task accomplished, her curiosity forces her to search her surroundings again.

There are always many people in the library: most cubicles, tables, lounge chairs, and couches are occupied. Yet still, she feels the eyes of one specific person watching her every move.

Nervously she closes the book, then slyly looks over her left shoulder at the area behind her. No one is there. Slowly she rises and peers over the cubicle walls on each side—no one is there either. She scowls, then remembers

Chapter 1

Lucy awoke to her cry of "No!" She sat up in bed and wiped the tears that soaked her cheeks. She looked around her room as the light of the dawn was beginning to strain through her blinds. She'd had the dream again: The dream that had been haunting her sleep for weeks now.

Sniffling, she reached for a tissue from her bedside table and blew her nose before she leaned back on her pillow, chewing on her thumbnail as she relived the dream in her mind.

The dream typically started with her perusing the shelves of books at the library. Standing in front of a specific row, she searches for a book that will carry her into an imaginative world of mystery. She begins to read the cover for 'The Sands of Crime' when she feels someone watching her. She stops mid-read as her heart beats faster. The hair on the back of her neck stands on end, and her skin crawls up and down her spine. She

1

stands still and uses her peripheral vision to see if anyone in her line of sight seems overly interested in her. When that doesn't produce an explanation for how she feels, she slowly looks from side to side for a more expansive view. She is disappointed that no one within the library seems remotely aware she's even there. With a sigh, she shakes her head to rid it of the silly notion and takes 'The Sands of Crime,' the most recent in the cozy mystery series she is reading, back to the cubicle where she left her purse.

The cubicle is one of many that are grouped in a section of the library. Some stalls have computers the public can use, and some are just cubicles where people can sit and work or read, as Lucy chooses to do.

In the dream, still feeling the observer's eyes upon her, Lucy self-consciously—and hopes with grace—sits in the cubicle chair and attempts to read the book's first page. But she feels about as comfortable as Lucy Ricardo did when she was in the Brown Derby and William Holden watched her eat spaghetti. She fights against the feeling of being watched, and after many stops and starts, she finally completes what is usually a simple task. With that task accomplished, her curiosity forces her to search her surroundings again.

There are always many people in the library: most cubicles, tables, lounge chairs, and couches are occupied. Yet still, she feels the eyes of one specific person watching her every move.

Nervously she closes the book, then slyly looks over her left shoulder at the area behind her. No one is there. Slowly she rises and peers over the cubicle walls on each side—no one is there either. She scowls, then remembers that someone is watching and quickly smiles, hoping to make a good impression. Slowly she sinks back in her chair.

No one ever looks my way, she thought sullenly to herself as she took a sip of water from the glass next to her bed. Admittedly, this lack of interest in her in the dream wasn't something new. She'd accepted long ago that she wasn't the type of girl to draw men's attention—especially the older she got. Long gone were the girlish days of flirting and dating she'd enjoyed in the past.

As a single, middle-aged woman who had dated forever but never met the man of her dreams, she continued hoping one day she would find that one man who would see beyond her flaws. Perhaps he would see what her friends saw and loved about her. Until then, she had grown comfortable with the solitary life and had put the idea of true love on the back burner. But if whoever was watching her in the dream was a guy—she was pretty confident was the case at this point, and possibly a suitor, then maybe this dream was a premonition of what was to come? Lucy smiled at the thought.

Then a look of fear replaced the smile. "What if the guy is a stalker?" She asked aloud and pulled her covers up around her neck as a slight chill ran through her body at the thought.

Lucy was a fan of true crime, cold cases, cozy mysteries, or any mystery. However, she had no desire to become a cold case herself. Having a stalker would be very inconvenient and not the kind of adoration Lucy wanted. With the fear of a stalker now fixed in her mind, she was determined to see this man's face so she could avoid him.

She continued with her review of the dream. She rose slightly from her chair. Anyone watching sees only her eyes as she scans the crowd a second time. She's looking for anyone with shifty eyes, sudden movements, rope, duct tape, or anything else listed in the cold case shows she watched.

She'd seen it multiple times in the tv shows and heard it in podcasts about true crime. They stalked the person, then kidnapped 'em, tortured 'em, then killed 'em. *Wasn't that how it happened?* Lucy shook her head to get herself back to reality.

"Stop!" She said aloud in her bedroom as she raised her hands in response to her thoughts. She was headed down a rabbit hole with the stalker thoughts when it really could be a future mate. She needed to concentrate on that, she thought. "Besides," she said aloud, "I don't live a life that would attract a stalker. I don't think so anyway."

With that settled, her thoughts returned to where she'd left off in the dream: sitting at the cubicle, she takes a couple of deep breaths to refocus and dives back into the mystery. She reads about the cute, young, yet chubby heroine who blithely goes through her day working in her bakery. She has the most eligible bachelors in town, vying for her attention as she solves case after case. She loses track of time, forgetting all about the eyes that watch her.

In the dream, she's just read about the first murder when with a startled jerk of her head, she gives an involuntary shiver. Her instincts tell her to look down at the carpet, which she does. Out of the corner of her eye, she spies brown leather shoes next to the cubicle. She

4

raises her eyes to the tan slacks that accompany them. Her heart begins to race, and her breathing becomes shallow. She doesn't want the Stranger to notice his effect on her or know she's scared if he's a stalker. But, she has to see who this person is in case he's a suitor! Yet, when she tries to look up, her eyes go directly to his shoes. She tries to force her eyes to move up the pantleg with immense effort, but they won't move unless the dream allows it.

If in the dream she ever gets to the point that her eyes will move to where she's about to see the Stranger's face and find out who he is, she wakes up. It was the same every time, night after night. Some nights she made it to the waist, sometimes just to the knee, but each night she'd wake before seeing his face. Afterward, if she tried to fall asleep again, then she'd dream it again. The second time, she always experienced a strong sense of fear or dread that scared her to her bones.

As the nights wore on, the dream would morph in different areas but was generally the same. Sometimes Lucy would find the brown shoes and tan slacks to her left, across from her cubicle, behind her, or at the end of the row of books. Still, her eyes refused to move quickly enough to get to the person's face —let alone his knees—before she woke. Even when she willed them to move faster in her dream, they gave no heed to her desire but always started at the carpet and slowly, very slowly, moved up the usual route.

There were a couple of noticeable changes in the library's configuration and where the Stranger was located in tonight's dream. Instead of standing close by, the Stranger was sitting over in a lounge chair, not just watching but intensely observing her. When it came time for her to look over her shoulder at the carpet for the now-familiar brown shoes, she was surprised to see drops of blood that grew in size, leading towards the shoes. She felt the familiar sense of dread wash over her. She tried to push her eyes to move quickly to see who was bleeding. Still, her eyes moved at a snail's pace towards the chair, up one leg encased in tan slacks seated in a chair, over the knee and the ankle that rested on it. Then her eyes slowly moved toward a brown belt with a silver buckle. Then her eyes took in a light blue button-down shirt with the collar open enough so she could see the clavicle at the base of his tan, muscular neck. The more she willed them to move, the slower they moved.

In the dream, she begged her eyes to continue up to the face but only saw the very tip of his chin before they stopped. She held her breath with the hope that tonight her eyes would relinquish their control, and she'd see the rest of the face. She remained still, holding her breath, willing her eyes upward when suddenly she heard her voice and woke up. *Who was this guy? Why did he stay hidden?* She asked herself repeatedly.

As she sat in bed, she could feel the rapid beating of her heart slow to a thump. . .thump, thump. Her fears began to dissipate from the bright light of day that permeated the room. She felt confident that even though she didn't see the man's face in the chair, he was the only watcher in her dream.

She rationalized that he didn't seem as menacing when he sat in the chair as when he stood close by. *But what did the drops of blood mean? Why did he watch her? Was he a friend or foe? Why the sense of dread? Why wasn't she allowed to see his face? Was it someone she knew? Someone who acted as a friend but wanted to hurt her? Was her life in danger?* So many questions.

Only when her phone alarm went off, reminding her that she had to get to work, did she climb out of not just her thoughts but her bed.

"I've gotta get a gun," she said to no one as she stood to stretch.

Chapter 2

Lucy parked her 4Runner in the usual spot in the parking garage and crossed the street towards her office building. Her workplace was in a very secure area, and she never worried about her early arrival or being the only one there.

Still thinking about the dream, she exited the elevator onto her darkly lit floor. She pulled open the fire doors and faced the vast darkened lobby. Then, with a flick of a finger, she chased the darkness away with the incandescent light and crossed the threshold.

As she moved towards her office, the dream played in the back of her mind, like white noise as she moved behind her desk, opened her Day Planner, and looked at her schedule for the day. Sighing, she fell back into the chair while exhaustion from lack of sleep rippled over her like waves on the shore. She allowed the dream back to the forefront of her mind and ran through what she remembered of it.

She marveled at how quickly the specifics seemed to fade from her memory. No matter how hard she tried to memorize the dream after she woke, it seemed like there were always missing patches. *I've got to write down every minute detail as soon as I wake up tonight,* she scolded herself, then heard the clang of her phone alarm that alerted her to Wall Street's opening bell. Her day had begun.

It was like any other Monday: the ritual of exchanging stories about the weekend with her colleagues as they passed by her door with their morning hellos, doing trades for clients, opening accounts, and assisting the two financial advisors assigned to her. She'd almost forgotten about the dream or at least pushed it into the back of her mind until the business of work began to lull. That's when she'd ask herself, *Was this dream a code? A riddle? A forewarning? Or was it just as it portrayed itself to be, a dream?*

"Hey, you okay?" Lori, the Cashier, asked as Lucy walked by her desk at the front.

In a haze from the lack of sleep, Lucy stopped and turned toward Lori. She walked up to the counter that separated the cashier from the rest of the office and said, "It's that darn dream again. I keep having it."

Lori frowned, "Dream? What dream?" As she set her large cup of diet coke on her desk.

"You know, the one about that stranger that keeps watching me?" Lori gave Lucy a confused look. "You know . . . and I can't see his face? I've had it for weeks." Lucy continued giving her clues.

"Oooh!" Lori said, "Thaaat dream." Lori's arms

were full of the mail she'd just returned from getting.

"Yeah, thaaat dream." Lucy looked at Lori in amazement, then said, "I can't believe you didn't remember." Lori had always been a good friend to Lucy. They were polar opposites; where Lucy was tall and slender, Lori was short and chubby. Lucy dressed casually and wore flat sandals; Lori always dressed to the nines with heels, jewelry, and false eyelashes. Although Lori's hair was perfectly styled, Lucy preferred to let the natural curl in her hair prevail. Where Lucy was a patriotic conservative, Lori considered herself to be a socialist. Lucy trusted Lori always to tell her the truth.

"So, you're still having that dream? And still not seeing his face?"

"Yes, and yes!" Lucy rested her arms on the counter with a sigh.

"I'm sorry," Lori said with a sympathetic look as she dropped the large bundle of mail on her desk, careful to avoid the cup of soda. A pile fell on Bingo, her service dog, which caused him to yip.

"Why are you sorry? You aren't in the dream or hiding his face," Lucy said.

"Well, I know that. I was trying to empathize with you." Lori rolled her eyes as she began to open the mail.

Lucy watched her in silence. Lori glanced up at Lucy as she sliced open an envelope and asked, "So, what are you going to do?"

"Now?"

"Don't be obtuse," she said as she rolled her eyes. "No, about the dream? What are you going to do to find out the meaning of this dream or who this Stranger is?"

Lucy thought for a moment before she answered, "Not sure. But I'm thinking that maybe I'll start going to the library and see if he's there," Lucy raised her eyebrows in question as she looked at Lori, who laughed. "No, really," Lucy said to convince her, "I think I may start hanging out at the library and see if Mr. Tan Slacks shows up."

"Well, that might not be a bad idea," Lori shrugged her shoulders. "What if he isn't there, though? How long will you continue to camp out at the library?"

"I don't know. But what else do I have to do after work? Might as well find my stalker, ya know?" Lucy said with a chuckle.

"Your stalker? Is that what you're calling him now?" Lori asked with a chuckle. "I thought you were referring to him as "the Stranger" or "Mr. Tan Slacks"? Either of those sounds more romantic than your stalker." They both laughed.

"Stranger, stalker, Tan Slacks, whatever. Doesn't really matter until I meet him and can make an educated decision."

"And how will you do that?" Lori asked.

"By camping out at the library, hellooo?" Lucy said with a "duh" look.

"Hellooo," Lori said and heaved a sigh. "How will you know if he shows up?" Lucy shrugged her shoulders. "What if this is just a dream and no one ever shows up?" Again, Lucy only shrugged her shoulders.

"I know that I could come out of this whole thing with pie on my face, looking the fool, but . . ." Lucy's voice trailed off.

"So, you're going to sit in the library and wait for a man whose face you've never seen. A man who you've only seen up to his chin, and you don't know his name. A man who may not even exist?"

Lucy snorted with a mischievous look on her face, "Why not? What can I lose?"

"Besides wasting time?"

Lucy smiled. "I have to find out what this dream is about, who this stranger is, and why I feel this strong pull towards him."

"Could it be because you're lonely? Desperate?" Lori asked dryly.

"Oh, be quiet," Lucy said and grimaced at Lori.

"You know you're crazy," Lori called after Lucy as she walked away.

Lucy smiled to herself as she walked back to her office. It hadn't occurred to her to see if there was anything to her dream until her conversation with Lori. It was a crazy idea, but one she thought had merit and could end the mystery and the sleepless nights. But, she could tell no one about this, except for Lori. But only Lori would know about her plan. Anyone else would think she was certifiable.

Waiting for the market to close that day took every ounce of strength Lucy had. It was challenging to focus and not daydream about what might be waiting for her at the Library that night.

Now that she'd decided to camp out at the library with the hope that the Stranger would show up, she couldn't wait to put this plan into action. She hoped that the dream would go away by her doing this or that she'd understand any symbolism in it. But, whatever she would gain from going to the library to do surveillance for "him" had to be worth it.

Chapter 3

Walking towards the library, Lucy could feel her heart rapidly beat against her ribs. The closer she got, the more she began to question her decision. It was such a strange thing to do, but she was desperate to get the reoccurring dream to stop so that she could resume sleeping through the night and not wake up crying every morning.

She glimpsed her reflection in the glass door of the library and smiled. Lori would've been proud. She wanted to be presentable in case this Stranger was there. Whether this would be a love connection or end up a missing person case, Lucy didn't know, but for some reason, the desire for romance seemed more potent than the fear of being stalked. So she chose to look on the fanciful side rather than the fatal and pushed forward.

Lucy entered the library with a casualness she didn't feel but wanted to portray if the Stranger was watching. It surprised her that at her age, she could still act silly when a man was involved. *Will I ever grow up?* She asked herself. *Hopefully not*, she responded to herself.

She glanced around at all the tables sporadically placed around the library. They were being used by both kids and adults either looking at or reading books. It never ceased to surprise her that so many people still came to the library in the internet age.

Instead of meandering about, she made a beeline for the same cubicle she sat at in her dream and was pleased to find it empty. As she set her book bag down, she glanced about to see if there were any men in tan slacks; There were skirts, shorts, jeans, skorts, and all different colors except tan. *That's okay*, she reassured herself. She was not going to let anything derail her from this mission. If he were out there, it would hopefully happen if she were supposed to find him, hopefully without any shock and awe on her part. With determination, she headed towards the row of books.

Slowly she walked down the row. She looked to the right as she always did in the dream. She allowed her eyes to trail over the visible spines of each book on the shelf. She knew exactly the spot to stop and the book to pull, 'The Sands of Crime' by Jillian Bates. She had already finished multiple books in the series, and this happened to be the next one.

She scanned her immediate area for any sign of tan slacks with her finger resting on the book spine. She paused to check if she sensed anyone, but nothing happened. There was no electricity, no shiver, no feeling of being watched. It was as if the universe had flatlined. As she stood and gazed at the row of books in front of her, she reminded herself that it was okay and continued what she was doing; it was for a good cause, her love life.

With the book in hand, she returned to where she'd left her stuff. Before she sat at her cubicle, she scanned the area once more. If the Stranger was there, she was going to see his face no matter what he wore. *Did it even matter what he was wearing? Maybe the slacks were there, so he wasn't naked?* She asked herself. But no one even looked close to how she imagined the guy in her dream. Her mind told her it was a waste of time and to go home. Her gut told her to stick it out that she'd know him when she saw him.

"What could one night hurt?" She mumbled to herself, then opened the book and began to read.

She paused in her reading to take a sip from her water bottle when she realized that she'd read as far as the third chapter. Not once while she read did her skin tingle or the hair on her neck stand up from the sensation of being watched. In the dream, she had only the first page before the sense of being watched stopped her. With a scowl, she slammed the book shut.

Immediately she heard, "Shhhhh!" She heard from behind her, then felt a tap on her shoulder, "You need to be more respectful of those around you and not disturb the peace," said the coarse whisper next to her ear.

"Aah," Lucy made the involuntarily sound when she looked up into the yellowed teeth that surrounded by an over-powdered face that had uttered the coarse whisper. The watery blacklined eyes and bright red lipstick showed signs of bleeding up from the frowning lips of one of the librarians. "Baby Jane?" Lucy asked without thinking.

"What?" The librarian asked, then pursed her lips.

"Sorry," Lucy responded in a loud whisper staring at her. The librarian gave a slight nod of her head and walked away. Lucy watched her retreat, stunned by her likeness to a Bette Davis character. She turned back to the book, then looked at the face of her phone. The library would be closing in about fifteen minutes with no sign of the Stranger. She had to accept the fact that he wasn't there tonight. "This isn't going to be an easy one-night event," she sighed to herself. She rested her face in her hands while the flood gates of self-pity opened.

Lucy's imagination had worked overtime. She hoped her dream was based on real-life and not an amalgam of all the men she'd known and fantasized about in her life. She fought the disappointment that flooded her soul as she returned the book to its shelf.

This is only the first night, she reminded herself. Not everything good happens right away. She had to work at those things that were worthwhile. She would come again tomorrow night, the next night, and the next night. She would keep coming until she knew one way or the other.

Chapter 4

Lucy didn't hear Lori call her as she passed the cage. She had just turned the corner when the door to the cashier cage opened.

"Lucy! Hey! Are you okay?" Lori asked.

Lucy stopped with a surprised look on her face and asked, "What?"

"Are you okay?" Lori asked, holding the door open with her foot.

She took a deep breath as she stopped and turned towards Lori, "Yeah, I'm fine. Why?"

"You just haven't seemed yourself lately. Are you still having the dream?"

"Yeah," Lucy answered as disappointment flooded her face.

"Are you still going to the library?" Lori asked in a hushed tone.

"Yes."

"But no luck?" Lucy only shook her head. "I've got to close this door. Come back here and tell me what's been going on." Lori closed the door and waited for Lucy to appear on the other side of her counter. "Tell me what's been going on. . . please."

"Nothing. Nothing is going on. I have been going to the library night after night after night and not one sign of the Stranger. Not one second of feeling someone watching me."

"Oh, I'm so sorry," Lori said sympathetically.

Lucy sighed then said. "I have read the first page of that cozy mystery so many times that I have it memorized."

"Why don't you read the rest of the book?"

"I can't. In the dream, I'm only on the first page in the first chapter. So I want to do exactly what I do in the dream so I can get an answer or closure or-or-or even clarity."

"Well. . . I don't think you have to be so literal about it. I'm sure the Stranger, if he shows up, won't know that you've read further into the story in real life than in the dream."

Shaking her head, Lucy held up her hand and said, "No, I've gotta do it as I do it in the dream. I cannot deviate from the dream. Especially if I want to find out what it's all about," Lucy said adamantly.

"So, are you doing it the same every night? Do you wear the same clothes, hairstyle, makeup?"

"Yup, the same clothes every night. I think they could walk into the library by themselves if they wanted."

"You haven't washed them?" Lori asked, horrified.

"Of course, I've washed them. Sheesh! C'mon, that's disgusting," Lucy told her, although she hadn't washed them. She was only in them for a couple of hours each night, sitting at a table, so she didn't think she needed to clean them—besides, they didn't smell. But Lori didn't need to know that. She continued, "I want to look good for when he sees me. But I gotta admit people are starting to look at me oddly—wearing the same clothes every night."

"Maybe you should change your clothes? Wear something different," Lori suggested.

"Perhaps," Lucy said thoughtfully. "I don't know what I look like in the dream since it is from my perspective. But, you might be onto something there," Lucy said thoughtfully.

****

Lucy walked into the library and sheepishly smiled at Mrs. Gable, an older librarian who sat behind the counter on the left side of the front doors. Her demeanor was the sweetest of all the librarians. Still, it only disguised the iron needed to guard the entrance to avoid any books leaving the building without being checked out.

Mrs. Gable raised her eyebrow as she deftly tucked a strand of her short grey-streaked hair behind her ear. She watched Lucy walk past her desk in her workout shorts, tank top, and sandals. Not Lucy's typical attire. "Is everything alright, dear?" she asked with concern in her voice and a surprised look on her face.

Lucy stopped and looked at the librarian and subconsciously entwined her fingers in the ponytail that held her curly hair back from her face before responding,

"Of course. Why do you ask, Mrs. Gable?" Her mind was on the row of books that held the key to her possible love match or her stalker. Only time would tell.

"No reason. You just seem a bit, umm," the librarian searched for the correct word, "a bit more casual today than normal."

"Oh, this?" Lucy nervously waved her hand in dismissal, then mumbled something inaudible. So much so that she didn't even know what she'd said and resumed her trek to the waiting book.

This marked night number thirty-nine of her nightly stranger watch, and she'd decided this would be the last night, so she'd worn her workout clothes. She doubted whether there was a Stranger in her future.

Lucy walked over to the cubicle and set down her book bag. Although the library was a bit more crowded than usual, her cubicle was available. Leaving her book bag on the small desk, she walked to the now-familiar row of books she'd walked to the previous thirty-eight nights. Once again, she was the lone visitor between the two bookcases. Half-heartedly, she trailed her index finger along the shelf, preoccupied with ending her nightly vigil.

Each night as she headed home after no sign of the Stranger, she began to doubt her plan and to curse the hope that would rear its ugly head, the hope that had revived her wish for romance. The hope she'd trained to stay buried deep within the recesses of her soul, where she'd hidden it as time passed and love continued to elude her.

Instinctively she pulled the copy of 'The Sands of Crime' as she had done thirty-eight previous nights. Then, with the book in hand, she returned to the cubicle and began to recite the now memorized words from the first page under her breath. With the thoughts that clouded her mind, she was oblivious to the slight tingling on the back of her neck. Deftly she plucked at the corner of the page until she held it between her thumb and index finger, then as Lucy readied to turn the page, she ran her finger along the page's edge.

"Ouch!" she said as she winced and rushed the cut finger between her teeth and gently bit the hurt spot to soothe the pain that accompanied the papercut. As she sucked on her finger, she glanced at the page she'd turned to, but nothing looked familiar. She re-read the page but didn't recognize any of what was on the page. Confused, she turned to the previous page. She didn't remember that either. Frantically she began to turn all the pages until she stared in horror at the title page. She'd pulled the wrong book!

"No! No, no, no," she said to herself in frustration. She hadn't pulled 'The Sands of Crime' by Jillian Bates, but 'Murder Calling' by Sarah Forrester.

"Shhh!" An older patron said with a frown.

"Sorry," Lucy grumbled back in the patron's direction. With an aggravated groan, she dropped her head in her hand, unable to believe what she'd done. She'd pulled the wrong book. *How'd that happen?* She asked herself. She was sure that she'd gone down the correct row. As she jumped to her feet, her chair loudly banged against the empty chair from the cubicle next to hers.

A patron in another cubicle leaned back on his chair,

with a scowl on his face, said, "Would you please keep it down!" But before Lucy could respond, the poor, grumpy patron was bombarded with multiple requests from other patrons at the library for him to keep it down.

Lucy giggled as she quickly walked over to the row that she'd pulled the book from only moments before. She was sure she'd gone to the correct shelf. She worried that she'd messed everything up for the night because of picking the wrong book.

Lucy stood in front of the familiar shelf blinking in disbelief; there on the shelf, as plain as day, was the title 'The Sands of Crime' in the same space she had returned it to the night before. She walked to the end of the row around to the other side with a confused look on her face to look for the Forrester mysteries; she found them on the bottom shelf. *It doesn't make any sense*, Lucy thought to herself. She would have noticed crouching down to get the book today. Deep in thought, she walked back to the location of 'The Sands of Crime.' *Maybe someone had accidentally misplaced the Forrester mystery in the Bates section*, she thought to herself. But, when standing in front of the Jillian Bates mysteries, she was eye-level with them and could not see any empty spaces where a book might have been.

As Lucy stood mystified at the situation, she slowly became aware of a tingle up her spine and the tiny hairs on her neck that began to stand up. Someone was watching her!

Chapter 5

"Lori, Lori, Lori, Lori, Lori, Lor—" Lucy stood in front of the counter, barely able to contain her excitement.

Lori handled all the investment checks that client's mailed in or dropped off for deposit into their accounts.

"What?!" Lori said with mock aggravation. "What do you want, ya weirdo?" Lori said, then laughed.

Lucy was way too excited to care whether she interrupted Lori's work or not; she had to tell her the news. "Guess what?"

"What?" Lori asked, looking at Lucy over her pink leopard-designed glasses.

Lucy gave a tight-lipped smile as she tried to contain her excitement, then said, "I felt someone watching me last night!" She shook her arms in excitement.

Surprised, Lori took off her glasses and, with a smile, said, "You did? Really?"

Lucy nodded her head emphatically, "Yes!"

"Remember to use your inside voice," Lori teased her. "Not everyone in the office wants to hear about your skin tingling." Lucy quietly danced and pantomimed her excitement instead.

"Now, tell me e-ver-y-thing," Lori emphasized each syllable as she set her work aside and rested her chin in her hands, and waited expectantly.

"I-I-It was nothing like what I thought it should be," Lucy began to explain. "I didn't wear the same clothes or-or-or fix my hair, noth--" Lucy began to stutter in her excitement to tell Lori her good news.

"Slow down," Lori calmly interrupted. "You don't need to speed through. I've completed all the deposits, so I have time. Unless you're worried, you might get a client call before you can tell me everything."

Lucy shook her head, inhaled, and began, "I felt someone watching me last night!"

"Did you see his face? Did you see the tan slacks and shoes?"

"No. Not at all."

Confused, Lori said, "But you felt the eyes on you."

"Yes, and it was totally unexpected."

"Unexpected? You've been going to the library for over a month for that specific purpose," Lori stated as she squinted her eyes in confusion. "How could it be unexpected?"

Lucy explained, "It was unexpected because I didn't do anything to make myself presentable. I wore my workout clothes; my hair was in a ponytail and not a speck of makeup. I only went because I wanted to finish out the week and then forget about the whole idea. I hadn't felt anything until last night."

"So, are you going back tonight then to see if he

materializes?"

Lucy laughed, unable to stop the light blush that covered her face, "Yeah. This time I'll be prepared."

Squinting her eyes, Lori asked, "What do you mean you'll be prepared?"

"I won't be in my sweats," Lucy said smugly.

"Oooh, so you're gonna get all dolled up again?"

"I don't know that *dolled up* is the word, but I won't be in my sweats; I can promise you that," she said assuredly.

"Okay," Lori said as she raised her eyebrows while looking down at her desk.

Chapter 6

That evening as Lucy readied herself for, what she hoped, would be a very lucrative night at the library, she couldn't help but smile as she looked at her reflection in the full-length mirror. She could see that her workouts and keto diet for the past seven months was paying off. For the first time in a long time, she felt attractive and confident. And she didn't mind the idea that someone might be watching her. Yet, she still didn't know if he was a friend or foe.

Lucy walked into the library and turned toward the row of cubicles she'd occupied for the past thirty-nine nights and stopped cold. All the cubicles were in use. In the cubicle she usually inhabited was a transient with her life possessions laid about her. It looked as though she had settled in for the winter. Lucy paused to decide how best to proceed, then, with a great exhale of air, headed towards a table with only one occupant.

"What else will happen to derail tonight?" she mumbled to herself as she set down her bag.

"I'm sorry? Were you talking to me?" The occupant

of the table did a double-take.

Lucy shook her head dismissively. "Is this spot taken?" Lucy asked in a loud whisper.

"No, please," the male occupant said as he motioned with his hand for her to take the seat.

"Thanks." Lucy quietly pulled the chair out and sat down, but not before she noticed his rugged attractiveness. *Was he laughing at her?* Lucy asked herself when she saw the suppressed smile on his face as he returned to his reading. *Did she look silly in her attire? Was something on her face, and he was too big a jerk to tell her?* Lucy felt herself get heated at these thoughts, then caught herself. *Relax*, she thought to herself.

"You have got to get out more," she told herself as she set her water bottle on the table and placed her bag on the floor next to her chair.

"What?" her handsome tablemate asked as he looked over at her.

"No-n-nothing, s-sorry," Lucy stuttered as she felt her face heat up from the slate blue eyes that seemed to pierce her soul. *Now he probably thinks I'm crazy for talking to myself—and aloud, no less*, she mumbled.

"Were you talking to me?"

"No." Lucy shook her head, mortified she'd done it again.

He smiled and returned to his reading.

Her heart fluttered from the exchange. As she sat at the table, she observed him from the corner of her eye; he looked tall, had short, brown hair with specks of grey, and his skin had the surfer-type tan. Although he wasn't your average handsome guy, he was attractive—especially to

Lucy.

Could he be the Stranger? She wondered as she felt an electrical shock race through her system. She couldn't tell if he was wearing tan slacks since he was seated, but he sure as heck wasn't wearing a light blue button-down shirt—that was blatantly obvious by the Deadhead t-shirt he wore that exposed his muscular arms. Lucy bit her lower lip and gave a slight shiver at the sight of them.

She had to see what pants he was wearing, then she'd know better how to handle the evening—or so she thought. As casually as she could, she took out a pen, then acted as though she were consumed with what she saw on her phone, and then used her elbow to knock the pen off the table.

"Oops," Lucy said with an embarrassed laugh. The handsome stranger looked up from his magazine with an inquiring look. "I've dropped my pen," Lucy explained. *Like he cares!* She screamed in her head. Then, with her eyes never leaving his and a goofy smile on her face, she bent over sideways in the pretense to reach for her pen.

When she was just below the table level, she looked at his legs encased in a pair of worn jeans. *Ugh*, she thought to herself. *It's not him.* She stretched her arm out to grab her pen with a sign, but it rolled further away from her. While holding onto the table with one hand and trying to remain in her chair, she walked her fingers along the carpet towards the pen. Finally, the tip of her finger touched the pen only to slip off, sending the pen rolling away further from her tough. She stretched for it. Before she could stop it, her chair tipped over, landing her on her book bag that she'd placed next to the chair.

29

"Ow," she quietly said.

"Are you okay?" The Stranger asked, alarmed.

Humiliated, she didn't respond but stayed where she was with the hope that he'd go back to his magazine. Then she could quietly get back in her chair and forget the whole incident. But Lucy wasn't that lucky. Before she knew it, he was beside her.

"Are you okay?" He asked again as he lifted her.

With her face blazing red and an embarrassed laugh, she stood next to the table, straightened her clothes, and responded, "I'm fine. Not sure what happened." She gulped and moved the book bag away from the chair while avoiding his eyes. She wished he'd go back to his magazine and forget she was there. But, instead, she quietly laughed as he set her chair right.

"Hm, I wonder if one of these legs is shorter than the other," he teased with a wink while rocking the chair, then held it for her to sit down before he returned to his side of the table.

After a few moments, Lucy self-consciously rose from her chair, aware of her table companion's presence, and walked over to the row of books that contained her copy of 'The Sands of Crime.' She hesitated in front of the book and waited for the familiar tingle down her spine.

"It has to be him," she said to herself. She closed her eyes and willed her body to tingle. "It had to be him," she quietly repeated. With her intense concentration, her breath became shallow, so desperate was she to feel that tingle. She'd been so patient and waited so long—she'd earned the tingling feeling, she reasoned with herself. "He must be the stranger," she repeated quietly.

With determination, she waited, and waited. . .and waited. Then just when she'd decided to give up, there it was. She looked at her bare arms and saw the goosebumps. Before she could stop herself, she gave a slight laugh of relief.

"Shhh!" She heard one of the volunteers as he stopped and glowered at her, his dark eyes glaring at her from behind his horn-rimmed glasses. His hair was black and straight and looked like whoever cut it had merely placed a bowl on his head and traced the edges.

"Sorry," Lucy whispered an apology as her shoulders rose to her ears. She placed a hand at her mouth to suppress the joyful giggle that threatened to explode out of it. He continued to glare as his short, plump body strained to push the cart full of books past the end of her row. Lucy didn't care. She was so happy to have felt the tingle. She pulled the book from its shelf and headed back to her table.

Setting the book down on the table, she couldn't suppress the smile that played around her lips with excitement or the giggle that escaped them, which caused her table companion to look over at her before returning to his magazine. She felt like a teenager. *Was this her dream?* Her heart asked.

Calmly she opened her book and pretended to read the first page, while inside her mind, she sang over and over, *La la la la la la la la*. Another giggle escaped the confines of her clenched teeth and lips; she placed her hand at her mouth to try and stop the joy that bubbled inside. Lucy ignored the voices in her head that told her this was nothing like her dream. She refused to listen. This was the first time she'd seen this guy here, and she'd gotten the tingle. The two had to go together. She would not lose thi--.

Lucy stopped mid-thought as she watched a tall, beautiful woman in her forties, with straight, long, brown hair, and dark eyes with a young girl and boy in tow, approach the Stranger and tap him on the shoulder, "We need to go," she said in a loud whisper.

The Stranger looked up and smiled at the lady, "Okay," he said and immediately stood and followed her out.

Lucy felt like a wrecking ball had just slammed into her as she watched him leave. She was devastated. Crushed. She could only look at the book on the table as she tried to hide the single tear that fell from her eye onto the book page. Her mind chastised her for ignoring its warnings. *But it was such a perfect setup*, she argued back. *She'd felt the tingle!*

The evening no longer felt magical as Lucy watched the tall Stranger follow his wife out the library door. Glumly she pushed the 'The Sands of Crime' into the middle of the table, lifted her book bag to her shoulder, and left for the night. *Obviously, he wasn't the guy*, Lucy sullenly thought to herself. And, just like that, she was back at the beginning.

Chapter 7

After having felt the goosebumps, Lucy returned to the library the next night and the next. Even though the Stranger had left with his wife, she couldn't help but hope that she would still have a chance at finding love with someone. Maybe the person that watched her was the man she'd been waiting for—the man she'd been dreaming of, and the handsome Stranger was just a warm-up act?

Even after the disappointment from the previous nights, with the flicker of hope barely sputtering in her heart, she went back the third night. *She had to go! He had to be there,* she told herself as, once again, she prepared for a night of reading the same page.

"Now, who's desperate?" She asked her reflection in the mirror before she left. She was almost out the door when her phone began to play AC/DC's *Thunderstruck.*

Lucy groaned when she saw who was calling. "This is Lucy," she said into the phone.

"Hi Lucy," said the voice from the other end of the line. "This is Brenda Nordstrom. I know it's after hours, but I had some trades I'd like you to execute tomorrow at the opening." Brenda was one of her more prominent clients. So for the next thirty minutes, Lucy sat at her table and wrote down the trade requests. As soon as the call ended, she contacted her boss and let him know about her conversation with the client. *Will I make it to the library tonight?* She asked herself as her boss said he'd contact the client regarding her requests and get back to her tomorrow.

Lucy entered the library later than she'd planned due to the call. It was another busy night with an almost to capacity crowd, unlike anything she'd ever seen before. She headed towards the row of cubicles only to find the same homeless person had set up camp in her cubicle again. *Why were the librarians allowing this?* Lucy scowled as the prospect of another fruitless night loomed in her mind. *Is it because I'm not following the script from my dream?* Why were all the other cubicles taken? That hardly ever happened. *What was going on?* She asked herself. *How could there be no available space?*

Lucy stood in the middle of the room in a quandary of where to go and what to do. She wanted to be alone like she was in her dream, but it didn't seem possible. Then she saw the table, the table she'd shared with the handsome Stranger. The attractive, *married* Stranger that is—the night before. She wanted to get back on track with her dream. She needed to do what she did in the dream to find her stalker or whatever he might be and move on with her life.

Again the table had one other occupant like the night before. *So much for being alone*, Lucy thought as she

34

trudged toward it with a defeated sigh. There was no way around it, and if she wanted to find answers to her dream, she'd have to share the space.

Lucy approached the empty chair across from the male occupant. She couldn't see his features due to the baseball cap he wore or that his body turned away from her. Instead, he looked focused on the material he was reading, so she quietly set her book bag on the table, only to have her keys crash against her metal water bottle inside the book bag. She winced at how loud it sounded in the silent, crowded tomb.

"Shhh!" Said the same librarian as before with a look that would have shot laser beams from her eyes to pulverize Lucy had it been possible. "If you can't be quiet, then you'll need to leave," she hissed.

"Sorry," Lucy said as her cheeks burned. It wasn't just the librarian who was staring her down, but every other person in her immediate area seemed to scowl at her. Lucy huffed aloud and plopped down in her chair. She blindly stared at the tabletop but listened with her ears in case Baby Jane happened to come over to throw her out. "Sheesh! What is her problem," Lucy said under her breath as her mood grew dark.

Lucy pouted with her chin resting in her palms when she heard a low chuckle to her left. She scowled at her tablemate with a sidewards glance then froze. It was him! The married guy from last night; she hadn't realized it was him. She craned her neck to see if his wife was anywhere nearby and was about to comment when he spoke first.

"Having a tough day?" he asked in an audible whisper with a smile that caused the hair on the back of her neck to stand up.

Lucy studied the Stranger before responding. "I've had better, I guess," she said with a sigh. *Just my luck to meet an unavailable man in the library who speaks to me*, she thought to herself.

"Shhhhh! This is your final warning, missy," the grumpy librarian hissed at her.

"Missy," her table occupant mouthed to her as he raised his eyebrows, with the devilish grin on his handsome face.

Lucy cringed from the loud reprimand that brought her shoulders to her ears. "Sorry," she apologized.

The Stranger chuckled to himself.

Lucy looked at him crossly. "Excuse me? Are you laughing at me?" She angrily whispered. *He might be cute, but I'm not his clown*, she thought indignantly.

Shaking his head, he swallowed the laughter. "No," he said apologetically. "Not at you, but with you. It's good to see someone else receive her wrath for a change," then gave her a conspiratorial smile.

Lucy squinted her eyes at him and asked, "Baby Jane gives you grief too?"

"Baby Jane," the married man said with a chuckle as he turned to look for the librarian she referred to with a nod of her head. "That's funny. And it fits so well."

"I've been here for the past six weeks," Lucy whispered across the table, "and I've never heard anyone get it but me."

He laughed aloud before he could stop himself and looked to see if Baby Jane was nearby. When he didn't see her, he turned back towards Lucy and quietly laughed.

She cocked an eyebrow at the sound of his laughter; it was so manly. Then warned him, "You're gonna get in trouble."

"Shhh! The same goes for you, mister," warned the librarian now known as Baby Jane. Lucy and her table companion looked at each other, surprised.

"Where did she come from?" The Stranger asked. Lucy shook her head. Then both covered their mouths and smirked as if they were sharing an inside joke.

When Lucy could control her laughter, she managed to say, "I'm surprised you'd get the reference of Baby Jane." She tilted her head at him curiously.

"Why, because I'm a man and shouldn't like old films like 'Whatever Happened to Baby Jane'?" He asked her.

Her eyes grew as big as her smile at his mention of the film's title. "Well, yeah. Is your wife a big fan of old movies too?" Lucy asked slyly, fishing for information.

"I hope so," he said matter-of-factly.

Lucy inwardly winced and asked, "You don't know? How long have you been married?"

"What makes you think I'm married?" he asked with a quizzical look.

"Well, I saw that lady you left with the other night. Her and the two kids," Lucy nervously explained. She felt the warmth creep into her face and calmly touched her forehead for any sign of sweat that usually accompanied a hot flash

"You remember me?" the Stranger asked, amazed, emphasizing the word remember.

Lucy's face was so red she feared her head would

37

explode, as she stuttered, "I-I-I . . . well . . ." He leaned back in his chair and chuckled with a pleased look on his face. This only flustered Lucy more. *Why is this handsome, married man teasing her?*

"You're quite cute when you're flustered," he said as he watched her struggle. "Did you know that?"

Why is he flirting with me so openly? How dare he think I'm desperate enough to chase a married man, she thought indignantly.

With a forced scowl on her face, she asked, "Where is your wife?" Then it was her turn to raise her eyebrows. She bit her inside cheek, then leaned back in her chair with folded arms and gloated.

This only caused the Stranger to cover his mouth as he snickered in a hushed tone and looked over his shoulder in the direction of Baby Jane before he whispered, "I don't have a wife."

"Yes, you do! I saw her last night," Lucy challenged him as she leaned forward.

Shaking his head, he said, "No, I don't."

Flustered, Lucy sputtered, "But. . . that woman with the kids last night. When she came up and told you it was time to go, you got up and left without an argument."

Her tablemate continued to shake his head with an annoying smirk on his face and a gleam in his eyes and said, "So only married men leave when a woman says it's time to go?"

"No. Not at all. But—," Lucy sputtered. "Stop changing the subject! Most handsome men—," she began.

"Oh, you think I'm handsome, eh?" the Stranger teased.

38

Agitated, Lucy responded, "I didn't say that. You said you didn't know if your wife liked old films when I asked you earlier. You—". *He did have a wife*, she told herself angrily. She was sure of that.

"You asked if my wife liked old movies, and I said that I hoped so. As in, when I have a wife, I hope she likes old movies as much as I do because I love to watch 'em," the Stranger patiently explained with his crooked smile and the maddening twinkle in his eyes.

"Well, why didn't you say that?" Lucy asked, exasperated.

"This was more fun," he said and began a chuckle that turned into a loud laugh. Just as Lucy was about to respond—

"Okay, you need to leave," Baby Jane bellowed as she walked towards their table. Her likeness to Bette Davis' character was uncanny. The long baby doll curls in her grayish blonde hair, the clown white face powder, and over accentuated red lips, not to mention the long fake eyelashes. Then there were the perfect circles of blush setting atop a body encased in a non-fitting suit of armor. That armor consisted of a shapeless brown skirt and top and her thick stockinged calves in sensible shoes. "You have disrupted this library for the last time. Get your things together and leave," she ordered. The Stranger looked at Lucy in good-humored surprise. "You, too!" She pointed at Lucy. "Get your things and go. You are banned from this library!"

Lucy's eyes widened in shock as she looked between Baby Jane and the Stranger. She'd never been kicked out of the library before. But her tablemate seemed to be taking it in stride, even enjoying it. His attitude was infectious. Before she realized it, they both began to giggle as they gathered their belongings and left their table in what was supposed to be the walk of shame. But they were laughing too hard to care.

"Goodnight, Mrs. Gable," Lucy called as she and the Stranger passed her desk and crashed out the front doors.

Before the doors closed, they heard Mrs. Gable, in her kind manner, say, "Now Jane, you can't ban people from the library for laughing."

Standing outside the library, Lucy and the Stranger stood and faced one another as their giggle turned into a full-on gut-busting laugh.

As she howled with laughter, she couldn't help asking herself if she was laughing because it was funny? Or nerves? Or attraction? Where did this guy come from?

"But ya are, Blanche, but ya are!" The Stranger said, mimicking Bette Davis in the movie. Lucy laughed, surprised by how like Bette Davis his imitation sounded. Then, when they began to regain some composure, they stood looking at each other and smiled. Lucy had not expected him to have a personality as well as looks.

"Did you hear that? Her name really is Jane," Lucy managed to say between bouts of laughter.

When their laughter subsided, Lucy sighed and turned to leave, "Thanks for making me laugh so hard. I really needed it."

The Stranger's brows furrowed with concern. "Is everything okay?" he asked.

Lucy guffawed and waved her hand in dismissal. "Yeah, it's all good. I just meant getting kicked out. I don't handle embarrassment well."

"Aaah, I see," he said, nodding his head slowly, "I think you take yourself too seriously."

This statement made Lucy bristle, and before she could stop herself, she said, "I do not!"

"Mmmmm. . ." the Stranger said as he moved his head from side to side in consideration, "I think you do."

"You don't know me," Lucy said indignantly. "You don't even know my name, and I don't know yours. Who are you to tell me I take myself too seriously?!"

"Whoa, whoa, whoa! Hold on there, little Miss Scorpio—" the Stranger said as he raised his hand as if to ward off any blows.

"How do you know I'm a Scorpio?" Lucy interrupted, "Who are you?" she demanded.

"Ah-ha! I was right. You are a Scorpio. Ha!" He said victoriously and turned to go.

"How'd you know I was?" Lucy asked as he walked away, but he didn't respond. She quickly walked to catch up, then stood in front of him to stop him. "I do not take myself too seriously either. I am fun! I'm very fun! I'm funny, too!" She said as if she were convincing herself.

The Stranger stopped and looked at her. "Nah, you don't take yourself too seriously," he said sarcastically. He walked around her, only to stop and turn back towards Lucy. He looked at her face covered with red blotches from her suppressed anger and chuckled to himself before he set his hand on her shoulder and said, "Relaaaaaax. I guessed you were a Scorpio because you seemed so intense. That is a sure sign of a Scorpio—not that I'm into astrology. It's just something I've learned over the years."

The Stranger paused as he watched Lucy sputter to herself, and began to respond, then he added, "Besides, it was just a guess. Your response to my comment confirmed it. That's all." He couldn't help but laugh when he saw how he'd gotten under her skin. He never imagined she'd be so much fun to tease. He smiled to himself as he turned to where his truck was parked, "See ya," he called.

"But wait," Lucy called after him. He stopped and gave her a curious look over his shoulder, "Who are you? What's your name?"

The Stranger turned and faced Lucy and walked towards her. He tilted his head as he judged how best to respond while a sly smile played on his lips, then said, "Jones, Davy Jones."

Lucy laughed before she could stop herself. She placed her hands on her hips as she squinted her eyes to try and take it all in, "Davy Jones? Like Davy Jones from The Monkees?"

Davy sighed and said with a sarcastic tone, "Yeah, as in Davy Jones from The Monkees or Davy Jones' locker from the Pirates of the Caribbean."

"I saw you roll your eyes," Lucy said as she pointed her finger. They stood looking at one another; Davy with his ever-present grin and a twinkle in his eyes and Lucy with her hands on her hips as she studied this impressively tall, handsome man who insisted on teasing her. "Do you really go by. . . Davy?" She asked and curled her lip up as if she smelled something bad. Finally, the smile left Davy's face.

"Yeah," he answered slowly, "what's wrong with

that?"

"Davy," Lucy repeated as she looked up into the night sky and pondered the name. Then looked at Davy and said, "Davy . . .Hm, okay."

Gone was the twinkle and smirk that had been present so much of the night as he said, "Hey." He looked dejected as Lucy turned away with a smile on her face.

"Goodnight," she called over her shoulder as her car's alarm beeped and unlocked her door. Without a glance backward, she got in and closed the door. Unable to contain it a moment longer, she began to giggle as she started the car. *Let's see who is so intense now*, she said to herself.

Chapter 8

The following day as Lucy opened the office, she had a bounce in her step as she thought about the previous night. What had started as another mundane night at the library ended in quite a different way. Lucy couldn't wait for Lori to get in so she could tell her about this exciting guy she'd met. The evening had been so unexpected. She hadn't thought about the stalker, the tan slacks, or even her dream once.

Finally, Lori and her dog, Bingo, appeared outside Lucy's office door. "Good morning," she said.

"Hey there," Lucy responded to Bingo cheerfully. She couldn't ignore those big brown eyes as they looked up at her with his tail wagging. He walked into her office expecting a treat. "Oh, I am so sorry, I forgot to bring anything again."

Lori laughed, "Again? You haven't brought anything for him yet."

"Oh, hi! I didn't see you come in," Lucy said with a smile. Lori turned and went into her cashier's cage. Lucy gave her time to get set up before she followed her and stood on the other side of the counter to share her good news about the night before.

The next half hour was the most brutal thirty minutes Lucy had spent in the past six weeks while she waited for Lori to settle in. She listened to some music on her laptop to try and help her pass the time, but it didn't work. The minutes seemed to drag by. *Didn't Lori know she had important things to tell her?* Finally unable to wait a moment longer, Lucy left her office and walked over to see whether Lori could chit-chat now or not.

"Ah! You're all set up," Lucy declared when she spied Lori sitting in her chair with Bingo settled in his dog bed. "I have some great news to tell you," Lucy couldn't help but smile like a Cheshire cat. It had been so long since she'd flirted with a man like she did last night or even had a man—a handsome man at that—flirt back so brazenly. And now that he'd told her he wasn't married— Lucy's head was swimming with the possibilities.

Lori looked up and said, "Oh? Did you meet your stalker?"

"No. Not even close. In fact, I didn't even think about the Stranger all night," Lucy confessed.

"You didn't? Why?" Lori asked, then took a sip on the straw from her ever-present extra-large coke.

"No, I didn't. Not once." Lucy couldn't stop the big grin pasted to her face, "I believe I told you about the guy I met at the library the other night?" Lori looked at Lucy over her glasses. "Okay, maybe I didn't meet him, but I occupied the same table at the same time he was there," Lucy told her. Before Lori could respond, she continued,

"Well, he was there again last night, and—."

Lori interrupted, "No, you didn't tell me about any guy. What guy? Is it the dream guy?" she asked.

"At first, I thought he was, but then when he left with a woman and two kids, who I thought was his wife, I figured I was wrong. Besides, there were no goosebumps," Lucy told her as she gently rubbed her arms.

"Wait, wait, slow down," Lori said, giving Lucy a confused look. "This guy left with a woman and two kids last night?"

"No. Two nights ago. He was sitting at the only table with any available seating, so I sat there too. I was bummed that nothing was aligning as it did in the dream; I mean, I couldn't sit in my cubicle, there was only this table, and a man was sitting there. So, I kinda plopped down at the table." Lucy proceeded to tell Lori about her last couple of evenings at the library. When she ended the story, they were both laughing.

"Sounds like you had a good night. Do you think he could be the guy from the dream?"

"Who? Davy Jones?" Lucy asked.

"Yeah. Is he the one?"

Lucy paused to consider the question. "Hm . . . no, I don't think so."

"Yeah? Why not?"

"Well, there's a lot of reasons why it couldn't be him. One, he wasn't sitting alone in a chair staring at me; two, there were no goosebumps—whatsoever, like I said before; three, I didn't do anything that I always seemed to do in the dream. In fact, I didn't think about the dream at all. Didn't even dream the dream last night," Lucy admitted not just to Lori but to herself for the first time.

"You didn't?" Lori asked.

"No," Answered Lucy, pleased with herself.

"Maybe you did dream it but don't remember," Lori suggested.

"I would know if I dreamt that dream, and I know I didn't. But that's okay. It was so much fun just to stand and laugh with someone and to flirt and be flirted with," Lucy said, then stopped.

Lori saw a shadow cross her face, "What's the matter?" she asked, concerned.

"I hope he isn't married. And I hope I see him again," Lucy said wistfully.

"You will," Lori assured her.

"I sure hope you're right. Maybe having a little social activity is what the dream was trying to tell me to do," Lucy said thoughtfully. She paused for a moment, then continued, "Well, I better get back to work. I just wanted to tell you about last night. Ciao!" Lucy cheerfully turned to go.

"Wait," Lori called after her. Lucy turned with raised eyebrows. "Are you going back to the library tonight?"

"Duh!" She said and turned to leave with Lori's laughter following her.

***

That night she was excited to go to the library. She found herself humming as she prepared for what had become her nightly routine and couldn't deny the excitement at the prospect of seeing Davy again. Although she knew very little about him, she couldn't stifle the smile that had been on her face all day as she remembered how handsome, manly, tall, and single he was —but he wasn't the guy in her dream, of that she was sure.

So, with him in mind, she applied the extra layer of mascara so that her eyelashes, what she had anyway, would pop around her blue eyes. She'd learned from the years of dating that where men were concerned, she needed to make use of all of her assets, no matter how small they might be.

Before she entered the library, she'd placed a baseball cap on her head hoping the cap would help her hide in plain sight if Baby Jane were anywhere on the premises.

Lucy entered the library with a group of people, and she both slouched and looked when she passed the front desk down to avoid eye contact with Mrs. Gable. But as luck would have it, Mrs. G. didn't seem to be there at that moment. Lucy couldn't deny the relief she felt as she continued her trek towards her new mecca. She'd forgotten all about the cubicle and only had eyes for the table.

Tonight Lucy only carried her purse and a plastic water bottle, to not draw attention to herself by making any unnecessary noise. She casually walked towards the empty table where she'd sat the night before but stopped.

"Hm," she said with a frown, "he isn't there." She could feel the joy she'd earlier felt drain away. She turned in a circle as she looked in all directions for any sign of Davy. Lucy's frustration at his absence began to seep through her pores as she hooked her purse strap on the back of the chair and pulled out the book she'd brought with her. She could not read that same page from 'The Sands of Crime' one more time, and this new cozy mystery showed promise of helping her pass the time while she waited for her stalker.

Lucy sat and read until it was time for the library to close—which was past her usual bedtime. Then, she stood and stretched and collected her purse, book, and water bottle to leave. She'd be exhausted tomorrow. But staying late was the sacrifice she'd have to make if she wanted answers to her dream and to see Davy again. Tonight it was all in vain though since there was no sign of either.

He didn't show up all week, much to her chagrin. What had seemed so bright, and exciting was turning to ashes. *He was just another flash in the pan, a beautiful memory*, she thought as she walked out the library door to drive home.

***

"I'm so confused. I don't know what to think," Lucy gloomily told Lori the next day.

"He hasn't shown up at all?" Lori asked with concern.

"No. I have been there every night so far this week, and nothing. And I've been staying until close, which is way past my bedtime, so I am exhausted," Lucy admitted as she rested her head in her hands and leaned on the counter of the cage.

"Maybe he's just another jerky guy?" Lori

suggested.

"Well, in his defense," Lucy said, thinking aloud, "he doesn't seem the type of guy to play someone."

"No?" Lori asked.

"No. I think he's a good guy. That's why his absence seems so suspicious to me. I have questions like What does he do that he's gone for so long? Is it because he lied to me and got caught by his wife?"

Lori raised her brows.

"But, he didn't seem the cheating type. Is there a type? Why would he lie to me, someone he doesn't even know? It just doesn't make sense."

"Was I supposed to be part of that conversation?" Lori asked.

"I just want answers. I'm tired of all the mystery."

"Oh dear," Lori said with dread. "You've only had two short conversations with him. Maybe you should slow down and not read into everything he does?" Lori suggested as she studied Lucy.

"Why do I always meet the guys who disappear?"

"I'm sorry," Lori said sympathetically.

"It's not your fault. Unless you're the reason he's disappeared," Lucy said glumly.

Lori snickered and said, "No, I had nothing to do with that." She paused then asked, "So, what are you going to do?"

With a shrug of her shoulders, Lucy lifted her head and said, "I honestly don't know. I am just so confused. I thought I'd gotten an answer to my dream—which I haven't dreamt since I met Davy, by the way. But now that he's disappeared, I'm not sure if I correctly deciphered any of the metaphors I thought were in the dream."

"Maybe there weren't metaphors in your dream? Maybe it was just a dream?" Lori suggested.

Cocking her head to one side in disbelief, Lucy said, "No way. You can't dream the same dream every night for weeks only to have it not mean anything." She stopped and looked down at her feet, deep in thought.

"So, what are you going to do?"

"I'm not sure, but I do know that I will go to the library for the rest of the week—which leaves only one more night, thank heavens," she said with a sigh. "He's got to turn up, or I am S.O.L."

"So, do you think he's the one from your dream, then?" Lori asked.

"No, not really. But the guy's a lot of fun, cute, and he enjoyed my company," Lucy stopped and gave a sigh, "I miss having guy friends."

Lori gave a sympathetic laugh, "That's understandable. But don't give up the idea that he could be the guy from your dream."

Lucy rolled her eyes and shook her head. "He's not."

"How do you know?"

"I know this because there are none of the signs. Trust me."

Lucy went to the library that night with little hope that Davy would show up. So when he didn't, she tried not to take it personally, but the disappointment was there. She had to remind herself that she couldn't get attached to every tall, handsome, funny, flirty, single—dare she think it, perfect male that showed her attention. If she did that, she'd turn into Baby Jane.

Instead, she decided she must have interpreted the dream wrong. Maybe she never saw the Stranger's face because the dream told her to stop watching all the true crime shows and get a social life. Or perhaps, the Stranger represented all the new, tall men in her future? Whatever the meaning, it would have to wait until she got back from a conference she had to attend for work the following week in Florida.

Chapter 9

Lucy walked onto the plane, exhausted. She'd been up late packing for her work trip to Florida. She wasn't in the mood to travel, but she didn't have a choice. It would be a week of back-to-back meetings with no chance to see the sites. Lucy hoped the change of scenery would help keep her mind off Davy Jones.

She'd read somewhere that it took a month to make a habit; soon, it would be a month since she'd last seen Davy. He wasn't a habit, not really. The two nights he'd been at the library and the fun they had together gave her hope that there were still good guys out there. But, unfortunately, his absence allowed all the doubts and fears from too many failed relationships to come flooding into her passionless life.

With her resolve to forget about Mr. Jones, she couldn't deny how good it felt to flirt with him and have him flirt back. That had been a badly needed shot of confidence. Something she'd lost after her last relationship went off the rails as it did.

After all these years, she still winced when she

remembered the night her boyfriend informed her that he was engaged to her best friend. It had come as such a surprise, and the pain had been so intense. She remembered sitting in the dark on her couch for three consecutive nights, numb as the hurt worked through her system. Eventually, she was able to push the pain to the very deepest part of her soul and continue with her life. But after that, her instinct was to avoid relationships at any cost until now. Between Davy and the dream, it seemed a door had opened she'd thought had been bricked up forever.

"Welcome," said Bertie, the older of the two flight attendants standing at the entrance. She motioned Lucy towards the aisle.

"Thank you," Lucy responded and smiled as she returned the memories into the deep corner of her mind where she'd placed them long ago.

Once she found her seat and had placed her carry-on in the luggage compartment above, she took her place in the aisle seat. She made herself comfortable and watched as passengers passed by, searching for their seating assignment on the plane. She was grateful her seat was closer to the door so that when they landed and disembarked, she could get off as quickly as possible.

While she waited for the plane to fill, Lucy pulled out the new mystery novel she'd brought with her to read. Eventually, her two-row mates came and took their seats next to her, and she could now lose herself in her book. Occasionally she'd look up to check out the passengers that were passing by her seat. Soon she lost herself in the tale of murder and mayhem, only coming back to reality when she heard the captain's announcement over the intercom for the flight attendants to prepare the plane for take-off.

Lucy took a break from her book to watch as the last group of passengers boarded the plane and walked past where she sat. She pulled her purse from under the seat to grab a Chapstick when it all came down on her, literally. Before she could react, she was crushed under the weight of a male passenger who seemed to plow into her. The collision pushed her into the person seated next to her. The passenger's body landed on her head, then rolled down her face into her lap, pulling her hair and pushed her purse and its contents off her lap. She felt as though she'd been side tackled.

"Hey! Watch it," she cried out as her hand reached for the spot on her head that felt as though a hammer had hit her. Then, with the weight of the male passenger still heavy in her lap, she tried to get out from under him and pushed back against a jumble of clothes and flailing body parts. In the chaos of everything, Lucy had grabbed hold of his waist to shove him off her, only to briefly feel the outline of what she thought was a gun.

"I'm so sorry," the male passenger said as he faced the aisle. He lifted himself out of her lap.

"Ouch!" Lucy gasped as his exertion pulled her hair that was tangled between his palm and her seatback.

"Sorry, 'bout tha—," the male passenger began to say when an ear-splitting scream cut the air.

"Oh, I am so sorry," said a young mom as she held a squirming toddler in her arms. The child was red in the face and crying as he waved a sippy cup. "I thought there was room for us to squeeze by." Again, she apologized as she looked at the male passenger that had righted himself from Lucy's lap—relieving the domino effect that had knocked her against her female seatmate in the middle, who leaned against the next woman pinned against the window.

"That's okay," he managed before another scream pierced the air.

The mother quickly took in the situation. "Oh, Charlie," the mother scolded the little boy in her arms, who continued with his tantrum. Finally, in his anger, he threw his cup.

"Ouch!" A fashionably dressed woman rubbed the spot on her head where the cup had hit. When the cup landed on her lap, the contents flooded her skirt. She bolted to her feet in shock only to hit her head on the overhead bin, causing her to collapse into her seat, and proceed to let flow a string of words one might expect from a soldier.

"I'm so sorry," the young mother said, mortified as she tried to wipe the liquid that had pooled on the lady's skirt. "I thought I'd put that lid on tight," she said as another passenger handed her the lid to the sippy cup.

"Don't touch me," the woman said through gritted teeth at the mom as she slapped her hand away. "You need to take better control of that little brat!"

Lucy rubbed her head as she watched all the commotion. At the same time, the person who'd just been in her lap attempted to calm the milk-covered passenger with the assistance of the older flight attendant as the younger flight attendant watched from afar.

What had hit her head? She wondered. *It was so hard.* She focused her eyes on the back profile of her attacker. He was leaning over to pull a carry-on down from the overhead compartment for the enraged, milk-covered woman. Then she saw the grip of a gun that an untucked shirt had previously covered. The attacker covered it quickly. Lucy gasped.

"Are you alright?" the woman that sat in the middle seat asked.

"Yeah. Yeah, I'm fine." With her elbow on the armrest, Lucy rested her aching head in her hand to think. *Should I tell the pilot now? Or after everyone had been seated?* She asked herself.

"Are you sure you're okay?" the male passenger that had been in her lap asked.

Still contemplating what she should do about the gun responded, "I'm fine." Then looked up with a weak smile.

"You!" They both said in surprise at one another.

"What are you doing here?" Davy asked.

"Traveling, obviously," Lucy said as she continued to rub her head. "What are you doing here?"

"The same," Davy said as another passenger pushed past him. His hand slipped from the seat back onto Lucy's shoulder, causing her to wince in pain. "Are you okay?" he asked again, concerned.

"Yeah. . . yeah, I'm fine. Just trying to recover from having a tank fall on me," Lucy said as she tried to rotate her shoulder. "I'm not sure which hurts more: my head, my shoulder, or my whole body," Lucy grimaced in pain before glaring at Davy. "Dude, do you always enter a plane that way?"

Davy chuckled, "No."

"Is everyone okay here?" Bertie, the flight attendant, asked, then continued before anyone could respond. "We need to get in the air. Would ya'll mind getting to your seats, please? We do have a schedule." Then she clapped her hands and began to direct everyone to their seats.

"I'll talk to ya later," Davy said as he side-stepped down the aisle.

"Sure," Lucy responded casually, but inside was excited that she'd seen him again—before the month was out. Maybe she wouldn't need to set any new habits now.

With all the commotion among the passengers and the flight attendant shooing everyone away en mas, Lucy didn't see where Davy sat on the plane. Lucy gathered her stuff back in her purse that had scattered when Davy had fallen on her. Then with her purse stored under the seat in front of her, she turned her attention to the torn pages in her book. Lucy was in a dreamy state when she suddenly remembered that he was the passenger that had the gun under his shirt. She immediately bolted upright but couldn't do anything because the plane was taxiing down the runway. First, she'd have to wait for the pilot to let them move about the cabin, then she'd find Davy and find out why he had a gun—if it weren't too late.

From her seat, she searched for Davy. She thought he'd walked towards the back of the plane but didn't see him. Lucy drummed her fingers on her armrest as she impatiently waited for the seatbelt light to turn off so she could confront him. She had to know about the gun she'd seen on him; it was her patriotic duty. Then if she didn't like his answer, she'd go to the pilot.

With her mission spurring her on, she headed to the front of the plane but stopped at the curtain that separated Coach Class from Business Class. She stood outside the restroom until the older flight attendant, Bertie, walked away before she slipped through the curtain. Slowly she walked towards First Class, checking each occupant in their seat. Davy wasn't there. She had to try First-class, so she quickly walked to the curtain and stepped through.

"May I help you?" asked a male voice. Lucy turned to see a male flight attendant who resembled a smaller version of Ben Affleck.

She looked at the name tag pinned to his shirt before she responded. "Uh, I'm looking for someone. Can you give me a minute, please, Bruce?" Lucy asked as she moved forward to see all the First-Class passengers.

"I'm sorry, you need to go back to your assigned seat," Bruce told her as he blocked her progression.

"It'll just take a second," Lucy said as she moved to step around him.

"The curtains are there for a reason, ma'am," Bruce said as he pushed her through the curtain back into Business Class. "Please see that she gets to her assigned seat," he told Bertie, who appeared out of nowhere. Then he stepped back through the curtain, and while keeping eye contact with Lucy, squeezed the Velcro on the curtain together until he disappeared from view. Lucy frowned at the curtain.

With a tired laugh, the older flight attendant looked at her. "You seem to be lost. May I help you to your seat?" she asked with a condescending smile as she moved aside for Lucy and followed her down the aisle towards her seat.

Moving down the aisle, out of the Business Class section, Lucy and Davy's eyes connected. She abruptly stopped. He ducked his head as if to hide from her. She glared his way.

"Keep an eye on this one," Bertie told the younger flight attendant, coming from the back of the plane, as Lucy dropped in her seat.

"Is everything okay?" the younger flight attendant asked in her soft drawl. Lucy rubbed her temples.

"Just keep an eye on her. She tends to wander about the cabin," Bertie said with a tick of her head in Lucy's direction.

"Sure thang," The younger flight attendant responded. "If there is anything you need," she whispered, slightly bending down to speak with Lucy, "please let me know. My name is Suzanne." She smiled big.

Lucy liked her immediately and smiled back at the kind flight attendant. "Thank you."

Now that she knew where Davy was seated, she attempted to continue down the aisle towards him, only to be stopped by Bertie. "I believe your seat is here," she said through clenched teeth.

"I just need to go see a friend of mine, real fast," Lucy said while she pointed towards the rear of the plane, but the flight attendant stood her ground until Lucy returned to her seat.

"Please put on your seatbelt," she directed Lucy. When she heard the click of the buckle, Bertie turned and went back through the Business class curtain.

Lucy nibbled on her top lip and leaned into the aisle

from her seat. She looked back to where she'd seen Davy. Their eyes met again, and he ducked his head.

"That's just rude," she said aloud. So what if she had only seen Davy twice before? He didn't need to hide from her.

Usually, she wouldn't have bothered him, but the situation was different now—even urgent. First, she had to know why he carried a gun and whether she should alert the pilot to this security breach or not. *Was he a hijacker? Is that how he brought the gun onboard—using his good looks to disarm the flight crew?* Lucy asked herself. If he was a hijacker, she needed to stop him. But first, she needed to ask him. *Would he kill her once she knew he was a hijacker? Is that what the dream had been trying to tell her?* She looked at the curtain to Business Class before she got up to make sure that Nurse Ratchet wasn't in sight. Stealthily she unbuckled her seatbelt, then stood, gulped some air, and quickly walked back to where Davy sat.

"I need to talk to you," Lucy hissed in his ear.

"I can't. I'm busy," Davy hissed back, not looking at her.

"Well, un-busy yourself, or I'll go talk to the pilot." Lucy stood and folded her arms as she tilted her head to one side and waited.

"About what?" Davy's voice raised an octave in disbelief.

"Talk to me and find out." He didn't move. "Okay then." Lucy turned to head back up the aisle.

"Okay, okay," he sighed. He grabbed Lucy's elbow as he stood, pulled her to the very back of the plane into the small galley, and backed her up to the most outer wall.

"What do you want to talk to me about?" He crossed his arms. Lucy could feel her face grow hot as she began to regret her decision. "Well?" he asked with a grim look on his face.

Lucy took a deep breath then asked point-blank, "Why do you have a gun?"

With lightning speed, Davy put his hand against her mouth as he mashed her even more against the wall of the galley.

"What makes you think I have a gun?" He asked in a menacingly low tone in her ear.

"Mum, ddddonddd mumnim," Lucy responded as she put her hands on his waist to push him away, but he didn't budge. *If only this were under better circumstances, I wouldn't mind such close proximity with him,* she thought, then tried to shake her head to get back into the moment at hand.

"What?" Davy asked as his eyebrows scrunched together in a scowl. Lucy tried to push his hand off her mouth, but he didn't release it.

"Mum, ddddonddd mumnim," she said again.

"What?" He asked. She scratched at his hand to pull it away, but it didn't budge. Then as if a light bulb went off, he slowly took his hand away.

"How do you expect me to answer your question with your hand on my mouth," Lucy hissed at him.

"Sorry." Davy backed away from her, then asked in a whisper, "How do you know I have a gun?"

"Because it slammed against my head when you fell into my lap," Lucy angrily whispered back. Both glared at the other.

"You couldn't tell that by it hitting you on the head," Davy stated.

"Okay, maybe not then. But when you lifted the luggage out of the overhead compartment, I saw it," Lucy admitted. "I accidentally grabbed it when I pushed you off my lap," she finished.

"Are you sure you felt a gun?" Davy asked with a wink.

"Eeew, that's disgusting."

Davy laughed.

"Besides," Lucy continued, "I just felt it again when you had your hand on my mouth, and I tried to push you away, so there," Lucy told him defiantly. The two glowered at each other until Lucy asked, "Why do you have a gun? How'd you get it through customs?"

Davy rubbed his hand across his eyes before he stepped back and studied her. Lucy stood still and watched his face expectantly; she could see that he was tired.

Davy buried his head in his hands, then looked up and said, "You need to go sit down and just let this go, okay?"

"And what if I don't? What if I go to the pilot and tell him about your gun?" Lucy mouthed the word gun.

Davy gave a heavy sigh and said, "Then I will arrest you."

"On what grounds?" Lucy asked indignantly. "You can't arrest me."

"Shhhh!" Davy put his hand on her mouth again.

"Stop putting your hand on my mouth!" Lucy said,

slapping his hands away.

"Okay, okay," Davy motioned for her to calm down, then continued, "I can, and I will arrest you if you don't go back to your seat and sit down for the rest of the flight." Lucy could see he wasn't kidding.

"Fine." She pushed past him, walked back up the aisle to her seat, and paused for a moment before she sat down and buckled her seatbelt.

Davy watched Lucy walk to her seat. He knew that hell hath no fury like a woman who was warned she'd be arrested if she didn't do as she was told, but he couldn't tell her what he was up to, at least not on the plane. So instead, he would try and tell her later if she'd ever talk to him again.

When Davy got back to his seat, he dropped down, looked at his seatmate next to him, and gave a sigh.

His seatmate, a chubby, balding older man, gave him a knowing look. "Women, huh?" he chuckled.

"Yeah, women," Davy responded as he rolled his eyes. He continued to watch Lucy. *She might become a problem*, he thought to himself.

Chapter 10

"Men!" Lucy said to no one in particular as she sat in her seat and fumed. *How dare he threaten to arrest her! Why was he carrying a gun? I should just tell the pilot and save the whole plane from crashing—if that's his plan*, she told herself. *He couldn't be a terrorist*, she reasoned with herself. *I didn't have terrorists for friends. I like All American warriors—soldiers, heroes. But not terrorists.*

Lucy refused to look in his direction for the rest of the flight. But she couldn't stop the multitude of questions that ran through her head: Who was he? Why'd he have a gun? How could she reason with a man with a gun? He threatened to arrest her; did that mean he was a cop? She must have been crazy to think they could be friends.

As soon as the plane's door opened, she was up and ready to disembark. She pulled her carry-on out of the overhead bin and pushed her way into the aisle. She had to get out of there fast. She'd made a fool of herself and wanted to disappear.

"So much for that friendship—never mind a

romantic interest," she glumly told herself as she stepped into the jetway, unaware of the slightly raised ledge. She hit it awkwardly, which caused her to fall right on her face. "Aaaagh," she cried as she fell. Her hands hit the surface before her elbow buckled from the pain in her hurt shoulder, and her head skidded into the floor—the same side Davy's gun had hit earlier. She saw stars.

"Ma'am," said Suzanne, the flight attendant, with a cute southern drawl as she knelt beside her, "are you okay?"

Lucy gingerly lifted herself to a sitting position. She winced when her palms touched the floor again. "Uh, I think so," she said as she looked at her scraped palms, oblivious to the passengers that walked around her as they sidestepped her luggage and the contents of her purse that had spilled.

"Are you sure?" the young woman asked with concern. "You're bleeding."

"I am? Where?" Lucy immediately felt her cheek and patted her chest.

"No, your lip." Suzanne pointed.

Lucy tentatively touched her lower lip with her tongue and could taste blood. "Oh, great." Lucy grimaced as her other hand dabbed at her lip and came away with blood on it. "I should go clean up, but I need to get my stuff first," she said as she observed the contents of her purse on the floor around her. Methodically she began to drop the items splayed all over the floor into her bag held open by the flight attendant.

Standing with her purse on her shoulder, holding her luggage handle, she turned to Suzanne and asked, "Is my cheek scraped?"

Suzanne studied Lucy's cheek, then said, "It's red, but I don't see any blood or scrapes. So it might just be a little rug-burn." She sympathetically winced.

***

As soon as the plane landed, Davy watched as Lucy quickly rose from her seat and left the plane. He felt terrible for how he'd spoken to her, but there was too much at stake. So he remained at the back of the plane with his two colleagues while they watched the flight crew begin to pull their bags from the overhead bins and exit the aircraft.

As Davy waited, Max, another Air Marshal on the flight, turned to him. "Who was the girl?" Max Felix quietly asked.

"What girl?"

"The one you took into the galley when you should have been doing your job?

"Don't worry, I handled it," Davy assured him.

"I hope you did." Max's face was void of emotion. Instead, they looked at one another as Sammy, an Asian man in brown dress slacks sporting a military cut, looked up from his personal phone. He was the shortest of the three but no less of a threat.

"What's going on?" Sammy asked, looking from one to the other.

"Just reminding Jones, here to keep his girlfriends at home and not bring them on flights," Max said as he cocked a brow at Davy before he turned and opened the overhead bin. Inside were three similar black backpacks. He handed one to each of the other guys before they walked off the plane. They still had their reports to write before their night was done. Every airport had an office for the Air Marshals to use.

Sammy chuckled, then said, "Yeah, dude. For a minute, I was worried for ya."

Davy shook his head in good-humored disbelief as he followed his two colleagues off the plane. At the end of the jetway, Davy paused and watched Max and Sammy walk down the terminal.

"You comin' bro?" Sammy asked when he saw he hadn't moved from the end of the jetway.

Max stopped and said, "C'mon! Let's get some chow. I'm starving."

"Yeah," Davy said, "right behind ya." He quickened his step to catch up with them.

Davy stood behind Max and Sammy on the escalator as it descended to the Luggage Claim level. He could see the passengers gathered around one of the carousels as luggage came down the ramp. Out of habit, Davy scanned the crowd then stopped at Lucy. She stood to the right of the exit; he could see her reflection in the window as she spoke on her phone. He saw her laugh and flail her arm about in some sort of gesture. Just as he stepped off the escalator, her call ended, but she continued to watch out the window. When he stepped off the escalator, he walked in her direction.

"Hey," Max called to him, "where ya goin'?"

"I'll catch up with you later," he told them over his shoulder.

Because it was dark outside, he could see her reflection in the window. And the closer he got, the better he could discern the look of disbelief that flashed across her face when she saw his approach.

"Here to thollow through with your threat?" She winced as she turned towards him with her hands on her hips.

"Look, I'm sorry about that. But I couldn't have you raising all that stink about my gun on the plane," Davy quietly explained as he moved closer to where she stood.

"Whatever," she said as she grabbed the handle of her roller bag and pulled it past where Davy stood.

"What happened to your lip?" Davy asked as he stepped in front of her.

"I thell," Lucy said, unable to pronounce her "fs" with the swelling in her lip. So instead, she tried to scowl at him.

"You thell?" Davy asked, confused.

"Yeth, I thell on the thloor as I letht the thlane," Lucy struggled to speak with her swollen lip. She didn't want it to bleed again and reached up to dab at it with a crumpled tissue.

"Oh, you *fell*. It looks kinda swollen," Davy said as he squinted to get a better look at it and slightly grimaced.

"Yeth, I thell," Lucy said, turning away so he couldn't see her lip.

Davy put his hand over his mouth to hide the snicker that wanted to escape and cleared his throat. When he felt he had it in control as Lucy moved past him.

"What do you care?" She asked over her shoulder, then winced as she touched her lip to check for more

69

bleeding.

"Hey! Wait," Davy called, "Hey!" He jogged to catch up with her, but she didn't stop until he grabbed her arm. "Can you stop, please?" he asked.

Lucy looked at his hand on her arm, then at him. "Let go of my arm," Lucy demanded.

"I don't even know your name," he told her. Lucy gave a disgusted sigh as she looked away. "C'mon, what's your name?" He let go of her arm and stepped in front of her.

"Lucy," she said reluctantly.

"Lucy what?" he asked.

"Just Lucy," she responded with a sideward glance.

"Just Lucy, huh? As in I Love?" he asked with a hint of a smile. He studied her face for a change in her mood. "Is everything okay? Do you need to put something on that?" He asked, pointing at her lip.

"It's thine," she said as she tentatively licked her lip, then remembered Davy was watching her. With a sigh, she said, "Look, you don't know me, and I sure as heck don't know you, so why don't you go back to your terrorist," Lucy paused as she gently placed her teeth against her lower lip and said, "friends." She continued toward the escalator. Davy paused, then, with a few quick strides, was able to block her path. Lucy glowered at him before she looked in her purse and pulled out her little tube of lip salve. "You tried to arrest me. Why would you care ith my lip is cut or not?" She quickly squeezed a healthy amount on her finger and dabbed it on her lip. "Mm," Lucy moaned with relief when the salve soothed her lip.

"C'mon, you can't be that mad. And I didn't arrest you. I only threatened to so that you'd go back to your seat," Davy explained apologetically.

"Who are you?" Lucy asked. "Definitely not the all-American boy you portrayed yourself to be at the library."

"Who says I'm not?"

"Does your sister know you carry a gun?" Lucy asked.

"Shhhh!" Davy said, "Please lower your voice."

"Ah-ha!" Lucy said victoriously. "If it were okay for you to have a gun, then you wouldn't constantly be shushing me."

Davy paused, then asked, "Are you hungry?"

Lucy studied his face, not sure what to do.

"Look, let me buy you dinner, and I'll try to explain everything."

Lucy saw a look of remorse in his eyes and said begrudgingly, "I could eat something, I guess." Then, with the help of the salve on her lips, Lucy noticed that her lip was more pliable.

"We can get something to eat upstairs," he said with a smile, then stood back so Lucy could get on the escalator before him.

Neither noticed Max and Sammy had remained where Davy left them, watching his interaction with Lucy.

"We better go turn in our reports for this flight," Max told Sammy, with a concerned look.

"Do you think she'll be a problem for him?" Sammy asked as Davy and Lucy disappeared at the top of the escalator.

"Time will tell," Max said as they headed towards an

exit around the corner from the escalator.

Lucy stepped off the escalator and moved to the side for Davy to step off as he approached the landing. Once off, he led the way to the food court, then stopped, and spread his arms wide, and proclaimed, "You can get whatever you want. Money is no object." He looked at Lucy with a silly grin.

"Obviously, if you took me here," Lucy said dryly. She heard Davy's soft chuckle. "Ouch!" She dabbed at her lip.

"What's wrong?" Davy asked with concern.

"Ooh," Lucy said in pain. "You know when you bite your lip, and then it seems like you just keep hitting that same spot again and again? Like there's no other place in your mouth for your teeth to hit?"

"Uh oh. But it looks better since you put the salve on it. Does it feel better?" Davy asked with empathy.

Lucy gave a little whimper and said, "Yeah."

"Well, let's get some food in ya. That should make you feel a little better, provided you don't bite your lip," Davy said as he led her further into the food court. Lucy moaned in agreement.

Twenty minutes later, with food in hand, they chose a table placed in a section all alone and faced each other to eat their food. After Davy took a big bite of his burger, Lucy began to pepper him with questions, "So are you friend or foe?"

"Friend," Davy said through a mouthful of food.

"Who do you work for? Why do you carry a gun? Who were those two guys you were with?"

Davy began to choke on his food and held his hand

up to stop her from going further.

"Well?" Lucy asked.

"Isn't your lip hurting you?" Davy asked, wiping his fingers with a napkin.

"It's feeling better," Lucy responded quickly. "Well?" She stared at him while she took a bite of an onion ring.

Davy took a big swig of his soda, then wiped his mouth with a napkin as he tried to figure out how best to handle her questions so they'd appease her curiosity. He couldn't afford her getting mixed up in this mess. It could ruin his past two years of work.

"Well?' Lucy asked as she leaned on the table and rested her chin in her hand. *Why did he have a gun? And why tell her—someone he didn't know—his deepest, darkest secrets? Or would he lie?* she wondered.

"Okay. . . it's not that big of a deal, but you had such a hissy fit on the plane," Davy began as he rested his chair on only the two back legs.

Lucy bristled at that accusation and said, "Hissy fit?! Are you kidding me? Ouch! Oh, ow," she said when her hand hit her cut lip.

"Sorry, *hissy fit* may not be the best word to use. . . at your, um, unease over something that didn't concern you—"

"Oh yeah, that's a lot better," Lucy said sarcastically.

"Anyway," Davy took a deep breath. He gave Lucy a look to not interrupt before he continued, "it is not as sinister as you might think—the reason I carry a gun on flights."

Lucy remained silent and cocked her head to one

side, waiting.

Davy continued, "I work for the government via the TSA." Lucy squinted her eyes in confusion and opened her mouth to say something, but Davy held up his hand to stop her. He continued, "I'm an Air Marshal."

"An Air Marshal?" Lucy smiled. "Mmm," she said as she wiggled her eyebrows.

Davy nodded his head, then asked, "Do you know what that is?"

"Yes," Lucy responded with a huge smile. "So, that's why you had a gun on the plane?"

Davy nodded. "Ya gotta keep it down, though. People aren't supposed to know who the FAMs are."

"FAMs?" Lucy asked, confused.

"Federal Air Marshals," Davy took another bite of his food.

"Is that what everyone calls you guys? FAMs?" Lucy asked.

Davy swallowed his food before he responded. "That or flyers."

"That is so cool," Lucy said with admiration as she continued to smile.

Davy gave an uncomfortable chuckle and said, "Thanks, I guess."

"And sexy."

"What?" Davy asked, surprised.

"Yeah, totally sexy. How long have you been doing it?"

"A few years."

"Were you in the military or something before that?" Lucy asked nonchalantly.

Davy nodded his head.

"The military?" Lucy asked, captivated.

Davy nodded as he ate some fries.

"Which branch?"

"I was in the Navy."

"The Navy?" Lucy asked while she dug in her purse. "Uh-huh. . . as a cook? Medic? Diver?" Lucy pulled out the lip salve and dabbed more on her cut lip. "The salt stings," she explained.

"No. I was in special ops," Davy said.

"Oh, you were an Operations clerk?"

"No. Special ops—operations," Davy told her. He continued to eat his fries.

"Special ops, huh? How special?"

"Pretty special, I guess," Davy responded without looking at her.

"Hm . . . special ops, and you were in the Navy, eh? Were you a Navy Seal?" she asked coyly as she leaned forward in anticipation of his answer.

Davy did a slight nod and answered, "Yeah."

"Shut up! Are you serious? O. M. G! And that's OMG for Oh My Goodness, not—" Lucy babbled in her excitement.

"Huh?" Davy looked at her, confused.

"Never mind. That is so cool. How long were you a seal?"

"Quite a while."

"Quite a while?" She asked.

"Yeah."

"So, you aren't gonna give me specifics, eh? Just very generic answers?" Lucy let out a heavy breath and relaxed back in the chair.

"What do ya mean generic?"

"Quite a while, a few years," Lucy mimicked Davy.

"I told ya I was a Seal," he said almost defensively.

"No, you said special ops. I guessed you were a Navy Seal. You didn't tell me. All you said was yeah when I asked. You could've gone into it a bit more." Davy rolled his eyes. Then she asked, "Why'd you get out?"

"Death in the family."

"Oh, I'm sorry. Wh-who died?" Lucy asked with a sympathetic look—which was tough after he told her he was special ops.

"My sister's husband. Left her with five kids."

"Five?" Lucy asked, incredulously, holding up her hand with all fingers spread as emphasis.

"Yup, five."

"Wow. So, you left your seal team to help your sister," Lucy stated as she nodded her head.

Davy took a bite of his burger and nodded. "Mhm."

"What a good brother," Lucy said while inside she was screaming, *you quit being a Navy Seal for that?* She knew she was a horrible person for having those thoughts, thus the reason she didn't say them aloud.

"It's what family does," Davy responded modestly.

Lucy grunted, then asked, "Is it the sister that was at the library?" Davy nodded and shoved the remainder of his burger into his mouth.

Lucy leaned forward and in a conspiratorial way and asked, "So, tell me this—" *This guy was way too good of a find*, Lucy thought to herself.

"Yes?" Davy asked as he saw the sparkle in Lucy's

blue eyes.

"Which was tougher: The Navy Seals or the five kids?" Lucy asked, then laughed at her joke. Davy laughed despite himself.

"Wait, you thought I was a cook in the Navy?" Davy asked in disbelief

Lucy shrugged.

"Do I look like a cook?" Davy asked incredulously as he leaned back in his chair and spread his arms. Again, Lucy just shrugged—she loved that she'd found a button of his to push.

"Are you gonna eat that?" Davy asked, pointing to her untouched burger. Lucy shook her head. "Do you mind?" He asked. She pushed the plate towards him.

"Have you ever been ma—" Lucy began to ask when her phone rang. She looked at her phone and rolled her eyes, "Excuse me, gotta take this," she said as she rose from her chair and moved away from the table with her back to Davy. He watched her walk away, unable to see her face or hear her conversation, but watched her free arm begin to flail about. Only a few minutes passed before she returned, frowning at her phone.

"Everything okay?" Davy asked curiously and chewed the last of Lucy's burger.

"Hm?" Lucy looked up from her phone, lost in thought. "Yeah. That was my office. They want me to come home tomorrow. They booked the flight for oh dark thirty tomorrow," Lucy blew out air in disappointment. "I was looking forward to some time away from the office." She sighed. "Oh well. . ."

"You have to leave?"

"Yeah, one of the guys I support is sick in the hospital, and someone needs to be there to help any clients that might call in," Lucy explained.

"You can't stay for a couple of days to relax and sightsee?" Davy asked.

"Are you?"

"I head back on a flight tomorrow," he said, "but you really should stay and sightsee."

"Nah, I gotta get back. The stock market's been so volatile lately that I really can't be away unless it's necessary," Lucy told him resignedly.

"Too bad. Florida is a great place to visit."

Lucy shrugged, "So I've heard. But it will have to remain an urban myth to me for now." Lucy gave a bitter laugh, then turned sideways in her chair, crossed her legs, and rested her arm on the chair back as she gave him an approving look. "Why did you tell me all that stuff about you and your work? Isn't the Air Marshal part supposed to be secret?" she asked.

"Yeah, but you threatened to go to the pilot, so I thought I should come clean with you."

"But you didn't have to. For all you knew, you might've never seen me again. And, if you're an Air Marshal, the pilot already knew you were on board."

"I think it's doubtful I won't see you again. I've seen you three times already in less than two months—now you're even on the same plane."

"Are you following me?" Lucy asked. Surprised, Davy looked at her for a second before he threw his head back and gave a loud laugh.

It had not escaped Lucy's attention that Davy didn't

L. K. Lawrence

respond to her statement that the pilot already knew he was on the flight. Instead, she slyly observed his actions as she finished her drink, then his phone rang.

Davy turned his phone over and said, "Ah! I need to take this," then put the phone to his ear as he stood. Lucy couldn't help but hear his side of the conversation, "Yeah," he answered, then paused before he said, "no big deal. I'll take care of it," He ended the call, then turned back to Lucy with an apologetic smile. "Sorry about that. But I think I better go submit my flight report."

Lucy stood and lifted her purse strap off the back of the chair and said, "Oh sure. I hope I didn't keep you from anything important."

"Nah, just have to finish some stuff up," Davy said as he casually hooked the black backpack onto his shoulder as they left the food court and moved toward the escalator. "So, you'll be heading home tomorrow?"

"Yup," Lucy responded glumly as she rolled her luggage on, then stepped on the escalator herself. "Will you be on that flight, per-chance?" she asked flippantly.

Davy laughed, "I sure hope not," he said as he stepped on the escalator closely behind her.

"Heeey!" Lucy said with a scowl.

"Sorry, that sounded worse than I meant it to."

"Uh-huh," Lucy didn't look at him. "I'm beginning to see why you aren't married." Davy gently pushed her but said nothing. Then, "Hey!" she said as she grasped the rail, so she didn't tumble forward.

"Where are you staying tonight?"

"Not sure; my hotel was in town. But now that I need to leave so early in the morning, I'll need to find a room here at the airport. Any suggestions?" She asked over her shoulder.

"You should ask the Concierge. They'll know where there are available rooms."

"There's a concierge at the airport?" Lucy asked, surprised.

"Sure. I'll take you to their desk." They rode the last couple of seconds in silence. Once off the escalator, Davy took the lead and headed through the doors away from the baggage claim area. They continued until they stopped in front of a desk with a sign that read "Concierge" above it.

"Well, here you go. Have a good flight home tomorrow," Davy said, then turned without another word and walked towards a door with the words No Admittance printed in thick block letters on it. Still, before he opened the door, he held his hand against the red light that glowed from a box at the side. Once the light turned green, he pulled the door open and disappeared behind it.

"Bye," Lucy said faintly to his retreating form. Something didn't seem right about the whole deal to Lucy. *Why would he tell so much information to someone he didn't know? Who is he?*

***

The next day Davy walked into the office at LAX amid catcalls, whistles, and applause from the other FAMs sitting at their desks. Word had quickly spread about the girl on the flight among the flyers. Davy looked at Max, who shook his head and held up his hands to say he had nothing to do with it, then nodded his head towards

Sammy, who sat laughing with the rest of the room.

"Is there no brother code with you?" Davy asked Sammy with mock hurt.

"No shame here, brother," he told him.

"Now your women meet you on your flights?" called Jerome, a pudgy Latin man who considered himself to be a Don Juan from across the floor.

Davy rolled his eyes before he responded, "Yeah, jealous?"

"You wish," Jerome chortled cockily. He was almost as tall as Davy but about ten years younger. He had his fair share of ladies in every airport even though he was married.

Later, as Max and Davy left the office simultaneously, Max asked, "How'd it go with the girl?"

"Fine."

"Is she someone you're dating?" he asked. They'd gone through the academy together before becoming Federal Air Marshals but hadn't worked together that much until Davy transferred into the LAX office.

"Nah. Believe it or not, I've only seen her a few times before yesterday."

Max let out a laugh and said, "Boy, it didn't look like that. Not the way she approached you. I was ready to pull my gun and come to your aid."

Davy chuckled and said, "She definitely says her mind. It took all my negotiating skills to get her not to go and report to the pilot that I was carrying a gun on the plane."

"That wouldn't have been an issue since the pilot already knew we were on board and carrying," Max said as he stopped and looked at Davy curiously.

"It would've drawn attention to me—which I didn't need—especially on a flight. Who knows how many phones would be recording the whole incident to post on social media?" Davy reminded Max. They stood at the entrance to the parking structure.

Max nodded his head in agreement and said, "I hadn't thought of it from that angle. Modern technology could really screw us."

"I hope I don't get written up for it."

Max guffawed as he shook his head and said, "Women."

"I know, right?" Both men turned and walked in opposite directions as they laughed in agreement.

Chapter 11

Davy sat across from Director Janssen, a man in his early sixties, who looked more like a friendly grandfather than the Assistant Federal Security Director. Dressed in a blazer, polo shirt, khaki pants, and loafers, he sat comfortably in a booth at McDonald's. In his younger days, he'd been one of the toughest Army Rangers in Ranger history. Nevertheless, Davy imagined this sixty-something guy could still hold his own in any fight. So he sat patiently and waited for Director Janssen to start.

"I know you were expecting someone else," Director Janssen said as he took his food off the tray, placed it on the table, then pushed the tray aside.

"Yes, sir, I was. I didn't expect to see you here. I usually report to another agent," Davy said as he took the lid off his salad.

"Since this operation is dealing with questionable activities within the government, I felt I should be more involved. I know someone like you, with the experience you have, we can depend on a professional job. Been undercover for what—two years now?" the Director asked.

Davy nodded his head. "Yes, sir."

"How are you handling working in your hometown?"

"I've never worked this way before," Davy admitted with a frown and took a forkful of salad.

"How do you mean?" asked the Director.

"Usually, when I'm working undercover, it's in another state or something. Here I have to worry about running into friends or family."

"Have you run into any family or friends yet?"

"You mean besides my sister and her five kids, my high school friends, buddies I served with?" Davy asked flatly.

"Ah," the director nodded knowingly. "Do you think you can do your job effectively, or is it too difficult?" Director Janssen asked as he lifted his coffee to his lips.

"I'm doing the best I can."

"Perhaps we should shut the operation down? Move someone else in and start over?" The director asked with concern. "I'd have to explain it to everyone why, but it is understandable," he reasoned aloud.

Davy exhaled. "Sir, I can do it. You don't need to shut it down. I just have to work it differently," Davy said as he rubbed his hand across his eyes.

"How? Did you change your name?" asked Director Janssen.

"I planned on doing that at first, but I think it would be too tough to maintain the two identities. So I just work very hard at keeping the two worlds separate," Davy said with a light shrug.

"Hm. That's a dangerous approach."

"I know, but what else was I to do? I'm in a very tough spot working in my hometown."

The director nodded his head, "I'm still not sure you're the right guy for this operation, though."

"I can do it, sir. After two years, I've finally gained their trust and will get to do more than just transport."

The Director started to say something, then paused, and said, "I'll be your contact instead of Smith for now."

Davy nodded his head in response. "Understood, sir," Davy stopped eating and looked at the Director.

"I'm also concerned someone compromised this operation."

"How do you mean?"

I was told that you might have been compromised?"

"By who? How?" Davy asked, alarmed.

"The girl."

"What girl?"

"The girl on the plane. The one that took you away from your job for about ten minutes—the one you pulled into the galley," Director Janssen raised his eyebrows.

"Oh, that girl. How'd you hear about her?" Davy set his fork down with a sigh.

The Director cocked his head to the side without a word and waited. When Davy didn't say anything, he continued, "I read the other flyers' reports. Both Stein and Felix mentioned it in their reports."

"Well, then you know about how I was pushed into her lap by that mother. The girl said she'd felt my gun and wanted to know why I was carrying one—before you ask, she's someone I've met at the library back home," Davy told him without looking up from the table.

Director Janssen sighed, then asked, "Is she going to be a problem?"

Davy looked up. "No, sir. As far as she's concerned, I'm an Air Marshal," Davy said, hoping he had handled it correctly. But, unfortunately, Lucy was not a young twenty-something girl that believed anything without question. It would take hard work to keep her off his track once he got back into town if that's how he chose to handle it.

"You're sure you haven't been compromised?" Director Janssen asked again.

"Anyone who wants to scrub this mission has never been undercover."

"I'm aware of that."

"It takes time to get in deep."

"I understand that," Director Janssen responded. "I'm not the one trying to shut down the operation."

"I appreciate that, sir," Davy responded.

"How do you think it's going?" The Director asked as he rested an arm on the back of the booth bench and looked at Davy as though he could read his thoughts.

"Since my transfer to LAX, I've been promoted within the organization. I'll be flying to Rome on my next flight," Davy told the Director.

"Why?" The director asked.

Davy shrugged his shoulders and said, "I don't ask questions; I just do."

"Is that a wise choice?" The Director asked.

"If you ask questions, they get suspicious," Davy

replied.

"What's the promotion?"

"Transporting the drugs through the airport without any difficulty," Davy said.

"Who are the drug carriers?" Director Janssen asked.

"Some of the flyers," he said gravely. "And some of the airport personnel."

Director Janssen sighed and said, "That's disappointing to hear, but we've had our suspicions. How many flyers do you think are involved?"

"Felix and Stein are my main contacts right now. With the promotion, I'll be able to find out who the head of the operation is and the other flyers that are involved," Davy said.

"You think you can find the head of this snake?"

"Eventually. For two years, I've played more of a gopher than anything else," Davy told the Director. "I keep my mouth closed and my ears open.

"Have they mentioned any names?" The director asked.

"Strega Straniera," Davy told him. "Not sure if that is the snake, but they do mention that name with some respect." Davy piled his food containers on a tray and slid out of the booth.

"Man or woman, ya think?" The director asked.

Davy shrugged. "I don't know enough Italian to tell, and no one states one way or the other," Davy said.

"I want to hear from you after your trip to Rome," Director Janssen instructed Davy as he stood, grabbed the tray with the wrappers and empty cup. "I don't need to remind you that this investigation is hazardous not only for you but for anyone you might associate with now and in the future. So try to keep your two worlds separate. If they find out you aren't who you've said you are, they'll kill ya."

"I'm aware of that, sir," Davy said. "That's why I work the way I do. I'm used to the danger.

"But is your family or your girlfriend?" The director asked seriously.

Davy bowed his head in frustration before he answered. "My sister is safe, and I don't have a girlfriend." But, of course, Davy was well aware of who the director was referring to as his girlfriend. *So why does everyone consider her his girlfriend?* They were just friends.

The director gave him a side glance with raised eyebrows before he said, "Well, keep me abreast of any changes or when you're ready to cut the head off the snake." Then dumped the trash into the bin and set the tray on top of it

"Will do, sir," Davy responded as he threw his trash in the bin. He knew all too well the seriousness of this operation—he'd been living it for the past two years. Smuggling drugs on one hand while helping his sister and her kids on the other. He had to continue to keep the worlds separate—one oblivious of the other. But the biggest worry was how to keep Lucy contained?

***

Lucy sat behind her desk, deep in thought. She'd been back from her trip for a week and still found the conversation with Davy unnerving. Why he'd told her so much about himself, what he did, and why he carried a gun. She'd kept the conversation to herself, unsure how to convey to anyone what she'd felt and thought at the time. That is until Lori stood in the doorway of her office, having just returned from taking Bingo for a walk.

As usual, she dressed in the latest fashion, in a light blue silk top, with a more oversized shirt worn over it with her fitted jeans and ankle-high boots with four-inch heels to make up for the height she didn't have. And as usual, her make-up was perfect. She let go of Bingo's leash as he walked further into the office to where Lucy stood, raised his front legs, and rested them on her lap for a moment to let her know he wanted to be petted.

"Is he supposed to do this?" Lucy asked while she scratched Bingo behind the ears.

"Sure. Why not?" Lori responded.

"I thought the dogs were trained to stay near their owners, that's all," Lucy responded.

"He's on medical leave," Lori said and laughed. "I have ruined all his training."

Lucy laughed. "So not surprised," she said.

"So, what's been going on with you lately?" Lori asked as she leaned against the doorsill.

"Nothin', just working," Lucy responded, not looking up.

"Are you sure? You've seemed a bit distracted since you came back from your trip," Lori stated with a concerned look.

That was all the prompting Lucy needed. "Oh, all right," and she told her all about the trip and her experience with Davy.

"So, he's an Air Marshal and a former Navy Seal? All the things you love most," Lori acknowledged. with a snicker. "What is wrong with that?"

Lucy couldn't help but blush at Lori's response. "Yes, he is all that. I acted the fool with my excitement at the news when he told me, but I couldn't help it. Imagine if you met Estee Lauder or some makeup icon and could get all the makeup and advice you wanted. I think you'd be just as excited as I was," Lucy said defensively.

Lori put her hand up to hide the laughter that escaped. She cleared her throat and said, "Yes, I can see the correlation between the two." But that was all she could get out before she began to laugh aloud. Just as she did, Bill exited his office next to Lucy's and looked at both of them in exasperation.

"Can you keep it down, please? You're a little loud." He told them and returned to his office, followed by a door slam for emphasis. Lori rolled her eyes while Lucy quietly laughed.

"What I don't understand is why he'd tell me so much, someone he's only spoken with a couple of times. In fact, he didn't even know my name until that night," Lucy said in a hushed tone.

Lori gave Lucy a shocked look and asked, "He didn't know your name?"

Lucy continued, unphased by Lori's reaction. "And I only told him my first name." Lucy proudly stated, then leaned against the credenza behind her desk, lost in thought as Lori scrutinized her.

"Are you still going to the library every night?" Lori

quietly asked.

"Yeah, duh!" Lucy guffawed.

Lori rolled her eyes and said, "I should've known better. Have you seen him?"

"No, not yet. But I do remain hopeful. I have to learn more about him and what he does, I guess. I find it so fascinating. I mean, c'mon, he's a warrior who isn't afraid to fight."

"You might not want to harp on about his service. He might not be comfortable with that," Lori suggested.

"Yeah, yeah, yeah," Lucy sighed in mock exaggeration and dropped in her chair as she rested her elbows on her desk. "Wait! Who says I harp?"

"Just sayin'," Lori said with raised eyebrows and turned to leave as she tugged on Bingo's leash, taking him with her. "What about the guy in your dream?"

"Oh gee," Lucy deflated back in her chair. "I'd forgotten about him, what with Davy and all his information. A navy seal always outranks a faceless stalker."

"What if it's a faceless Navy Seal?" Lucy watched Lori's chubby frame shake with laughter as she retreated into the Cashier's cage.

"Hahaha! Very funny," Lucy said to the closed door.

She understood to not harp—as Lori would say, on about his service. *But gee, this is like kryptonite*, she said to herself. She needed to learn more about Air Marshals; what did they do? How often they flew? How many on a flight? What were the tools of the trade? And to who did they report? The rest of the information would need to come from him.

As Lucy went through her day, her mind would often return to Davy and how best to play it. Finally, she realized that her best bet was for them to be friends since she was sure he wouldn't be interested in her romantically. If they were friends, there would be no expectation, and perhaps he'd tell her more.

With that decided, she needed him to show up at the library so she could build on their friendship—and then she'd ply him for more information. She crossed her eyes at that idea, but who knows, it might just work. *Good luck with that*, she told herself.

That night in the library, she waited at the table where she'd met him twice before. *Will he show up?* She asked herself. Or would he avoid her after their meeting on the plane and in the airport? Especially since she'd made such a fool of herself when he told her his history.

***

Max and Sammy guided Davy towards an old warehouse near the pier where many cargo ships had docked. Davy made a mental note of the surrounding area and the location to put it in his report to Director Janssen.

As they approached the warehouse, he could see more detail. There were two large sliding doors on the front end, probably for receiving shipments, an upstairs, and a couple of side doors. Davy headed towards the front with the sliding doors out of instinct but was stopped and redirected to the first side door. He looked at Max questioningly.

"We rarely use the front doors," Max explained as he

directed him to the side entrance.

"No need to, really," Sammy stated with a shrug from behind.

Davy didn't expect to see what he did when he entered the warehouse behind Max. He stopped as he took it all in. There weren't bales of drugs as he'd expected, but multiple skeletons of classic cars—all at different stages of being refurbished and about a dozen mechanics working on them. Maybe he had this group all wrong? *Perhaps they are really a Podunk operation that I've wormed my way into*, he thought to himself.

"So, you refurbish cars here?" Davy asked while scanning the large room. He was breaking his first cardinal rule by asking a question.

"That's the cover, bro," Sammy responded as he stood beside him.

"What's upstairs?" Davy asked when he saw the stairs at the back end of the warehouse.

"Living quarters and the rest of the operation," Max told him as they got closer to the stairs. "Down there is the accountant's office," Max said as they passed a small hallway that had a door at the end of it.

"Someone lives here?" Davy asked, amazed.

"Yeah, Junie. Her husband started this whole operation," Sammy told him.

"Her deceased husband," Max corrected Sammy.

"But you'll never need to have contact with the accountant," Sammy told him. "In fact, you'll probably never be here again," he concluded.

"Why not? Isn't this where the packages are?" he asked.

Max stopped walking and turned to him. "The packages will be dropped at your place by Sal and Johnny in exchange for the money you'll receive from a third party. We brought you here to see the operation, so you're more familiar with the process, that's all."

"So, the front of the operation is the classic car refurbishment?"

"Yeah," both Max and Sammy responded in unison. Davy nodded his head.

They proceeded up the stairs with Davy sandwiched between Max and Sammy. Once at the top, they walked through the first set of double doors into an office.

"This is where the boss can be found on most days," Sammy explained just as a petite blonde entered.

"I'll meet the boss?" Davy asked, looking from Max to Sammy.

Max and Sammy exchanged looks before Max started to say, "Not the bo—," but was interrupted by Junie entering the area.

Davy looked at the petite blonde with appreciation. She wore a white tennis outfit with a three-color design that went up the left side and fit like a glove over her curvaceous form. The golden hair down her back accentuated her tanned body. The tennis shoes she wore had a slight heel that added a minute amount to her short stature. He was captivated by the beautiful white smile, the big brown eyes that stared back at him.

Junie stopped in her tracks when she saw the three men. She hadn't expected the new guy to be so tall and rugged-looking. She beamed at Davy as if he were the only one in the room.

"Well, well, well, who might this tawl drink of water be?" she asked in a nasally Southern drawl almost identical to the Steve Urkel character from a nineties sitcom.

"This is the new guy," Sammy told her.

"Oh? How new?" She asked with a smile pasted on her face. Davy fought the urge to laugh at the sound of her voice.

"He's only worked in the field, but the boss promoted him," Max informed her.

Junie cocked an eyebrow, then asked, "The boss?"

Sammy and Max nodded.

"Well, I am very pleased to meet you," she said as she sidled up next to Davy, hooked her arm through his, and gently pulled him towards the couch while Max and Sammy looked on.

"Just sit right here, next to me. I want to get to know you better," Junie said with a smile that could melt butter. Davy willingly sat down next to her.

"We were just gonna show him the rest of the warehouse," Max informed her.

"That's okay," she said smoothly, "I'll show him."

"I should probably stick with Max and Sammy— don't want the boss to think I'm—," he started to say but was stopped by the woman's finger to his lips.

"Don't ya'll worry 'bout the boss," she told them dismissively, then turned to Davy and said, "I'm Junie, by the way, or June-bug if you like."

Davy smiled big in response to her flirting. "I'm Davy." He told her. If he didn't listen to her speak, then she was quite attractive.

"Davy?" she asked, "I like your name. Mind if I call you Davy Honey?"

"N-n-no, not at all," he stuttered and gave Max and Sammy a confused look. They returned the gaze and shrugged.

***

The week passed with no sign of Davy. And again, Lucy was back into her old routine of going to the library and waiting. But this time, it wasn't for a faceless stranger, but a man with a face and a history that movies and Lucy's dreams were made of.

Lucy didn't read the same book while she waited for Davy to reappear but instead searched the internet on her laptop for information on Air Marshals. She learned about their training, what they wore, what they did, their salaries, and the type of guns they carried. It was as sexy as she'd thought it would be. To her anyway, if not to the actual flyers as they were called. And so, it went day in and day out. Until one Sunday, she didn't bother going. It was a day for her to take a break and rethink her plan.

***

It's like nails on a chalkboard, Davy thought as he listened to Junie respond to his question. "I was born and raised in Georgia but moved out here as soon as I could because of work," she told him as she batted her long lashes from across the table.

"Was that the same work you do now?" He asked.

"Well, it was my husband's idea that I work," Junie told him as she took a sip of water.

"You're married?" Davy asked.

"Me? No," Junie said with finality as she made a face.

"But you just mentioned your husband," Davy stated, confused.

Junie giggled. "Oh, he died."

"You started working at the warehouse after that?" Davy asked as casually as he could.

Junie gave Davy an evaluating stare, then said suspiciously. "You sure do ask a lot of questions."

"How else will I get to know you?" he countered.

"Oh," Junie giggled. "I guess that is the only way." Her laugh turned into a bray. Junie reached her bony hand across the table and playfully tickled the back of Davy's hand with her claw-like nails as she cooed. Davy feared his face would give away his discomfort of listening to the Urkel voice emanating from her beautiful face. He knew this was only the beginning of some very long nights ahead. *How will I survive?* He asked himself.

Later that week, driving in his truck Davy called his former contact, Joel Smith. He was the agent Davy used to meet with before Director Jansson.

"How long have you been seeing this Junie?" Joel asked.

"Just a week, but it's killin' me," Davy told him.

"How so?"

"Do you remember that Steve Urkel character from that nineties show?" Davy asked.

"Uh, yeah, the skinny kid with the big glasses?" Joel

answered hesitantly.

"Yup," Davy said.

"Why?" Joel asked.

"Imagine this beautiful typical California girl, or Georgia Peach as she claims, but when she opens her mouth, out comes that Urkel character. And, she has a southern drawl that draws it out." Joel was laughing so hard Davy pulled the phone away from his ear. When Joel had stopped laughing, Davy said, "Makes me homesick for the water boardin' days."

"Dude, it can't be that bad. Is she a smoke show?" he asked.

Davy exhaled and said, "If I remember right, yeah. But I can't even tell anymore.

"You can't tell?" Joel asked.

Dude, it's only been a week, and all I see when I look at her is Urkel."

"Maybe you should cut her loose?" Joel suggested between bouts of laughter.

"Oh man," Davy said with a slight chuckle, "if only it were that easy."

"So, you're dating her?"

"She works at the warehouse. This might be the break I've needed for this operation."

"Is the sacrifice worth it?" Joel asked.

"Sacrifice? You mean dating her?"

"Listening to her voice—."

"Man, I don't know. What I do know, though, is I should never have to pay taxes again after dealing with this crazy." Joel only laughed on the other end of the phone. "On the bright side, she should be a good source of information," Davy concluded.

"There ya go. I knew you'd find the reason to stick with it. You always do," Joel told Davy.

***

Lucy stayed away from the library for a couple of weeks until she decided to tempt fate and see if there was any sign of Davy. With little hope of him being there, she went directly to the library from her workout; she was sweaty and messy and not fit to be seen in public. She only planned to drop in, take a quick look to see if he were there, then leave. It had been weeks since she'd last seen Davy. Without a flesh and blood man in sight, the dream had started up again. She was back to the faceless stranger and restless nights.

"Well, hello there," Mrs. Gable said as Lucy walked past her desk. "We haven't seen you for quite some time."

"Hello Mrs. Gable, I've just been busy with work."

"Aren't you casual today," Mrs. Gable said as she noticed Lucy's sweaty appearance. This caused Lucy to blush and zip her sweatshirt all the way up and put her sunglasses on in hopes that no one else would recognize her.

"I won't be here long—," Lucy said as she backed towards the table through the crowded library. She turned in the direction of the table and stopped in her tracks. A man was seated at her table. *Is it him?* She asked herself. She held her breath as she approached the table while she subconsciously crossed her fingers. She couldn't see his face. *Is it him? Is this the dream?* She asked herself as she moved around people, and her heart began to pound.

She was almost to the table when the man looked up and repositioned the baseball cap on his head. Lucy stopped cold. It wasn't Davy. With a sigh of disappointment, and without looking where she was going, she turned and crash into another patron sending books and sunglasses flying.

"Oh, excuse me," she said as she crouched to retrieve her sunglasses.

"No problem. I should've watched where—," said the deep voice of the other patron as he crouched down at the same time. Their knees knocked together, which pushed both off their balance onto their backsides.

"Aaah," Lucy said as she fell backward.

"Hey! It's you! Where ya been?" They said over each other.

Lucy did a double-take in comical surprise. "Where've I been? Where've you been?" She asked in shock as she stared at Davy, who sat across from her. *He's back!*

On the floor surrounded by books, they looked at each other in silence as smiles spread on their faces. Lucy casually reached for her sunglasses that had skidded further away when she fell. Then they both began to laugh.

Lucy asked, "Are we in a Doris Day Rock Hudson movie?" and laughed some more.

Davy's laughter stopped cold as he gave her an intense look, "Does that make me Rock Hudson?" he seriously asked with a cocked eyebrow, no longer laughing.

With a chuckle, Lucy said, "Oh, sorry. Bad choice. Um—how about a Katherine Hepburn Cary Grant movie?" she asked with a snicker.

"Uhm, yeah, I don't think so—not sure that's any better." Davy gave a deadpan response, which made Lucy double over in laughter.

"You do know your Hollywood history," Lucy said with admiration.

"Shhhh! Shhhhh!" Said Baby Jane as she angrily marched towards them.

"Now, Jane," Mrs. Gable said in a loud whisper just a short distance behind her. "I saw what happened, and it was just an accident of them bumping into each other." Mrs. Gable put her arm around Baby Jane and redirected her, "I think I saw some books that a patron had left on the floor in the Psychology section. Would you be so kind as to return them to their correct shelf, please?"

"Bu—," Baby Jane started to say, but Mrs. Gable raised her index finger to stop her.

"Just over there, Jane. Thank you." She said and lightly pushed Baby Jane forward. After Baby Jane had walked away, Mrs. Gable turned back towards Davy and Lucy, still seated on the floor. "Okay, I've bought you enough time for you to gather your stuff. In the future, please keep your joviality down for the other patrons, okay?" She smiled sweetly and walked away.

While Davy's attention had been on Mrs. Gable and Baby Jane, Lucy took the opportunity to put her sunglasses on. She felt she had to hide how bad she looked after her workout. Davy began to pick up the books he'd dropped when he and Lucy had collided. Lucy, with sunglasses in place, began to assist him.

Davy quietly chuckled as he stood with his arms full of books, cocked his head, and with a crooked smile, said, "I've missed this."

"You missed what? Us banging into each other or me?" She smiled big at the prospect of being missed.

"You, of course." Davy chuckled and continued, "You're the only one who gets my movie references," Davy said in a casual tone.

"That's the only reason you noticed my absence? Great." Lucy asked, deflated. Davy looked at her blankly. *Typical man*, she thought disappointedly, then asked again, "So, where ya been?"

Davy sighed then said, "I can't begin to tell you." *She has no idea how true that statement is*, he thought.

Lucy couldn't hide her self-conscious smile as she looked up into the handsome face of this tall man she hadn't seen for so long; A man who had almost admitted that he'd missed her. "So, you aren't upset at me for what happened the last time I saw you?"

Davy looked at her confused, "What happened last time?" he asked.

"At the airport—on the plane," Lucy said as she looked down at her tennis shoes.

Davy gave a quiet laugh, then answered, "No, of course not. What made you think that?"

"Seeing you."

"I don't even know you to be upset at you," Davy waved his hand in dismissal.

"That's good to know."

"Shhh!" Both looked over to see Baby Jane staring

them down with her finger to her lips as she scowled. Then, they looked at each other and laughed.

"She's ba-ack," Lucy said in a sing-song voice and giggled.

"Good to see that some things haven't changed," Davy said with a wink. "I owe you some tea, I believe. Wanna go get some?"

Lucy had forgotten she was in her sweaty and possibly smelly by now, gym clothes, and no makeup. "Sure," Lucy said with false confidence, then grimaced.

"Great, let me put these books back, and we can go," Davy said with the easiness that came naturally to him.

Lucy waited as Davy disappeared down one of the rows only to reappear from a different library area altogether a few minutes later. "Sorry, I had a lot of books. I don't like to leave them for the librarians—even Baby Jane—to have to put back since I pulled them," he paused for a moment as he put his hand on the small of her back to direct her towards the doors.

"Aren't you Mr. Thoughtful," Lucy said flippantly, although down deep she was impressed.

As they passed Baby Jane, he leaned down and whispered in Lucy's ear, "But ya are Blanche, but ya are!" Lucy couldn't stop the laughter that burst out of her.

"You two need to leave. Don't come back until you can control yourselves and respect the rules," Baby Jane scolded as she followed behind them. Davy held Lucy's elbow as he pulled her out the door, where they doubled over with giddy laughter. She hadn't expected this comfortable comradery with someone she barely knew. Yet, she couldn't deny how natural it felt to be with him.

Once outside, she waited to see what he'd do next; would he still want to get some tea, or had he changed his mind? She crossed her fingers with the hope that he would still like to get tea and that the moonlight would be kind to her sweaty appearance. Then, slyly she removed her sunglasses and hoped he didn't care or notice.

"Ooooh," She groaned aloud. She couldn't stop all the questions that were running through her mind.

Davy stopped walking and looked at her, "Are you okay?"

She hadn't realized she'd groaned that loudly. "Yeah, I'm fine. Why?" She asked, playing dumb.

"I thought I heard you groan or something."

"Groan? Me? Nooo, why would I groan?" Lucy asked, unable to look him in the face. They continued to walk towards their parking spots in silence.

"So, do you want to drive over to Starbucks together or separately?" He asked.

"Umm, let's drive separately, but not to Starbucks. Instead, let's go to, um, Coffee Bean and Tea Leaf. They have better tea, in my opinion," She leaned toward him in a conspiratorial manner as she spoke.

"Coffee Bean and Tea Leaf, it is then," Davy said with a wink that reminded her of Jimmy Stewart in *It's A Wonderful Life*. "I'll follow you. Where'd ya park?" He waited for her answer, unaware that he'd lost her for a second to George Bailey.

With a pleasant sigh, she returned to the present day. "Just over there," she said, surprised he was so easygoing.

"Great. I'm just over there." He pointed in the opposite direction. "Give me a few minutes to drive over here, and then we can leave, okay?"

"Sure." Lucy watched as he jogged to where he'd parked. She couldn't deny her growing attraction to him. *Oh dear*, she thought to herself, *am I getting a crush on this guy? I'm too old for that.*

Lucy waited in her car for the headlights of what she hoped was Davy's truck. Soon she heard the light tap of a horn as the headlights filled her rearview mirror, making it difficult to see to back out of her spot. Cautiously Lucy backed out and hoped he left her enough room so her bumper wouldn't hit him accidentally. She sighed with relief once she straightened out her tires and moved towards the parking lot exit.

With her in front, they formed a caravan—of two cars—in the mile drive to the Coffee Bean, then pulled into two consecutive spots close to the front doors of the establishment.

"That didn't take long at all," Davy told her as they exited their cars and walked towards the doors.

"Yeah, it's pretty close. But, even though you can't sling a dead cat without hitting a Starbucks, I prefer the Coffee Bean."

"Hm. I haven't been to one before, so I'll let you know what I think," Davy said as he opened the door for her.

Lucy gave a short laugh. "Uh oh, should I be nervous?" she asked as they stepped inside and up to the counter.

"Hi there," the barista greeted them. "What can I get for you?"

Davy gestured for her to go first, so Lucy moved in

front of him and said, "I'll have a large chai tea with almond milk and one Stevia, please." After she'd ordered, Lucy opened her purse to dig for her wallet to pay, but Davy stopped her.

"It's on me this time," he said casually.

"Thanks," she said, then stepped back so Davy could place his order.

"These two orders," he said, waving his hand, "are together, and I'll have what she's having." He told the barista, then pulled his wallet out of the back pocket of his well-worn jeans. Lucy walked to the end of the counter to wait for the completed drinks. As soon as Davy had paid the barista, he walked over and stood beside her.

While they waited for their drinks, Davy looked around the shop and asked, "Come here often?"

Lucy giggled, "Do I come here often, eh? Is that your best pick-up line?" She asked through her giggle. At first, Davy looked at her, lost to the humor, then he began to laugh, the kind of laugh that came from deep in his belly. It was good to hear his hearty laugh since Baby Jane usually suppressed it.

"Ah, I get it," Davy said and continued to laugh. "What I meant was, do you come here a lot? Often? As in, is this your hang out?" He accentuated the last bit with finger quotes.

Lucy's eyes sparkled with delight as she responded, "I understood what you meant. It just struck me as funny." She picked up her drink that had been set on the counter and motioned for Davy to grab his.

They walked over to two comfy leather chairs set against one of the walls with drinks in hand. Davy collapsed in his chair as Lucy curled up in hers. She felt chilled from the sweat that had cooled and dried on her body and shivered for a moment as both hands closed around the warm paper cup.

"Mmm," she said as she felt the warmth of the first sip of tea go down her throat. "This tastes so good." She continued to take small sips of tea and then waited for the after-taste of the anise that she loved.

She watched as Davy sat with his head resting on the back of his chair and his eyes closed. She studied his features; they weren't your average good looks, but more of an acquired taste type of look, she thought to herself. Lucy could see the strands of grey that were in his hair and at his temples. She studied the lines that crawled from the corner of his eyes from years of squinting at the sun. She saw the smile lines that encased his mouth, the lines that crossed his forehead, and the odd age spot that peaked through his golden tanned skin that belied the youthfulness he portrayed.

Davy sat up with a start, "Oh, sorry 'bout that. I think I dozed off for a minute." Then he reached for his tea and took a sip.

Lucy watched for his reaction, then asked, "Do you like it?"

Davy tilted his head back and forth as if considering how to answer before he nodded his head. "Yeah. Yeah, I think I do—especially that after taste. What is that?" He asked, searching Lucy's face.

"I like it too. It's anise." Lucy responded with a grin. This was one more thing they had in common. They sipped in companionable silence. Davy rested his ankle

107

on his knee and continued to sip his tea in silence. Finally, when Lucy couldn't stand the silence any longer, she asked, "Why are you so tired? Did you fly today?"

Davy nodded his head, "Yeah. I've been flying a lot."

"That explains why I haven't seen you at the library for so long," Lucy carefully pointed out and saw his body slightly tense up.

"I've been there, but our schedules haven't meshed up until tonight," he lied. He couldn't tell her the real reason he had been away—as well as his concern for her safety. He had to be careful who he let into his life to avoid any dangerous situations that could happen, should his work-life ever cross over to his private life.

"I was worried that you were trying to avoid me after the flight and our conversation in the airport," Lucy stated.

"The flight?" Davy queried.

"Yeah, you know "the flight," Lucy told him. He squinted his eyes in response. So Lucy tried again, "THE flight. The one where you ended up in my lap."

"Oh ho ho," Davy said with a knowing laugh, "THAT flight." He wiggled his eyebrows which caused Lucy to blush.

"Yeah, that flight," Lucy snapped, flustered by him. *Why is he so maddening with his teasing*? she asked herself.

Davy softly chuckled, then took another sip of his tea, "Mmm, that is good." And set the cup on the table between them.

"Yeah," Lucy continued, "since I hadn't seen you, I

figured you were avoiding me." She looked at Davy with the hope that she was wrong in her assumption.

Davy laughed. "Avoid you? Not at all. Just busy with work."

Lucy expelled a sigh of relief and continued to sip her tea. Then just for her own reassurance, she asked, "Honest?"

"Honest," he reassured her.

"So, tell me this," Lucy began, interrupting Davy's reverie, "Why did you tell me so much about you and your job when we were at the airport?" She looked at him curiously. "You told me earlier tonight that you didn't know me well enough to be angry at me. So, why'd you say so much to a stranger then?"

Davy shrugged as he ran his hand through his hair, leaving some standing before he answered, "I don't know. You're easy to talk to, I guess. Were you uncomfortable with what I told you?" He asked, turning his head towards her.

"Nah, not really. Just a little surprised—at first. Then, when you were telling me all your cool history, I loved it." Lucy grinned at Davy as she rubbed her hands together in glee.

"Oh no. Are you a groupie for men in uniform?" He asked.

Lucy blushed. "Honestly? Yup. I am. I can't help it. But not just any guy in uniform. The-the fearless ones— the-the ones who've seen battle, the ones I know would protect me." Lucy stopped and looked at Davy as he silently watched her.

"Anyone who puts on the uniform is most likely

willing to protect you whether they see action or not."

"I know. But ya gotta love a man in uniform, with stubble, and just that edginess he seems to have when he's gone through hell and back," Lucy said with a dreamy sparkle in her eyes.

Davy sniggered. "Oh man, you've got it bad," and sipped more of his tea.

She gave an embarrassed cough and then continued. "I never really paid attention to the military when I was younger. Not until the Iraq war, that is. I remember standing in the gym-where I worked—watching the news as our military rolled into Iraq. I was so overwhelmed with the idea that these people were willing to give their lives for me—someone they didn't even know. I was overwhelmed with gratitude, humility, and the testosterone that seemed to come through the tv. Yes, I know women fought too, but it was the men that caught my attention."

Davy nodded his head as a crooked smile played on his lips. "I see."

"I guess it turned into hero worship, in a sense." Lucy scrunched her face up as she searched his face for any reaction. When he remained silent, she tried to explain more to pull herself out of the hole she was afraid she'd dug for herself. "My dad was part of the greatest generation—he was always my hero." Lucy scrunched her eyebrows together.

"Your dad should be your hero—especially those guys. They are the true heroes," Davy told her sincerely.

Lucy bobbed her head in agreement. "But you know I've always loved King Arthur too. And all the stories about the brave knights and chivalry—"

"You do know that King Arthur didn't really exist, right?" Davy asked as he tilted his head with a questioning look.

Lucy gave an exasperated sigh and responded, "Yes. I know he didn't really exist. But there had to have been someone those tales grew from." She stopped and gave Davy the sweetest smile and continued, "That is the man that I imagine him to be." Davy rolled his eyes.

"So, what do you do for work?" Davy asked her.

"I work in finance."

"Doing what?" He asked.

"I work in the background; with the clients and getting the paperwork completed, I do trades, move money when requested, stuff like that. Nothing really exciting."

"Do you like it?"

Lucy responded without a pause, "It's alright, it pays the bills, so—." She shrugged her shoulders. "I like the people I work with."

"That always helps," Davy said, taking another sip of his tea.

"How 'bout you? Do you like what you do?" Lucy asked as she concentrated on Davy's facial expressions.

Davy nodded his head. "Yeah, for now."

"For now?" Lucy questioned him.

"Yeah, for now, it's interesting. I like the adrenaline rush. But that could always change."

"Ah, so you're a glass half full person, eh?" Lucy asked as she searched his face for confirmation.

"Nah, not really. It's just that there are always

politics in everything. I like my job as long as I don't have to deal with the politics," he said.

Lucy nodded. "Yeah, I get that. I don't like office politics either. And, trust me, in my office, we've got plenty."

"Like what?"

"Well, for instance, the men in my company tend to promote based on looks. And since I'm not one of the pretty girls, it's tough to get recognized," Lucy said with a frown.

"Jealous?" Davy asked with a mischievous look.

Lucy said, "Pfft, probably."

Davy laughed. "At least you're honest," he said with a note of admiration. Lucy took a sip of her tea. "How long have you been doing what you do?" He motioned towards her with his hands.

"What? Finance? A long time, years," Lucy said, then paused, "I can't believe I've done it as long as I have."

"I know. Same here," Davy said in agreement. Again, he leaned his head against the back of the leather chair and closed his eyes.

"Do you wanna go? You seem tired," Lucy asked quietly.

Davy raised his head and looked at Lucy, "Not unless you do. It's nice here," He responded as he looked around the room with its warm tones and soft lighting.

"Yeah, it is. The only bad part is that you get so relaxed that when you're ready to go to bed, you have to drive home," Lucy said with a slight giggle.

Davy nodded.

They sat in friendly silence with spurts of conversation for the rest of the night, asking each other questions about a multitude of subjects. Just as two friends.

"Do you mind if I get your number?" Davy asked as they stood outside the coffee shop near their cars.

"Sure!" Lucy responded quickly, then casually continued, "why would I mind?" Then recited her number to Davy. "Can I get yours?"

"I can't give you my work number because that phone is supplied through the government, and we can't have personal stuff on it. But I'll text you from my personal phone."

"Why can't you give me your personal number now? What if I don't know it's you and ignore the text?" Lucy asked as she looked at him with crinkled eyebrows and her palms up.

Davy couldn't stop the laughter that burst out of his mouth before he said, "It isn't anything sinister, I promise. I had to change my number and haven't tried to memorize it yet. I'll make sure you know it's me." Lucy gave a sigh of relief, which caused Davy to laugh. "Boy, I should've never told you what I did for work," he said as they walked to Lucy's car.

"You should've never fallen into my lap on the airplane, thank you very much," Lucy stated as she gave him a cockeyed grin and pulled her car door open, then plopped inside on the seat. Davy grinned and lightly tapped on the hood of her car as he headed to his truck.

Chapter 12

Four days later and Lucy still hadn't received any text from an unknown number. She knew he was busy just from the little conversation they'd had that night at the coffee shop, but he had asked for her number. She tried to be patient, but with the patience of a gnat, waiting for him to text her was excruciating.

This guy was a sexy hero, and even if it never progressed to something more than friendship, at least she'd have a sexy friend. *A girl can never have too many sexy guy friends*, she reminded herself. He'd have to do until she found the stranger in her dream, then she'd let him go—maybe. *Hopefully, the stranger in my dream will be sexy and brave,* she thought with crossed fingers.

Because she still had the dream some nights, Lucy restarted the ritual of going to the library every night. But to be honest, she'd long given up reading each time. Instead, she'd take her laptop and work as she sat at the table in the hope that Davy would appear.

***

Davy walked up the stairs in the warehouse to find Junie exiting the doors at a brisk pace and ran right into him. "Hey!" He said as he grasped her shoulders to steady her so she wouldn't fall off her four-inch heels.

"Oh dear," she said in her best distressed southern belle accent. "You saved me," smiling up at him with adoring eyes.

"Of all the gin joints in all the world—," Davy began.

"Huh?" Junie said. "What are you talkin' 'bout? Gin joints? How old are you?" she asked with a disgusted look on her face.

Davy let out a disappointed sigh and mumbled, "Lucy would've gotten that."

"Huh? Who?" Junie queried, then her face turned mean, and she asked, "Are you cheating on me?"

"What?" Davy played innocent. "What're you talkin' 'bout? How could anyone cheat on someone like you?" He asked as he picked her up in a big hug.

Junie laughed as her mood quickly lightened, "Oh you, put me down." She giggled as Davy set her down.

"Let's get going so we can get the shipment in time," Davy told her.

Junie smiled. "I knew you were a good bet."

Davy looked at her confused, "A good bet?"

"Well, yeah. A good bet for a boyfriend."

"Ah."

***

"Are you in love with this guy?" Lori asked Lucy one Saturday as they casually strolled in the mall between stores.

"No-ho," Lucy answered without hesitation. "Not at all."

"I don't know," Lori countered as she stopped and studied Lucy, "I think you are."

"Nope," Lucy said as she smooshed up her face. "I don't know enough about him, and I am too old to just fall in love." Lucy walked ahead of Lori and Bingo and stopped in front of a clothing store window, then wistfully said, "I need to get new clothes. I hate mine!"

"Especially now that you have a boyfriend," Lori teased. Lucy turned and glared at her with hands on her hips.

"For your information, I haven't heard from him since he asked for my number and said he'd text me from his personal phone. Granted, due to his job, he may be flying. He told me he could be assigned flights with as little as an hour's notice. But surely, he has a couple of seconds before, during, or after a flight to text me."

"No, you don't like him, do you," Lori stated flippantly with an innocent look.

"Oh, shut up," Lucy said with a laugh.

***

"As soon as we land, we'll need to go meet with our contact," Max lowered his voice as he leaned over the armrest towards Davy.

"Is that Strega?"

"No," Max said.

"Who am I gonna meet then?" Davy asked.

"Paolo."

"Who's that?"

"An Italian connection."

"Why do I have to meet him? When will I meet Strega?" Davy asked.

Max sighed then answered, "I should've never told you about Strega."

"Why?"

"You may never meet him. I haven't."

This was not what Davy wanted to hear. He needed to meet Strega Straniera to get the head of the snake and end this operation before the Feds did. But how? Everyone seemed to mention him, but no one had met him. Maybe he'd have to force the issue, get Junie to use her influence, and arrange a meeting. Whatever he did, a meeting with Strega needed to happen sooner rather than later.

***

"I finally got a text from him," Lucy announced as

she put in the code to the Cashier's cage where Lori was sitting behind her desk. Since Lucy was Lori's backup, she had the combination to the lock that kept the cage secure. When she needed to tell Lori something that was for her ears only, she would use the code to enter; This was one of those times.

Without looking up, Lori asked, "A text from who?"

"Davy! Davy Jones!" Lucy shoved her phone in Lori's face. Lori promptly leaned back to focus her eyes on the phone.

"Is that him?" She asked as she pointed at the text on Lucy's phone.

"Yes," Lucy said.

"Is this the first one he's sent you?"

Lucy sighed and said, "Yes."

Lori gave her a confused look and asked, "How long ago did you give him your number?"

"He asked for my number over a month ago—when we went for tea."

"Wow, so you waited a whole month for him to text you, Ms. Patience-of-a-Gnat?"

Lucy shrugged her shoulders. "He's just a friend," Lucy explained as she concentrated on the text.

Lori rolled her eyes and smirked as she said, "Yeah, right."

Lucy's head shot up from her phone, and she said indignantly, "He is! He is," Bingo got up from his dog bed and walked over to Lucy and leaned against her legs; He was trained to do this when his

owner was agitated. Lucy saw those big brown eyes
as they looked up at her and the little wag of his curly
tail and bent down to give him some love.

Lori laughed and said, "He's supposed to do that
to me when I get agitated. Not you." Lucy stuck her
tongue out at Lori, which made her laugh more.

Lucy went back to her office and sat on the
credenza behind her desk as she reread the text
message she'd received:

> But ya are Blanche, but ya
> are...

Only one person, other than Lori, knew about that
conversation. So it had to be Davy. What should her
response be? Can hers be as clever as his? She stared
at the message on her screen, then replied:

> Mr. Jones? (pls
> read with stuffy Brit
> accent)

Yeah, that was creative, she thought to herself.
She waited for a response, but there was none, so she
put her phone down and went back to work,
disappointed at the one-line text. Soon her day blew
up, and she forgot about the one text from Davy until
she was able to clock out for the day.

Later that night, Lucy walked out of the gym
much more relaxed than she'd been when she first
got there. Especially after a particularly tough HIIT

class. She was sweaty and regretted she hadn't washed off her make-up since the mascara and eyeliner were now in dark circles under her eyes and very noticeable in the rearview mirror.

"Oh," she groaned aloud in her car, "I really need a shower. I stink." With one last glance in the mirror, she turned the key in her ignition when her phone chimed. She pulled it out of her sweatshirt pocket and looked at the display:

LOL! Is this I love.?

LOL! Ya got me. It's Lucy.

Lucy didn't know another way to find out where he'd been, so she just flat out asked:

Where ya been?
Flyin'.

You've been gone forever.

Lucy held her breath as she waited for his response.

I know. Wanna get some
tea and catch up?

Lucy let out a sigh of relief and replied:

Sure! When?

*In ten minutes at the Coffee
Bean?*

Lucy was grateful he couldn't hear her groan as she replied:
Sure. See ya then.

"Wow, he wants to meet in ten minutes," Lucy said to herself in disbelief, "great." She looked at her reflection in the rearview mirror and grimaced at the image that looked back. She took the lid off her water bottle and tipped it onto a corner of her workout towel, and tried to wipe away the dark makeup, but it wasn't going as smoothly as she'd hoped and left the skin under her eyes red from the rubbing. *Maybe if she wore her sunglasses?*

Lucy pulled into the Coffee Bean parking lot next to what she thought might be Davy's truck. The last time she'd seen it, it had been dark, and her attention was otherwise occupied, so she hadn't noticed the color or even the make of the truck. But she knew it was a truck.

"It doesn't really matter. We're only friends," she reminded herself with resignation as she looked in the rearview mirror one more time before Lucy pulled on the baseball cap she kept in her car for times like this.

Upon entering the store, Lucy walked right into the end of the line of people waiting to place their orders. She circled around to the big easy chairs they'd sat in the last time, only to find them empty.

She looked around the store and saw no sign of Davy. *Maybe he's in the restroom*, she reasoned with herself as she walked over to the restroom, turned the knob, and pushed the door open. Obviously, he wasn't in there. She closed the door and turned to look around the room again. She was curious about what had happened to him. She thought that had been his truck outside but wasn't sure. Thinking perhaps he hadn't arrived yet, she sat down in one of the big leather chairs to wait for him before she ordered. Thirty minutes passed, and still no sign of Davy. She pulled out her phone and typed:

Where are you?

While she waited, she ordered a chai tea, then made herself comfortable in one of the leather chairs—saving the other for him. With the last sip of her tea, she looked at her phone for the twentieth time and heaved a sigh. Lucy looked toward the entrance, willing him to walk through the door before she reluctantly typed:

Is everything okay?

Lucy set her phone on the arm of the chair as she sat and stewed over Davy's absence. *Why didn't he show up? He was the one that asked to meet.* She was both worried, annoyed, and cold since she hadn't had a chance to take a shower yet after her workout. She'd been willing to meet him as is, raccoon eyes and all, but he wasn't there.

Lucy walked up to the counter and asked the teenage barista, "Did you see an older guy come in here a little bit ago?"

The teenager gave her a bored look and said, "Yeah. He's over there." He pointed to a section of the store she couldn't see from the chair she'd occupied. Why hadn't she thought to look there before now?

"Thanks," she said with a smile as she dropped a dollar in the tip jar and turned in the direction he'd pointed, then stopped dead. The only person in the area indicated by the barista was an elderly gentleman with white hair. "Hey, that's not the guy I meant," she said as she charged up to the counter.

"What?" The teenager asked, annoyed.

"That guy is elderly. I was asking for an older man," Lucy explained patiently.

"Ma'am, most of the guys in here are old to me," he said as he rolled his eyes. "You're old to me."

"Excuse me?" Lucy said indignantly, but the kid just turned and walked into a room off to the side. With a huff, Lucy reached in the tip jar and removed the dollar tip she'd earlier left and returned to her chair and waited one more hour before she headed home.

Lucy tossed and turned in bed that night, unable to get the missing Davy off her mind. It had been a couple of days since his last text. She was concerned as to why his texts were so sporadic. Had something happened to him? Was he okay?

She'd just fallen into a light sleep, and the dream had just begun when she started to hear beeping in her dream—beeping that continued until she awoke to realize it was her phone. The front was all lit up. She reached for it on her bedside table and squinted from the brightness. Then, groggily she touched the screen to open the text message:

I'm so sorry.

Who is this?

It's Davy.

Lucy frowned when she saw his response, then typed:

Oh.

I'm sorry.

I waited a long time.

*I'm really sorry about that.
But I got called on a flight
at the last minute.*

*You should've texted me. I
waited for hours.*

Hours? Really?

. . .

*Wait, is that how you let me
know you're giving me the
silent treatment?*

> *(sigh) No. You'll know when
> you're getting the silent
> treatment from me.*

*I couldn't use my personal
phone until we landed.*

> *Uh-huh.*

Lucy pulled herself into a sitting position and stared at the phone, unsure how she should respond. With her finger poised to tap something, she pondered what it should be when her phone beeped, and another text message appeared:

> *Forgive me?*

Before she could type a response, the phone beeped again.

> *I'll text you when I'm back
> in town.*

Lucy typed the only response that came to mind that early in the morning.

Wait!

What?

*You weren't even in town
when you asked me to meet
you for tea??!!*

*I told you I was in town but
was called on a flight and
didn't have time to text you.*

Lucy looked at Davy's text in disbelief. She didn't know whether to be flattered that he'd asked or insulted that he'd left her hanging like that. Had it not even crossed his mind to let her know that he wouldn't be able to make it? Or did he think so little of her that it didn't matter? She stared at his text.

*Hello? Are you there?
Lucy?*

You owe me two teas now.

LOL! You got it!

Lucy placed her phone face down and leaned back against her pillow. She couldn't deny the disrespect she felt he'd shown her—to ask her to meet for tea then disappear on a plane. However, she also couldn't deny the flood of relief she felt having heard from him.

***

Davy smiled as he set the phone down on the bedside table. He adjusted the pillow behind his back as he turned the sound up on the TV. Then laughed when he realized that he'd turned the sound down while he texted Lucy as if she could hear it. He yawned and rubbed his eyes as he contemplated whether he'd have time to grab some z's before he caught his flight home. After he'd arrived in Rome and located Max and Sammy, he'd been up all night being introduced to the Italian operatives by Paolo.

Maybe he should've texted Lucy before he got on the flight, he thought as he went over the events that returned him to Rome: He'd been on his way to meet Lucy when Max called.

"Jones," Davy answered.

"We need you to come to Rome," he heard Max's voice from the other end of the phone.

"Okay."

"You have to bring a package."

Davy couldn't believe his luck. This was what he needed to impress those with power. He had to show them he was trustworthy. "Sure," he said. "Where do I get the goods?"

"You'll find them in Morris' locker. Just put it in your backpack and get on the flight leaving for Rome in one hour," Max instructed him.

"Got it," Davy said and did a U-turn as soon as he could to change directions and headed to the airport. He didn't have much time to get there, check-in, get the package, and get on board. He'd text Lucy from the flight telling her they wouldn't be able to meet, after all, he told himself as he pushed the accelerator down.

Davy checked his watch, then called the office at LAX to confirm the flight time for the trip to Rome.

"You're scheduled to be a flyer on the six o'clock flight tonight. Are you just finding out about it?" Sharleen, the assistant to the flight coordinator, told him over the phone.

"Uh, yeah. I just got the call."

"You better get in here. The flight won't wait for you," Sharleen told Davy.

"On my way."

In this operation, the flyers recruited by the ring were often used to transport the drugs, since they could get in and out of the airports without going through customs. The fact that Max had called and asked him to transport this package to Rome affirmed his belief that they were beginning to trust him. This would be his first trip to Rome without Max and Sammy in tow.

Davy parked his truck in the parking structure, but before he exited, he made a call.

"Director Janssen."

"Hello, sir? This is Jones,"

"Yes," the director said.

"I thought I should let you know that Max called and asked me to bring a package to Rome."

"To Rome?"

"Yes, sir," Davy said. "I'm just heading into the airport now to catch the flight. The package is already there."

"At the airport?"

"Yes, sir. He told me that it was in one of the old lockers." Davy left the cab of his truck and did a quick jog through the terminals towards his office.

"Hm," The director responded, "So they're storing the drugs on the premises?"

"Before transporting anyway."

"What do you do with the package once you're in Rome?" Director Janssen asked.

"He didn't say. I'll just wait for further instructions. But this is a good sign they're trusting me." Davy professed as he stepped through the office door. "I better go, sir. I wanted you to be aware of the new development."

"Keep me updated," the director told him, then hung up.

***

Sal Vortelli stood outside the warehouse with his phone to his ear. He was an extremely overbearing man at six foot six inches but as bald as an egg. Johnny leaned against Sal's car and observed him on the phone. Then, for the first time, he noticed that Sal's head was very round, and his ears stuck out.

Johnny started to snicker as he realized Sal reminded him of a huge Charlie Brown. But, of course, he'd never tell him that if he wanted to live.

"Yes. Max confirmed that Jones would be on the flight to Rome tonight." He listened for a few minutes, then said, "Got it. We'll make sure it's there." He listened a couple of minutes longer, then pulled the phone away from his ear and tapped the cover to disconnect the call.

"Was that the boss?" Johnny asked as he rested his sandaled foot on the bumper of the red Chevy Nova.

"Yeah," Sal said as he approached Johnny.

"So, why'd they send Jones to Rome?" he asked.

Sal stepped up to where Johnny leaned against his car, placed his hand under his armpits, lifted and tossed him like trash away from his car. "What have I told you about touching my car?" He asked angrily.

Johnny pushed himself up after doing a face plant into the ground. He spat out the gravel that he'd eaten and muttered, "Sorry, Sal. I forgot." He stood and slapped his hands against his legs to rid them of the dirt and cautiously dabbed at his knee that showed speckles of blood where his pants had torn when they'd scraped the ground. "So, why'd they send him to Rome?"

"They wanna see if he'll follow direction," Sal growled. "Get in. We got an errand to run."

Chapter 13

"Hey, bone-gerno," Lucy said in a loud whisper as Davy approached. It had been so long since she'd seen him it was a nice surprise to see him again.

"Bone-gerno? What's that?" He asked as he sat down at the table where they first met.

"It means good morning in Italian," Lucy explained as she returned to the open book.

"Ooh, you mean buon jurno, not bone-gerno,"

"That does sound more familiar," Lucy said thoughtfully and smiled appreciatively at Davy.

"But it's not morning now, it's evening. How do you say good evening?" Davy asked.

"Hm," Lucy said thoughtfully. "I haven't gotten that far."

Davy chuckled. "Oh, I see. What are you reading?" He asked as he pulled Lucy's book towards him.

"I told ya, I'm learning Italian." She opened her water bottle and took a swallow.

"Why?" He asked as he flipped through the pages.

"Because I want to," Lucy said haughtily as she tightened the lid of her water bottle.

"Why don't ya learn something you can use?"

"Like what?"

"Spanish. You'll have more opportunities to use that than Italian."

"Not if I'm in Italy," Lucy said smugly.

"Uh-huh. When will you be in Italy?" Davy furrowed his brow in disbelief.

"I don't know, but it could happen. And, when it does, I'll be prepared," Lucy said. Davy laughed aloud.

"Shhhh!" Baby Jane said. Davy and Lucy looked at one another and convulsed into silent laughter.

"Why is it with you I act like a teenager?" Lucy whispered to him.

Still laughing, he shook his head, shrugged, then asked, "What other words do you know?"

Lucy gave a cocky shrug of her shoulders and said, "Try me."

"Okay then," Davy said as he cocked a brow, "let's see what you know."

"Go ahead," Lucy said with confidence, "I've been studying this for a month." Lucy squared her shoulders and rested her clasped hands on the table and waited.

"Okay," he said and turned the page, "Spiacente." Davy looked up from the book and waited for her to respond.

"Hm . . . uh, let's see . . . spee-a-chen-tay," Lucy repeated aloud, then thought for a moment before she said triumphantly, "Open!"

"Wrong. It means *sorry*."

"That's okay. I'm just warming up. Give me another one." Lucy smiled.

"Okay . . . primavera."

"Pasta!" Lucy smiled.

"Spring," Davy said and watched a shadow cross her face.

"Hm. Another."

"Mangio."

"Jump."

"Jump? Are you sure?"

"Yeah, final answer," Lucy said with a giggle, "Mangio means to jump."

"You've studied this for a month?" Davy asked. Lucy nodded her head. "Did you open the book when you studied?" He looked at her quizzically.

"Yeees!"

"Tu," Davy said and waited.

Lucy grinned and said, "That is too easy. Tu is two." She held up her index and middle fingers.

"No. T-u means you, not the number two. That would be due eh."

Lucy furrowed her brows and frowned. "Argh! I knew that!"

"Yeah, I can see that. Let's try a different approach. How about I give you the English version, and you translate it to Italian.

"Now you're talkin'," Lucy said as the confidence returned. She wiggled in her chair as if to prepare for the challenge. "I'm ready."

"You weren't ready before?"

"I wasn't warmed up. Now I am, so shoot!"

Davy chuckled then said, "Hello."

Lucy gave him an odd look, then said, "Hi. What's the word?"

Davy rolled his eyes and gave a soft chuckle. "The word is *hello*,"

"Oh," Lucy giggled, "uh . . . don't tell me. I know this, *Grazie*."

"Grazie?" Davy questioned her.

"Yeah," Lucy responded with pride, "Hi!"

Davy shook his head. "I hate to burst your bubble, but *Grazie* doesn't mean *hi*; it means *thank you*. *Ciao* means *hi*," he said and watched Lucy's face fall.

"Okay, maybe I need to do a bit more studying," Lucy said as she looked away, defeated.

Davy bit his lower lip to hide his smile. When he'd gained control, he said, "Yeah, a bit more studying should do it."

"Do you know Italian?" Lucy asked.

Davy tilted his head from side to side and said, "A bit."

"That's all I need—a bit of help."

Davy chuckled, "Yeah, sure. I'll help you study—when I can, but I would suggest you study on your own as well."

"Of course! Course I'll study. I do know this stuff. You just caught me on a bad night," Lucy assured him.

"Uh-huh. I'm sure. Hopefully, you'll have a better night next time," Davy said with a wink.

"Oh shut up," Lucy said with a scowl.

"Shhhh!" Baby Jane scowled at them as she passed behind their table. Davy and Lucy looked at one another and quietly snickered.

"But ya are Blanche," Davy said in a loud whisper. Lucy covered her mouth to muffle her laughter.

"Here's a question for you," Lucy said to him.

"What's that?" Davy asked.

"What's this all about?" she asked as she pointed to the whiskers growing on his face.

"This?" Davy asked as he rubbed his hand across his chin.

"Yeah."

"What, you don't like it?"

"I didn't say that," Lucy said with a flirtatious smile.

Davy's eyes squinted as he looked at Lucy with a curious smile, "Then what?"

"No, it's good. But I thought you had to be clean-shaven for your job."

"We have to look like every man, so we don't stand out," Davy explained.

Lucy couldn't stop the giggle that escaped. "Every man, huh?"

***

Davy walked through the front doors of the hotel Nazionale Rome. He approached the counter, where an older, overweight Italian man with a huge shock of black hair sat as he read the newspaper.

"Buongiorno," Davy greeted the man upon approach.

"Come posso aiutarla?" the hotel clerk asked.

Davy searched his tired mind for the translation.

135

"Uh, how do you say . . . um . . . Um, a room, I need a room. . .um, ho bisogno di una stanza?" Davy told the clerk. He laughed to himself as he thought of Lucy and her Italian.

"Come posso aiutarla?" The bored clerk asked as he continued to read the newspaper.

Davy wasn't sure what the clerk asked, "Ripetere, per favore?"

The clerk looked up from the paper at Davy, then asked again, "Come posso aiutarla?"

"Do you speak English?" Davy asked, "Lei, uh . . . parla uh, Inglese?" As he spoke, he noticed that the clerk had hair growing on the bulb part of his nose. Involuntarily he reached up and rubbed the end of his nose to make sure no hairs were growing there.

"Si! Si parlo Inglese," the clerk said as he nodded his head. He looked at Davy for the first time as he began to speak in broken English, "I-I do spake Inglese—English," and gave a hint of a smile.

"I need a room, please. Um. . . Ho bisogno di una stanza, per favore," Davy had memorized this on the plane ride over.

"Va bene," the clerk said. "Avete una prenotazione?" He asked. Davy gave him a blank look. "Um, how you say. . . do you have a reservation?"

"Ah!" Davy said with relief, "Yes."

"Nome?" The clerk asked.

"Nom eh?" Davy responded.

"Si, si, nome, per favore."

"Nome, nome, no—oh, you mean name?" Davy asked.

The clerk smiled and bobbed his head, "Si! Name."

"Jones, Davy Jones." Davy waited as the clerk looked at his computer. He'd been up seventy-two hours straight, and all he wanted to do was get a little shut-eye before he had to meet up with Paolo later that night.

Davy unlocked the door to his room and, without thought, dropped his bag, and fell face-first on the bed that seemed to fill the space as the door slammed shut into the darkness that greeted him.

The vibration of his phone against his room key slowly permeated Davy's sleep as he began to stir into consciousness. Groggily he reached for his phone and looked at the face. He'd only been asleep for three hours. The phone continued to vibrate. He slid his finger across the front of it and croaked out, "Hello?"

"Is this Davide?" the voice on the phone asked.

"Who's this?" Davy asked cautiously.

"It's Paolo, your guide."

"What time does the tour start?" Davy asked as he moved to a sitting position.

"Nine sharp. Meet me at the Fontana di Trevi."

"Gotcha. What time is it now?" He asked as he looked at the watch on his wrist.

"Seven forty-five," Paolo said.

"Got it." Davy hung up. He stood and stretched to his full six-foot-five inches. With his shirt untucked, he lifted it to remove the holstered Sig Sauer inside the waistband of his pants. He'd been so tired when he arrived; he hadn't even removed his gun before he fell asleep. He now pulled out the gun, ejected the magazine, and confirmed that its chamber was clear before he set it on the bedside table.

He chastised himself for the lack of security and safety he'd been taught over the years—he knew better than to fall asleep with a loaded gun in the waistband of his jeans.

Needing to shower before his meeting that night, he had just wrapped himself in a towel when his phone beeped. It was a text from Lucy.

Are you back in town yet?

No.

Hm.

Do you need something?

No. Just curious. I thought your trips were only overnight.

They are. Why?

Well, you still owe me tea. And I wanna make sure you aren't trying to welch out of it. Hehehe

Davy smiled to himself. *If only his life were that easy*, he thought.

LOL! No, I'm not welching. I've been busy with work.

Uh-huh. Whatever.

138

Davy chuckled as he read the text, tossed his phone on his bed, and headed to the shower. He didn't have much time before he had to meet Paolo. As Davy showered, he went over in his mind the last time he'd seen Lucy. He liked her ability to make him laugh and relax, where when he was with Junie, he felt like her pet—always having to perform.

"Oh, Junie," he groaned aloud and rubbed his hand across his eyes. The sacrifices he made for his job.

A little while later, dressed in dark clothing, Davy hugged the darkened doorways, streets, and shadows as he made his way to the Piazza di Trevi. He hoped the growth of facial hair would help him look less like an agent for the government. He'd left his hotel earlier than needed since he'd never been to the fountain before and was going at night.

Once in the vicinity of the Trevi Fountain, he moved through the shadows on the periphery of the piazza or square as it's known in English, as he searched the location for any suspicious anomalies. The moonlight illuminated the white marble of the statues Michelangelo had so beautifully carved as part of the Fontana de Trevi adding new dimensions and shadows not seen during the day. Davy paused for a moment in awe of the beauty before him. The water had was off for the night, so there wasn't the white noise of it cascading out of the mouths of fish into the pool below. This was both good and bad; good because no one would be able to enter the area without him noticing or hearing their approach, and bad because anyone would be able to hear his movements if he weren't careful.

He wasn't sure exactly where Paolo would be in the locality. The lack of daylight made every little nook and cranny around the fountain seem ominous. They were a perfect place for someone to hide. However, since he was so early and didn't see anyone, he stealthily stepped into the shadows that swamped a small luggage shop's doorway. He waited with the assumption he was there alone.

As Davy waited for the minutes to pass, he was aware of the way the full moon's reflection off the white marble lit up the area with an ethereal glow that kept him in the shadows. Even in the dark, the fountain still had a romantic quality to it. Again his thoughts returned to Lucy and her Italian. He imagined how much she'd enjoy this and then silently chuckled at the thought of her using the little Italian she knew on the Italian natives. He was slightly startled when he heard the sound of someone speaking and chastised himself for letting his guard down. Now wasn't the time to think about Lucy.

The doorway where he waited was a great vantage point to see anyone near the fountain and its surrounding area. He pressed himself further into the shadows as the voices drew near. He rested his hand on his holstered gun as the voices approached. Then relaxed when he saw it was only three teenage boys passing through the square. He checked his watch. It was nine-fifteen. Where was Paolo?

Davy exited the safety of the doorway's shadows when it became apparent that Paolo wasn't coming. Instead, he'd return to the hotel and contact Max to find out what his next move should be. Carefully he retraced his steps and exited down the first darkened walkway, still staying close to the shadows. He paused, for a moment, to gather his bearings, then froze when he felt the barrel of a gun held against his temple.

Chapter 14

"What happened to you?" Lucy asked, surprised at Davy's appearance after two weeks of his absence: His hair and beard were longer. He sported a black eye that had turned purplish yellow and a bruise by the right corner of his mouth that camouflaged the cut on his lower lip.

Davy gave her a lopsided grin and said, "Would you believe I ran into a doorknob?"

Lucy rolled her eyes and said, "You're too tall to have your face hit the doorknob."

"Did you already get your tea?" he asked with a wry smile that went all the way up to the twinkle in his eyes. He hadn't realized how much he missed Lucy; he missed their banter, her straightforwardness, and wit. He missed talking about movies with her, her awkwardness at times, and her laughter. She was a breath of fresh air after the filth he was around most every day. Davy needed someone to lighten his mood after the last week.

During his time in the military, he'd seen some pretty gory sights, but they all paled in comparison when he'd been unable to stop the butchery of Paolo before his very eyes. He'd followed a hunch coming to their tea place in search of her. When he saw her sitting in the big leather chair, it took a conscious effort to seem carefree.

"No. I waited for you, and waited, and waited," Lucy said with mock exaggerated exhaustion as her head lolled back on the chair back.

Davy laughed. "I'm sure you survived." He plopped down in the leather chair next to hers.

"You disappear for weeks on end and come back with long hair and a beard. I almost didn't recognize the 'every man,'" Lucy said as she emphasized with finger quotes.

"You don't recognize me?"

"Let's just say you aren't boring."

"Who wants to be boring?" He asked.

"Obviously not you," Lucy said as she studied him then, with a concerned look, asked. "Are you on drugs?"

Davy's face exploded with laughter. "What makes you think I'm on drugs?"

Lucy motioned at his appearance with her hands. "Well, all this: your longer hair, beard, your disappearance, stuff like that."

Still laughing, Davy said, "I can assure you I am not on drugs."

"Just making sure," Lucy said, still suspicious.

"C'mon, I'll buy you your tea," he said as he stood. Lucy lifted her hand towards him so he could pull her out of the chair. She loved the feel of his hand around hers and the way he could make her feel so light with his strength. She sighed as she rose to her feet.

"Were you out of town this whole time?" Lucy asked

as they stood in line.

"In and out."

"I see."

"You do?" Davy asked.

"What can I get you?" the snowflake barista interrupted as she adjusted her horn-rimmed glasses with a tattoo that covered her hand and went the entire length of her arm.

"He's paying," Lucy quickly stated with her thumb over her shoulder.

"Yes, I am," Davy said with a slight laugh as he proceeded to give the order for both their teas.

"I'm impressed," Lucy said as they moved to the area of the counter to await their order.

"Only this time?" Davy asked.

Lucy rolled her eyes. "No, I'm impressed that you remembered my order."

"It's not too difficult. You get the same thing every time."

"So do you," Lucy quickly pointed out.

Later as they sat at a table—other customers have commandeered their two comfy chairs—Lucy attempted to find out where his cuts and bruises came from.

"So, what really happened to your face?" she asked.

"You don't like it?" Davy asked.

Lucy snickered and said, "I didn't say that." She tilted her head as she studied his face, "In fact, I think I do like it. It takes away the pretty boy look you didn't have."

Davy looked confused, then laughed despite himself and said, "Wait, what?"

"It adds character to your face, I think," Lucy said as she gave him a wide-eyed look. "That is once I get past all the hair."

Davy chuckled as he sipped his chai tea. It felt good to be silly and let his guard down for a bit. "Okay, okay, I get it. You don't like all the hair."

"I didn't say that. Just getting used to your scruffy look," Lucy said as she scrunched her nose.

"Have you ever been married?" Davy asked.

"No."

"Why not?" He asked.

"Why haven't you been married?" Lucy asked, turning the question back on him.

"I have," Davy said without a missed beat.

This confession stopped Lucy in her tracks. She looked at him in shock. "Wait. What? You have?"

"Yup," Davy responded without looking at her as he drank his tea.

"I knew it! I knew you were married," Lucy declared with a huff. "Why'd you tell me you didn't have a wife?" Lucy asked, then stopped cold. *Oh no*, she said to herself, then asked aloud, "Do you have a husband?" She gulped. Tea sprayed from Davy's mouth, and some came through his nose; he laughed so hard. "Eeew," Lucy said as she wiped the tea from her t-shirt, the table, and the lid to her tea. "That's disgusting." But Davy snorted with laughter. Lucy rose from her chair and walked over to get more napkins. She didn't understand what was so funny.

When Lucy came back to the table, Davy wiped the tears of laughter from his eyes and muttered, "Do I have a husband. Oh, that's good." He reached up and touched the bruise at the corner of his mouth and winced with pain as he wiggled his jaw. "It hurts to laugh," he told her. Lucy handed him the napkins to wipe the table.

"Me-thinks the man doth laugh too much," Lucy said, confused by his reaction. "You did say you weren't married, but now you say you had a wife. I'm confused," Lucy said in a serious tone.

Davy saw the twinkle in her eyes disappear. "I did have a wife, but she left me when I was in the military."

"Oh, I'm sorry. Why didn't you tell me at the beginning?" Lucy asked as she tried to lighten the mood that had settled at their table.

Davy drank the rest of his tea before he responded, "Sorry. I guess it was kinda fun to mess with you," he said sincerely.

Lucy looked at him surprised, "You were messing with me? Seriously?" She asked. Davy only chuckled.

Lucy rolled her eyes while she muttered under her breath, "Messin' with me." She didn't smile but pursed her lips and glared at Davy. "So, are you gonna tell me how you got that shiner et al?" She asked as she waved her hand to encompass his whole face.

"Et al?" Davy asked with furrowed brows.

"Yeah, it's Latin for *and all*,"

"Ooooh," Davy said as he nodded that he understood, "I see. How many languages do you think you know?"

"Enough to be dangerous," Lucy said caustically.

"You are dangerous, that's for sure," Davy admitted.

Lucy hesitantly smiled and said, "Well?" She watched his face as he contemplated what to tell her.

146

"I shouldn't tell you anything," he said somberly.

"Why not?" Lucy asked.

Davy bit the inside of his lip in contemplation, then decided it was too dangerous to tell her anything. He'd already said too much when he told her he was a flyer. So, he decided to lie. Not his favorite thing, especially with friends, but he couldn't take the chance of her getting hurt.

Davy took a deep breath, then said, "I was in a fight." He looked down at the table to avoid her eyes. Besides, that was kind of the truth.

"You were in a fight?!"

"Yeah."

"That's what you were so concerned about telling me?" Lucy asked with disbelief.

Hesitantly Davy responded, "Well, yeah. It's not something I'm proud of. You already think I'm into drugs. I don't need you to think I'm a ruffian."

"Ruffian, huh?" Lucy said as she contemplated Davy's avoidance at looking at her. Then she asked, "You were embarrassed you lost?"

Davy's head shot up, surprised. "What? I lost? No! Are you kidding me!"

"Oh. There it is," Lucy said with a playful smile.

"What?"

"That cocky seal attitude," Lucy said teasingly. "It got under your skin that I'd think you'd lost a fight," Lucy couldn't stop the giggle that bubbled out of her mouth.

"No, it didn't," he responded a little too quickly.

"Hahaha! It did," she said in a sing-song voice. Davy gave her a sidewards glance. "Hahaha! Someone's ego's bruised." Lucy stood up from her chair to throw her empty cup away and danced her way to the trash bin and back, with a huge grin on her face, "I bet you did lose the fight. Why else would you have a black eye and that nasty bruise on your mug?" Suddenly Lucy's face lit up. "I bet that's why you left the military; in fact, you didn't leave but were kicked out because you suck at fighting."

"Okay, that's it. You better run because you won't like it if I catch you," Davy said and jumped up from his chair. Lucy screamed, then laughed as she ran out the door with Davy in pursuit.

Once outside the coffee shop, Lucy ran towards the park next to the parking lot where there was grass. She felt it was her best option in case she ended up being tackled. Davy was still in pursuit as Lucy approached the fountain with two fish perched on top with water shooting out of their mouths.

Laughing, Lucy said, "Look, I'm sorry. I didn't mean that you were awful at everything."

"Too late," Davy replied with an evil laugh. "You want attitude; you're gonna get attitude."

She kept the fountain between them. "C'mon, I was just playin'," Lucy tried to reason with him. But before she could say another word, he stepped into the fountain, where the water came to his knees and began to walk across it to where she stood with her mouth open in shock. He grabbed her wrist, she tried to slip away, but he grabbed the back of her shirt and wouldn't let go.

"Stop!" she told him through laughter. "I'm too old for this. People our age don't act like this."

"Speak for yourself," he told her with no mercy. Then pulled her back towards where he stood until the back of her legs felt the fountain base. "This is how we handle dissent where I come from," he said. Without another word, he pulled her into the fountain right on her backside, into the water, and dunked her head in the water.

"Ach!" She sputtered, spitting out water as her head rose above the waterline. She struggled to gain her balance with her water-drenched clothes. Davy had stepped out of the fountain after he'd dunked her.

His laughter was empty as he held out his hand to help her up. Lucy carefully stepped out of the fountain in her now squishy shoes. She was furious that he'd put her in the water, but she knew she needed to be a good sport. Besides, the look on his face stopped her from saying anything. *Maybe she'd pushed him too far with her teasing.*

Lucy stood next to the fountain, confused by his reaction to her teasing. He said nothing else, only turned and walked away. She waited for that mischievous smile from him, showing all was well, but he never looked back. Lucy watched his retreating figure as she quietly began to shiver.

***

"I think it's worse than we thought, sir," Davy told Director Janssen gravely.

"What have you learned so far?" Director Janssen asked.

"It's not just the LA office that drugs have been smuggled through. It looks like there are multiple flyers at multiple airports that use their access to the planes to move the cargo."

"Do you have proof to back this up?"

"Not enough, sir. I'd like to get more. I do have some videos that I've recorded on my phone that I can send you, though," Davy said.

Director Janssen thought for a moment, then said, "I'll get back to you on where to send what you have so it will remain confidential."

"As far as I can tell, the received drugs are transported through Europe and eventually brought back into the country via another route."

"We didn't know that. Is this something new?"

"Yeah, I think so."

"What's your next move?" The Director asked.

"With my promotion to organize the flyers and my new connection with Junie—."

"Who's Junie? What happened to the other woman?" the Director interrupted.

"Junie is a woman who runs the warehouse on the pier where they break up the drugs for distribution, and she's taken a liking to me. So I'm using that as leverage to get further inside. As far as the other women—she's just a friend. Someone I want to stay clear and safe from this whole thing," Davy said with determination.

***

Davy sat in his assigned seat on the plane and watched a couple a few rows up in Business class, who seemed out of place. He'd woken from a restless night in a bad mood. He couldn't get his last meeting with Lucy out of his head.

Why had she gotten under his skin so bad with her teasing, he asked himself. What did he care what she thought of him and his service or how he looked? He shouldn't have seen her so soon after the Paolo ordeal. It wasn't like him to react the way he did to a bit of teasing. Besides, she hadn't meant anything by it. *She was just having fun*, he reasoned to himself. He needed to apologize to her.

"I like her, I mean her friendship—I like her friendship and don't want to lose it," he said aloud.

"Like whose friendship?" Martin, a flyer seated near him, asked.

"What?" Davy asked as he gave Martin a confused look.

"You said you liked someone's friendship and didn't want to lose them," Martin told him.

"It's nothing. Just thinkin' aloud," Davy said, embarrassed Martin had heard.

Martin gave a short laugh, "Uh-huh. I'm sure."

Humiliated, Davy tried to change the subject as he leaned over and told Martin, "You might want to watch that couple up there in the second row. Something seems odd about them."

"I thought you weren't working this flight," Martin said with a knowing chortle.

"I'm not, but I still have eyes."

"Sure, boss," Martin told him, "I'll watch that couple." Davy put his seat back and pretended to sleep to avoid the blush he felt coming.

But Davy couldn't deny the shame he'd felt after the way he'd treated Lucy. He'd started to reach out to her multiple times in the last couple of days but always stopped due to the awkwardness he felt over his reaction to her teasing. Was it awkwardness? Or was it fear she wouldn't accept his apology? This was so not like him! He'd been a Navy Seal, for heaven's sake! Seals aren't scared of anything, especially women!

"Dammit!" Davy slammed his fist down on the armrest of his seat.

"I'm sorry?" the lady sitting in the seat across the aisle from him asked with an alarmed look.

"Nothing, sorry," Davy apologized and waved his hand, "just thinkin' aloud." Davy rose from his seat to walk down the aisle. It bothered him that he was afraid of a woman's reaction. Was he afraid of losing her friendship? Or just losing her? Davy walked towards the back galley; he couldn't stop himself from huffing at the thoughts in his mind.

"You okay, bro?" Jordan, another flyer who stood in the galley area, asked as Davy approached.

"I'm not afraid of a woman," Davy said to him, clearly agitated.

Surprised, Jordan asked, "Did someone say you were?"

"What?" Davy asked as he leaned against the back wall of the galley.

"Afraid of a woman?"

Davy shook his head and sighed, "Women!"

"Yeah," Jordan said as he huffed, "pfft! Women." Both stood in silent comradery while they observed the activity in the cabin.

Davy remained standing at the back of the plane after Jordan returned to his seat and tried to calm himself down before he went back to his seat.

Having returned to his seat, Davy decided to take a chance. He lifted his phone from where it laid on the tray table and cautiously typed:

You there?

It had been almost a week since Davy dunked her in the fountain. She felt some remorse about teasing him but didn't contact him in case he was still mad. Lucy avoided confrontation of that nature like the plague. So, when she saw the text message from him, she was relieved that he'd forgiven her. Her pulse soared as she happily typed back:

Who wants to know?

Lucy smiled at her response; clever yet aloof? But he didn't respond. As the seconds ticked by, Lucy grew concerned that she'd gone too far again. He really didn't know her yet, so maybe she should cool her wit and be boring and blah. However, just as these thoughts flooded her confidence, her phone lit up:

LOL! Me. And you know who that is.

Then thirty seconds later, another text appeared:

Hey, I wanted to apologize for dunking you in the fountain.

Really?

*Yeah. I have this thing I'm
dealing with from work.*

And?

*And? Nothin'. If I told you,
I'd have to kill you.*

Jk

When Lucy saw the *Jk* in his text, she couldn't help but laugh. He was serious so often and had been through so much, yet he could keep up with her on any discussion about film and could be as funny as the best of them. While lost in these thoughts, her phone lit up again:

*Wanna meet for some apology
tea when I'm back in town?
My treat.*

*Yeah, but bring your good
humor this time.*

Yes Ma'am!

Don't call me Ma'am! LOL!

Lucy waited expectantly in case he texted anything more, but nothing came.

Davy smiled at his phone before placing it face down on the airplane tray next to his laptop. She was just what he needed to take his mind off the investigation. Since he wasn't working the flight as an Air Marshal, he leaned his head against the seat back and close his eyes, smiling.

***

Davy entered the small Chinese food restaurant in Mesquite, Nevada, to see Director Janssen seated in the only booth in the place that faced the door. There were three tables placed against the other three walls. The only other person in the place besides the owner and his wife was an extremely large man with a plate piled high with every option of food that had been placed in the meager buffet. Davy squinted against the bright lime green that covered the walls.

He'd just exited the plane from another trip to Rome when his phone beeped with the message to meet the Director at the specified location. He didn't even have time to go home as the message told him to leave directly from the airport. Six hours later, he pulled into the small dirt parking lot in front of the small restaurant.

"Hello, sir," Davy said as he slid into the booth on the opposite bench seat. "I came as fast as I could."

"Did you have a successful meeting in Rome?" He asked, skipping past any small talk.

"More of the same, but I didn't see Max or Sammy anywhere. I thought they'd be there," he said.

"Our intel has lost track of them. We aren't sure if they're even alive," Director Janssen said gravely.

"You're not sure if they're alive?" Davy asked, alarmed.

The director nodded his head. "They went to Rome and disappeared off the radar. Have you heard anything?"

Davy shook his head. "No, I thought they'd been transferred."

"If you can, try and poke around. See if you can find out anything."

"Will see what I can do," Davy said, concerned. "But I'm not a detective. I'm an undercover agent and can't blow my cover."

"Just see what you can find out, if anything. But don't blow your cover or put yourself in unnecessary danger."

"Yes, sir," Davy said. He bit his tongue to not repeat himself. These guys just didn't get how dangerous undercover work can be. They can't expect an agent to play homicide detective when they're undercover.

The Director nodded his head and asked, "Did you find out about the next shipment?

"Yeah, I forwarded it to you."

"Great, we'll take care of it," the Director said. "When do you go back?"

"To Rome?"

"Yeah."

"I don't know if I'll be going to Rome again. It looks like they want me to concentrate my efforts here in the US."

"That makes sense if the smuggling operation works like you think it does. Do you think you can get more names of the players?" Director Janssen asked.

"I should since I'll be vetting any new recruits," Davy said.

"Good. How's it going with the woman at the warehouse?" The director asked.

"As good as can be expected," Davy said with a shrug.

"We think she might be more important than originally thought. We need you to put more effort into that relationship. Let the other woman go."

Davy looked at him bewildered and asked, "What other woman would that be?"

"The one from the plane."

Davy nodded his head in acknowledgment. "Sir, that was a one-off. She had only been on that one flight and just by chance," Davy explained.

"That may be so, but we can't take a chance of this operation being compromised by some woman who has a crush on you."

"Crush on me?" Davy asked, astonished, "We're just friends."

"Whatever it might be. It can't happen again," the director said firmly.

"Yes, sir," Davy said and exited the restaurant.

***

"How's your Italian coming?" Davy asked as they jogged along the beach.

"It's better than it was. Wanna test me?" Lucy responded a little breathless as they slowed to a walk.

Davy laughed. "Okay, how do you say hello?" He

asked as he picked up a shell and threw it in the water.

"Ciao," Lucy responded proudly. Davy cocked an eyebrow at her.

"How do you say good morning?" Davy asked.

"Buongiorno," Lucy said without a pause.

"Not buon gerno?" Davy raised his eyebrows.

"Ha ha," Lucy said. "No. It is pronounced buon jerno." Lucy continued to walk along the shore.

"How do you say thank you?" Davy asked as he jogged after her.

"Grazie."

"Very nice. See how much easier it is to learn when you actually read the book?" Davy asked.

"Oh, be quiet. I did read the book before," Lucy said as she playfully punched him.

"Ouch," Davy said.

Lucy looked at him in mock disbelief. "Seriously?"

"Hey, do you want to go to the shooting range with me sometime?"

Lucy stopped in her tracks. "Are you kidding me?"

Davy stopped and turned towards her, "No. Do you wanna go sometime?"

"I'd love that, but I have to be honest and say that I haven't been shooting that much. You might need to give me some pointers."

"Note to self, do not let Lucy handle a gun unsupervised," Davy said as he continued over the sand towards the bike path.

"Note to self: You're a goof," Lucy called to Davy as he laughed out loud. She loved his laugh and couldn't contain the smile on her face or the giggle that burst out.

"So . . . back to me," Lucy said as they approached a bench just off the beach path.

Davy chuckled and asked, "Isn't it always about you?"

"I don't think so, but it should be," Lucy told after him as she sat on the bench. Davy continued on the path as he watched the ocean undulating over the sand; Lucy patiently watched him. She knew he'd realize soon she wasn't there—she hoped he would anyway. Eventually, he became aware she wasn't next to him, stopped, and looked around. When he saw her on the bench, she waved, and he walked back to where she sat.

Davy laughed, "Okay, back to you," he said and sat next to her.

"When will you take me shooting?" Lucy asked, her eyes bright with excitement.

"When I have time, I guess." Davy stretched out his long legs out, adjusted his baseball cap, and leaned his head back with closed eyes so the sun shone on his face directly.

"And when will that be?" she asked as she observed his muscular, long legs in his running shorts appreciatively.

"Not sure."

"Why not?"

"Because I work and travel, so I don't have a lot of time."

"So do I, work, that is. Not much travel," Lucy responded impatiently.

"Besides, you might not be able to shoot the first time you go," Davy said as he looked at her through

159

squinted eyes.

"Then, why the heck would I go?"

Davy puckered his eyes as he considered how to tempt her. Then with a sudden thought, his face brightened, and he said, "Because there'll be a lot of former military guys there. Guys with guns," Davy said to entice her, "I know how you like military men." Davy wiggled his eyebrows as emphasis.

Lucy began to blush. "I don—," she stopped and looked at Davy, then asked, "Former military, huh? With guns?"

Davy laughed, "You are so transparent."

Lucy beamed at Davy. "What can I say?" Davy closed his eyes and returned to bask in the heat of the sun on his face. Lucy hummed a mindless, happy tune as they sat in companionable silence. "So, why can't I shoot the first time I go with you? Is there an initiation or something I have to go through?"

Davy guffawed and lurched to an upright sitting position, "You are so funny. Why would there be an initiation for you to target practice?"

"Well," Lucy shrugged, "I don't know. I mean, would I need to date one of those hunky guys or something?" she asked with hope.

"Or something?" Davy asked as he gave her a sideward squinted glance.

"Just a date, nothing else," Lucy told him sternly.

Davy shook his head, "Why would you think there'd be an initiation? We aren't a fraternity."

"Ah, but I think you are," Lucy told him knowingly.

"So, you think there's an initiation?" Davy asked.

"Why else wouldn't I be able to shoot the first time?"

"Because it won't be just you and me. The other guys'll be there—they mean business and always want the women to stay away. Besides, I'll be going there to sharpen my skills."

Lucy huffed out a blast of air and asked, "If the guys don't want girls there, then why do you want me to come?"

"Thought you might like it," Davy told her.

Lucy angrily rose from the bench. "Seriously? You're throwing the spinster a bone? Giving me a thrill?" Lucy accused him before she waved him away and charged down the beach path.

"Well—." Davy's voice raised an octave as he held out his arms in a helpless gesture and trotted after her.

"I don't believe you," Lucy said with disgust.

"Are you the spinster?" Davy called after her.

***

Lucy pushed the auto-dial for Lori's number before she remembered that Lori was out of state helping her mother. She quickly disconnected the call and stared at her phone.

"Now, who do I call?" She asked herself. As she contemplated who could help her with this dilemma, she walked along the beach, oblivious to passersby, until she heard her name called.

"Lucy? Lucy. Is that you?" Lucy continued to walk, deaf to her name being called. "Lucy! Lucy!"

Startled, her head shot up. She stopped walking and looked about, unsure if she'd heard her name or not.

When she saw who'd been calling her name, a big smile appeared on her face as she said, "Annie! What are you doing here?"

Annie was a woman Lucy had worked with at a previous firm. She was a tall, dark-haired beauty with big blue eyes. She'd had much more success as an actress in a previous life than what Lucy had. She was what those in the business called a "triple threat": she could sing, dance, and act, and boy could she sing. The two ladies came towards one another and hugged.

"How have you been?" Lucy asked Annie as they sat on the bench near the path Lucy had previously run on.

Annie gave a short laugh of joy and responded, "Great! How are you? It's been so long."

Lucy laughed in return, "I know. What are you doing in this area?" Annie lived in the beach area further up the coast.

"I'm taking a surfing class."

"A surfing class? Down here?" Annie nodded her head. "Don't they have surfing classes up where you live?"

Annie gave her throaty laugh and said, "Of course they do. But the Groupon I found was for a class down here," she paused before they both broke into laughter, like old times. Annie gave Lucy a searching look and asked. "So, how's it going for you? Any men in your life?"

"I'm so glad you asked," Lucy said with a chuckle.

Annie rolled her eyes. "I should've known."

Lucy told her about the dream and Davy Jones and all the ins and outs of their relationship. She concluded the whole story with, "but I'm not really sure you can call it a relationship. We are just friends." Lucy finished and looked at Annie, who'd sat quietly and listened as she told her tale. "Well? So, what do you think? Should I be concerned when he doesn't respond to my text? I asked my brother, but he really wasn't any help." Lucy watched Annie's expression as she puckered and unpuckered her lips.

"You say you're just friends, right?" Annie cautiously asked.

"Yeah. Just friends," Lucy told her defensively as she studied a couple rollerblading along the path.

"It sounds like you want more than just friendship," Annie said with a laugh. Lucy loved her friend but hated how she always cut to the core. Annie never let Lucy get away with anything.

"No. Not at all," Lucy said a bit too defensively.

Annie laughed. "Uh-huh." Annie stood up, placed one of her legs on the back of the bench, and began to stretch.

"Honest. He's just a friend—it's nice to have a guy friend." Lucy looked out at the ocean, unable to look in Annie's all-knowing face.

"You forget that I know you. You are the biggest flirt I've ever known." Just as those words came out of Annie's mouth, the breeze blew the end of a strand of her curly hair right into her mouth. She removed it and placed her hair in a ponytail with the elastic band she'd worn on her wrist.

"I am not!" Lucy answered, offended. Annie only laughed in response. "Besides, like I told you, he approached me. I didn't approach him." Lucy took some deep breaths of the salty air and felt an instant calm.

"Whatever." Annie gave a soft chuckle, which was maddening to Lucy.

"He did!"

"Well, if you're only friends, then he's not obligated to respond all the time. You just have to be patient—something I know that'll kill you—and wait for his response."

"Why does everyone think I don't have patience?" Lucy asked, exasperated.

Annie laughed and responded, "Because we know you."

"Huh. We'll see," Lucy said, deep in thought.

"I can almost see the wheels in that conniving brain of yours turning," Annie said as she studied Lucy's face.

"I need to learn more about him," Lucy said more to herself than to Annie.

"What do you mean?"

"Well, at this point, I only know what he wants me to know."

"I thought he did an information dump when he bought you dinner at the airport?" Annie asked.

Lucy gave her a get real look, paused, then said, "He still only told me what he wanted me to know." Lucy began to tap her chin with her forefinger as she contemplated her next move.

"Oh no," Annie said with a note of trepidation, "what are you thinking?" Lucy didn't respond. Even though it had been a few years since she'd seen Lucy, Annie knew too well what happened when Lucy got that look on her face. Annie looked up at the bright sky and groaned.

"The problem is I don't really know who he is. I need to find out by doing the due diligence I'd be expected to do at work."

"Oh no, did you really just say due diligence? I knew I should've just let you pass by without saying a word."

"How rude," Lucy said as she scrunched her face with a look of displeasure.

Annie held her hands up in retreat and said, "As long as it doesn't involve me. I remember too well what happened last time."

Lucy looked at Annie and said, "It was years ago and only happened once. Besides, they didn't keep us in jail— didn't even charge us with anything."

"Still too close of a call."

"Well, if you're chicken—," Lucy said with a smirk.

Annie laughed as she stood to leave. "Some things never change with you."

"Is your number still the same?" Lucy asked innocently.

Annie groaned as she collapsed back on the bench beside Lucy and looked heavenward. In a sigh, mostly to herself, she said, "Oh dear." She blew out the air in her lungs, turned to concentrate on Lucy, then responded weakly, "Yes."

Lucy chuckled and jumped up from the bench, which startled Annie. "Great! It's really great to see you, but I gotta go. I'll give you a call," Lucy called to Annie as she trotted down the path.

Annie shook her head as she watched Lucy leave.

"Oh dear, what have I gotten myself into?"

***

"Woohoo! Hi Davy Honey," Junie called and waved from across the little room where she sat wearing an outfit as if she were preparing to go into surgery. He wouldn't have guessed it was her if it weren't for her Urkel voice that could not be mistaken for someone else's.

Davy observed the scores of men and women opened packages, cut, weighed, and re-bagged the much smaller portion of rock cocaine for resale. He had no doubt the workers in the room were illegal immigrants. Junie had guys who made regular trips to the border to pick up the illegal immigrants and hired them for these dirty jobs.

Davy held his sleeve over his nose and mouth as he picked his way towards her through the tables. A cloud of smoke rose from the cocaine they were cutting. "I didn't realize you would come in here to help cut," he told her as he approached.

Junie pulled her masked down as Davy leaned down to kiss her. "Of course, how do you expect things to be done correctly?" She said and pulled the mask back up. Davy put the sleeve back up to his mouth and nose as a pretext as he wiped her kiss from his lips.

"Would you like to go to the shooting range with me tonight?" he asked.

"Eeew," she exclaimed loudly. "Why would I want to do that?"

"I thought you'd like to spend more time together outside of the warehouse," he answered, grateful she couldn't see the frown on his face.

"Honey," she said in her nasal voice, "I've got work to do. And you should have some work to do as well. Have we received any drop-offs lately that you need to deliver?"

"I've brought all I have."

"That's good. You need to be more careful with the deliveries. We don't want to lose any more to the Feds," she scolded.

"I didn't know they were gonna confiscate it," he said defensively. Never mind the fact that he'd alerted them to the delivery. But he had to play it safe for everyone involved.

"Well, everyone makes a mistake, and you've made yours. Just make sure there isn't a second time," Junie said as she stopped her task and looked at him to stress her words.

Davy's ire was raised by the words of this little munchkin, and it took all his strength to let it pass without a rebuttal. "You're right," he said abruptly. "I'm heading to the range. I'll talk to ya later."

Davy exited the room with a sigh of relief. It sickened him to see the workers taken advantage of and to have to turn a blind eye. *When had he become so soft?* He asked himself. These types of operations used to never affect him. What had changed? What had changed him? The only thought that crossed his mind was Lucy.

Chapter 15

As Davy parked his F-150 next to a jeep that had so much dirt on it, you couldn't tell what color it was; Lucy took note that all the cars that were parked nearby were filthy and masculine.

"Doesn't anyone wash their cars in this group?" She asked Davy as they exited his truck.

"Why?"

"They're all so dirty. Bluuck," Lucy said as she accidentally brushed against one of the cars.

"This is an outdoor shooting range, not a shopping mall. The guys here don't care about clean cars," Davy explained.

"A shooting range I don't get to use," Lucy reminded him. "Why is it you wanted me to come again?" Lucy yawned.

"You said you wanted to learn how to shoot a gun."

"So, you changed your mind? You're gonna teach me to shoot?" Lucy asked with excitement. Davy had texted her and asked if she'd like to go to the shooting range with him the night before. When she read his invite, she quickly accepted and hoped he'd changed his mind about her only watching. The prospect of getting to shoot with someone who had so much experience and could give her some pointers was more than she'd thought possible.

"Unfortunately, no. Like I told you, this is mostly for me." They walked towards a tall wooden fence with an iron gate you could see through to the other side. Davy held the gate open for Lucy to enter, then lead the way towards a camouflage-painted building almost the length of the fence.

"Let's go in here," Davy instructed as he pointed towards the entrance in the wall of the building.

"Where?" Lucy asked.

"Here," Davy repeated.

"Question," Lucy began. When Davy stopped and looked at her, she continued, "When something is camouflaged, isn't it supposed to be hidden or blend in?"

"Yeah," Davy answered hesitantly, not sure where she was going with her question.

"Well, I can see this building. I don't think the camouflage worked." Davy rolled his eyes and groaned. Lucy snickered and innocently asked, "What?" Her spirits were high at the thought of spending time with Davy and watching his friends.

Still shaking his head from the bad joke, Davy told her, "You can sit and watch, okay? And keep your jokes to yourself, please."

"Oh, great. This should be loads of fun for me—watching you," Lucy said sarcastically.

"I told you that you wouldn't get to shoot."

Lucy blew out a heavy breath and said, "I thought you might have changed your mind when you invited me." She rolled her eyes like a teenager.

"I promise I'll bring you another time. But this time is for me. This is how I'm able to keep my skills fresh. We don't just shoot at targets, but also work scenarios of what could happen."

"Yeah, yeah, yeah," Lucy said with less excitement as she followed him through the building to a picnic table that had been set off to the side behind a lower wall where whoever was shooting would stand.

"You'll be out of the way here."

"I'll be out of the way?" Lucy asked incredulously. "Gee, you make me feel so wanted. You invited me, remember?"

"I'm sorry, I didn't mean that," Davy apologized as Lucy plopped down with a huff on the bench closest to the smaller wall. "I promise to bring you here and let you shoot sometime soon, k?"

"A'ight," Lucy replied. Davy did a double-take when he heard that.

"A'ight?" he asked. Lucy just smiled. She saw him physically relax when she did. This reminded her not to be so ornery.

Lucy watched Davy walk towards a group of men she hadn't noticed before standing outside the smaller wall. About twelve of them, all dressed in t-shirts, jeans, or khaki pants with cowboy boots or the camel-colored boots the military wore. Most also wore baseball caps with dark sunglasses—either hanging from a cord around their neck or set on the bill of the baseball caps. She observed all the handsome men with their guns holstered as they stood around and talked or laughed. She felt her head swim from all the testosterone and was thankful for her sunglasses that hid the dazed look in her eyes.

A couple of the men were on the same side of the small wall as she was as they readied their rifles and set them on the second picnic table at the other end of the building. When Davy approached them, she could hear them greet him. Davy said something in response. They all glanced over at her and laughed. Mortified of why they looked at her, she weakly waved and smiled.

After a few minutes, the men began to separate, and Davy walked back to her. She briskly waved him over and asked, "Did you tell those guys anything about me?" she asked nervously.

"Like what?" Davy asked, confused.

Lucy looked at Davy over her sunglasses, "Really? You don't remember?"

Davy started to laugh, "Oh, that. No, they know nothing about your hero worship."

"Why'd they all look over at me and then laugh?"

"I had to tell them who you were and why you were here. These guys are all protective of who sees them here."

"But why'd they laugh?" Lucy asked nervously.

Davy gave an embarrassed chuckle and said, "Just guy talk." Davy waved it off. "Please sit here quietly and be sure to wipe the slobber from your chin so they don't notice, and you'll be golden," Davy said. "Oh and put these on." Davy handed her a pair of headphones.

171

"Do these play music?" she asked as she turned them over in her hands.

"Uh, no." He said.

"Do I really need 'em?" she asked.

"Trust me, you will. Once we start, you'll be glad you have them."

"A'ight," she said as he walked away.

He turned around and gave Lucy a curious look, then asked, "When did this start?"

"When did what start?"

"This a'ight that you keep saying."

"I don't know. Problem?" Lucy asked smartly as she lowered her sunglasses and looked at him with raised eyebrows.

Davy held up his hands in surrender, unable to stop the guttural laugh before he said, "No, no problem. Just curious." Still laughing, he turned back towards the group of men.

Lucy frowned as she watched Davy walk towards the others with no indication to introduce her to them—but only point her out. She heard the muffled sound of their conversations and then a burst of laughter. She prayed her sunglasses would hide the dreamy look in her eyes as she watched these men in action.

With the targets set in preparation for their competition, they all put on their ears and eyes, as she learned they were called, and stood back to watch until their turn. Lucy saw for the first time where the targets were placed; they were the ones she'd seen before with the circle that had a bullseye, then to the right of her, she saw piles of what looked to be blocks or dirt or

172

something—they were too far away for her to really tell what they were. But she knew the men had been fussing over them before the organized shooting began.

After all the guys had emptied their clips, they proceeded to where the targets had been placed to retrieve them and compare shots. Lucy wished she could hear their trash talk but knew it was probably quite colorful. Still, she took her ears off just in case she could hear some of their jabber.

Lucy watched these warriors with their scruffy beards, God-like builds, and impressive firepower lined up outside the wall. Almost in unison, they put on their eyes and ears and started to fire. The sound jolted Lucy back to reality, and she rushed to put her headphones on— although her ears were already ringing from the sound.

Their stance showed they knew what they were doing—at least in Lucy's eyes, and the targets were so far off she couldn't tell whether they hit them or not. The gunfire soon became white noise to the fantasy going on inside her head. That is until they stopped, holstered their guns, and began the comparisons with much laughter. *Oh, how I love watching these men*, Lucy thought with a sigh. Davy made major points today by bringing her.

She watched as all the men seemed to relax; some came back to her side of the wall where they lifted a cooler onto the same picnic table that held many of their rifles. She was grateful for her sunglasses that hid her sideward glances. At the same time, she pretended to look at her phone as they opened the cooler. She'd expected to see it full of beer, but it was full of water on ice.

"So, what did you think?" Davy asked, who had left

the group and approached her bench.

She'd been so absorbed in her observation of these wonderful specimens that she hadn't noticed Davy's approach from the field. She wasn't sure what to say that wouldn't make her sound like a pathetic groupie, so she didn't answer. Instead, with the headphones Davy had given her to use that still covered her ears, she pretended not to hear him.

She motioned to them and mouthed, "What?"

Davy mouthed to her, "Take off the headphones."

"What?" she mouthed back, and under cover of her sunglasses rolled her eyes.

Davy reached across the table with both hands and pulled them away from her head and set them on the table. "I said, what did you think?"

"Oh," Lucy feigned surprise that she'd still had them on her ears, "so that's why I couldn't hear you," she said with a nervous laugh.

Davy sat on top of the table near where she sat on the bench. She moved up to the table and took a deep breath. "I thought it was amazing." Davy laughed. Lucy blushed.

"I'm glad. Is there anyone specifically you liked?" He asked with a gleam in his eyes.

"Like I'm gonna tell you. You'll just make me feel stupid for it."

"No, I won't. C'mon, you can tell me."

Lucy turned towards Davy with a sincere look and asked, "You promise?"

The smile on Davy's face faded as he said quietly, "I promise."

With a deep sigh, Lucy told him, "All of 'em."

Davy gave a hard blink and asked, "All of 'em?"

Lucy started to giggle quietly and said, "Yes, all of 'em. They are some of the most handsome men," she paused to take another deep breath, then continued, "I have seen in a long time." She let out her breath like a dreamy sigh. "Just amazing." She glanced over at Davy, who had a look on his face that hinted at worry.

"Oh," was all he said. "Really?"

"O.M.G. dude! I'm messing with you. Yes, I like all these men, and I love watching all the shooting, but I still wish I could shoot."

Davy let out an audible sigh of relief. "So you're seriously not a drooling mess?"

"Puuuuleeeease," Lucy said and rolled her eyes as if he were crazy. There was no way on earth she would let him know that her previous answer had been the truth. Then she asked, "Are we gonna leave now?"

"No, there is one more exercise we're gonna do. I think you'll find this interesting to watch."

"What is it?"

"You'll see."

"You just want me to adore you and your friends longer, doncha." Lucy said, "Men and their egos." Davy got up to leave. "Hey!" Lucy grabbed his hand to stop him.

"Yeah?"

"You didn't say anything to the guys about my goofiness, did you?" She asked.

Davy gave a light chuckle and said, "No. That secret is safe with me."

"Jones! We're gonna start. Do you want to do time?"

the man who seemed to be the leader of the group called over to Davy as he stood next to the table.

"Yeah. Be right there." Before he walked away, he tapped the table and said, "Put your ears on and watch this. I think you'll really like it."

"Gotcha," Lucy said as she placed the headphones back over her ears and gave him the thumbs-up sign.

For the next two hours, Lucy watched each man go through the timed exercise. She learned that these piles weren't really piles of rubble but of different pictures that would either pop up or turn around. The pictures could be a woman and child, a robber, a jihadi, an old lady, etc.

Man after man went through the exercise, while Mark, the man with the stopwatch, timed each one with Davy tracking the time. That is until it was his turn.

Lucy hadn't been aware that she held her breath when Davy stood ready to run through the gauntlet. She marveled at his ability to react so quickly and to make the correct decision as to whether to shoot or not. When he'd reached the final position where a bad guy hid behind the head of a woman and was able to shoot him in the head without any harm to his captive, she involuntarily applauded. The other men turned and looked at her.

"Oops, sorry," she mouthed to Davy when he turned around.

"Looks like you've got a cheering section there," Mark said with a tic of his head in Lucy's direction.

"She's just never been to one of these before," Davy explained embarrassedly.

"You've never brought a friend here before, let alone a woman." Mark studied Davy's face.

"What? She's just a friend and wants to learn to shoot," Davy said defensively.

Mark nodded his head and said, "A friend, huh? Okay." Then one of the other guys called to Mark. Mark raised his hand to signal them to wait a moment, then lowered his sunglasses and gave Davy another look.

Davy met his gaze and said with a chuckle, "A friend." As Mark walked away, he looked over his shoulder and nodded his head in mock belief with a slight grin still on his face.

Davy holstered his weapon as he ambled over to where Lucy patiently waited. Lucy watched his approach with admiration. *He looks so sexy*, she thought to herself.

"Ready to go?" he asked without looking at her, but she didn't move.

At first, Lucy didn't hear his question. She was so lost in appreciation of him.

So he stopped and turned back to her and asked again, "Luce? Ready to go?"

Lucy jumped, startled out of her fantasy, and managed to say, "If you are," Lucy wrinkled her nose from the pungent scent of gun powder that hung in the air like smoke from a brush fire.

"Yeah, let's go," Davy said as he continued towards the gate. Lucy quickly jumped up from the picnic table and followed him.

Walking outside the gate where all the vehicles were parked, Lucy had a much better appreciation for them, now that she knew who the owners were. She chuckled to herself as they walked through the unpaved parking lot, kicking up small rocks and dust as they made their way to

Davy's truck.

Once inside the truck, they rode in silence until Lucy asked, "So, you do this every week?"

"When I'm in town," Davy answered without looking away from the road.

"Have you ever had to use those skills on a flight?" Lucy asked as she slightly turned in her seat and watched his profile as he drove.

"No," he lied. *There were some things he'd done that she really didn't need to know*, he reasoned with himself.

"Why do you time everyone?" Lucy asked.

"Most decisions are made in a split second. We have to be ready when that happens."

"How was your time?"

Davy took his eyes off the road a second to look at her before he shrugged and responded, "It was alright," was all he said before he returned his attention to the road.

"Alright, eh? Who's was the best?" Lucy asked flirtatiously.

"I don't know," Davy said gruffly.

"Then how do you know you weren't the best?"

"I just do."

"Hm," was all Lucy said. She worried that he was in a mood. The last time he'd been in a bad mood, she'd ended up dunked in a fountain. She needed to change the subject and get him laughing again.

The two sat in silence while Davy drove onto the five freeway. Lucy wracked her brain for a light subject to broach as she watched him maneuver amongst the cars from one lane to another. She had an idea.

"So, tell me this," she began and turned toward him.

Davy turned his head with a questioning look and asked, "Tell you what?" Then looked back at the road.

"What's with all this hair growth?" She asked and looked at his handsome profile. "Are you rebelling against your parents?

Davy gave her a strange look as he said, "What?"

"Well, usually it's teenagers that grow their hair out in rebellion against their parents. So, I just wondered if you've been grounded or something." Lucy chuckled at her own joked.

Davy shook his head and said, "I told you I need to look like your *every man*." He accentuated with finger quotes.

"Not *every man* has long hair and a beard," she said as she mimicked his finger quotes. Davy gave her a sidewards glance and raised an eyebrow. "Okay, most of the men might have beards nowadays, but not long hair."

"You don't like my hair?" Davy asked as he ran his hand through his longish locks.

Lucy slowly shook her head as she grimaced, "I don't mind the beard, but the long hair, not so much. Ya know you'll never get a girl when you look like a scruffian."

"What's a scruffian?" Davy asked.

"Look it up. Your picture will be next to it," Lucy told him and gave him a posed smile, then changed her position so she could rest her head on the headrest.

Davy gave her a searching look then asked, "What kind of girl do you think I would attract?"

Lucy sighed and said, "I'm not sure. I guess it depends on what your type is." Davy didn't respond. "So, what's your type?" Lucy turned her head and looked at him.

"Hm, what's my type?"

"Yeah. What attracts you? What was your ex-wife like?"

"Oooh, well, that was a long time ago. I don't think her looks are really in play anymore."

"Why not? You liked them enough to marry 'em. C'mon, you can tell me," Lucy prodded with a smile.

Davy took in a deep breath and said, "Well, she had long brown hair, was about five feet four inches tall, slender build, brown eyes, pretty smile, and these long—"

"Okay, okay, I get the gist—she was gorj," Lucy interrupted. She didn't realize that it would bother her to hear him describe the woman he'd loved and who'd left him while he was out serving our country.

"Gorj?" Davy asked curiously.

"Gorgeous," Lucy stated with a frown, but when Davy looked at her, she gave a fake smile. *I shouldn't have asked about his ex-wife. I'm nothing like his type*, she told herself as she tried to suppress the wave of depression that was on the verge of drowning her.

"Ah, I see," Davy said with a knowing nod.

"Are you still in contact with her?" Lucy asked. *Aargh*, she told herself, *stop asking about this woman!*

"Who? My ex?" He asked. Lucy nodded. "No. After the divorce, she left with the guy she cheated on me with, and that was that."

"Do you miss her?" It took all of Lucy's strength to not hit herself for asking yet another question about his ex.

"No."

Hm, he didn't even hesitate, Lucy thought. "So, what are you looking for in a woman now, or are you even looking?" *What am I doing?* Lucy asked herself as she braced herself for his response.

"Someone who can quote a line from a movie, first of all," he said with a wink before he turned his attention back to the road as he maneuvered towards an exit lane.

"You're so full of it," Lucy responded. *Great comeback*, she told herself.

"What? Why do you say that?" Davy asked with feigned innocence.

Lucy did an involuntary laugh and gave Davy a knowing look. "I know what you're up to."

"You know what I'm up to?" Davy asked without taking his eyes off the road.

"Mm-hmm." Lucy watched out the window as Davy turned off the exit onto a surface street.

Davy gave a short chuckle then asked, "And what would that be? What am I up to?"

"You're avoiding the question."

"I am? What was the question?" He asked.

"Seriously?" Lucy shook her head at his avoidance of the question.

"No, really. What was the question?" Davy asked while they were stopped at a red light. He leaned back against the door as they studied one another. Lucy watched as a slow, relaxed smile appeared on his face without a word said between them. She gave a closed-mouth smile back. The light turned green, and the truck slowly accelerated. He asked a third time, "What was your question?"

"Oh, look, there's Café Rio," Lucy said as she turned her head in the direction of the café.

Laughter burst out of Davy. "Now who's avoiding the question," he stated.

"Whatever," Lucy said with an embarrassed laugh. This may have saved her from an awkward situation.

Davy held the door for Lucy as they entered the restaurant. It turned out they'd come at the right time because they didn't have to wait in line. They were able to get right up to the counter and get their food. At the register, Lucy realized she hadn't brought her wallet. She stood in front of the register and began to pat her pockets, hoping Davy would come to the rescue.

"Ma'am," the teenager with a ring in her nose and black lipstick began, "that'll be ten dollars and forty-five cents unless you want a drink."

"Um, I'll just have water," Lucy said.

"Ten forty-five, please," the teen repeated.

Davy watched with amusement at Lucy's discomfort. He wanted her to sweat a little bit. *It's good for her*, he told himself. But when she finally turned to him, with her eyes that seemed bluer than normal, he acquiesced.

"I've got it," he said as he moved her aside.

"Sheesh," she mumbled under her breath, "Took ya long enough."

Davy laughed and stepped up to the register. "These two orders will be together. How much do I owe ya?"

Lucy gave a sigh of relief. She knew he'd pay for her

meal, but she didn't want to assume that he would. However, she'd get back at him for making her sweat.

Once they had their food, they found around, painted table in a back corner surrounded by windows. As they ate, the tension lifted. Neither had realized how hungry they were until their first mouthful.

"Wanna go for a bike ride after this?" Davy asked with a mouth full of salad.

"What'd you say?" Lucy asked, squinting at Davy.

"After this," Davy said as he waved his fork over both their meals and dropped some salad bits, "wanna go for a bike ride?"

"Eeew! Really? Can you keep your food on your plate, please?" Lucy covered her mouth as she laughed to ensure that no food would escape. Davy snorted. "That'd be fun, but I don't have my bike with me?"

"Neither do I, but we can rent them at the beach," Davy suggested. "It'll be a nice change after the heat on the shooting range."

"Who's paying?" Lucy asked as she gave Davy a coy look out of the side of her eye.

Davy rolled his eyes and said, "I am."

Lucy danced in her chair as she softly clapped with pleasure. "Okay then, I'll go."

Chapter 16

Lucy straddled the bright yellow beach cruiser Davy had rented for her while she waited for the clerk in the rental shop to adjust his bike to fit his six-foot-five frame. The beach seemed particularly busy, and the bike shop was down to very few bikes when they got there. She was pleased with hers but knew Davy was having a more difficult time finding a bike that would work.

While she waited, Lucy looked around at all the different people that moved about on the sand and the bike path. It was a beautiful day and others obviously, had the same idea that Davy had suggested for them. Lucy raised her face towards the sun and felt the warm breeze lightly trip over her skin. She breathed the salty sea air in deeply, and as she let it out, the stress from the past week began to melt away.

Lucy loved the beach and the briny smell of the ocean. It wasn't often that she had a free Saturday to go to the beach or have a friend to go with her. She closed her eyes and began to drift along with the breeze when the repeated tin sound of a bike bell penetrated the peaceful moment. With an agitated sigh, she opened her eyes and looked in the direction of the bell.

Lucy doubled over with laughter when she saw Davy in his jeans, big military boots, and plaid shirt sitting on a large pink with blue and white daisies beach cruiser scowling. "I love it!" she laughed and applauded.

"Great, then you ride it and let me have yours," Davy said as he pushed the bike towards Lucy.

"No way! I love yellow. This is just perfect for me," she said as she patted the handlebar, put her foot on one of the pedals, and pushed off. "This was your idea," she called over her shoulder.

Davy sighed as he awkwardly peddled the brightly colored beach cruiser in pursuit of Lucy. He watched as Lucy effortlessly moved the bike between pedestrians and other bikers. He was thankful for the bright-colored bike she rode, which made it easier to keep her insight. It was especially easy in the more populated areas where people seemed to gather in clumps as they watched the volleyball games, barbequed, swam, and surfed. Everyone was enjoying the day.

Finally, they'd reached a section of the bike path further from the beach where the crowds had thinned. Davy watched Lucy lazily weave from side to side on the path as he cautiously peddled up next to her.

Lucy gave Davy a sidewards look and smiled at him. "I think this may be your best idea yet," she told him.

"Even better than the gun range this morning?" Davy asked.

Lucy paused, then inhaled through her teeth as if to wince before she gingerly answered, "As much as I loved watching all those amazing men, I think I'd have to say yes." She nodded as if to accentuate her answer.

"Really?" Davy answered in disbelief. "Wow."

"Just bein' honest," Lucy said apologetically. Davy laughed, which caused Lucy to look at him. "What?" she asked.

"You're way too easy to please. Not many women are that easy," he confessed.

"Well, my love language—not that you care—is actions. I prefer actions over gifts," Lucy told him in a matter-of-fact tone without looking at him.

"Ah, so I've been feeding your love language," Davy said with finger quotes before his hands returned to the handlebars, "without even knowing it. Good thing I don't care," Davy said as he moved his bike a little closer to her, unable to pass up the opportunity of getting under her skin.

Lucy glowered at him before she answered, "Don't ruin the moment. This is too good of a day, and I am too happy to let your comments mess with my mood." Davy laughed out loud as he stood up and began to peddle ahead of Lucy.

"Wanna take a break up here?" He asked as he motioned to a rest point with a picnic table and restroom facility nearby.

"Sure," Lucy said as she followed Davy over to the side and peddled backward to put the brakes in motion. Davy leaned his pink bike against the sandy, metal picnic table and disappeared into the restroom. Lucy thought it best to wait with the bikes for him to return before she went in and used the facilities.

As she sat on the bench and waited for Davy, she was glad that she had worn sandals with her jeans and t-shirt since this helped keep her cool. She slipped off the sandals and dug her toes into the cool sand where the table had been set. As her toes peaked up through the sand, she noticed that her nail polish had chipped and even disappeared on a couple of her toes. She quietly growled and reminded herself that she needed to put more effort into the little things.

Sitting on the bench, lost in her thoughts, she heard voices approaching from the parking lot located above the area where they'd stopped. She looked up to see two men and a petite woman make their way down a path that had been created over time as people looked for a quicker way to the beach.

"You're sure he was down here?" The big guy asked as they approached.

"Yeah," the little man said impatiently. Lucy looked away to avoid them, thinking she was eavesdropping.

The two men wore jeans, the bigger one was the size of a mountain, and the other guy was scrawny, short, and smoked a cigarette that he tossed into the sand as they reached the bottom.

"It better be him," the taller and bigger guy said with a menacing tone. "Or you'll be next." The trio now stood near the table. The bigger man wore black sunglasses and a wife-beater tank top that exposed the two sleeves of tattoos covering his muscular arms. He seemed to be the same height as Davy but was bald, with ears that stuck out. Lucy watched him with curiosity; he reminded her of someone, but she couldn't put her finger on who it was.

He lifted his sunglasses and looked at Lucy. Then flashed a smile exposing a set of beautiful white teeth, totally unexpected from a rough-looking guy with a toothpick protruding from his mouth.

Lucy gave a half-hearted smile back but hoped that Davy would come out soon so they could leave. She'd wait to use the restroom—she wasn't comfortable with these characters who had just shown up.

"There he is!" The gorgeous, petite blonde drawled as she excitedly trotted over to where Davy had just exited. "Hi, sweetie! We've been looking for you." She stood in front of Davy, wrapped her arms around his neck, and pulled his head towards her until their lips met in a kiss. Lucy's stomach dropped to her knees as her eyes grew big in surprise at the sight before her. She forced her eyes to look away as she began to shiver from a cool breeze. So, this was Davy's type. *I should've know*n, she said to herself. *Why does her voice sound so familiar?*

"What are you doing here?" Davy asked as he pulled away from the beautiful, petite blonde with manicured toenails in wedged sandals. Davy darted a look in Lucy's direction. How would he get her away from this situation?

"Davy," The big guy said with disdain from where he sat on the edge of the dirty picnic table.

"See, I told you it was him," the little guy said as he adjusted his loose-fitted Hawaiian shirt. He reached into the pocket and pulled out a packet of Camel cigarettes, tapped it against his hand, and pulled the cigarette that popped out and put it in his mouth.

"Hello, Sally," Davy said with a sneer. Lucy watched with wide eyes as the mountain stood and the two squared off.

"Don't call me that," the big guy looked at Davy and said, "Where ya been? You were supposed to find out which of your flyers told the Feds about the big shipment."

"Who said I didn't?" Davy challenged.

"Why you been hiding if you got the information?" Sal countered.

With one arm still around the little blonde, Davy could only put the other hand up to caution the big guy and nod in Lucy's direction. "Cool it, man. I've got the info." Then he turned towards Lucy and told her, "You wanna go use the restroom, and I'll watch the bikes?"

"Nah, it's okay," Lucy said as she watched the little blonde attached to Davy. Self-consciously she slipped her polish chipped toenails back in her sandals, stood, and reached for her bike. "I'll leave you to your friends." Lucy walked her bike to the cemented path, straddled it, and stood with one foot poised on the pedal.

"You don't need to go. Just give me a few minutes," Davy told her. Instead, Lucy waved and pushed the peddle down to ride in the direction they'd just come.

"Who's she?" Lucy heard the blonde beauty drawl in her nasally tone.

"Just a friend," Davy responded flatly.

Those words rang like a jackhammer against a paved road in Lucy's mind. Now she knew where he saw their friendship; it was a huge disappointment, not a surprise, but typical.

"It looked like a date to me," the blonde accused in her Urkel voice.

"She's just a friend, Junie bug," Davy said to placate her as he drew her close in a one-arm hug.

"Okay then," she purred as she wrapped her arms around his waist and squeezed.

"Junie," the big guy said firmly, "Davy and I need to talk business, go with Johnny."

"But Sally, I wanna stay with Davy," she said with a pout to the big guy.

"Go with Johnny. We need to talk," Sal said and gave a dismissive nod to Johnny to take Junie away. He and Davy watched the two awkwardly climb back up the path they'd just descended. Then Sal turned towards Davy and said, "I told ya not to call me Sally."

Davy rolled his eyes and said under his breath, "Whatever you say, Sally."

Sal gave Davy a dark look before he asked, "What's the information?"

Davy shrugged his shoulders as he turned and sat on the bench and rested his arms behind him on the table before he responded, "The Feds confiscated the shipment."

"We already know that," Sal said with contempt as he looked down at Davy. "How did the Feds find out about the shipment? We lost millions of dollars and the boss ain't happy."

"I'm working on that." Davy stood and nonchalantly walked over to the water fountain and leaned down to take a sip. He needed to stay out of Sal's reach. "Obviously, there's a snitch," Davy straightened and wiped the back of his hand across his mouth.

"Obviously," Sal stated sarcastically. Davy gave a

slight shrug and looked at the ocean; he could feel Sal's frustration. "I told 'em you'd fail. It's too much for a lousy frog," Sal chided Davy.

"Maybe, maybe not, but you'll never know because I'll only tell your boss," Davy said.

***

"Are you sure that's what you heard?" Annie asked through the phone.

Lucy looked out her office window with her cell phone to her ear and nodded her head. "Yes. I heard it with my own ears. He had no idea I was there. As far as he knew, I'd cycled back to the bike rental shop." Lucy began to pace in her office.

"Tell me again what you saw," Annie directed Lucy.

"A beautiful snack time girl mackin' on Davy," Lucy told her irritably.

"Yeah, you've already told me about the girl. I meant about the big guy—what was his name again?"

"Sal. . . Sally. But he didn't like being called that. And the little guy was named Johnny."

"And what were Davy and this Sal guy talking about?" Annie asked.

"Some kind of shipment that the Feds had intercepted and Davy finding out who the snitch was, but he said he'd only tell the boss what he found out. Which Sal didn't appreciate because that's when he started making digs at Davy's special ops experience," Lucy told her.

"Then they started to fight?" Annie asked with

interest.

"Yeah."

"Who said what to bring them to blows?" Annie asked.

"I could only hear bits and pieces, not enough to put it together. But, I could tell that they didn't like one another," Lucy told her.

"Gee, ya think?" Annie asked sarcastically.

Lucy laughed. "Yeah, I guess that's kind of apparent."

"So, then what happened? Who won the fight?"

"Well, if you ask me, I'd say that Davy did, but neither of them walked away bruise-free. I'd never seen guys fight before—in person. It was kinda gross to see them hit each other and the blood—," Lucy trailed off, lost in thought.

"Ew, I bet."

"Yeah," Lucy gave an involuntary shudder.

"So, what are you gonna do?" Annie asked.

"Do? About what?" Lucy asked as she sat at her desk and rested her head in her hand.

"About Davy. Looks as if he's crooked."

Lucy felt her stomach clench up at the thought that Davy was dirty. "He can't be," she said with decisiveness.

"How do you know that? From what you told me, it sounds as though your hero is a dirty, scumbag drug dealer," Annie told her through the phone.

"He can't be," Lucy repeated as she felt her throat tighten and fought the tears of disappointment that were nearby.

Have you heard from him since then?"

"No," Lucy responded sullenly. "Not one word. Should I reach out to him?"

"Why not? Because of the little snack time girl—as you call her—it's fairly obvious that you and he are just friends." Lucy smarted at those words. Unaware, Annie continued, "So why not? Or, have you lost interest in him because of his dirtiness or his girlfriend?" Lucy didn't respond. "Lucy? Are ya there?" Annie queried. "Lucy?"

Hearing Annie refer to that blonde as Davy's girlfriend tore her insides apart, but she couldn't think about that now. "Hm?" She answered absently.

"Uh oh," Annie said with dread, "what are you thinking?"

"Who is he? I don't know him that well, but what if the little I know about him is all a lie?"

"I think you know who he is now. Maybe that's the true Davy?" Annie prompted.

"I refuse to believe he's like that. If you only saw him when we're together. If you only knew him."

"You don't even know him. How would I?" Annie asked.

"Something else has got to be going on. I can't believe he's crooked," Lucy said stubbornly.

"Are you sure it isn't your crush talking?" Annie asked.

"Crush! I don't have a crush," Lucy retorted stubbornly.

Annie gave her throaty laugh. "Yeah, right. You don't have a crush."

Lucy scowled at her phone then placed it to her ear. "I don't. We're friends."

Annie's maddening laugh could be heard before she responded, "Uh-huh." Lucy sighed in frustration. "So, what are you gonna do? Anything?" Annie inquired.

"I have to. I have to find out who he is," Lucy stated.

"Oooh, that's what I thought you'd say," Annie said with a groan.

"And, I'm gonna need your help."

"I should have never said hi," Annie mumbled under her breath.

Chapter 17

Davy sat alone in the office at LAX, writing up the report on his last flight, when he heard the door open. He looked up in time to see Sammy stumble through the slim opening and lean against the wall. Davy looked at Sammy's appearance with alarm: His face was bloody and disfigured from the swelling, blood covered his hair, and he held his right arm, which was wrapped in bloodied cloth protectively against his body, his clothes barely draped over his body.

"Dude, what happened to you?" Davy asked as he rushed from his desk to catch Sammy before he hit the floor. "What happened to you? Who did this to you?" He asked as he carefully leaned him back against the wall.

With Sammy secured, he pulled his gun from its holster. Cautiously he opened the office door to see if anyone was in the hall waiting, but it was empty. He ran down the hall to the main entrance into the office, but no one was in the vicinity—all was quiet. He returned to the office and deadbolted the door before he holstered his gun and returned to Sammy, who was barely breathing.

Through swollen, bloodied lips, he said, "They got Max."

"Who got Max?" Davy asked as he began to do a check on Sammy's injuries. "We need to get the paramedics," Davy said as he quickly retrieved his phone from his desk, his jacket from his chair, and began to call the airport paramedics. As he waited for an answer, he put his phone on speaker and set it aside. He knelt next to Sammy and gently laid him on the floor with his jacket underneath his head.

Davy pulled one of the other flyer's jacket off the back of their chair and gently laid it over Sammy's torso to try and prevent shock. Then he began the first aid he'd learned in the military. He gently grabbed Sammy's bloodied right arm to put it under the jacket when he saw, for the first time, that the bloody cloth was covering a stub that had formerly been Sammy's right hand and raised Sammy's arm to try and slow the loss of blood from the blood-drenched rag.

"Where's your emergency?" He heard the operator ask.

Davy reached for his phone from the floor, but it slipped through his bloodied hand and clattered on the floor. "Hold on," he said as he wiped his hand on his pant leg and reached for the phone before he remembered it was on speaker. "I need paramedics in the FAMs office asap." He yelled.

"They killed Max," whispered Sammy.

"What are the injuries?" the operator asked.

"I have a FAM that's down with serious injuries,"

Davy said into his phone. "What did you say?" He asked Sammy.

"I asked what the injuries were," responded the operator.

"Not you. Please just get the medics to the Field Air Marshal office asap," Davy yelled at the phone, then asked Sammy, "Who killed Max?"

"The I —," he began.

A loud bang on the office door interrupted Sammy's response. Davy looked at the door, startled by the banging, and reached for his gun when he remembered he'd dead bolted the door.

"It's the EMTs," the Operator yelled over the noise at him, followed by hard banging.

"Open up!" The EMTs called from the other side of the door. Davy quickly rose and unlocked the door.

"Sorry about that, but I had to take precautions when Sammy came in looking like this," he said as he motioned to where Sammy laid.

"How'd this happen?" asked the first paramedic as he knelt next to Sammy.

"I don't know."

***

Davy sat in his darkened living room and stared out the big picture window of the home he'd rented while he worked undercover. He sat and observed the quiet neighborhood he'd become familiar with since the operation began. With the murder of someone like Max, he knew things were beginning to boil. It wouldn't be long before the operation would come to an end, and he could get his life back to normal. Whatever that was.

He thought about Max and Sammy. What had hit the nerve with the crime ring? Had it been the confiscation of the huge drug delivery? He let the exhaustion he'd held at bay for so long wash over him like a wave. This would be his last undercover operation. *I'm too old for this*, he thought to himself. So lost in his thoughts, he jumped when his phone beeped.

Wanna get some tea?

Davy smiled as he read the text message, then his brows furrowed. He looked out the window at the darkened street and chewed his inner cheek. He'd never made the mistake of mixing his personal life while working an operation before, and now he knew why. The daily danger of looking over his shoulder was not an easy life. But add civilians, and it was impossible. His phone beeped again.

Hey, ya there?

Are you in town?

Should he answer her text, he asked himself, *or should he cut ties and disappear*? He stared at the text messages as he contemplated this quandary he'd put himself in. On the one hand, he really enjoyed the time he spent with Lucy. Yet, on the other hand, the operation was heating up, and he couldn't afford to blow it because of some goofy girl. His phone beeped a third time.

> *Dude! Are you not texting*
> *anymore?*

Davy was aware that he walked a very thin line as well as an extremely dangerous one. He should have never allowed himself a social life outside of all the players in the operation, no matter how lonely or stressed he was. He'd been working this covert operation alone for so long—he shouldn't endanger others—hadn't planned on endangering others. But when he'd moved into that neighborhood, he hadn't planned on Lucy. He enjoyed spending time with someone that wasn't dirty from the illegality of their actions. She was a breath of fresh air, and selfishly, he'd put her in danger by their friendship.

Davy typed a response to Lucy's text, then stopped and backspaced until his text disappeared. He had to step back and cut off all contact to keep her safe. He heard another text notification, but without looking at his phone, he closed his eyes as he pressed the side button and heard it shut off.

***

Lucy scowled at her phone as she walked out of her kitchen towards her couch. Ordinarily, Davy responded in a timely manner to her texts, but he hadn't responded to any that she'd sent over the last couple of days. *Is he traveling?* She asked herself, then shook her head in denial. That shouldn't matter; even when he traveled, he still managed to respond to her texts. *Have I done something to upset him?* He'd been gone for quite a while this time. If only she knew where he lived, then she could drop by and see if he were there.

Lucy plopped down on her couch as her index finger repeatedly swept upward on the face of her phone. "Nate the skate," Lucy said into her phone once the ringing stopped.

"What!" He answered with mock irritation on the other end of the line.

"I need your opinion on something."

"Whaaaat," he continued to pretend he was bothered, but since Nate worked from home, it was usually okay to give him a call when she needed his advice. He wasn't only Lucy's brother but her friend and confidante in the matter of men—since he was one.

Lucy ignored his irritation and said, "Why would a guy not respond to my texts?"

"Because he's smart." Nate gave his goofy laugh.

"*Nathan!*" Lucy said with her own mock version of exasperation. "I need your opinion on a guy and his texting habits."

Nate sighed then asked, "Who's the guy?"

"Remember that Air Marshal I told you about?" Lucy asked and was met with silence, so she continued, "You know, the one I met at the library and then ran into on the plane?"

"Oh. The one you're stalking?"

"I'm not stalking him. I was on a legitimate trip and did not know he'd also be on that flight. In fact, I didn't even know he was a FAM then."

"FAM?" Nate asked.

"Yeah, you know—Federal Air Marshal, also known as FAM," Lucy explained. She could hear Nate chuckle over the phone. She stilled herself for the barrage of quips she was sure she'd get from him. Nate took after their dad in many ways, the most being that he had a fun sense of humor.

"A FAM, huh?" he finally asked. Lucy didn't say anything. Nate could make her laugh at herself, but this time she really wanted some sort of answer or direction as to how to deal with this guy. "What was your question, again?" Nate asked.

Lucy pulled the phone from her ear and looked at it, confused. This was so not like him. Cautiously she asked, "Are you okay?"

After a slight pause, Nate told her, "I broke off my engagement to Dreena."

Surprised, Lucy asked, "Why?"

"Turned out she'd gotten married to some rich guy in her country."

"So, *you* broke off the engagement?" Lucy asked, confused.

"Yeah, why?"

"Well," Lucy paused before she continued, "if she was married, why didn't *she* break off the engagement?"

"What about this FAM?" Nate asked, changing the subject.

"FAM?" Lucy asked, surprised by the abrupt subject change. "Oh yeah, the FAM. Um," she paused again.

"What's his name?" Nate asked.

"Davy Jones."

"Like from the Monkees?" Lucy could hear his laugh.

Lucy rolled her eyes and answered, "Yes, like from the Monkees."

"So, what about him?"

"Well, we are friends and have texted quite a bit and done multiple activities together."

"And?"

"Well, he stopped responding to my texts," Lucy whined.

"What'd you do?" Nate asked.

"Nothing."

"Really?" Nate asked doubtfully.

"Well, nothing that I know of," Lucy responded as she stood and began to pace around her living room.

"Uh-huh."

"I don't," Lucy said defensively.

"Were you dating him?" Nate asked in a flat tone.

Lucy paused before she asked, "Did I wish I dated him or actually dated him?"

Nate remained silent.

Lucy gave a choking sound then said, "No. I wasn't dating him, okay? We just spent time together as friends, doing activities."

"So, then he's not obligated to respond to your texts—not that he would be if you were dating."

"Lot of help you are," Lucy told him glumly as she plopped herself down on her eight-foot couch she'd owned for a billion years.

"Just keepin' it real, like you always do for me."

"Yeah, yeah, yeah. Thanks for nothin'."

"Mm-hmm," Nate answered absentmindedly.

"And I'm sorry about your girl." Lucy sat up on the couch.

"Oh well." He said. Lucy could hear the sad tone in his voice.

"But I did point out the red flags. Especially when you have a long-distance romance with someone in another country." Lucy had told him repeatedly that there were too many red flags regarding his girl, but Nate was such a romantic and looked at the world with rose-colored glasses. He always looked for the best in people. Even after all his heartaches, he was still full of hope—where romance was concerned. Not Lucy. She was more cynical and doubtful about any romance, which probably worked against all her relationships.

Lucy heard the dial tone in her ear as she walked to the counter in her kitchen and set her phone down on the breakfast bar. She loved her brother Nate and all the support he gave her as she struggled with her efforts to find love. Like her, he understood heartache. But he had been absolutely no help in this matter.

The next day Lucy went for a long jog in the hope of clearing her head regarding Mr. Jones and his silence. At the end of her run, she stopped and stared out towards the ocean, baffled. She hated games and couldn't imagine Davy was the type to play them. What should she do? Forget about him? Report him to the police? Or accept the fact that she really did like bad boys? She couldn't forget the conversation she'd watch him have with that Sal guy. What was that all about? Those people didn't seem like the kind he'd naturally hang with—especially since he seemed so comfortable when he was hanging with her. *Should I consider turning him into the police or report his girlfriend as a lost munchkin?* She thought jealously.

Lucy loved the waves with their mesmerizing undulation. It pulled her closer and closer. She ignored the sand that spilled into her shoes with each step and, without thought, eventually carried the shoes in her hands. She stood barefoot on the firm sand near the surging waves and could feel the coolness of it between her toes.

Lucy welcomed the breeze that swirled about her. She filled her lungs with the salty air and her ears with the roar of the waves as she walked along the shore and felt her mind start to clear. As she walked, her mind worked through the dilemma until a thought began to take hold. Everyone accused her of this, so maybe she should do a version of it until she resolved the issue.

Okay, she told herself, *I will stealthily follow him, but only to find out who he is and what is going on, but I can't tell anyone. Okay, maybe just Annie—and Nate, but no one else.* Lucy could feel her mood lighten with this new idea and, with a lift in her step, changed direction.

Chapter 18

Lucy jogged to her 4Runner, unable to calm the excitement she felt with the ideas that ran rampant in her mind. Once inside, she paused before she put the key in the ignition. She needed a plan, but first, she needed to decide what her starting marker would be. The ideas bubbled over each other. She loved the adrenaline that now pumped through her body—maybe she didn't even need her 4Runner right now, she chuckled to herself. She was so excited to begin this new adventure; she felt she could've run home from the beach.

As she drove through the canyon from the beach, she began to organize her plan. She realized the only way she'd know how to deal with this male creature that intrigued her would be if she found out more about him. She stared at the road and tapped her fingers on the steering wheel as she organized her thoughts. She must start following him and find out what he did with his time away from her—which was more than his time with her.

Later, as Lucy sat at her dining table and stared at the

face of her phone, she debated as to whether she should try and text Davy once more before she initiated her plan to learn more about her mysterious friend. With a grimace, she began to tap into her phone:

Are you there?

Then held her breath and waited. . . and waited. . . and waited. With a disgusted huff, she stood and went to her fridge to get a cool drink. She pulled out a Powerade Zero and slowly drank from the bottle as she listened for the ding that would notify her of a text message. After so many sips, she replaced the bottle and plopped herself onto her comfy couch—and still no ding. Before she could stop herself, she was typing in another text message:

Davy? Are you okay?

Lucy hated the feeling of gloom that tickled the circumference of her brain. *We're just friends*, she repeated to herself while she washed off her makeup and climbed into bed. *It was too good to be true*, she thought to herself as she stared up at the darkened ceiling.

It was always in the hours of the night when she felt the loneliness begin to cover her like a weighted blanket. With a shaky sigh, she sniffled as a tear rolled down the side of her cheek. Angrily she reached up and swiped it off.

"Don't you dare have a pity party now," she angrily reprimanded herself. "You've got a plan, and you can't look for the man through tears."

***

"I told ya to be careful with that girl," Agent Smith told Davy as they relaxed on the bench outside of the tennis court. Through their sunglasses, the two men pretended to watch a couple playing.

"We're just friends," Davy explained. He hadn't seen Joel since Director Janssen decided that Davy needed to report to him. Before then, Agent Joel Smith had always been his contact. They'd served together overseas. When Joel left the service, he had immediately joined the DEA and risen through the ranks quickly. Since he'd been Davy's Seal commander before he retired, he knew him well, so when he heard that Davy had left the seals, he quickly recruited him into the DEA. Davy could've risen through the ranks just as quickly, but he preferred being out in the field rather than being stuck behind a desk.

"She's put not just you, but herself, in danger," Agent Smith said as he stroked his full beard.

"I know," Davy agreed as a tennis ball landed on the grass in front of him.

"What are ya gonna do?" Joel asked as he scooped up the ball and tossed it over the high chain-link fence to the waiting couple.

"Thanks!" They called and waved at the guys.

"I'd like to get her out of the picture," Davy said.

Agent Smith returned to the bench and sat with a look of resigned disbelief before he asked him, "How?"

"I wanted to stop all contact," Davy responded

without looking at Joel.

"But?" Joel asked.

Davy paused and lifted the water bottle to his lips for a drink to delay his response. "I tried to stop contact, but there were extenuating circumstances."

"Extenuating circumstances?" Joel asked as he lowered his sunglasses and looked at Davy.

"Ya know," Davy tried to explain, "she's not your average woman. She's not like anyone you've ever met before."

"Uh-oh," Joel said. He hadn't heard Davy speak about a woman like that since the situation with his ex-wife and daughter.

Davy's brow furrowed, "What do you mean by uh-oh?" Joel cocked an eyebrow. Davy looked at him confused, then surprised before he answered, "Dude, no. It's not like that. We're just friends," Davy raised his hands in resistance to the idea.

Joel adjusted the ragged bill of his baseball cap and resumed watching the tennis match as he pursed his lips in silence.

"But, there is the extenuating circumstance," Davy said. Joel leaned forward and rested his elbow on his knee as the other hand-picked at the grass between his feet. When Davy didn't continue, he looked up at him expectantly. Davy cleared his throat and blurted out, "I think Sal and Johnny are watching her."

Joel looked at him in disbelief, then lifted his cap and scratched his scalp through his thick mane of brown hair before he replaced the cap on his head. "You should have told me this first, bro. Are you sure?"

208

"Pretty sure." Davy nodded his head as Joel's eyebrows raised in question. "Sure enough that I increased my contact with her."

Joel gave a quick tic of a movement with his head towards Davy and asked, "The Italians, huh?"

"Yeah. Should we get the Director on the phone and let him know?"

"Why?"

"Because it looks like I've really screwed up. I walked too tight of a rope this time. Got too cocky," Davy said solemnly.

"You haven't heard?" Joel asked.

"Heard what?"

"The Director's gone back to DC. You only report to me," Joel told him. He noticed the slight shift of relief in Davy's shoulders.

***

"I want you two to find out where Davy spends his time when not with us," Junie told Sal and Johnny.

"Why, boss?" Johnny asked. "If he ain't here, he's probably on a plane."

Junie swung her tennis racket hard at Johnny, hitting his shoulder and breaking the frame of the racket.

"Ouch!" Johnny said.

"Look what you've done!" She yelled at him. "Just do what I tell ya!"

"Do you want us to watch his house then?" Sal asked from a chair out of Junie's reach.

"Only if he's there. Otherwise, follow him but don't

let him know." Junie set the broken racket down on the couch opposite Sal. She picked up the emery board off the table next to the couch and, without looking at Sal, told him, "And make sure he isn't dating anyone else."

Sal and Johnny exchanged looks. "Yeah, sure, boss."

"If he is, I wanna know."

Sal and Johnny left Junie's office and walked down the stairs in the warehouse in silence. Once on the ground floor, Johnny turned to Sal and asked, "Are we gonna tell her about that girl we've been watching?"

"Nah," Sal told him. "We're gonna wait until Davy makes a mistake, then let him know our displeasure which'll please the boss."

Chapter 19

Lucy woke at two in the morning to the hard, staccato beat of rain on her roof and balcony. She laid in her bed and enjoyed the sound of the rain beating against her bedroom window before she left the warmth of her bed. When she did throw the covers back, she could feel the brisk air in her room. Without turning on her bedroom light, she wrapped her robe about her and walked over to her window to peek out. She marveled at the passion shown by the torrential rain storming against her balcony and window. She loved the fury storms seemed to express, and it didn't matter if she were outside or inside. But her preference was to be home when it rained because it felt so cozy.

With a sigh, she turned away from the window and switched on the light to begin her morning ritual before she left for the office. Crunches came first in her routine, so she laid down on the floor of her bedroom. While on the floor, she zoned out due to the small amount of sleep she'd gotten the night before. Then she heard the beginning strains of AC/DC Thunderstruck as her two-thirty alarm hit. She stared at the ceiling as she started her first crunch, only to find herself staring at a big black spider that was rapidly moving about the ceiling.

Lucy's irrational fear of spiders kicked in as she bolted up from the floor with a speed that surprised even her that early in the morning. She ran to her hall closet to get her vacuum so that she could get rid of it. She shivered at the thought of the spider, but with the long hose attachment on her vacuum, she wouldn't need to get too close to annihilate it. Since it was so early in the morning, Lucy had to be cognizant of her neighbors below and try not to make too much noise—but this was an emergency. It was either her or the spider that wouldn't leave her bedroom that morning.

"Where has it gone?" she asked aloud when she returned with the vacuum. Slowly she turned and searched every nook and cranny of her room. "Ah-ha! There you are," she said as she spotted the little creature on the doorsill. "Trying to blend in, are we?" she asked while, with trembling hands, she moved the hose closer and closer to where the spider waited, unaware of its imminent departure from this world. "Gotcha!" Lucy said victoriously and grimaced as the vacuum sucked in the eight-legged menace. It would be a while before the involuntary shivers would stop—so much for today's workout, she told herself.

After returning the vacuum to the hall closet, Lucy sat on her bed. She flipped through the shows available to her via her Roku on her tv when her phone dinged. She was still in her cotton pajama bottoms and t-shirt, having not begun to get ready for work. She hadn't felt like washing her hair that morning, so she would just put it in a ponytail and call it good for the day. While she sat and looked for something interesting to listen to, she heard her phone ding again. It was so early in the morning that she assumed it was merely a notification of someone's post on Facebook, so she just ignored it. Then her phone began to ding multiple times.

> *Are you there?*
> *Luce, you there?*
> *I don't have much time.*
> *Look, I'm out of town for a*
> *while.*
> *Sorry for the si--*

Lucy stared at the phone in shock. It had been so long since she'd heard from him that she'd assumed it would be her plan that would bring him back in her life.

> *Oy! Where've you been!*

While Lucy waited for his response, she noticed the "oy" in her text. "I really do need to slow down on the British shows," she said aloud.

> *Davy? Are you okay?*

Lucy watched her phone with the hope that Davy

would respond, but time ticked by and nothing. She would send one more text and see if he'd respond.

Twenty-four hours later, when Davy still hadn't responded to her last text. She sat and fumed while she stared at her phone. *This is absolutely maddening. Why isn't he responding? Why didn't he finish his last text? What is going on? Who is this guy? He didn't seem the type to just ghost a woman, especially when they were friends.* Lucy decided it was time to act.

She scrapped the idea she'd previously drafted as her plan. Instead, she would keep it simple and just watch and follow him. She had to follow him and learn his schedule. Multiple times they'd discussed his travel as a FAM, and how he dealt with the parking at the airport, so she felt she had a pretty good idea of where his truck would be parked, and that would be her first step.

***

Lucy drove around the airport parking lot where Davy had mentioned he usually parked when he worked. She drove up and down each row in search of his truck for what seemed hours but was probably only twenty or thirty minutes until she finally found it. She was sure it was his truck because of the baseball cap that sat on the dashboard space in front of the steering wheel—that had to be his. She'd seen him wear the ragged dark blue cap with a faded spot on the front where some patch had formerly been. She'd always meant to ask him what had been there but kept forgetting. Besides the distinctive spot on the baseball cap, she'd seen him place the cap on his dashboard multiple times. She confidently backed into a spot a couple of rows away, so she'd be sure and see him when he returned.

Lucy wasn't sure how long she'd been waiting for Davy when she realized her eyelids were getting heavy. Had she been asleep? She quickly checked for Davy's truck—it was still there. She gave a sigh of relief, then looked at her phone; it was twelve-thirty in the morning. She had to do something to stay awake, so she jumped out of her car and began to briskly walk up and down the row of cars to get her blood moving to stay awake. After a couple of jaunts along the long row, she felt invigorated and climbed back into her truck.

She leaned back in the driver's seat and relaxed with her head against the headrest when her eyes immediately began to close but flew open when a nearby car alarm began to squawk. Instantly she sat up in the seat and reached for her phone.

"What are you doing again?" Annie asked drowsily.

"I'm at the airport waiting for Davy to return from his flight," Lucy said as she opened the door of her car and stepped out.

"What time is it?"

Lucy looked at the time on her phone, then said, "One forty-five in the morning. Did I wake you?"

"It's one forty-five in the morning. What do you think?" Annie said, followed by a yawn.

"I'm sorry. I took a chance that tonight might have been one of those nights when you didn't sleep well." Lucy told her as she did lunges around the perimeter of her truck.

"What are you doing?" Lori asked with curiosity.

"I told you. I'm at the airport waiting for Davy." Lucy answered as she stretched against her truck.

"But why? Why are you doing that?" Lori asked.

"Too many questions about the guy. He jumps up at the oddest times to run off, and then I don't see him for days or weeks," Lucy said.

"Doesn't that go with his job as an Air Marshal? He told you there would be times when he was only given an hour's notice to get on a flight."

"True, but he says that he has some seniority since he's done it for so long. So, one would think that he'd be able to pick and choose the schedule he wanted instead of being at their beck and call," Lucy explained to Annie.

"What are you going do when he gets back?"

"Follow him," Lucy's tone was very matter-of-fact as she opened her truck door and climbed back inside.

"Where?"

Lucy looked at herself in the visor mirror and grimaced. She licked her index fingers and lightly rubbed them under her eyes to get rid of the makeup that had smudged there. "Wherever he goes. I want to find out where he lives and why all the secrecy."

"What secrecy? You're just friends. It shouldn't matter what he does on his time. You're acting a little crazy here," Annie informed her.

"It shouldn't matter, but it does," Lucy told her.

"But why?" Annie asked, exasperated. "Doncha think stalking him will be a huge turn-off to the guy?"

"I'm not stalking."

"Really?" Annie challenged.

216

"Well, it's not meant to be stalking."

"Uh-huh." Was all Annie said.

Lucy scowled. "Since you're up, why don't you come wait with me?" Lucy asked.

"It's almost two in the morning," Annie said in disbelief.

"And you're up, so why not? What else are ya gonna do?" Lucy reasoned with her.

"Well, sleep for one."

"Ah, c'mon. You can do that later."

"No, I work later—like you," Annie said.

"Ya have to get up now anyway, so come sit and watch with me."

"No, you get up at this time. I still have four more hours before I have to get up," Annie told her.

Lucy gave a loud sigh.

"Oh, alright," Annie said as she gave in partly out of curiosity and partly because if she were there, she could keep Lucy from doing anything crazy. "I must admit that I am curious as to how you're gonna do this. Where are you parked?"

Lucy gave Annie the row and building she was in and told her to hurry. Since Annie lived less than five miles from the airport, it wouldn't take her long, so Lucy made herself comfortable and readied herself for a night of waiting.

Twenty minutes later, Annie startled Lucy out of her reverie when she knocked on the passenger side window. "Open up," she said.

Lucy clicked the lock button on her door to release the lock. "I'm so glad you came. This will be fun," Lucy reassured her with a smile. But did a double-take when Annie climbed into the front passenger seat clad in her cartoon doggy-covered pajamas and fluffy slippers. "Glad you didn't dress up or anything. Luckily, we shouldn't be expected to get out of the car, so your pajamas and slippers should be safe," Lucy said.

"Problem?" Annie asked, giving Lucy a don't-mess-with-me look.

"No, no, none at all," Lucy looked away so Annie wouldn't see the face she made. "I just didn't take you as the doggy PJ-type person."

"You so owe me for this," Annie grumbled under her breath as she settled in her seat, then changed the subject and asked, "Any sign of him yet?"

"Not yet," Lucy said with a sigh, "this may not have been the best idea."

"Ya think?" Annie asked.

Lucy watched out the windshield at Davy's truck as she thoughtfully said, "He might not come back today."

"You're kidding, right?" Annie asked in disbelief.

"Well . . ."

"Give me strength," Annie muttered under her breath. "So, which car is his?" She asked.

"That one over there," Lucy said as she pointed toward the dark blue F-150 truck.

"Are you sure that's his?"

"Yes. I memorized his license plate so that I wouldn't get it confused with this other truck that's always parked at the Coffee Bean."

Annie studied the truck for a moment, then gave Lucy a mean side glance. "Well, I'm gonna sleep until he shows," Annie said as she moved the back of her seat almost flat and closed her eyes.

"You're just gonna sleep? I was hoping you'd talk and help me stay awake," Lucy said as she watched Annie place her pillow against the door and relax with her eyes closed.

"Beggars can't be choosers," Annie mumbled.

"Gee, thanks," Lucy said and stuck her tongue out at Annie.

The girls waited; Annie slept while Lucy watched. The sun began to light the parking structure with still no sign of Davy. Lucy looked at her phone, then reached over and nudged Annie and said, "It's six in the morning. You better go."

Annie rubbed her eyes and tried to stretch in the confined space before she asked, "And, what are you going to do?"

"I'll work remotely from here," Lucy told her while she turned in her seat to reach into the backseat. She pulled an open tote bag that rested on the bench seat, which she placed in her lap and began to dig through it. Contained in this bag were her computer, daily planner, pens, and a notebook.

"You came prepared," Annie observed.

"I had to. I can't leave and have him get back and disappear. That'll put me back at square one," Lucy explained as she pulled out her laptop and handed it to Annie.

"What do you want me to do with this?" She asked.

"Just hold it," as Lucy set her other items on top of the laptop before she returned the tote from where she'd retrieved it.

"What are you gonna do if he doesn't come back for a week?" She asked as she opened her door, stepped out, and set Lucy's laptop and stuff on her seat.

"Hm," Lucy paused as she settled back in her seat, "I hadn't thought of that. I know I can't stay here a week, especially with the high cost of parking."

"True," Annie said, then looked at her wristwatch, "I better get going. Text me if he shows up," she said and closed the door. Lucy watched her walk away in the rearview mirror.

Lucy looked at her phone; she was late for signing into work. She hoped the Wi-Fi would be available in the parking garage, so she'd be able to work. If not, she'd have to leave and go to the office. She tried to connect once, twice, and then a third time, but her laptop wouldn't connect to the Wi-Fi—if there was any.

Hm, she thought as she looked around for another option. She couldn't leave yet—didn't want to leave yet, not with Davy's truck still there. Lucy set the laptop on the passenger seat and exited her truck to better view any other possibilities. That was when she noticed the maroon range rover back out of a spot closer to the outside wall of the parking structure.

"Maybe if I park over there, I can catch any available Wi-Fi," she said to no one in particular and jumped into her truck and quickly backed into the open parking spot. Once there, she realized that her view of Davy's truck was not as good as at the previous spot, but she couldn't change now. She had to sign in to work.

She opened the hatch door to the back of her 4Runner

and sat with her legs hanging over the edge, dangling as she opened the Dell computer that rested on her lap. Cautiously she pushed the Wi-Fi button to see if she had internet.

"Success," she proclaimed loudly, then looked to see if anyone were around to hear her. With a smile on her face, she watched the Google page appear on her desktop. She was in business. She scooched herself further into the back of the 4Runner and leaned up against the wheel well so that she see Davy's truck through the side window. *This wasn't the best setup, but it was better than nothing*, she thought to herself. She was determined to find out more about him.

***

Davy watched as the passengers exited the plane. Although he could have disembarked with the passengers since he wasn't working as a FAM on the flight, out of habit, he waited to be one of the last to leave. Before he exited, he looked back to see the plane empty except for the flight attendants. There were no flyers on this flight, which struck him as odd. Not every flight had a FAM or flyer, but since it was coming back from South America, he'd assumed it would.

"No one told me we had a FAM on this flight," the pilot said as he walked next to Davy down the jetway.

"It looks like you didn't. I wasn't working this flight." Davy told him.

"You didn't work this flight?" he asked, concerned.

"No, I was just a passenger this time. Besides, if I'd

been working, I'm legally required to let you know. You know that."

"Hm," the pilot nodded in agreement. "When one of the flight attendants told me you were on board, I just assumed--."

"Davy shook his head and reaffirmed. "Nope, I was just a passenger."

"Looks like you've been up to your old tricks?" Chuck said. He'd been a pilot in the Navy the same time Davy had been there.

"It's that obvious?" Davy asked as he reached up and felt his lip.

"How else do you think I knew?"

Davy exhaled then said, "That won't make my sister happy. The kids get too scared when they see my face cut and bruised."

"How can they tell the difference?" Chuck said, then slapped Davy on the back as he walked away.

"Haha—oh!" Davy involuntarily groaned and winced, "Don't make me laugh."

Davy lifted the backpack and placed it cautiously on his shoulder as he limped over to the escalator. He always tried to take the stairs down, but this time he was glad for the escalator so he could rest his leg for a few minutes before the long walk to where he parked his car.

Lucy stretched as she stood by her truck. The stock market had just closed. She'd been sitting in the back of her 4Runner since six that morning with sporadic breaks to get the blood circulating in her lower half. She jumped when her phone began to play the tune Thunderstruck.

"How's it going?" Annie asked from the other end of

the line.

"Ooooh, my butt is so numb. I have been cramped in the back of my truck since you left this morning. Do you realize that I've been awake over thirty-five hours?"

"Thirty-five hours?! You must be exhausted."

"Not yet. I don't feel tired at all," said Lucy as she lightly jogged to get the blood moving.

"Any sign of Davy?" Annie asked.

"Not yet," Lucy said as she stifled a yawn. *I may have spoken too soon,* she thought to herself.

"How much longer are you going to stay there? You need to get some sleep soon," Annie said.

"I know, I may ne—" Lucy stopped mid-sentence as she saw Davy limping down the row of cars towards his truck.

"You may need to do what?" Annie asked. When Lucy didn't answer, she asked again, "Hello? You may need to do what? Lucy?"

Lucy had taken the phone from her ear as she ducked down between two cars, but she could hear Annie yell her name. "Oh, sorry, Davy is limping. Hmm—I wonder why he's limping?" She asked in a whisper, then continued, "towards his car right now."

"Why's he limping?" Annie asked.

"I don't know," Lucy responded, "But that's not all, his nose has a band-aid on it," Lucy said as she crouched and followed Davy as he limped along. "His face looks bruised, but it is hard to tell with all his facial hair, and he's limping."

"You already said that," Annie told her.

"What is it he does that he gets so beat up? And so

often? Are passengers really that rough on his flights?" She wondered aloud.

"What do you mean?" Annie asked.

"This isn't the first time I've seen his face bruised. But it is the first time I've seen him limping." Lucy moved between cars in an effort to keep pace with Davy as he limped along. When he'd reached his truck, she stopped behind a car and watched his slow movement to dislodge the backpack from his shoulder. "I wonder if he'll respond to my text?"

"You're gonna text him? Now?"

"Yes," Lucy whispered into the phone. "Hold on." She took the phone and quickly began to text a message:

Where are you?

Lucy remained behind the car as she watched Davy wince as he pulled his phone from his front jean pocket. He looked at the phone and gave what could be construed as a cock-eyed grin but was difficult to tell with the swelling in his face. Unable to stop the smile on her face at the sight of that goofy grin, she told Annie, "He just smiled when he saw it was a text from me."

As Davy maneuvered the phone in his hand, he dropped his keys and gave an audible groan before he punched in:

Just got back in town.

Lucy knew she should stop it there since she knew he was back, but her fingers began to tap a return text and hit

224

send as if they had a mind of their own.

> *I didn't know you'd left. Wanna*
> *get some tea?*

> *I can't. Pretty tired from my*
> *trip.*

Lucy rose up from her crouch enough to see him lean against his truck. She spoke into her phone, "Are you still there?"

"Yeah. What's going on?" Annie asked in a whisper.

"Why are you whispering?" Lucy asked her.

Annie laughed, "I didn't realize I was. Guess that shows you that I'm listening."

Lucy gave a victorious giggle, then became serious and said, "He can barely move. It looks like he's been in a fight, again."

"Are you satisfied? Are you gonna leave him alone now so he can nurse his wounds?" Annie asked while Lucy was already texting Davy again.

> *Wanna go with me to my dance*
> *class tomorrow night?*

"I just asked if he wanted to go with me to my dance class," Lucy whispered into the phone as she tried to hide behind the side view mirror of a van.

"Do you have a dance class?" Annie asked.

"No, but I'll find one," Lucy said as she watched Davy's truck back out of the spot and stop.

Uh, sure. What time?

> *I'll text you the information. I need to take this call.*

Lucy looked up from her phone to watch Davy's truck as it sped towards the down ramp to exit the parking structure.

"Lucy, are ya there?" Annie asked from the phone.

Lucy lifted the phone up to her ear and said, "Yeah. I'm here. What's up?"

"I thought you were gonna follow him."

"Oh shoot! That's right," Lucy said as she scrambled to get into her truck and leave the parking structure. Then she stopped, "It's no use. I blew it," she told Annie glumly. "I've been awake for thirty-six hours so that I could follow him, and I just let him leave without following him."

"Don't be too hard on yourself," Annie told her. "You can try after the dance lesson tomorrow."

"Oh, that's right," Lucy said with relief. "I thought I'd really screwed it up."

"Now you can go home and get some sleep."

"Great idea. The lack of sleep is starting to hit me. And, I'll have to go into the office tomorrow, so I need to be rested." Lucy ended the call, set her phone on the passenger seat, started her car, and followed the same route that Davy had taken to the exit.

As Lucy waited for the ticket person to give her change, she studied the street, wondering which direction

Davy's truck turned. Deep in thought, she asked, "Who are you, Mr. Jones?"

Chapter 20

Davy could hear the faint melody of Benny Goodman's Sing, Sing, Sing seeping through the dance studio doors while he paced in the lobby waiting for Lucy. He'd managed to get a few hours of sleep before he woke to his phone beeping a notification of a text message from Lucy with the dance studio's address and the class time. Then another text, all in caps, DO NOT BE LATE. So, there he was. But, where was she? Mindlessly, he watched the door as he rubbed his leg in an attempt to loosen the muscle that had been sprained on his most recent trip. He couldn't limp around Lucy without a barrage of questions. But there was nothing he could do about the bruises on his face except removing the band-aid that had been on his nose.

Why did I agree to dance lessons—especially with my sore leg? He asked himself. This wasn't like him; women didn't ask him to dance classes. He didn't dance. He was a Navy Seal. *We don't dance. We capture, monitor, track, even kill if necessary, but we don't dance—let alone jitterbug. What is she doing to me?*

Davy's mood started to darken, "Oooh," he groaned, his chin dropping to his chest. He paused in his pacing as he relived the fleeting visit with the little Steve Urkel sound alike.

"What did you do to your lips?" Davy asked when he saw Junie's overly puffy lips.

"Lip injections," she responded as she lifted her face to his expecting a kiss.

Davy recoiled. "I think I'm getting a cold," he lied in avoidance and kissed her on the cheek.

Junie pouted; at least he thought she pouted. With all the Botox injections in her face, it was tough for him to see any emotion unless he heard her voice.

"Why won't you kiss me?" She asked her voice grating down Davy's spine.

Davy gave a couple of light coughs and pointed to his throat, and said, "Cold." He cleared his throat as he backed out of her office.

Standing in the lobby, Davy gave an involuntary shiver as he remembered her lips. *I deserve the Congressional Medal of Honor if I survive dealing with Junie,* he told himself. He looked around the lobby, then peeked through the slight sliver between the doors that lead into the room where six other couples were attempting the jitterbug.

Lucy burst in through the front door of the studio and said, "Sorry, I'm so late."

With a sigh of relief, he said, "I was just getting ready to text you. I thought you'd blown me off."

Lucy laughed. "You wish."

"What's all this?" Davy asked as he looked at Lucy dressed in a straight skirt, loafers with ankle socks, and a light short-sleeved sweater.

"Do you like it?" she asked as she did a twirl. She wore dark red lipstick and very simple make-up but had fashioned her hair in a style that she thought would have been worn during the forties.

Davy smiled. "You should have told me you were dressing up," he said.

Lucy's eyes lighted up. "You would have dressed up too?" She asked.

"No," he said flatly. "Is this get-up the only reason you're late?" He asked.

"I thought my friend Annie was gonna come, but she had to cancel at the last minute. Some family emergency. Or, maybe it was a dog emergency. Anyway, she'll be here later," Lucy explained.

"Ah, I was actually gonna meet one of your friends?"

Lucy laughed and said, "Yes, you were." Lucy looked at his face and the cut over his temple, the discoloration on his nose. She stated, "Surely that can't be from another doorknob."

"What, this?" Davy reached up to touch his face but winced at the movement from his stiff body.

"Yeah, that." Lucy reached up and pushed her finger in his temple.

"Ouch," he said as he pulled back from her touch, then let out an involuntary groan as he winced once more.

"What did you do to yourself?" Lucy asked as she scrutinized Davy.

"Would you believe Pilates?" Davy asked as he tried

to mimic Don Adams from *Get Smart*.

Lucy shook her head with closed eyes, then looked up at him with a scrunched face and said, "No. I wouldn't believe that."

"Hm. I was that close," Davy answered still in the voice of Don Adams from the series *Get Smart*.

Lucy couldn't help but laugh, then stopped and said, "Seriously, what happened? You're looking older than usual."

"Heeey," Davy said, then winced and put a hand on his ribs.

Lucy was about to respond when the doors to the dance studio opened. She and Davy stepped aside and watched as the couples exited the studio, and those who'd been waiting in the lobby rose to enter. "I guess that's our cue. Ready to Jitterbug?" Davy asked as he stepped back and motioned for Lucy to enter before him.

The teacher had just taught some of the dance moves and turned on the upbeat tune of Benny Goodman's "Sing, Sing, Sing." Both Lucy and Davy stood in the first position and heard the slight beat of the drums. The teacher had told them to listen to the beat and let it put a little bounce in their steps.

Davy, although stiff, tried to keep the beat while Lucy bounced in place and looked at each other with goofy grins on their faces. Davy reached for her hand, and they began to move—whether they were doing it right or not didn't matter as they laughed and enjoyed the sounds.

When they came to the part of the dance where they'd push against each other's hands and spin in the opposite direction, the teacher stopped the music and had the couples practice it a few times before she turned the music back on. The more they danced, the more Davy's body seemed to loosen up, and he was able to move without as many moans and groans.

Once again, Lucy and Davy faced each other as they waited for the music to begin to play. Lucy's face hurt from all the smiling she'd been doing from the beginning of class.

"Alright, class," the dance instructor called out to everyone. "Remember, have a bounce in your steps, and once your hands connect for the spin, push off each other like you're polar opposites." The instructor then gave the signal, and the faint beat of drums could be heard as Davy and Lucy began to dance together badly.

"Ouch!" Lucy yelled through laughter and the music. "You keep kicking me," she continued to giggle.

"Stop stepping on my toes, and I'll stop kicking you," Davy yelled the suggestion as they both laughed.

"Okay, get ready," the instructor called. "It's about time for the spin."

"Ready?" Davy asked with a devilish grin.

The instructor paused for a moment then yelled over the music, "Spin!"

Right on cue, their hands met, and Davy spun her, and she spun him, but when she came around, he had his phone to one ear and a finger stuck into the other talking as he walked through the double doors, leaving her without a word.

Lucy stopped and stared after him, shocked that he'd just leave her, just like that, leaving her mid-spin. She jumped when the teacher spoke to her.

"What happened to your partner?" She asked as she approached where Lucy stood, rooted in shock.

"I-I-I'm not sure," she stuttered, then hastily walked towards the still swinging double doors that led to the lobby.

"We can find you another partner," the instructor called after her.

Once outside the building, Lucy stopped in time to see Davy's truck drive past the building's front entrance toward the parking lot exit. She began to move towards the parked cars when she saw Annie walking towards her. She walked briskly to meet her. It was then she noticed that Annie held a German shepherd dog on a lead.

"We've got to go! He just left." With an odd glance at the dog, Lucy continued past Annie at a brisk pace.

"Oh! Don't you look cute," Annie exclaimed when Lucy walked towards her.

Lucy had forgotten her attire and stopped when Annie mentioned it. "Thanks," she said with a huge smile. "We have to follow him," Lucy told her abruptly.

"I just parked," Annie said as she turned and did a slight trot to follow Lucy.

"Where'd you park? Whose dog is that?" Lucy scrunched her eyebrows as she slowed her pace enough for Annie to catch up.

"My neighbor's. I told him I'd watch his dog, but then you called, so I brought him with me." Annie explained as she struggled to keep up with Lucy and pull the dog along at the same time.

"Where's your car?" Lucy asked as she scanned the poorly lit parking lot.

233

"Over next to that red Miata," Annie said louder as she hurried to catch up. "Where's your car?" Annie asked as she caught up with Lucy.

"I took an Uber because I thought you'd be here or I'd get a ride from Davy," Lucy told her.

"Where is he?" Annie asked. Lucy motioned towards the line of cars that waited for their chance to exit onto the street. "Oooh," Annie said as she stood next to her car.

"Okay, what's his name?" Lucy asked as she watched Davy's truck stopped at the exit.

"Davy. Did you forget?" Annie asked, puzzled.

"Not him, the dog." Lucy rolled her eyes. She thought she was done with dogs when Lori moved. Lucy stood next to the passenger side of an older green Saab and waited for Annie. She heard the alarm beep and opened her door.

"Oh," Annie laughed. "Sarge," Annie said as she opened the back door for the dog to get in the car.

"Oh," Lucy said with a look behind her. "We've gotta catch up with Davy," she told Annie impatiently.

"Okay!" Annie put the car in gear and sped toward the parking lot exit, then stopped and asked, "Which direction?"

"Left. It's clear. Go," Lucy ordered as she scanned every lane for his F-150. Annie pushed the gas pedal down and shot out of the parking lot. Sarge yelped in the back as he hit against the back seat.

"Oh, sorry, baby," Annie said to Sarge. "Is that his truck?" Annie asked as they pulled up next to a big dark truck.

Lucy craned her neck and said, "I'm not sure. It's so

dark, and I didn't see his license plate—which I've memorized." Annie glanced at her in disbelief before she looked back at the road. Lucy rubbed her hand on the window to remove the condensation that had gathered since they'd entered the car. "Pull up closer to the cab so I can see if it's him," she instructed. Annie slowly moved her car forward as Lucy lowered her window just enough to look through. "I still can't see. Can you move forward a little more?"

"If I go any further forward, I will be in the middle—," Annie said. Before she could finish her sentence, the light turned green, and traffic began to move.

"Great. Get behind the truck, so I can see the license plate," Lucy instructed. Annie slowed her Saab down until the truck was a car length ahead of them. As soon as the coast was clear, she moved into the lane behind the truck. Waiting until the cars ahead of them moved out of the way.

"We've got to get closer to the truck so that I can see the license plate," Lucy told Annie as she rocked in her seat to move the car closer.

"I'm trying, but this car behind his won't budge. So I can get any closer," Annie continued to try and maneuver her car behind the truck. "If I get close enough in this lane, do you think you'll be able to see his plate?" She asked. "You can roll the window down and stick your head out if that will help," Annie said. She hesitated a moment, then added with a snicker, "You'll make Sarge totally jealous because I won't let him stick his head out the window."

Lucy gave Annie a dirty look, then said, "Very

funny. Jus-just drive." Lucy rolled the window further down and tried to read the license plate, but with it being dark, the traffic moving in stops and starts, she eventually had to put her head out the window to see if that would make it any easier. At that moment, she noticed the car that remained in front of Annie's was an old red car.

Lucy pulled her head back into the car as she sat back in the seat and said, "That's odd."

"What's odd?" Annie asked as she maneuvered the traffic.

Lucy shook her head and said, "Nothing. Just do me a favor and follow the car next to us." *Why did she see that car so often?*

Annie let the red car pass them, then another car before she moved back into the lane behind them. She looked at Lucy, barely able to stay in her seat as she leaned from side to side and looked out the window. "Like this?" she asked.

"Perfect. Have you done this before?" Lucy asked, impressed by her skills of trailing the cars. "I do think that truck is Davy's. So, keep following it. We need to see where he goes."

The girls followed the train of cars that grew and shrunk as Davy turned and weaved through the streets, but the old red car remained steady the whole time.

"I can't keep doing this," Annie complained. "I need to get home and take Sarge for a walk."

"You were walking him when I came out of the studio. He doesn't need to be walked for a while now," Lucy said matter-of-factly. "Please just follow for a little while longer."

Annie didn't respond but kept driving, then said, "Just a little longer, then I really do need to leave."

Lucy smiled to herself and said, "Thank you! I really appreciate it. You know I'll cover your gas," she told Annie and emphasized it by tapping Annie's arm so she'd look at her and see she was sincere.

Annie smiled and said, "I know you will." That was the moment Sarge decided to try and climb into the front seat. "Sarge! You get back there and stay! Why aren't you in your seatbelt?" she asked as she looked into her rearview mirror. "I need to pull over and put him in his seatbelt," she said.

"No! Please keep going. I'll put him in his seatbelt," Lucy said as she twisted in her seat and leaned into the back seat. "C'mon Sarge, get in there. Good boy. Now . . . hold on. Don't lick me! I don't know where your tongue's been," Lucy said. Annie chuckled as she listened to the commentary. Soon Lucy turned back around in her seat and sat down, red-faced, and declared, "Okay, he's all safe in his seatbelt."

Just then, Davy sped up, "He's going faster. I'm not sure I wanna go that speed," Annie said to Lucy.

"Just follow—," Lucy began, then stopped when she saw the red car peel off the train and turn right. "Hey! Where are they going?" She asked as she watched them drive down a darkened industrial street. "What's Davy doing?"

"He's slowed down, thank heavens. But he's turning around now," Annie said as Davy came to a light and did a U-turn.

"Quick! Ya gotta keep up with him!" Lucy yelled.

"Don't yell at me! I'm following him." But the light turned red before they could make the turn. Lucy, again, turned around in her seat as she watched him drive in the opposite direction. Suddenly she felt rammed against the passenger door as Annie did a quick U-turn. "Ugh," she moaned, "you could've told me you were gonna do that. What if my door had opened and spilled me into the street?" She asked as Annie sped up.

"But it didn't, and you didn't, so it's all good," Annie said with a cocky laugh.

Lucy to look at her with concern. "Have I created a monster?"

Annie continued to follow Davy with at least two other cars between her and his truck. "I think I may have found a new hobby," she declared.

"Which is?" Lucy asked, then before she could answer, said, "Don't lose him! He just turned!"

"I saw him. Relax. I got this," Annie said in a self-assured tone.

"I hope so because we can't lose him. We may not get this chance again," Lucy said in a low whisper.

Annie looked at her confused and asked, "Why are you whispering?"

"I don't want him to hear us," she said as she intently watched Davy's truck slow way down and turned onto a residential street. "You may want to hang back more since there are no other cars between us," she suggested.

"I know what I'm doing, thank you," Annie said with authority. Lucy gave a slide glance and raised her eyebrows but said nothing as Annie slowed down and turned off her lights.

"Wait. Why'd you turn off your lights?"

"So, he won't see us. I saw it on a Lifetime movie once," Annie said without taking her eyes from the road.

"You saw it on Lifetime, so it must work," Lucy said as she rolled her eyes.

"Don't roll your eyes at me," Annie scolded. "It must be working because he doesn't seem to be aware of us. See?" Annie pointed to a ranch-style home where Davy had pulled into the garage and exited his truck as they silently rolled by. At least, Lucy hoped it was silently.

"Let me write down his address so I can check on him without putting you and your pooch in harm's way," Lucy said as she searched for a piece of paper. "Don't you have a napkin or something I can write on?" she asked as Annie continued to roll past his house. At the corner, she turned around and slowly drove past again. "I need a piece of paper and a pen," Lucy began to squawk.

"Hold on a second, I think I have one here," she said as she stopped her car in the street, in front of Davy's house, in front of his big picture window, and began to dig in her purse. When she didn't find what she was looking for, she turned to the cupholder section in her console.

"What are you doing! You can't stop here! He'll see us," Annie loudly whispered at Annie. "He's gonna notice the car stopped in the street." Annie reached up and turned on the overhead light.

"Are you crazy?" Lucy asked as she reached up and

turned the light off. "He would definitely have seen that."

"Oh, he will not," Annie assured Lucy. "He won't even know we're here."

"He better not," Lucy said angrily.

"Oh look, the eyebrow pencil I thought I'd lost." Annie held it up victoriously and was about to put it in her purse.

"Give it to me!" She grabbed the pencil and wrote the house numbers on her hand. "Now we need to go see what street this is," Lucy directed.

Davy stood to the side of the big picture window in his living room and watched the green Saab that had stopped in the middle of the street. He'd noticed it long ago behind the Nova. He wasn't sure who it was until the light went on inside the car and he saw for a quick moment Lucy angrily gesture to some woman—who must be Annie—then it went dark. He didn't stop the laughter that emerged from within. *She is sure full of surprises*, he thought to himself, does this mean he has to move now?

Chapter 21

Lucy leaned forward and pinched her shoulders back to stretch. She'd been sitting in the same position, in her car, for over four hours as she waited to see Davy's truck pull into his driveway.

She'd learned from a previous text conversation that he would be back in town tonight but would be arriving late. She wasn't sure why she felt so strongly that she had to see him pull into his drive, but she did. She didn't expect anything exciting to happen; he would probably just go to bed, which would be her cue to go home. She still had a job and had to get up early to get there. So, she leaned back in the driver's seat and prepared to wait.

The quiet of the night and the comfort of her seat helped Lucy to relax. She stared out her windshield into the dark, lost in her thoughts, when she saw a car turn onto the road coming towards her. In the nights since Lucy had been watching Davy's home, she'd learned that he didn't live on a busy street. Very rarely did cars travel into his neighborhood, but those that did had a definite destination. They would promptly turn into their drive and pull all the way into their garages if they had one. There never seemed to be any through traffic. So, when Lucy saw a car approach and turn out its lights, it caught her curiosity.

"I need to watch more of the Lifetime channel," Lucy said aloud to no one. She watched as the darkened car got closer and waited for it to pass so she could see who was in it, but it stopped just before Davy's home. The car remained motionless, with no light emanating from it whatsoever. Lucy leaned forward in her seat in concentration and waited. *Who is that? What did they want*, she wondered. Carefully she rested her arms on the steering wheel, careful not to hit the horn as she continued to observe this dark visitor.

Slowly the passenger door opened, the silhouette of a man slinked out, leaving his door ajar. Lucy lowered her window to listen, but there was no sound. Even the engine was quiet as if it were an electric engine. An electric engine in a classic car? Lucy watched as the man scurried around the back of the car, like a rat, up the side of Davy's front yard, then with only a bit of a struggle, climbed over the fence that blocked off his backyard from the street. As the man was about to fall over to the other side of the fence, something dropped to the ground. She watched as he returned to his starting position to pick up the dropped object, tuck it inside his shirt, and struggle over the fence again.

It was so dark that all Lucy could see were shadows, but there was something familiar about the guy. She wondered where'd she seen him before as she waited for him to reappear. After a couple of minutes, she saw a bundle thrown over the fence and land on the grass, followed by the man as he struggled to pull himself over the fence.

What had originally been a quiet attempt by him soon turned into the rattle of the fence as the joints banged against each other as his shoes clawed their way up the wooden slabs. His lack of athleticism had screwed up the silent mission they seemed to be on. Lucy looked up and down the street, expecting to see the light go on, or a curtain move with a neighbor's curiosity, but nothing— dogs didn't even bark. *This really is a private neighborhood*, she thought in amazement.

Once over the fence, he returned to the waiting car with the bundle, the trunk opened, and he dumped the package inside before he quietly pushed the trunk lid down with the faintest click. Then scurried around to the passenger door and climbed in. Lucy couldn't see any of his features as there was no glow from the dashboard lights to illuminate them. Somehow they'd managed to turn off all the lights in the car that would have given any clue to their identity. But she couldn't deny the feeling that she'd seen him before.

Lucy strained her eyes to pick out anything that would stick out, but the street was too dark. Then the car, instead of driving forward—where it would pass by Lucy—went into reverse and did a quick turn. Only then did she see that it had a dark paint job, possibly red, but maybe purple or brown? The glimpse of color was too quick before the car completed the turn and sped back up the road it had just come down. When it was a few blocks away, she saw its lights come on as it turned off the road out of sight.

Now Lucy was awake. She checked her phone; it was only ten-thirty. *Why would that guy carry a package back and forth with him, especially when he could barely climb over the fence? Maybe it wasn't the same package? Was he leaving one and picking up another*, she wondered. There was only one way to find out. Was there enough time to find what the guy had left in Davy's backyard before he got there? With the street so quiet, she didn't worry too much about being seen but still pulled on her baseball cap just in case. She opened her door to get out, only to be stopped by the chime that reminded her the key was still in the ignition, the overhead light was on, and she hadn't unlatched her seatbelt.

"James Bond, I'm not," she said to herself as she undid the seatbelt, then leaned back and pushed the little button on the overhead light, which plunged her truck into darkness. Purposely she put the key in her jeans pocket to ensure it didn't get lost and quietly closed the door, but not completely. It would be easier to pull the door open if, for any reason, she had to get out of there quickly.

With adrenaline pumping through her body, Lucy crossed the street and stood in the shadows of the trees. She'd never done anything like this before. Why was she doing it now? She walked with stealth towards Davy's home, staying close to the chain-linked fence that ran along the property line. She avoided any bushes but tripped over one sprinkler head and did a face plant right into his grass with a soft "Oph" that escaped her. Slowly she raised up to her knees to catch her breath and continue when she noticed the smell of dog poop.

"Oh no," she said under her breath. "Maybe this wasn't such a good idea after all." She didn't seem to be as good at it as she'd imagined. *Does Davy have a dog,* she asked herself. She didn't remember him ever mentioning he did. Sitting back on her heels, Lucy checked her hands to ensure they were clean and looked around where she sat before she put her hands out to push herself up into a standing position. That was when she saw the little gift some Fido had left setting in the grass; she'd missed it by inches. Lucy checked her jeans pocket to make sure her car key was still there and continued on toward the house.

To the right of the house was more of the wooden fence she'd watch the other guy climb over previously. So she was aware she'd be doing some climbing, but hopefully, she wouldn't be as pitiful at it as he'd been. She walked up to the fence and saw some sort of mechanical apparatus set next to the fence. She wasn't sure whether it was the HVAC or water heater, but whatever it was, she could use it as a step for climbing over the fence. She'd just have to remember to wipe off any footprints that might be left so Davy wouldn't be suspicious.

Lucy placed both hands on top of the wooden fence frame, set her left foot on the metal box, lifted herself up quickly kicked her right leg over the top of the fence. She made it up and straddled it in a very uncomfortable way. She quickly brought her other leg over and pushed off, only to land into a spider web. Lucy put her hand to her mouth to stop the scream that wanted to escape, then started to jump around to quickly wipe off the web and any spider that might have been there. Her scalp crawled with the fear of an arachnid being anywhere on her. She wanted to cry but had to continue on with her search. With one last shiver, she carefully walked the length of the side of the house.

As Lucy turned the corner, she ran into a built-up wood patio encased by a wooden railing growing out of the backside of the house. The patio stayed level with the house as the backyard sloped down. Cautiously she followed the patio's edge around to the six steps that lead up to it. She carefully stepped on the first step and searched to see if a package was near the sliding doors or the barbeque, but there was nothing. She went up a couple more steps and still didn't see any bundle. *Maybe it's under the patio?*

With a curiosity not normally felt in regards to looking for anything under a patio, she knelt down on a step to look into the blackness beneath. But it was too dark to see, and she was too chicken to risk meeting what might be lurking under there. Sitting back on her knees, she realized that she'd either need to come before it got dark or remember to bring a flashlight if she wanted to search for a package under there.

Having decided the next move, she stood and dusted the dirt off her pants and checked herself for any little crawling things. That's when she heard the engine of a truck pulling into the driveway, breaking the silence.

"Oh crap," she said as she turned towards the side of the house where the portion of the fence was the other man had crossed. She hoped to avoid any spider webs this time. She could see the lights from the truck shining through the slats in the fence, which meant that was the side the garage was on. If he parked in it, then she could climb over the fence and be gone before he even knew she'd been there, she hoped. But he didn't pull into the garage. Instead, he parked on the cement drive outside of it. She abruptly retraced her steps back to the side with the spider web. With a look of dread on her face, she slowed her approach to the fence as she cautiously maneuvered anything that might harbor those eight-legged demons.

Lucy stood on the other side of the fence and heard the truck door close, then the beep of the alarm being set. She heard his footstep up the short climb to his front door, then the creak of the screen door as it opened. She waited until his front door slammed shut before she looked at the fence for a way out.

Alarmed, Lucy realized she didn't have the ready metal box to give her a boost over the fence. She knew she didn't have enough upper body strength to pull herself up. Her heart began to beat a little faster at the thought of Davy catching her in his backyard and how she'd explain it. She froze in her spot, indecisive as to what she should do. Then the decision was made for her when a window on her side of the house lit up.

In a bent-over position, Lucy again retraced her steps to the back of the house, around the patio, and over to the other side. It was there that she found a wooden box she assumed the other guy had placed there to assist him in getting over the fence. She noticed as she stepped up on the box that the fence on this side of the house was much higher than on the other side of the house.

Lucy made sure she had solid footing on the box

before she tried to pull herself up enough to swing her right leg up so that the calf hung over the other side. Then she strained to pull herself into a lopsided sitting position on top of the fence as she moved to lift herself up enough to bring her left leg over, the pant leg fabric caught on an exposed nail. She wiggled her leg in an attempt to get it released from its captor's hold, only to find it steadfast. Without the needed upper body strength to help maneuver her, she hung in the precarious position with her leg still hooked on the fence and thanked God for giving her long legs.

Standing there in the splits position, she reasoned the only thing she could do was try to yank her leg free of the nail. She was overtly aware she didn't have the strength to unhook it, and she couldn't alert Davy. Yet, with the pain pulsating through her hips, she took a drastic step and, with both hands, pulled with all her might on the fabric to free it. Finally, she heard the sound of ripping material and felt her leg's immediate release, which caused her to fall to the ground.

Lucy laid on the ground for a moment before she rose to a sitting position and looked at the status of her left pant leg, which now sported a slit from the knee down. Gingerly she opened the split fabric and noted a patch of fabric must still be attached to the nail on the other side. She tried to reach over and blindly feel for the nail so she could dislodge the piece of fabric and take it with her, but she was unable to find it.

Disgusted with herself, Lucy slightly limped down Davy's drive as quietly and carefully as she could, still in the shadows. She crossed the street and pulled the

4Runner's door open without making a sound. She felt her jean pocket and sighed with relief as she pulled the key out. *This had been a long day*, she thought as she pulled away from the side of the street and returned the same way she'd come to avoid driving past Davy's home.

On the drive home, she couldn't stop wondering where the bundle was that the guy had left.

***

Davy set his protein shake next to the keyboard and dropped into the chair, ready for his already long day to end. But before he could call it a day, he needed to check the videos from his security cameras. He moved his neck to pop some of the kinks out, rubbed his hands up and down his face vigorously. Looking at his watch for the time, he stifled a yawn. He had to see whether the bundle had been picked up or not before he could go to bed.

When he moved into the house, he'd known people from the drug ring would need access to his backyard to drop off the drugs and pick up the money, so he'd built the fence for that very reason. He'd expected them to show up and retrieve their packages, but for his own enjoyment, he didn't include a gate in the fence so he could observe their ingenuity in gaining access to his backyard. So far, no one had complained about it, but he noticed when Sal had to retrieve a package, it was Johnny, the little guy, who had to climb his fence to get it and leave the money.

Unbeknownst to both Sal and Johnny, in each package of money, he included a type of tracking device included in the glue that held the bands around the money so he could follow its progress and see where it ended up.

He typed in his password and moved the mouse about as he clicked on different icons before he leaned back in the chair to finish his protein shake and watch. He laughed at Johnny's attempts to climb over of his fence. Then paused and rewound the security film to watch Johnny one more time when his phone chirped.

"Jones," Davy spoke into the phone. "They've picked up the package with the tracking device inside. I just finished watching Johnny's comical extraction of it from my place—how he's still alive with this group is beyond me." Davy sniggered. He listened to the voice from the other end as he absent-mindedly released the pause on the video and watched his screen. He'd just taken another swig of his protein shake when he spits it out—spraying it all over his computer screen. He stood from both the shock of seeing her on the screen and having his drink all over his equipment.

"What is she doing?" He raised his voice in exasperation. "Let me call you back," he groaned into the phone as he stared at the screen. "She's gonna kill us all."

Davy's phone chirped again. "Yeah?" he answered to hear Joel's voice on the other end.

"Who's the woman in your backyard?" He asked.

"Ooooh," Davy groaned. He had hoped to get rid of that footage before Joel saw it.

"Well?" Joel asked.

Davy sighed, "That's her."

"Her who?" Joel asked.

Davy paused. "Her."

"Ah," Joel said. "How does she know where you live?"

"She must've followed me. I never invited her here," He admitted to Joel.

"You have to move. I'll send you the location of your new home in one hour."

"That won't work. I need to be here for the exchanges," he told Joel.

"What are you gonna do about your woman?" Joel asked.

"Don't know. But maybe it won't matter if no one else has seen her. And, maybe this was a one-time deal?"

"We can't be sure of that, though. What if the Italians have seen her?" Joel questioned.

"I think we're okay. When she was here, they'd already gone. My front cam shows their car driving off."

"You need to make sure. And you need to stop her from any more visits," Joel told him firmly.

"Gotcha. I'll get her to stop coming over, then I'll pull all the troops from overseas, balance the budget, then run for pre—," Joel interrupted Davy.

"Okay, I got it. I'm asking the impossible." Joel laughed, then continued, "You have your hands full with that one, but you started it," Joel reminded him.

Davy sighed as he shut down his laptop. He was tired and frustrated that he'd screwed up the operation with his fondness for Lucy. "I think I'd have better success fighting terrorists," he confessed to Joel.

Joel laughed out loud, "I don't envy you, bro."

"She's truly a different experience from my ex—she fascinates me and scares me at the same time," Davy admitted. Joel remained silent on the other end of the line.

"Welcome to my world," Joel said in commiseration with Davy.

"I didn't know you were dating someone," Davy said.

"Woah, not me, bro. But when you date someone our age, you're not in Kansas anymore. Those women do not play," Joel laughed at his statement.

Davy gave a snide laugh and said, "I hear ya. It's a whole new experience for me."

"Wait, dating? So you're dating her?" Joel asked.

"Dating? I didn't say dating," He protested. "We are not dating. She is a friend, that is all," he adamantly protested.

"I think I heard you say you were dating her," Joel chuckled.

Suddenly he had a headache. "I better go for a run," Davy said, exhausted, and disconnected the call.

Davy enjoyed running in the stealth of night on the dark, quiet streets. It gave him a chance to think things over without all the distractions. It was a time for him to clear his mind, but he didn't seem to be able to do that since he'd met Lucy. *Why can't I get this woman out of my mind?* He asked himself. She wasn't the most attractive woman he'd ever known. Yet he couldn't forget her blue eyes and how they lit up when she spoke about something that interested her. Or the twinkle in her eyes when she teased him. Their banter was easy, and they had so many of the same likes and dislikes. He chuckled at the memory of her on the plane. *Yeah, she is a force to be reckoned with*, he reminded himself. Davy stopped suddenly and put his hands to either side of his head and growled loudly up to the sky.

"We are not dating!" He repeated in frustration. "I don't need this in my life right now." Then he stopped abruptly as his hands dropped to his sides, deep in thought as he turned around and mumbled to himself, "What am I gonna do about her?"

***

By the time Lucy got home after climbing into Davy's backyard, it was well after midnight, and she had to get up in a couple of hours to get to work. Once in her bedroom, she collapsed on her bed and looked up at the ceiling. She kept replaying in her mind what she'd seen and done. She removed her jeans and took a good look at the tear in the pant leg. *So much for these*, she thought to herself and tossed them into the dirty clothes hamper. She reached down to remove her sock and saw the blood smear from where she'd cut her leg while exiting Davy's backyard.

"Eeew," she said aloud as she reached for a tissue and began to dab at her leg. "I didn't even know I'd hurt myself. Must've been the adrenaline," she said aloud and limped into her bathroom so as to not get any blood on her carpet and so she could wash her leg. It was a small cut, so she covered it with gauze that she repeatedly wrapped over it and returned to her bed. She felt a wave of exhaustion wash over her as she looked at the clock on her bedside table that read one-thirty. When her head hit the pillow, she slept the sleep of the dead.

Chapter 22

A week had gone by before Lucy was able to continue her due diligence on Davy. Again, he wasn't responding to her text messages, so she thought he was either out of town or busy. He didn't seem to stay silent for too long, though, so she wasn't that concerned yet.

However, because he hadn't responded to her texts, she wasn't sure where he was, and, for her plan to work, she had to know that. So she decided to go search for his truck at the airport in the parking structure where he normally parked. She drove up and down all the levels looking for his truck but didn't see it anywhere. *Maybe he's home,* she thought to herself. She drove over to his home and waited in the same spot that she'd been a previous night. She waited, and waited, and waited. The time ticked on until it was almost one in the morning, with still no sign of Davy. *Where is he?*

The next night she did the same routine of first driving around the parking lot—still with no sign of him.

Then drove through the other parking structures at the airport as well. She needed to see where he was. *Was he okay?* She wondered.

Davy had just pulled into the parking structure and parked when he saw Lucy pass by in her 4Runner, a row away. Instinctively he ducked to avoid her seeing him before he remembered that he'd changed his car. The truck was parked in the garage at his house, and he'd purchased an older grey Jeep Cherokee to drive to and from work in case Lucy did what he was now witnessing her doing. It had been tough not responding to her text messages, but he had to try and cut all contact with her. It was for her own safety. He sat in his car until he saw her leave his parking level before he got out. He headed towards the airport terminal to prepare for the flight he was scheduled to take to New York as a FAM.

Davy pulled the baseball cap with the letters AZ sewn onto it lower over his eyes as an added precaution and zipped up his oversized sweatshirt in case he saw Lucy. He also took a totally different route, which would take longer, to get to the office.

He missed her, but that was the sacrifice one had to make in the career he'd chosen. Davy had resigned himself to the loss of contact with family and friends over the years. Lucy would just be another casualty in his life.

"Oh, you didn't get the message?" Peggy, the assistant to the supervisor, told him as she set the book she'd been reading aside and lowered her cat eyeglasses.

"What message?" He asked as he removed his sweatshirt and baseball cap.

"Your flight was canceled due to mechanical issues.

I left you a message letting you know." Peggy lifted the glasses up to her eyes and consulted the clipboard on her desk.

"When?" Davy asked while he took his phone out of his pocket to look for any voicemails.

"As soon as we found out that the flight had been canceled," she responded defensively. She hated being questioned by these cocky guys as if she hadn't done her job.

"Just put me on another one then," he told her irritably.

"Sorry, all the others are already staffed by flyers. Looks like you get some time off," she told him coldly. Davy stood motionless for a moment as he decided how far to push this, unaware of the questioning look from Peggy. She didn't like him as well as some of the others because of the cocky attitude he'd displayed in the past. She didn't care for his average good looks or the fact that he didn't flirt with her as the other guys did. He'd always been so quiet when he wasn't cocky that he came across as a little awkward. She'd learned to expect it from the type of guys that did this kind of work. These guys were a different breed—an acquired taste, perhaps. "Are you okay?" She asked, hoping that he'd either go into the flyer's office area or leave so that she could return to the book she was reading.

"What?" Davy asked as he remembered where he was. "Oh, yeah. I'm good. Just got a lot on my mind. So, I don't have any flights today?" He asked. Peggy only smiled at him. "Well, okay then, I'll take off." Peggy continued to smile. Davy turned in the awkward silence,

"Okay, see ya tomorrow."

"Sure," Peggy called as he walked away. "I'll call you if you're scheduled." She gave a sigh of relief as the door closed behind him. She gave a sigh of contentment as she returned to her mystery romance, 'Dying to Fly.'

Now that Davy didn't have to work, he decided to do a little surveillance for himself. It had been a week since he'd seen the surveillance video of Lucy on his property or had answered any texts from her. Tonight he'd begin watching her place to make sure she wasn't engaging in something she didn't need to be embroiled in.

Davy drove to Lucy's neighborhood and parked down the street from her place, keeping it in his line of vision. Driving the Jeep would help him stay incognito and allow him to follow a bit closer with her unaware. He could see that her car was not in her parking spot, so he accepted that it would be a long night without sleep. He gave an exhausted sigh as he reflected on how this job was aging him.

Davy opened a Slim Jim that he carried in his car for just such instances, along with a bottle of water, and began his long vigil. The hours ticked by as he watched this family neighborhood go about its activities. Kids were riding their bikes in groups of three or four, mothers took their babies for strolls, fathers playing with their kids in their yards. Davy watched all this with a longing he'd never felt before. He regretted never giving thought to have a family of his own after his marriage broke up, that and the baby they lost.

She was the prettiest little girl he'd ever seen in his life—yes, he was a bias daddy, but it really was true. With her dark hair and aqua blue eyes. He smiled at the memory of the sweet grin that would spread across her face when she'd hear him say her name, "Grainne." She would kick her legs and wiggle, begging for him to pick her up.

She was four months old when he left for Iraq, and that was the first time he hated his job, knowing he'd be away from her for so long. But his wife promised to send him pictures of her so he wouldn't miss out on all the changes she'd go through. He'd just returned to the base after a couple of days mission and had set his gear in his tent when he received a message to call his wife. That was the call that changed his life forever. When he heard the news that his sweet baby girl had died in her sleep, Davy was devastated—he could hardly think or function. It was one of his buddies that got the C.O. to authorize him to catch a flight back to the states immediately for his baby's funeral and time to grieve.

After the funeral and before he'd returned to Iraq, he knew his marriage was in trouble as they both dealt with their grief differently. Where he had to be busy and not just sit there and grieve, his wife, so overwhelmed with grief and self-blame, rarely got out of bed. She couldn't deal with the corrosive sorrow that made it feel as though she were trudging through sludge each day.

His wife's mother had suggested they go to grief counseling, where the therapist had given them ways to work on their marriage even after he was gone, but Davy wasn't sure if it was helping. Although Karen began to get out of bed and return to her normal routine, their marriage still struggled. Davy knew that when he had to return to Iraq, it was going to be a very tough conversation with his wife, Karen.

When that time came, she didn't want him to go. She accused him of loving the military more than his family. He tried to explain to her that it was his duty and not that he loved the military more than his family. But to be honest, he needed to get away from the omnipresent grief that was everywhere he looked in that house, in his wife's eyes, in the pitiful looks everyone seemed to give him.

"Babe, you know that's not true," he told her.

"It is true! You don't care that our baby is dead!" His wife screamed at him through her sobs.

Davy attempted to take her in his arms and console her as he said, "There is no one I love more, but I have obligations. If I don't return, then I'll be considered AWOL."

His wife pushed him away from her. "Your daughter has only been gone a couple of months! How can you leave? I need you here," she sobbed.

"Karen, I'm sorry. I hate that I have to leave—,"

"No, you don't! You only care about yourself! You weren't here when she died! You weren't the one to find our baby in her crib dead," His wife accused him.

The guilt rolled over Davy like a wave. "Karen, I'm sorry I wasn't here. I'm sorry we lost our little girl more than you know. But my staying here won't bring her back," he tried to reason with her. He knew she was grieving and pulled her into his arms against all her struggles to remain free of him until she began to be calm. They stayed like that for half an hour as she sobbed until he heard the cab honk outside.

"It looks like your taxi's here," Karen's mother

quietly told him as she entered the living room where they sat.

"Babe, I gotta go," he said hesitantly.

Karen looked up at him with the pain blazing from her eyes before she pushed him away. "Go! Just go!" Were the last words she yelled at him before he left. Then she ran and locked herself in their bedroom. That was the last time he saw her.

At first, he emailed her every day, as instructed by the therapist. She would answer his emails as they tried to heal the hurt they felt and save their marriage, but soon they went from every other day to once a week, then once every two weeks, to once a month, if that. Their marriage crumbled, then crashed when he received divorce papers in the mail. He called to speak with her about it, but she'd disconnected her phone and only communicated through her attorney.

From that time on, it was all about his work. That is until he received word that his sister's husband had died of a massive heart attack, leaving her with five kids to raise alone. As much as he loved the excitement of his naval career, his family needed him. So, with much-concealed regret, he retired from the Navy to help her.

Luckily, he wasn't unemployed long before Joel had approached him about doing undercover work. He leaped at it. For years he'd been able to straddle both worlds—even when his sister's second marriage broke up, leaving her with two young kids to raise.

Now, he was older, ready to retire, and nothing to show for it. He heaved a heartfelt sigh, sat up, and stretched. *Enough of these melancholy thoughts*, he told himself. He didn't need that right now. Davy checked his phone and did a double-take when he saw the time. *Where is she?* He asked himself. He wondered if she'd gone to his place to snoop around some more.

He'd just decided to drive home to see if she were there when he saw headlights in his rearview mirror. He quickly ducked down in his seat and waited for the car to pass. Instead, it slowed down, then stopped after it pulled into her parking spot. It was Lucy.

Dressed in dark clothes, Lucy stepped out of the car, pushed the hood of her sweatshirt off her head, and stretched as she stood outside her 4Runner. Then climbed the steps to her place and went inside. Davy watched as the lights went on in different windows before they finally went dark.

He stared at Lucy's place with a frown on his face. *Where has she been? Why dark clothes? And, why is she getting home so late?* He asked himself, dreading the answer he felt he already knew. Drumming his fingers on the steering wheel, he realized that a wrench had been thrown into his life. And it was this crazy woman, Lucy. What was she up to?

Everything had been going as it should with his undercover work until that fateful night at the library when he met Her. Now he'd have to deal with her. How does he save a woman that doesn't want or think she needs to be saved?

He held the phone to his ear and waited. He knew it was late, but this needed to be handled right now.

"Hello?" He heard the sleepy voice on the other end.

"Smithy, it's me," he said into the phone.

"Is everything okay?" Joel sounded more alert now.

"It's the woman," Davy said gravely.

"What woman?" Joel asked.

"You know, The woman," Davy stated. He hated having to do this, but it was necessary.

"Ooooh," Joel said. "You're girlfriend."

Davy growled. "She's not my girlfriend."

Joel heaved a sigh. Davy could hear him rub his face in irritation before he answered, "What's going on?"

"I need to have some time away from the FAM job. I think she's still snooping around my place. I need to get back in contact with her in order to stop her."

"You understand that this will be your last undercover job," Joel told him.

Davy sighed, "I know. I screwed this one up," Davy admitted with disappointment. His heart just wasn't in it any longer, not since he met Lucy. "But the bright side is that I won't need to fly overseas anymore. I have strong proof that the head of the snake, to quote the director, is here, not in Italy."

"That's great news. We need to get rid of that scum."

"Just let me deal with Her, then we should be able to make the arrests." Davy knew that by his reference to Lucy as "Her," it would objectify her so they wouldn't look at her as his girlfriend, hopefully. *Had Johnny and Sal seen her*, he worried.

"Okay. I'll arrange for your time off, and you let me know when you're ready to move."

"Will do," Davy told him as he disconnected the call. "She should be staying put for the rest of the night," Davy said aloud as he started his Jeep and pulled out of his spot on the street.

***

Davy waited outside the parking structure at Lucy's work. He had followed her over in the morning to make sure she went to her office, then came back just before she left so that he could follow her after she left work. He'd slept for a few hours, so he felt a bit more refreshed than he had yesterday until his phone rang.

"Hi honey!" came the nasal voice through his phone.

Davy scowled, then said, "Hi Junie."

"I haven't seen you for a few days."

"I'm sorry, I've been busy at the airport," Davy lied.

"I don't like you working there anymore. I think you should stop." He could hear the pout in her voice.

"I can't stop, you know that. I've been told the boss wants me to continue to move stuff through the airport. It's easier if I'm there."

"When am I going to see you again?" she asked. Davy's head dropped to his chest despondently. When he didn't answer, she accused him, "Are you seeing that girl?"

Davy's head shot up. "What girl?" he asked, although he was sure he knew to whom she referred.

"Tha-that ugly amazon we saw you with," she sputtered.

Davy yawned. "Be nice. She's not ugly, and no, I'm not seeing her," he lied again. Yet, it was the truth in a sense. Technically, he hadn't seen her for a few hours. He had to keep Lucy safe.

"Well, okay. But don't stay away too much longer. I

miss you." she purred.

"Don't worry. I won't." He disconnected the call and set his phone, face down, on his dash. He looked forward to when the operation was over, and he didn't have to hear that voice anymore.

Davy relaxed back in the seat and waited for Lucy. Joel had arranged a leave of absence for him from flying so he could get Lucy under control—which Davy didn't really have faith would be possible. Somehow he needed to alleviate her curiosity and turn her interest elsewhere. However, first, he wanted to find out how much she knew about him. How was he to know that she'd try to be an amateur detective? He groaned at the work ahead of him. Being undercover in the cartel had been easier than what this was going to be.

Step one, reactivate their text conversations.

Davy had just paid for fifteen more minutes on the meter when he saw the 4Runner exit the parking structure. He looked at his watch, and it was two-twenty on the dot. He pulled out of his spot and followed her, leaving three cars between them.

He found himself smiling as he tracked Lucy into the parking structure where he usually parked and slowly drove between rows of cars. *Is she looking for my truck*, he wondered?

"I have got to stop being such a creature of habit," Davy said aloud. He managed to keep a row of cars between them, and with him driving the Jeep, she seemed oblivious that he was there.

After leaving the airport, she headed to her place and pulled into her parking spot. Davy gave a sigh of relief that maybe she was in for the night. Maybe he'd been wrong about her and what she was up to. Maybe her climbing over his fence was a one-time-only thing. He decided to stay put until it got dark just to make sure and began to relax in the comfort of his leather-covered driver's seat. He felt the pangs of hunger and pulled out another Slim Jim from his ever-ready stash in the glove compartment and prepared to wait.

***

Lucy awoke from her nap and checked her phone. It was six o'clock. She needed to leave and head over to Davy's home by seven to see if those guys came back or if she could get into his backyard and look for that package again.

"I better wear old dark clothing tonight," Lucy said as she searched through her dresser drawers. "Ah-ha!" She pulled out a dark blue hoodie. "I forgot I had you," she said as she held it up and turned it around. "Now, for some pants. I need something I won't care if it gets torn." In the nights past, she hadn't seen any sign of that car, so she hadn't made any attempt to climb Davy's fence, but her gut told her the car would be there tonight, and she needed to be prepared. "No new jeans tonight." She said as she continued to open and close the drawers searching through each one. Then she remembered the boxes she'd put some clothes in last summer that were too small for her. She carefully lifted it down, holding it away from her body to avoid any contact in case an odd spider appeared. She set it down, took off the lid, and saw a pair of black sweats on the top. She crossed her fingers and held them against her.

"Perfect!" she said as she turned them about, noticing the discoloration on the right thigh.

Davy sat up in his seat and stretched as he grabbed his water bottle from the passenger seat. He looked at his phone. It was seven o'clock, the sun was going down, and it appeared Lucy might be done for the day. With a sigh of relief that he had been wrong about her intentions all along, he set the water bottle into the cup holder, locked his seatbelt into place, and turned the key in the ignition.

At seven o'clock, dressed in dark clothes with her water, some snacks, a flashlight in her bag, and her phone in hand, Lucy stepped outside her front door. She was ready for another long night of waiting for the mysterious car to show up at Davy's home. She walked towards her car, then, as an after-thought, tapped a message and waited for a response. After a couple of minutes, Lucy tapped in a second text.

Davy leaned forward in focused surveillance at the image of a cat burglar that she portrayed. His eyes squinted with intense scrutiny.

"Who are you texting now?" He asked himself quietly. Within seconds his phone chimed, and a text message appeared on the cover.

Are you in town?

She leaned against her car as she waited, but when it seemed that there would be no response, she scowled and dropped the phone in her bag, opened her car door, and tossed it onto the passenger seat. She had one leg in the car when her phone beeped with a text notification. She froze, had she heard correctly, she wondered. She cocked an ear; there was another beep. Lucy scrambled for her bag on the other seat. Once retrieved, she stepped out of the car, set her purse on the vacated driver's seat, and dug through all its contents for her phone. It beeped again just as she grasped it and disentangled herself from the items in her bag.

Lucy stepped away from her car as she used her thumbprint to unlock her phone. She opened her text app with the firm hope of who'd sent the text only to see they were ads from companies she'd previously purchased goods, not Davy.

Davy watched her head drop to her chest while her hands dropped to her side. He could see her dejected posture as she leaned against the side of her car in contemplation as she stared heavenward.

Davy looked down at his phone and tapped a quick message, then quickly looked for Lucy's reaction:

I am.

The text notification interrupted Lucy's reverie. She looked down at her phone with a heavy sigh as she unlocked the screen and then tapped the messaging app. At first, she didn't believe her eyes and pulled the phone closer to make sure she saw it correctly.

Davy saw a smile begin to appear on Lucy's face before she did a little dance and hugged the phone to her chest. He chuckled to himself as he watched her. This was why he enjoyed spending time with her. He enjoyed how easy it was to please her and her mostly positive outlook on life. Before he could stop himself, he tapped out another text:

> *What are you doing? Wanna*
> *get some tea?*

> *Oh, I can't tonight. Have plans.*

"You little liar," Davy said aloud as he read her text. "I can see you. What are you doing tonight?" He looked up and watched her curiously, then decided to call her. He held the phone to his ear and watched her stand beside her open driver's door, look at the phone as it rang, and not answer it.

> *Answer your phone!*

> *No. You're not the boss of me.*

Davy watched in awe as Lucy laughed at her text and did a little pose. He shook his head in disbelief and softly chuckled. "Not the boss of you," he muttered to himself.

Lucy was very pleased with her response to Davy. Now he would not expect her to show up at his home if he were there. This way, she'd be able to wander around freely. She dropped her phone back in her bag and moved it to the passenger seat before she climbed in her 4Runner and headed to Davy's home.

It was dark when Lucy arrived in Davy's

neighborhood. With as few street lamps as there seemed to be, Lucy felt a nervousness she hadn't before as she pulled into a spot that allowed her to see Davy's house.

Davy pulled into a spot half a block behind where Lucy parked. He hadn't told her he wasn't working, just that he was in town. He'd expected her to head back to the airport to try and find his truck, but she came here. Turning off the engine, he sat back in his Jeep and waited for her to make her next move. He didn't have to wait long.

Having learned her lesson, Lucy turned off the dome light before opening her door to exit her truck. Quickly she crossed the street, hoping no one saw and was just about to step on Davy's lawn but stopped with her foot in mid-air. She looked down at the lawn to make sure there were no gifts from any neighborhood fidos. She took a few steps towards the middle of the lawn when she realized that the porch light wasn't on and paused. *Why did the house seem so dark and lifeless?* She wondered but continued over to the fence at the side of the house she'd climbed over a week ago. She needed to see if there was any package left for Davy in the back. *Was Davy aware that questionable characters were using his place as a depository?*

Davy watched Lucy as she stood rooted in one spot and contemplated his house. *What is she doing?* he wondered. Then he quietly exited his car and clung to the shadows as he moved closer to his property, but before crossing the street, he scanned the area from where he stood. Everything looked normal until he spotted the familiar Chevy Nova. He looked at the car, then at Lucy as she stood on the lawn. He maneuvered his way over to the Chevy Nova to find it empty.

Davy's head shot up over the top of the car. If they weren't in the car, then they were in the backyard. But why were both of them there? And, where was Lucy? She no longer stood on the lawn. Davy could see Lucy's car still parked in the same spot; it was empty as well.

He let out an exasperated sigh and moaned, "That woman is gonna be the death of me." He quickly crossed the street, still in the shadows that lined the edge of his property, until he came to the fence that separated the backyard from the front. He easily vaulted over the wall and landed quietly on the other side.

Lucy moved slowly along the side of the house then paused when she heard the screech of nails as Johnny pulled boards apart on the patio. She froze. The loud whisper of two male voices could be heard just around the corner of the house into the backyard. She wanted to see who was there. Was it the same guy as before? Who was with him? Was he leaving another package? If so, where did he put it? Then, as she was about to turn the corner, a hand clamped over her mouth, and an arm wrapped about her waist pulling her back from the edge of the house. Her heart stopped.

"Be very quiet," A voice hissed in her ear. Lucy tried to struggle but was held so firmly she was unable to move. She and her captor stood still as they heard one of the parties swear, then the sound of feet as they thudded along the yard, paused then a light rattle of the fence before the thuds of their feet on the concrete of the drive and ran away. Her captor pulled her backward to the wall she'd just climbed over. She could feel his hold on her relax.

Lucy pushed her captor's hands away and spun around. "You! What are you doing here?" She asked in a furious whisper as she stared into Davy's face.

Davy looked at her in disbelief before he asked, "What am I doing here?" Lucy opened her mouth to respond, then remembered that she was the trespasser and closed her mouth. Inwardly she was thankful that it was dark, and he couldn't see how embarrassed she was to be caught snooping around his property.

Moments later as Lucy sat on the steps of the patio at the back of his house. She watched as Davy stood with his back to her. She couldn't help but admire the nice silhouette he cut in the moonlight, but now wasn't the time to get lost in that fantasy, especially as angry as he seemed at her. She slyly knelt on the stairs, near where one of the boards and been torn away and tried to look through them under the patio to see if she could see any packages under it. If she'd only remembered to bring the flashlight, she put in her bag.

"What are you doing?" Davy demanded. He'd finally gotten his temper under control, only to turn around and find her on her knees, looking under the patio. Startled, Lucy looked up at him and sat back on her heels. *At least she has the decency to have a chastised look on her face*, he thought to himself. "Well? Why were you trespassing?" Lucy didn't respond but sat on one of the steps. "What were you going to do when you came face-to-face with the intruders?"

"How'd you know I was here?" Lucy challenged.

"I fol—," Davy began to say then stopped himself.

"You followed me?" Lucy glared at him angrily. "Why are you spying on me?"

Davy began to sputter an answer, then stopped. "Hey! I'm not the one in the wrong here. You have no right to be on this property uninvited." Davy glared at her. "I could call the cops and have you arrested."

Lucy knew he was right, but her embarrassment at having been caught wouldn't allow her to back down. "That's your answer to everything—arrest me. Then why don't you? Why don't you call the cops?" she rose to her feet and challenged him.

Davy stood with his hands on his hips and head bowed to his chest to calm his temper, then asked, "Why did you trespass? Do you do this a lot?"

"No, I don't do this a lot. This is the first time," She mumbled and looked away. She knew it wasn't the first time, but did he? "But don't worry, it won't happen again." She stormed down the steps and crossed over to the same side of the house where the two intruders had escaped over the fence. She hoped that the box would still be there, and she could use it to help her get a clean escape. Davy followed her as she indignantly walked to the fence, and with an inward sigh of relief, saw the box was still there, stepped up, then turned and said, "Go ahead and call the cops. Tell 'em they can come arrest me. But I won't wait here. I'm going home." With that said, she flung her leg over the fence, and then her body followed. She landed with a heavy thud on the cement and let out a heavy "Oph" as she laid on the cement, having the wind knocked out of her.

Speechless, Davy peered over the fence at Lucy on

the ground. He'd never seen her like this before, but he hoped his threat to call the police would cause her to pull back and let him do his job without worrying for her safety.

"Are you okay?" He asked as he watched her push herself to a standing position.

"I'm fine," she huffed over her shoulder as she awkwardly trotted towards her car. She didn't care if anyone saw her now. She just wanted to get home and lick her wounds and deal with the embarrassment she felt, as well as the possibility that she'd be arrested.

Davy watched Lucy drive away before he returned to his backyard. He stopped at the side of the patio where the board had been pulled out in search of the package he'd already retrieved and turned over to Joel.

Typically when Sal and Johnny left a package, they knew they could come back two days later and pick up a bundle of money in exchange for leaving another bundle of drugs. He was supposed to take that bundle and have one of the FAMs carry it to another drop. They must've learned that the last drop-off didn't happen but came back for the money anyway—only to find nothing.

Unbeknownst to Davy, the intruders had returned to the neighborhood with the thought that they'd looked in the wrong spot for the money and watched Lucy run across the lawn into her car and drive away. They followed her.

"She doesn't have the package," Johnny noted.

"I can see that," Sal barked back at him.

"So why are we following her instead of waiting for Davy?" He asked.

273

"I told ya, she might come in handy later."

***

Hey Luce, ya there?

Davy looked at the text he'd just sent. It had been a couple of weeks since the incident at his property, and Davy thought he should check in with Lucy to make sure everything was okay. And, if he was honest with himself, he missed their banter. As stressful and dangerous as his life could be, it was good to have a release—Lucy had become that to him.

Lucy? You doin' okay?

Back at work, Davy decided to wait until he was on the flight before he would text her again. Finally placed in his Business Class seat, Davy impatiently waited for the fasten seatbelt light to go off so that he could check his phone for any response from Lucy. While he waited, he reviewed the last time he'd seen her and how she'd gone off in a huff when he chastised her for trespassing on his property. It couldn't have worked out better, as far as getting her to distance herself from him if only to save her life. He couldn't have her around the people he associated with at this time because they were so evil and dangerous and gave such little value to anyone's life that wasn't theirs.

When the fasten seatbelt light went out, he turned his phone over and saw that there was still no response from her. That wasn't like her. She usually responded in a timely fashion. She must really be mad at him. *This is for the best*, he told himself. She would be safe now, and he wouldn't have to worry about her. But, if he let her go now until the operation was over, would she still be around afterward? Would she forgive him and be friends again? Did he want to be just friends? He sat in his seat and contemplated these questions.

***

Lucy had just got comfortable on her couch for a night of watching one of her favorite movies, 'Cinema Paradiso.' She needed to watch it; she needed to bathe herself in the beautiful story, almost like a salve for the embarrassment and frustration she still felt, even though it had been a couple of weeks since she'd last seen Davy. She'd totally blown it with him. She knew it was her fault and still suffered from the humiliation of having been caught trespassing.

As the beginning credits began to play, Lucy looked at the two text messages Davy had sent. She should've responded as if nothing had happened, but she didn't. Instead, she let her pride get in the way. She admitted she'd been in the wrong but couldn't stifle the questions in her head as to who this guy was. Why was he in so many fights? Was he a good guy or a bad guy? Did she really want to lose his friendship? Were they just friends? Could they ever be more?

Lucy burrowed further under her heated throw, ready to lose herself in the story when her doorbell rang. She put the movie on hold and quietly walked to the door, then looked through the peephole to see who was on the other side of the door. When she saw who it was, she paused for a moment before she slowly opened the door.

"Hi," Davy said with an apologetic grin. Lucy looked at him as he stood on her doorstep, holding a large chai tea in each hand. "I think I owe you a tea," he said as he pressed the cup towards her. She didn't move to take it. When he saw her lack of response, he took a sip from the one he held close to his body and said, "Mmm, this is really good." And grinned, hoping to entice her.

Lucy couldn't stop the smile that appeared on her face. She pushed her screen door open and asked, "Do you want to come in?" Davy smiled and stepped through the door as Lucy made room for him to pass. As soon as she closed the door behind him, he handed her the other Chai tea. It felt warm in her hands, and she could smell its wonderful aroma.

Davy looked around the living room encased by windows on one wall and a fireplace with a television mounted above it on the other. His large stature suddenly made the room feel crowded and the high ceiling not so high. He looked at the picture frozen on the TV, at the light gray colored dining room walls that led into the open kitchen, then back to the living room where an oversized couch faced the television with a large ottoman in front of it to rest one's legs.

"This is a nice place," he said. "I like your style."

Lucy softly chuckled as she watched this tall, handsome, masculine man talk about her decore. "Thanks," she said.

"What are you watching?" he asked as he looked at the picture on the TV.

"Cinema Paradiso," Lucy said with a wistful smile.

"Cinema Para-what?" Davy asked as his face scrunched, and he cocked an ear towards her as if he hadn't heard correctly.

Lucy laughed aloud, "Cinema Paradiso. It's an Italian movie with subtitles." She smiled and slightly shrugged her shoulders.

"Is it any good?" He asked as he studied the picture frozen on her TV.

Lucy gave a dreamy sigh, then said, "Yes. It's wonderful."

"What's it about?" Davy asked as he gave her an evaluating stare.

Lucy returned to the end of the couch where she'd been sitting before Davy arrived. She placed her tea on the black stool she used as a table. "It's a love story." Davy rolled his eyes. "It's a story about a man's love for the movies. It's absolutely wonderful," she told Davy. Then, when he didn't make any motion to leave, she asked, "Wanna watch it? It just started, and I can start it over." Lucy smiled at Davy encouragingly. This would be the first time they'd watched a movie together if he stayed, she realized.

"Sounds interesting," Davy said as he sat towards the center of the couch. "Do you want me to turn off the lights?" He asked as he stood still holding his tea.

"Sure, if you'd like, or you can leave them on— they're over by the door—it's the middle one," Lucy pointed in the direction he should go. "It's a good movie either way." She smiled at him. *He's so easy to warm up to*, she thought to herself as she watched him walk over and flip the light switch.

Together they sat in just the glow from the television, in silence, for the next two hours and watched the movie. Neither spoke as they read the subtitles to follow the story. Midway through, Davy looked over at Lucy. He couldn't help but smile as he witnessed how entranced she was with the film; he watched her face as it reflected every emotion played on the screen. *She really is something*, he thought to himself with a smile.

Lucy could feel him looking at her. She pulled her eyes away from the screen and looked at him and, with a smile, said, "It's good, isn't it?" Davy nodded. Lucy's attention immediately returned to the screen.

Davy continued to gaze at her for a moment longer before he returned his attention to the screen. He liked how comfortable he felt with her and that they could watch a movie and not need to talk.

"As much as I love movies, would you believe I've never sat through a foreign film before?" Davy confessed as the word *Fine* appeared on the screen.

"Really? How'd you like the subtitles?" Lucy asked as she sniffled and tried to hide her tears from the final scene. She leaned over and pulled a tissue from the box on the ottoman.

"At first, it was awkward, but soon I got the hang—hey, are you okay?" he asked when she wiped her eyes.

Embarrassed, Lucy laughed and tried to brush it off. "This movie gets me every time," she sniffled, then wiped her nose.

Davy turned back to the television. "You're right. It was a good movie," he said as they continued to watch the credits scroll up the screen.

Lucy sniffled and said, "It's just such a great story. I love the ending." She hiccupped a couple of times.

Davy softly chuckled as he rested his arm on the back of the couch and lightly brushed her shoulder. "Do you cry every time you watch this movie?" He asked.

Lucy felt the warmth of his hand on her shoulder and looked at him to see if he was making fun or was sincerely sympathetic. He just looked at her and gave an understanding smile. She began to feel flustered and needed to deflect whatever it was he was sending her way.

"Why aren't you crying? Are you heartless?" She asked to lighten the mood.

Davy laughed and loudly whispered, "I'm crying inside."

Lucy laughed and said, "Sure. Inside." She rolled her eyes, so he'd see.

Davy laughed again. He pushed the ottoman so that it was only in front of Lucy. Then sat on the edge of the couch with his forearms resting on his knees.

"Sorry," he said, watching her adjust her position on the couch with the new placement of the ottoman. Then as if to share a secret, he leaned sideways towards her and said, "Between you and me, I did get a little choked up. But if you ever tell anyone, I'll deny it."

"Ah-ha! So you are human!" Lucy jabbed her finger into his shoulder triumphantly and pushed him away.

"Course I'm human," he said as he stood. "Where's your trash can?" He asked with the empty paper cup in his hand. Lucy pointed to the trash can in the kitchen. Davy walked over and dropped it in, then reached for hers, which she handed to him and watched him toss it in, then turn in the direction of the door.

"Thanks for the tea," she said as she stood to walk with him.

With his hand on the doorknob, Davy turned to Lucy with a sincere look and asked, "So, are we okay?"

She nodded. "We're okay." Davy reached out and pulled her into his arms for a quick hug. Lucy felt a strong current of electricity rush through her. Casually she pulled away to see if he'd felt it too, but he seemed oblivious to it.

"Where were you the other hundred times I watched that movie?" Lucy gave an awkward laugh.

"Should've texted," he said, then stopped and told her, "I'm glad we're okay." After a pause, he continued, "You know I wouldn't turn you into the police for just trespassing, right? At least the first time. I like to think people can change." He pulled the wooden door open.

Lucy feigned shock and gave a light punch to his side. His arm automatically moved to block it. "I can't believe you." Davy gave his boyish grin to Lucy's frown, then asked, "So, why didn't you tell me it was you when you had your hand over my mouth?"

"It wasn't safe to have a full conversation. I just needed you to stay still and quiet—which is a chore in itself," Davy said with a George Bailey wink.

Lucy couldn't stop the laugh that escaped with his blatant teasing. "You better go before someone gets hurt," she told him with a big smile on her face that had replaced the tears from earlier.

Davy pushed the screen door open and stepped onto her front stoop, then turned and said, "I had a really good time tonight. We need to do it again sometime."

"Yeah, yeah, yeah," she said as if to throw it away but continued to smile. Davy laughed out loud, waved, and walked down her steps into the night. Lucy watched him disappear before she closed the door and glided to bed.

As Lucy laid in bed, she smiled at the memory of Davy watching the movie. She'd glanced at him throughout it to see if he was as caught up in it. He seemed to be involved in the story, which pleased her. She appreciated not talking, especially when she got choked up as the story progressed and could hide her emotions from him. That is until the last scene; that scene got her every time as the main character watched the gift the older man had left him, and the theme music swelled. But, he didn't seem to mind that she was teary. Then her mind fast-forwarded to the hug, and she gave a languid sigh. *Yes, all is right with the world*, was her last thought before she fell asleep.

Sal and Johnny watched Davy descend Lucy's stairs from their position in a dark corner of the parking lot, giving them a direct view of her building.

"Are we gonna go visit her?" Johnny asked as he drew on his cigarette then blew the smoke out the window where he let his hand that held the cigarette hang out.

"No," Sal said as he backed out of their spot. "We have to find out who has our money first."

"Maybe she has it?" Johnny suggested.

"We'll see," Sal said as he slowly passed Lucy's building.

Chapter 23

Lucy opened up the back door of her 4Runner and placed the two bags of groceries on the floor between the seats when she heard the beginning bars of AC/DC's Thunderstruck. She scrambled for her purse and pulled out her phone.

"Pronto," Lucy answered.

"Hello?" Davy said into the phone as he relaxed on his couch.

"Come va?" Lucy asked.

"I see you've started your Italian lessons again," Davy said with a chuckle.

"Come va?" Lucy repeated, unphased.

Davy sighed, then said, "I'm fine."

"In Italiano, per favore." Lucy interrupted him.

"In Italian? Maybe I don't know that much to have a conversation."

"Pfft. Per favore," Lucy said in disbelief.

"Really?" Davy asked, but she remained quiet. "This is so silly," he muttered, then with a deep inhale of air, said, "Sto bene tu come stai?" He heard Lucy giggle on the other end.

"Sto bene tu . . .sto bene tu, hm. I know that come stai means how are you. What is sto bene tu again?"

Davy chuckled then said, "Sto bene tu means I'm fine. I can see your studies are going really well," he teased her.

"Shut up," she said loud enough to be heard over his laughter. "Good thing you think you're funny."

"No, sei tu quello divertente."

"What does that mean?" Lucy asked.

"Look it up," Davy said, then sniggered.

"You can be very irritating at times. But you already knew that, didn't you?" Lucy said, annoyed.

"What are you doing?"

"Just finished—" Lucy stopped when she noticed the old, red sports car idling nearby.

"What? Just finished what? Hello? Lucy, are ya there?" Davy asked after a couple of seconds of silence.

"Uh, yeah. I'm here," Lucy answered as she tried to see the two men that were inside the car. Why were they following her? "Hm," she said into the phone.

"What's up?" Davy asked with a note of concern. Then, when Lucy didn't respond, he asked again, "Luce? Everything okay?"

"What? Oh, yeah. Yeah, it's all good."

"You seem distracted. What's going on?" Davy asked curiously.

"It's probably nothing, but . . ." she said as she continued to watch the Nova.

"But what?"

"Ah, it's—," she said.

"Lucy. What is it?" Davy asked as he sat upright on the couch.

"It's probably nothing, but—." Lucy closed the back door, climbed into her 4Runner, and locked the doors.

"But what, Lucy? Talk to me. Are you okay?" Davy stood up from the couch, concerned.

"Well, what are the odds that the same car would be most every place I am?" She asked.

"You have a car following you?"

"I think so, but I could be overreacting. Aah, it's probably stupid. Forget I mentioned it. I'll talk to you later," Lucy pulled the phone from her ear.

"Luce! Hey Lucy," Davy called from the phone.

Lucy put the phone back to her ear, "Yeah?"

"What kind of car is it?"

"The one that's following me?"

"Yeah."

"I don't know; it's red, old, and sporty."

"Can you take a picture of it and send it to me?"

"Why?"

"So, I can see what kind of car it is. I'm curious," Davy said. He didn't want to mention who he thought they were.

Lucy quickly snapped a picture of the car with her phone and sent it to Davy. "Did you get it?" she asked.

"Yeah."

"Do you know what kind of car that is?" Lucy asked.

"Yeah, It's a Chevy Nova. So you're sure this is the same car you've seen everywhere?" Davy asked.

"I think so," Lucy hesitantly responded. "But maybe

I'm paranoid, and it's just a coincidence," she explained and relaxed against the seatback.

"Probably. I wouldn't worry 'bout it," Davy told her reassuringly.

"Mm," Lucy grunted.

"Wanna meet for lunch?"

"As long as you're buying, sure," Lucy said as she turned the key, and the engine came to life.

Davy chuckled, "When have I not bought?" He asked as Lucy snickered. "Meet me at that Mediterranean café."

"Okay, at one? I need to drop these groceries off at my place."

"Okay, see ya then." But, unfortunately, the smile on his face was replaced with grave concern.

Davy looked at the phone he held in his hand, then tapped in a series of numbers and held it to his ear.

"We've got a development that I didn't expect," he said, then listened to the voice on the other end of the phone.

***

Davy watched the soccer game from the sidelines. He hadn't liked the idea of meeting Joel at the game, but he needed to update him on the latest developments with the operation. And when Joel suggested it, Davy agreed the game would be an innocent place to meet, less conspicuous, perhaps. So while waiting for Joel, he moved up and down the field behind where all the parents sat. He pretended to watch and cheered. Then he saw Joel approach the field from the parking lot. He gave a slight tip of his head at Joel to confirm he knew his position and turned his attention back to the game.

"Let's make this quick," said Joel as he stepped up to Davy's side. He wore a blue t-shirt with a black skull that dripped down the front and a pair of dirty, torn jeans with flip flops, a worn baseball cap, sunglasses, and his beard was now plaited into one braid. His hands were in his jean pockets as he casually viewed the players on the field behind his Oakley sunglasses.

"Gee, you shouldn't have dressed up for me," Davy said sarcastically.

"You're lucky I dressed at all. I could've come in my boxers," Joel said. It was tough to tell if he was kidding or not as his beard hid any glimpse of a smile.

Davy shrugged and cocked a brow. "I know this isn't convenient, but I think it warrants some attention," Davy told him as he kept his interest on the field. Both men clapped and cheered with the crowd as one of the teams made a goal, then moved with the group down the field as the mothers looked at Joel with suspicion.

"Great job on blending in," Davy muttered to Joel as they watched the mothers give them a wide birth when they passed.

"Is it your girlfriend again?" Joel asked as he expelled air out in a sigh.

"She's not my girlfriend, and yes," Davy said, embarrassed.

"I thought you'd handled this," he stated as his lower lip reached up and smoothed down over his mustache repeatedly.

"It's different. Sal and Johnny are still tailing her."

"Are you sure that the car is the same one?"

"Yeah, I had her text me a picture of it." Davy pulled his phone from his pocket and showed the picture to Joel.

"Did she say it'd been following her or is that your perception?" Joel asked as he studied the picture.

"Those are my words. She only mentioned it in passing, but it did cause alarm bells to go off that she'd notice it. She isn't the type to be into cars," Davy said and found himself smiling.

"You told me they were following her a while back," Joel reminded him.

"True, but now that she's noticed it, they're no longer hiding from her."

"You'll need to stop flying so you can keep better tabs on her," Joel informed him.

Davy nodded. "I guess you're right. But I can't watch her all the time."

Joel gave him a concerned look before he asked, "Dude, is there more to this friendship than you're telling me?"

Taken aback, Davy responded defensively, "No. No, not at all. She's just someone I met who's become a friend. Just someone I like spending time with, but ro-romantic interest? None." Davy felt himself choke a little on the words. *I can't be interested in her*, Davy thought to himself. *She's just a friend*.

"We have a huge problem. You sure she's not a ringer of some sort?"

Davy bit his lip to stop the chuckle that tried to escape at the thought of Lucy as a ringer. Then, when he could control his voice, he said, "Yeah, I'm sure."

Joel cocked his brow, then frowned and said, "It's not good that we now have an innocent civilian possibly involved. You are sure she's innocent, right?"

Davy couldn't hide the slight smile that tripped across his face before he said, "Yeah. If you knew this woman, you'd know she couldn't possibly be involved in anything like this."

Joel looked at Davy for a moment before he asked, "So what do we do? Or do you already have a plan?"

The two men stood in silence as they watched the crowd cheer as the ball flew into the goal box. Then they turned and walked back towards the parking lot.

"What about Junie Urkel?" Joel asked with a grin without looking at Davy.

Davy chuckled, "Junie Urkel, that's good."

Chapter 24

Davy watched Lucy struggle to pull her bike out of the back of her 4Runner. She'd taken the front wheel off to make it fit. He'd felt bad when he watched her struggle to put it in her car at her home. Now, as she struggled to pull it out of her truck, he fought the urge to be the gentleman and help her, but he knew he couldn't give away his position. He needed to stay put, out of sight, and disengaged to keep her safe. So he rented a non-descript car to have even more anonymity. He was hiding in plain sight.

Lucy pulled the bike from her car and set it on the ground, then paused for a moment to gaze at the ocean and soak it in. It was a gorgeous day, and the sun was hot for that time of year. After a short break, she returned to her car and pulled out the front tire. She held the tire in her hand then lifted the bike frame with the other hand to slip the tire into the hooks that would attach it to the frame. But it wasn't as easy to put the tire on as it had been to take the tire off. Now she couldn't get the parts to line up and hold the bike up simultaneously. She had to get them back together if she was going to go for a bike ride.

The more she tried to fit them in, the more the bike seemed to fall apart. Soon the chain was off its track, which meant she had to put that back on before she could ride it. She turned the bike upside down and rested it on its seat and handlebars. She'd gingerly placed the greased chain on what she thought would be third gear when her nose began to itch. Without thinking, she rubbed it. She sighed with disgust when she realized grease from the chain covered her fingers, which was now smeared all over the end of her nose and upper lip. It left her looking like Charlie Chaplin's little tramp—at least around the nose and mouth area. *This is why I'm still single.* She used the back of her hand to wipe the grease from her upper lip and nose.

Lucy tried to put the tire on her bike once more but still couldn't get the grooves hooked onto the space allocated for them on the wheel. So she stood with her hands on her hips, unsure of what to do. Then she noticed a surfer a couple of cars down with his wet suit stripped down to his waist.

"Excuse me," she called to the surfer, but he didn't hear her, so she called again, "Excuse me!" She walked towards him. "I'm sorry to bother you, but I can't get the wheel back on my bike. Can you help me?" She gave him her sweetest smile. Although she was sure he was only in his twenties and very immune to her smile, she still hoped he'd be able to help.

"I'll try," he said.

"It's just over here," she said as she led him back to her truck. She knew it wasn't safe to trust strangers, but he seemed nice enough, and he was only half-dressed. So what harm could he cause?

"Let's see," he said as he picked up the tire she'd left on the ground and looked at the front of her bike. "Oh yeah, this is easy to fix." Then, without another word, he connected the tire to the body of the bike. Lucy blinked her eyes, surprised at how easy he'd made it look.

"Wow! You were so quick. Thank you," she said as she took hold of the bike.

"It was easy," the surfer said as he shrugged his shoulders with bashful indifference and turned to go.

"Oh, before you go, can we make sure the chain is all connected? It came off as I tried to get the wheel attached." When she'd said this, the surfer turned back and reached for the bike. He pushed it forward and backward, then knelt and moved the chain to a different row of teeth before he stood and rolled it forward.

"Why don't you take it for a quick ride around the parking lot to see if it's working?" He suggested to her.

"Do you mind?" she asked.

"Not at all. I'll just finish changing while you check it out," the surfer said as he flashed a beautiful white smile against his tanned face.

Lucy climbed on her bike and began to peddle. At first, she felt the chain kept skipping links. As she tried to look down at the chain to see if it was still on the gear teeth, she lost control of the bike. She almost ran into a blue sedan that was parked to the side of the parking lot but quickly swerved, barely missing the front fender. It seemed the teeth of the gears and the chain seemed to merge, and from that moment on, it was as good as gold. Lucy turned the bike around and found the surfer dressed in shorts and a t-shirt sitting in the back of her 4Runner where the bike had been, waiting for her return.

"It works perfectly," she pleasantly exclaimed.

Davy pulled the baseball cap he'd worn down over his face when he saw Lucy begin to lose control of her bike and almost crash into his rental. Just his luck that she'd practically ruin his surveillance disguise. He sat up in the seat and readjusted his hat, and watched the surfer leave and Lucy close the back door on her car. Then, she headed down the bike path that ran parallel to the beach with the bike in tow.

Just as she swung her leg over the bike bar, her phone rang. Lucy pulled it out of her pants pocket and answered, "Hello?"

"Hey, what're you up to?" he asked.

"Who's this?" she asked.

"Who's this?" he repeated to her, "Who do you think it is?"

"Oh, hey. Where've you been?" She asked while pulling the bike to the side of the path without getting off it.

"Where are you?"

"I'm at the beach. Where are you?" She asked coyly.

"I'm at the beach," Davy answered smugly.

"You're at the beach? Which one?" Lucy asked excitedly.

"The one near that Mediterranean café," he answered.

"Shut up! That's the one I'm at. Where are you?" Lucy asked as she looked around.

"Where are you?" Davy asked strategically.

"I'm just headed down the bike path. I'll turn around, and maybe we can meet up," Lucy suggested. "Wanna?" Lucy asked as she awkwardly turned her bike.

"Sure."

"I'll see you in a couple of minutes," she told him and hung up.

Davy quickly exited his rental. He couldn't let Lucy see him getting out of a car that she almost ran into—if she even remembered virtually hitting the vehicle. He jogged over to the bike path that led down to the beach and spotted her walking up the steep path towards him. He contemplated whether he should go down and meet her or not. As he waited for Lucy, he thought he saw two guys he recognized leaning against the lifeguard hut. He squinted against the brightness of the sun to get a better look, then reached for his sunglasses that rested on the bill of his baseball cap. He pulled them off only to drop them. He quickly stooped to pick up the glasses and moved aside to get out of the way of a group of people exiting the trail just ahead of Lucy. With his sunglasses in a place, he looked for the two guys—who'd disappeared. He scanned the area and couldn't see any trace of them. Maybe he'd just imagined them, he told himself.

"Hey there," Lucy called to him with a smile and a wave as she approached him. "I can't believe you're here the same time I am without us coming together. What are the odds of that happening, I wonder?" She asked.

"Yeah, what are the odds?" he dryly responded as he

searched for the two guys.

"Wanna go rent a bike so we can ride?"

"Nah," he said. "Why don't we go do something else?"

"Sure, like what, though? It's such a gorj day," Lucy said as she dismounted from her bike.

"Gorj?" Davy gave her a curious look.

"Yeah, gorj, as in gorgeous."

"What, you couldn't just say gorgeous?" Davy teased her.

"Shut up," Lucy said, then bit her lower lip to hide her grin as she walked past him with her bike.

"Where did you park?" Davy asked, although he already knew.

"Just over here," Lucy pointed to her 4Runner in the second row. They walked to her truck and heard the two beeps of her alarm disarming. Lucy rolled her bike around to the back and pulled the hatch door up. She leaned down to take the front tire off when Davy stopped her.

"What are you doing?" He asked.

"I need to take the front tire off so that I can get my bike in the back," Lucy told him.

"Here, let me show you an easier way to do that without removing your tire." Lucy cocked an eyebrow at him inquisitively as she leaned her bike towards him.

Lucy watched in amazement as Davy lifted her bike and maneuvered it in such a way that it fit perfectly in the back—with the front tire still attached. "Hey! That is so cool! How'd you know to do that?" She asked him in admiration.

Davy grinned and said, "We learned it in the Navy."

"Liar," Lucy said without missing a beat. They both laughed. "So, what are we gonna do?" She asked.

"Well, I thought I could take you shooting."

"No way! Serious?" Lucy asked, unable to hide her excitement.

"Yup," Davy said, thankful for his sunglasses that hid the pleasure her reaction gave him.

Lucy did a quick little jig and leaned in to give him a quick hug, which surprised Davy. Before he could respond, she said, "I need to use the facilities before we go. I'll be right back, watch my car." Without another word, Lucy jogged over to the restroom situated next to the path they'd just vacated.

With her absence, Davy decided to follow a hunch and walked to another row of cars. He jogged from one end to the other in search of the red Chevy Nova. If it were there, then he'd know he hadn't imagined those two thugs at the beach. As he jogged along, he didn't see it and sighed with relief. He turned to head back to where Lucy was parked when a stiff breeze came along and blew his baseball cap off his head. As he ran to grab it, a Volkswagen van pulled out of a parking spot in the back of the lot. Davy steered clear of it, then stopped and watched it move towards the exit; that was when he saw the red Chevy Nova hood as it peaked out between two large trash bins next to the exit. Davy jogged back to find Lucy leaning against her truck, patiently waiting for him.

"Where'd ya go?" She asked.

"I thought I saw someone I knew," he casually said. It was kind of the truth, he thought to himself. He had thought he saw someone he knew. Now he'd confirmed it. "C'mon, let's go."

"Want me to follow you?" Lucy asked. "Where's your truck?"

Davy had forgotten about his rental and that he was supposed to observe Lucy from afar. He had to think quickly. "Why don't you go home and drop off your bike. I'll come pick you up, and we'll go together rather than take two cars. Parking can be difficult at the range," Davy continued to scan the area for Sal and Johnny.

"At the range? Are you kidding me? It's a dirt parking lot," Lucy stated, confused.

"What?" Davy asked, only half-listening to Lucy.

"At the shooting range, the parking lot," Lucy said as a nudge.

"Oh, that parking lot. We aren't going to that range. We're going to an indoor one," Davy explained. "Let's get going before it's too late, okay?" He said as he opened her door, hoping that she'd get in with no further comments and they could leave without Sal and Johnny knowing.

Chapter 25

Lucy rushed home and pulled her bike out of the back with a strength she didn't know she possessed. "He's taking me shooting," she sang to herself as she changed into what she thought would be appropriate shooting attire, then sat on her steps and waited impatiently for Davy.

Thirty minutes later, as she paced back and forth on the sidewalk in front of her steps, Davy's truck pulled up to the curb. She trotted towards it before he could exit his vehicle. "Let's go," she said. "I've been waiting forever!" Lucy walked around to the passenger side, pulled open the door, and climbed in.

Davy laughed, "I wasn't that late."

"It's been thirty minutes, and you said you'd be right behind me," Lucy argued.

"Well, I'm here now," Davy stated the obvious. Davy put the truck in gear and pulled away from the curb with a smile on his face. He did enjoy her enthusiasm.

"Let's go! Let's go shoot!" Lucy could barely

contain her excitement.

Davy held the Bullseye Shooting Range door for Lucy as she entered. Her heart was beating quicker than usual with excitement, and she stood aside to make room for Davy to approach the counter just to the left of the door.

There were two guys and a girl standing behind the counter, all dressed in casual clothes.

"Hey, man," one of the guys said to him as he reached out and shook Davy's hand. Lucy looked at the man with his rugged looks dressed in a 'don't tread on me t-shirt' and worn jeans. He sported a big grin upon seeing Davy and said, "Good to see you, brother, been a while."

"How ya been?" Davy enquired with as big a smile on his face.

While Davy and his friend caught up, Lucy looked around. Bullseye Shooting Range was a no-frills place with racks of different shooting gear spattered everywhere. To the right of the counter was a wooden case full of different types of handguns. To the right of that, another counter with shotguns under glass. Lucy walked over and gazed at all the guns in the wooden rack, then headed towards the shotguns where a man in glasses and a biker mustache stood in front of the counter with another man sporting a huge pot belly stood behind it. The man with the belly handed the man with the glasses one of the shotguns from inside the case. He held the shotgun up so he could look through its sites.

Opposite the counters was a wall of windows where the actual shooting range could be observed. It was divided into twelve separate stalls where people stood and were either loading their guns or shooting them. Lucy watched them all longingly through the glass, antsy to get in there and shoot. She'd always dreamt of being a marksman. Was this the beginning of accomplishing her dream?

Lost in her fantasy, Lucy jumped when Davy put his hand on her shoulder. "Ready?" He asked.

"Yes. I can't wait," she said, moving towards the door that opened into the range.

"Wait, we need to get some gear first," Davy said as he grabbed her arm to stop her progress. Lucy gave him a questioning look. "Yeah, come over here. We need to get some eyes and ears." Davy led Lucy back to the counter they'd passed that was near the entrance.

"Eyes and ears?" Lucy asked.

"Hey Jan, can we get two pairs of eyes and ears, please?" Davy asked the lady that was behind the counter. Under hooded eyes, Lucy quickly assessed Jan, who seemed to light up when Davy spoke with her. She was in her thirties, Lucy guessed, with an athletic build wearing jeans and a t-shirt. She had a golden-brown tan and long dark brown hair pulled back in a ponytail pulled through the back of the baseball cap she wore with the Bullseye Shooting Range on the front of it, and she wore no makeup. Lucy inwardly rolled her eyes as she listened to her flirt with Davy—who soaked it up like a sponge.

"Do you want to pay for everything before you leave?" Jan asked Davy with a big smile.

"Nah, I'll take care of it now." Davy flashed his smile at her. "Hey, this is my friend's first time shooting. Can we get a good lane for beginners?" Jan handed a basket like what you'd use in the grocery store over the counter full of targets, the eyes, and ears, and at the very bottom of the basket a .22 pistol and a box of ammo that went with it.

"Sure, take the two over against the wall," Jan said with a smile, then gave Lucy an up and down look as she sussed her out.

"Great, thanks," Davy said as he handed Lucy the eyes and ears out of the basket. "You need to put these on before we go through that door."

"Okay," Lucy said as she put the safety glasses on and placed the headphones over her ears. She remembered at the outdoor shooting range when he'd insisted she wear them then. She saw that Davy was speaking, but she couldn't hear what he said, "What?" She asked, pulling one earphone off her ear.

Davy just shook his head with a silly grin. "Just wear 'em," he said as he placed his eyes and ears on, then picked up the basket and escorted Lucy into the shooting range.

Lucy's adrenaline was high as she stepped through the door, fueled by the smell of gun powder that hung in the air. She looked at the stalls as they passed by; some were occupied and beneath were piles of spent shells. Finally, she stopped and looked at Davy, who motioned for her to continue towards the end of the row.

"Okay," Davy said in a louder volume as he placed the red basket on the bench set against the wall behind them. "Let's go to the end one, and you can shoot from there." Lucy moved to the very end stall between the wall and a wooden partition with a small counter set in the middle connecting the wall and the partition. Davy put the .22 pistol on the little counter. Lucy reached out to pick it up but was stopped by Davy, "Don't touch. I have to teach you gun safety before you do any shooting," he told her. Then he turned back to the basket, pulled out the box the size of a Rubik's cube, and set it on the counter next to the gun.

Lucy lifted the box from the counter, "Wow," she said, "that's heavy. Are we gonna use all this ammunition?"

Davy gave her a get "real look," then answered, "I don't think so, but we can shoot as long as you want." Lucy quickly clapped her hands with pleasure.

As luck would have it, the other shooters seemed to have left the range, which left it eerily quiet. Davy motioned Lucy to remove her headphones and place them around her neck as he'd already done to his.

"Now, I don't have to yell so you can hear me teach you about gun safety." For the next ten minutes, Davy showed Lucy how to operate the pistol and the safety features. She tried to be patient, but he took so long with what she considered the boring stuff—she just wanted to shoot. She'd belonged to the NRA when she was younger, and her dad and taken her to shoot, so she wasn't stupid about it. But, Davy seemed to enjoy being an instructor, so Lucy bit her tongue to avoid making any smart remarks and let him instruct her.

Finally, Davy pushed a button on the side of the partition that brought a type of binder clip on a wire rushing towards her. When it was just in front of her, he stopped it, then turned around and pulled a target out of the basket, clipped it in place, then pushed the button, sending the silhouette of a man back down the alley.

"Now," he said, turning to Lucy, "you need to load the clip, put your ears back on, and we'll begin to shoot, okay?"

Davy pushed the box of ammunition and the empty clip in front of Lucy. Lucy picked up the empty clip and opened the box of ammo. The bullets were so small, and there were so many of them. Hesitantly she pulled one out and pushed it in the clip, then looked at Davy for confirmation. He nodded his head. She continued until the clip was fully loaded and pushed it into the handle of the gun. Then with a mischievous side glance, she placed her hands as Davy had shown her and slowly brought the gun up to the middle of her chest and pushed it out directed at the target.

"Don't close your eyes," Davy stopped her.

"I thought you were supposed to close one eye," Lucy said.

"Do you want to do it your way or the correct way?" Davy asked seriously.

"The correct way, of course," Lucy answered humbly. "Sheesh," she mumbled quietly. At that moment, a group of people came into the range and took possession of the available spots.

"Sorry, but you can't play around guns," Davy told her apologetically.

"I know." Lucy could feel the atmosphere thicken and her mood dampen.

"Now, what I want you to do, is keep both eyes open and look down the barrel of the gun. Do you see the three white marks at the end of the barrel?" Davy asked as he moved and stood behind Lucy with a hand on each arm.

"Yeah," Lucy managed to say. Her senses were tingling with the close proximity. It was almost a sensory overload with the excitement of shooting and now his hands on her arms. It took her a behemoth effort to concentrate on the target and not how good his hands felt on her arms.

"Those are the sights, and you want to align all three of the lines so that they're even across the top." He crouched down to where his chin almost rested on her shoulder, so they both could view the lines, and gently placed his hands over Lucy's as he helped her align them, "Like that, okay?" Lucy only nodded. "Now, with both eyes open, are lined up all three marks, and the middle one is where you want to aim." He waited as Lucy moved the gun, his hands now returned to her forearms. "Okay, now slowly squeeze the trigger," Davy told her, then gently slid his hands up both her arms before they disengaged themselves altogether, leaving an odd coldness in their wake. Lucy slowly squeezed the trigger. Only after she released the trigger did she realize she'd been holding her breath.

"Did I hit it?" Lucy asked.

"Looks like it. But go ahead and empty the clip before we bring the target forward and see how you did." Lucy raised the gun and aimed, but Davy put his hand on her arm and said, "Remember, when you shoot in succession, don't lift your finger from the trigger, but continue to hold it and then exert the pressure for each shot." With that said, Davy lifted his hand. Once again, she noticed the absence of his touch. She shook her head to clear it and began to squeeze the trigger until she heard a click letting her know the clip was empty.

"Ah-ha!" she said, pleased as she set the gun down on the counter, "I did it. Now let's see how I did, k?" She smiled at Davy, almost childlike in her excitement. Davy pushed the button, and the target seemed to zoom towards them.

Lucy smiled as she looked at the target of a human silhouette hanging in front of her. She hadn't done too bad, she thought, but she waited to hear Davy's assessment of her skills.

"Hm, not bad at all," he said with a smile. "You can feel confident that anyone you shoot at will never walk away with their spleen intact," Davy said with a wink and a chuckle.

"At least I hit the target," Lucy said in good-humored defense as Davy refilled the clip.

"Let me show you how it's done," he said with a cocky tone to his voice as he playfully moved Lucy out of the way. Davy removed Lucy's target and replaced it with a new one. Then pushed the button on the partition and moved it further back than where Lucy's had been—almost to the end of the alleyway.

"Show off," Lucy grumbled loud enough for him to hear. Davy chuckled then fired in rapid succession until the clip was empty while Lucy watched in awe. "Let's see how you did, Mr. Humble," Lucy said as she pushed the button on the partition and the target again zoomed towards them.

Lucy stared at the cluster of holes located center

mass, as they called it, on the target in admiration. She hesitated to say anything to Davy since he stood beside her. With all the strength she could muster and without looking at him said with a shrug, "Eh, it's alright." Then released the target that was still attached to the large binder clip.

"What?" Davy asked in a loud voice.

She could feel Davy's gaze on her and fought her natural inclination to look at him. Instead, she picked up the empty clip and began to dig in the box of ammunition.

"I said, it's alright," Lucy told him again louder.

"Oh ho," Davy said as he laughed, "just alright, huh?" Lucy gave a slight giggle before she felt his arm around her shoulders as the other arm encased her waist, and he tried to tickle her.

"Stop!" she choked out through laughter. "We're not supposed to play around guns," she reminded him.

Still pinned in his arms, Davy said, "Is that a challenge I hear?"

Lucy regrettably pushed away from him and said, "Scared of being shown up by a woman?" She knew she was in a losing battle, but there was no way she could back down from this challenge, no matter how badly she lost.

"You're on," Davy told her and slid the gun in front of her. "I'll even let you go first."

"Gee, thanks." Lucy rolled her eyes sarcastically and turned to retrieve another target from the basket. For the first time since they arrived, Lucy realized they were alone in the shooting gallery.

They took turns shooting for the next ninety minutes. Lucy continued to lose but sustained the challenge, pleased with the lighthearted teasing from Davy and laughter between rounds.

Lucy had just finished her turn when Jan, the girl from the counter, approached them and announced, "We're closing in ten minutes." Lucy hadn't seen her enter, but Davy nodded in her direction, which caused Lucy to turn and see her. Again they were the only two in the shooting range.

"Oh, okay," Davy said as he laughed out loud and removed the headphones he'd placed around his neck. He nudged Lucy and motioned for her to remove her headphones and put them in the basket, "Let's go get some dinner."

They decided on a small café that served California cuisine, and both ordered the Chinese Chicken salad. Once the food arrived at their table, there was silence as they devoured the food. You could hear the music playing in the background more clearly as the other diners left. Finally, it was only Lucy and Davy who remained at their table. With the plates almost clear of food, they both seemed satiated and leaned back in companionable silence.

Lucy began to hum along with the Michael Bublé cover of Nat King Cole's When I Fall in Love that could be heard from the speaker above their table. Lucy quietly sang along as they put the remainder of their salads into boxes to take with them.

"Do you believe in that?" Davy asked as he watched her.

"What?" Lucy asked with a questioning look.

"When you fall in love, it will be forever."

Lucy nodded her head. "Yeah. Do you?"

Davy gave a slight frown then answered, "I thought I did."

"You don't anymore?" Lucy asked in disbelief.

Davy shook his head.

"Just because your first marriage didn't work out doesn't mean your next one couldn't be a forever love."

"Have you been in love?" Davy asked and took a swallow from his glass of water to avoid looking at Lucy.

Lucy tried to hide the hurt that flamed over her face before she answered. "No. No, I've never been in love. I've had lots of crushes but never love." She trailed off at the realization that she had never been in love.

"Why not?" Davy asked as he leaned back in his chair and scrutinized her.

"I don't know. Haven't we already discussed this?" Lucy wanted to change the subject.

"Hm. I don't remember if we did."

"I'm sure we have. Let's talk about something else, like why you get beat up so much," she suggested sitting in the chair.

Davy chuckled and studied Lucy as she acted preoccupied with the fake marble design on their table. "If you've never been in love, then why do you think it could be forever?" He watched for her response.

"I thought guys didn't like to talk about this kind of stuff?" She asked with a curled lip.

Davy shrugged. "You don't have to answer. I was just curious. You seem to have an ideal of how love is." Davy rested his folded arms on the table and waited.

"Well, as corny as it sounds, I know that when I do

fall in love—if I do—it will be forever, and I will give my heart completely." Lucy looked at Davy with raised eyebrows and a gently pursed mouth as she stood and prepared to leave the little café. Davy watched her walk away with a warmth he found unsettling.

Once in his truck, Lucy rested her head on the back of the seat and, with a relaxed smile, watched Davy as he drove. *Today had been such a fun day*, she thought to herself. She hoped he felt the same and that her idea of forever love didn't scare him away.

"Thanks for such a great day," she said.

Davy took his eyes off the road for a moment and said, "I had a good time too." He turned his attention back to the road and traffic with a slight smile playing on his lips.

That was when his phone beeped. He casually glanced at it in his hand, then checked both his side and rearview mirrors. He glanced at Lucy, who had twisted back in her seat where she faced forward.

Davy's phone gave off a barely audible chirp, "Yeah?" he answered. Then listened before he responded, "Cartel?" Davy gave a loud groan, then said, "Now is not a good time for this." He looked in both mirrors again before he pushed his foot down to accelerate the truck. "I see them. They're a couple of cars back. Do you know if there are others?" He asked before he began to weave in and out of traffic.

Lucy became alarmed as he swerved in and out of traffic at a speed higher than was legally allowed. "What are you doing?" She demanded as she tightly gripped the armrest on the door. "Did you say cartel?"

"Don't worry 'bout it," Davy said without looking at her.

"Why are you going so fast?" Lucy asked angrily.

"I wanna get you home. It's past your bedtime," he said with little thought as he concentrated on the road ahead.

"That's okay. You don't need to drive so fast. I'll be okay. It's barely dusk," Lucy said. Davy continued to weave through the traffic, all the while picking up speed. "You better slow down," she warned. But he only increased his speed. "Who are you running from?" Lucy demanded.

"I'm not running from anyone. I don't run," Davy said in a flat tone before giving her a side glance.

"Well, it looks like you're running to me," Lucy stated as she looked out the passenger side window, and her heart began to beat a little faster. Davy swerved the truck over to another lane, launching Lucy's face into the door window, leaving a makeup mask on it. "Dude!" She yelled at him. "What is going on? Are you trying to kill me?" She lifted her arm to wipe off the smudge her face had just left.

Davy continued to watch through the mirrors when his phone chirped, "Where are the cops? Why aren't they stopping this guy?" He asked, then listened to the other person's response. "He's staying on my tail."

Lucy looked out the back window of the truck cab to see what was chasing them. At first, she didn't notice anything but the normal traffic. The more she watched, she noticed a silver sedan that duplicated every move Davy made. "Who's in the car?" She asked as she tipped her head towards the traffic.

"What car?" Davy asked.

"The one behind us that makes every move you make!" Lucy yelled at him over the noise the truck made as he sped up even more.

"Just some people I don't care to see right now. Don't worry; you're okay." His phone chirped. "They're close," he said into the phone, "get 'em off my tail. I've got cargo." Davy clicked the phone off again.

"What did you do? Why don't you want to see them?' Lucy fired at him as she watched him drive up the ramp and enter the freeway, only to increase his speed even more. "Wait, cargo?! Did you just call me cargo? Who are you?" Lucy demanded, but Davy ignored her.

Davy's phone chirped again. He quickly answered it, "Where are you?" Again, he listened as the person on the other end of the line spoke before he said, "And the cops?" He asked, then nodded his head, "Can you handle them?" He hung up without saying goodbye.

Lucy stared at him with her mouth open. She didn't know whether to be attracted to him at this moment or scared as the truck sped through traffic. "What's going on? Are we gonna die?" Lucy asked uneasily as Davy pulled the truck through the two right lanes and exited the freeway.

"Not tonight," He responded. He proceeded to do a rolling stop at the end of the ramp before he turned right and drove down the darkened street next to the freeway. Then turned left off that road onto another road that had no streetlights, pulled over off the street, turned off the truck's engine and lights, and parked. He slightly lifted his shirt to expose a handgun holstered. He placed his hand on it at the ready.

Lucy's heart was beating one thousand beats per minute as they sat parked. Neither moved nor spoke. *Who was this guy? Why had she thought she could trust him?* Was he gonna hurt her? She gulped. She needed to be able to run if he made any moves toward her. She felt for the door handle very slowly to see if it would move or if he had locked her in.

"Don't open that door," he commanded her without a glance her way. The tone in his voice told her he wasn't kidding around. Slowly she released the handle and placed both hands in her lap. Lucy sat in silence for what seemed like hours, watching Davy. Suddenly two cars sped by, followed by two cruisers flashing their colorful lights.

Davy's phone gave another barely audible chirp that he answered instantly, "Yeah, we're a go." Then hung up. Lucy stared at him in shock. *Who was this guy?*

As the cars disappeared down the street, Davy turned on the engine and backed out of the road. Then, without turning on his lights, he sped in the opposite direction until they came to the busiest part of the downtown area. He pulled the truck over to the sidewalk, where there were lots of pedestrians.

"Go into that bookstore," he said and pointed to the store on her side of the truck, "wait for one hour, then call an Uber and go home."

"You can't take me home?" She asked, confused.

"No. Ya gotta go. Now." Davey urged her as he leaned across and opened her door. When she didn't move, he gently pushed her before he said, "Please, ya gotta go now."

Lucy slid out of the truck onto the sidewalk, shocked by how the nice afternoon had taken a one-hundred-and-eighty-degree turn. She turned to see Davy reach for her door and begin to pull it close, but stopped and said, "Lucy! Go inside the bookstore. Remember what I told you to do. I gotta go." With that, he closed the door and pulled into traffic, and sped off. She watched as he finally turned on his lights.

"Who are you!" Lucy said, then turned and did as he told her, unaware of the ever-present Chevy Nova idling at the end of the block.

Chapter 26

"It was crazy," Lucy told Annie as they entered the dog park with Sarge. "We'd had such a great day, he seemed relaxed and . . ." suddenly she stopped and looked around. "This is the dog park?" She marveled at the beautifully manicured lawn surrounded by the elegant wrought iron fence. "This is better than the parks for people," she said, turning a full circle.

Annie laughed, "Just be careful where you step. Most people pick up after their dogs, but there might still—"

"Eeeew!" Lucy lifted her left foot and looked. "Oh, that is disgusting," she grimaced as she drug her foot along the grass to remove the crap that clung to her shoe. "These were new shoes," she lamented.

"Sorry, but I did try to warn you," Annie said as she unhooked Sarge's collar so he could run freely. "Why don't we sit down," she said as she led Lucy towards a bench. "You can scrape your shoe on that if you'd like," Annie explained as she pointed at a small metal divider placed next to the bench.

"Thank heavens," Lucy said as she scraped her left shoe across it again and again before she lifted her foot to check for any residue.

"So, you were telling me about your date with Davy," Annie said teasingly.

"It wasn't a date. We're just friends," Lucy told her.

"Uh-huh. Sarge! Stop that," she yelled at Sarge as he nipped a smaller dog, then she looked at Lucy expectantly.

"Well, after the shooting range, then everything just changed."

"How so?"

"Well, we'd just finished dinner and were in the truck when he got a call on his phone, which didn't really ring but chirped. Have you ever heard a phone chirp before?" Lucy asked.

"I don't think so."

"I was so surprised when he answered his phone. I mean, how in the heck did he even hear it? I mean, it was a chirp—a barely audible chirp at that. Yet he'd answer it every time. I barely heard it. It was so quiet and to hear it in his truck—."

"Anyway—," Annie interrupted Lucy's tangent. She was used to them and had learned the best way to get her back on track was to interrupt rather than wait for her to finish.

"What? Oh, where was I?" she asked.

"His phone had chirped."

"Oh, that's right." So Lucy proceeded to tell her about the ride and the calls and everything that happened until he dropped her at the bookstore.

"You heard him mention the Cartel?" Annie asked.

Lucy nodded. "Yeah, I swear."

"But then, he just left you on the street and told you to get a ride home?" Annie asked, shocked.

"Well, yeah. And then he sped off in traffic. I haven't heard from him since. Who knows what happened to him after that."

"Maybe he's dead," Annie suggested. "If not, he should be. What kind of man leaves his date on the side of the road to find her way home?"

"I know, right," Lucy said in agreement. "But again, we weren't on a date, and he left me on the sidewalk, not on the side of the road, technically.

"So, what are you going to do the next time he calls or texts? Are you going to meet him or write him off?" Annie asked, then said, "Wait, don't answer yet." She rose from the bench and called to Sarge, who obediently ran to her. She put the leash on him and said, "Sit!" Then she sat and looked at Lucy, "Well?"

"Well, what?" Lucy asked. She'd lost her train of thought as she watched Annie.

"What are you gonna do the next time Davy contacts you?"

"Probably meet him," Lucy said lightly, then laughed. Annie shook her head. "What?" Lucy asked good-naturedly.

"What are you gonna do if he leaves you in the street again?"

"He didn't leave me in the street," Lucy corrected her.

Annie looked at her curiously and asked, "What

about those people you saw at the beach? What about June?"

"He doesn't know I know about that or his girlfriend June bug," Lucy said her name sarcastically. "As far as he's concerned, I rode away on my bike." Lucy reminded her.

"Don't you think it's strange?"

"Of course. But I don't know what to do. I've never been in this situation before."

"You better be careful. This could go in several different directions—and none of them good," Annie said with concern. She had known Lucy long enough to be familiar with the irregular situations she had a knack of getting herself into and felt it best to warn her, although it wouldn't do any good.

That night Lucy's dream turned into a nightmare. The dream started as it always did with her in the library, then it changed. Suddenly she was hiding from someone—not Mr. Wonderful. She crouched down low at the end of a bookshelf. She glanced at her hand and saw that it was covered with blood. She slowly crawled along the aisle. With each movement, she could feel her body tremble as if she'd collapse at any moment. Finally, she came to the end of the book aisle and, with fractured breaths, cautiously looked around the back of the bookcase. Suddenly she was lifted off the floor by the pointed toe of a cowboy boot in the middle of her stomach.

She cried out in pain, "Davy!" Then let out a blood-curdling scream as a hand grabbed her hair and pulled her head back. She stared into Sal's face and saw him lift his other anvil size fist and watched it descend until she felt this crashing pain against her temple, and everything went black.

Lucy bolted upright in her bed, drenched with sweat and trembling so hard her bed frame was shaking. Quickly she leaned over and turned on the light on her bedside table and welcomed with relief the light as it chased away the dark. The dream seemed so real that all Lucy could do was sit in her bed and sob. This was the only way she knew to rid herself of the intense emotions the nightmare had caused. She could no longer call it a dream. She reached for her phone but didn't know who to call. She looked at her phone's face; that showed it was one-thirty. Annie would kill her if she woke her this early again. *Who will help?* Exhausted, she sat in her bed as tears rolled down her face.

With fingers that trembled, she typed:

Are you there?

Are you there!!

She sat back and waited. The nightmare kept playing in her mind. She put her hand to her stomach to assuage the pain she thought she felt, only to remember that it hadn't really happened. Solemnly she waited in her bed, not moving but hoping that she'd get a response. She jumped when her phone chimed.

Yeah, I'm here. Wassup?

Are you okay?

> *Yeah, I'm fine
> now.*

What's the matter?

Lucy?

> *Sorry, I'm okay—just a bad
> dream.*

*About me? Gee, I told ya I'd
give you a rematch with the
target
shooting.* 🙂

Lucy lightly laughed at Davy's response. Then, she felt her body begin to relax with the reassurance that he was okay.

> *Where are you?*

> *In my truck. Just returned
> from a flight.*

> *Do you need me to come
> over?*

Lucy smiled at his text, then blew her nose before she responded.

> *No, I'm good. Thanks.*

Goodnight.

Davy frowned at his phone. He'd never received a text from Lucy like that before. He set his phone aside, put his truck in reverse, and then drove towards the parking lot exit.

It only took Davy thirty minutes to get to Lucy's place at this time of day from the airport. Her street was quiet, so he parked in a spot to have a good line of vision to her home. He could see the light on in one of the windows. With Sal and Johnny aware of her, he wasn't comfortable getting texts from her like that, especially at such a late hour. He would wait and watch to make sure she was okay for the rest of the night until she left for work.

Lucy tried to sleep, but as soon as she'd fall asleep, the nightmare would start from the beginning and end with her scream. She feared falling asleep because of the pain she'd experience in the dream and the fear that would flood over her that something had happened to Davy. With relief, she heard the beginning strains of AC/DC's Thunderstruck signaling that it was time to get up.

Lucy dragged herself into the bathroom and looked in the mirror. She recoiled like a vampire from a cross in horror at what stared back at her from the mirror. The pale color of her face accentuated the dark circles under her eyes. Her hair looked as though she'd put her finger in an electrical socket. What miracle would make her presentable for the office, she wondered to herself as she tried to moosh the curls into some sort of style. She looked at herself and groaned aloud.

As Lucy prepared for work, her mind went over the nightmare, again and again. She needed to decipher what it all meant. She was surprised that she'd call out for Davy as she did. Did that mean he was there in the library? Or was it wishful thinking on her part that he'd save her? Why would she think that in the dream? The questions walked through her mind like a slow-motion parade, but the reoccurring question was always, who is Davy? What was his secret?

Lucy didn't recoil as much the next time she looked in her mirror. But instead, she gave a weak smile at her reflection. It looked as if the makeup she'd spackled on her face covered all the signs of no sleep and with her hair tamed into a ponytail. She grabbed her keys and walked out the door.

Davy sat up in his truck when he saw Lucy step outside her door. He was surprised to see the exhaustion that seemed to permeate from her as she descended the stairs, then paused by the driver's side door before she opened it and slid in behind the steering wheel. He grabbed the baseball hat he kept on his dashboard and put it on his head to disguise himself before turning the key and starting the truck motor, ready to follow her. He hoped she was too tired even to notice, but to be safe, he'd stay three or four cars away from her. Slowly he pulled away from the curb and followed Lucy down the street before he turned off and shadowed her with a block between them. First, he wanted to make sure she made it to work safely; then, he'd go home and grab some sleep.

Chapter 27

"Headquarters wants to end this operation," Joel told Davy as they sat on a bench on a cliff that overlooked the ocean.

"Why so soon?" Davy asked; he'd only been out a couple of years. These operations are known to take five years or more.

"We've been quietly arresting the flyers that are involved not to alarm those yet to be arrested. But we've got to get the head of this ring before we close it completely," Joel told him.

Davy nodded his head but remained silent.

"Do you think you could rouse Strega out of hiding?"

Davy nodded again. "I think I can if I steal enough from him." Joel cocked an eyebrow. "Sal and Johnny hate me since the Feds confiscated that big shipment of drugs. They blame me since I'm the supplier's contact," he explained.

"Do you think you can finish this and live, or should

we just pull the plug now?" Joel asked with concern.

Davy started to say something, then stopped. "Of course. I might be the worse for wear, but I'll live," he said, surprised at Joel's comment.

"We'll need to speed it up then. Do you think that's possible?"

"We have that big shipment that's coming in," Davy said thoughtfully. "I can tell them the supplier wants more money, or he'll stop the transport."

"Do you think that will bring the Strega's head out of the hole?" Joel asked.

"It should. This shipment's huge. It's been all over the world to launder it, and now it comes here."

"This is gonna get very intense. I'll assign a team to shadow you again," Joel told him.

Davy nodded and bit the side of his lip as he contemplated the future.

***

"It's the oddest thing," Lucy told Annie as they sat in a small Italian restaurant waiting for their food.

"What is? That he's never at his house? That these guys keep dropping off packages? Or that you're stalking him?" Annie asked as she bit into a breadstick. "I'm starving."

"All of it, I guess, except for the part about me stalking him," Lucy told her.

"Well, he was there the last time—you know, when he stopped you?"

"True," Lucy said thoughtfully. "That was fortuitous

for me, I guess."

"Why do you say that?" Annie asked.

"If he hadn't been there, then I could've seen where they put the packages, and then I could have seen what is in them." Lucy frowned in thought.

"Those guys could be dangerous."

"If they're dangerous, then what is he doing with them, Annie?" Lucy asked.

"Maybe you should just forget about those packages and him," Annie said.

Lucy furrowed her brow. "It's too late for that— forgetting about the packages. But him?" Lucy shrugged her shoulders.

"I think you like this guy more than as just a friend," Annie accused her.

"What if I did? What difference would that make? I told you about Junie."

"Yeah," Annie said in agreement. "But, if he is so into that little snack time girl, why would he spend so much time with you? Why would he bring you tea? Why would he care if you were mad or not?"

"I know. Why?" Lucy asked.

Just then, the waiter came with the food they'd ordered. It smelled so good. Lucy had forgotten how hungry she was as she took her first bite of the Caprese salad.

"Oh," Lucy moaned, "this is so good."

Annie nodded in agreement, then asked between bites, "So, what are you gonna do?"

Lucy set her fork down and scrunched her lips to one side in thought. "I'm not sure. But something's going on.

I don't know if I need to go to the cops or what?"

"You can't go to the cops. What would you tell them?" Annie asked.

"But, what if it's drugs that are in those packages?"

"Do you really think Davy would be a drug smuggler?" Annie asked, amazed.

Lucy sighed, "I truly hope not. He doesn't seem like it, but—,"

"If he's a drug smuggler, then you'd better run. That is the last thing you wanna get involved in. I watch those true crime shows. That could really end up bad," Annie warned.

"I know. I watch those shows too," Lucy said as she leaned on the table and rested her chin in her hands. "But, I gotta find out what is going on."

"No, you don't," Annie replied. She took a drink of her water as she studied Lucy, who was deep in thought. "You're going back there, aren't you?"

"I have to," Lucy said with determination. "I do like this guy, and even though he has his little girlfriend, and I don't have a life, I need to do this."

"Why?" Annie asked, confused. "Why put yourself in danger to save him for the little one?"

"Because he's my friend."

"He was a Navy Seal. I'm sure he can handle this without you and your financial knowledge—totally two different worlds there," Annie said. Lucy gave her the "get real" look. Annie continued, "Seriously, what are you gonna do if you get in a dangerous situation? Put in a trade? Open a new account? Hit them with your planner or collection of pens?"

Lucy scowled at her, then her face brightened. "Hopefully, it won't come to that. Especially if I have someone to keep watch while I go and look," Lucy told her with a slight hopeful grin.

"Are you crazy? You think I'm gonna put my life in danger like that? Especially for a guy I have no chance in hell with?" Annie asked in disbelief.

Lucy smiled as she rubbed her hands together mischievously. "Neither of us will have a chance with him, but isn't it our patriotic duty to stop crime when we see it happen?"

"Patriotic duty? Get outta here." Annie said with a dismissive wave and waited expectantly. "Are you serious?" She asked in disbelief.

Lucy smiled and wiggled her eyebrows in anticipation. "Yup. Do you wanna come and be on the lookout? It would really help," Lucy said to convince her.

Annie rolled her eyes as she weighed the idea and options before she said, "You're gonna go whether I go with you or not, though, aren't you?"

Lucy nodded her head. "Annie, you don't even need to get out of my car. I'll leave the keys, so if anything happens, you can get away, k?" Lucy continued to convince Annie to come. Even though Lucy would still go alone if she had to, she would feel safer knowing that Annie was there if something happened. "But, I'm sure nothing will happen."

As Annie slid out of the booth, she dryly said, "Famous last words."

***

Sal seethed as he watched Johnny fall to the ground as he came back over the fence from Davy's backyard empty-handed, once again. He charged out of his car, unable to contain his anger anymore.

"There's no money a—," Johnny started to say as he approached Sal with his hands spread wide only to be met by Sal's huge fist against his jaw. Johnny flew back as he crashed to the hard ground. "What I do?" He asked as he held his jaw.

"I don't wanna hear it! He has stolen from us for the last time," Sal stood over Johnny with clenched fists.

"What are we gonna do about it?" Johnny asked, rubbing his jaw. "She's not gonna be happy."

"We aren't gonna tell her. We're gonna fix it ourselves," Sal picked Johnny up by his collar and stared him in the eyes to

"How? She's gonna know we don't have the money, and one of us will pay."

"It's not gonna be me," Sal said with a threatening tone in his voice.

"So, what are we gonna do?" Johnny asked as he made a wide circle around Sal, who stood like a mountain in the middle of Davy's front yard.

"Get his attention," Sal growled and turned back towards his car.

"How?" Johnny asked as he opened the passenger side door.

"Take what is his, then make him pay for it." With Sal's long legs, in a little over two strides, he was beside his car. Sal yanked the door open, then turned back towards Davy's house and said, "He's stolen from us for the last time."

***

Davy answered his phone with caution when he saw Sal's name appear. "Yeah?" was all he said.

"Stopped by your place the other night?" Sal said in his deep voice.

"And?" Davy responded.

"You weren't there, and neither was the package," Sal revealed to him. "Where were you?"

"Not that it's any of your business," Davy said irritably, "but I was working."

"If you were working, then where's the money you owe us?"

"You'll get it," Davy responded.

"We better. The boss ain't too happy with you not following through on your part."

"I always follow through. Not my problem if you don't have the money. I just have to leave it for you to pick up."

"I told the boss you weren't the right person to handle the deliveries," Sal said, "I knew you'd screw it up or steal it."

"What'd you call for?" Davy asked impatiently.

"Like I said, I stopped by your place."

Davy sighed. "So. You missed me?"

"You weren't there, but a lady was. She's been there a couple of times."

"What lady?" Davy asked as he tried to keep any

emotion out of his voice.

"My question is, does she have the stuff? Is she the one we should contact?"

Davy's heart began to pound in his chest. It had to be Lucy. Why was she at his place? Davy inwardly groaned. How was he going to protect her if she wouldn't stay out of his business? "I don't know who you're talking about. Maybe you've been going to the wrong location."

***

"Okay, I'll just be a minute," Lucy told Annie as she pulled into her parking spot. They'd already stopped off at Annie's so she could change into some dark clothes.

"I'll just come in with you," Annie said as she began to open the door.

"Nah, it'll just take me a couple of minutes. I promise it won't take me long," Lucy told her as she exited her truck.

"You better hurry. I don't want to sit out here all night," Annie called after her as she watched her walk up the stairs and enter her apartment. She pulled her phone out of her purse and resigned herself to checking her messages while she waited.

Annie was unaware of the passing of time until she noticed her battery level was showing bright red. That's when she realized it had taken Lucy longer than it should to change her clothes; she tapped in a text before her phone died and hoped it went through.

Hurry up!

Within seconds she heard a chime and looked over to see the outline glow from Lucy's phone as it laid face down on the driver seat. Frustrated, Annie reached for the door handle to get her when, at the same time, she saw the screen door to Lucy's place open.

"You better be ready," Annie muttered as she sat back expectantly.

But it wasn't Lucy who exited out her door. Instead, a man with bleached blonde hair and a dark goatee wearing an open Hawaiian shirt over a blue wife-beater tank top. He was followed by Lucy, who stumbled out the door as if pushed, still in the clothes she'd worn to dinner. She was followed by a mountain of a man that resembled Charlie Brown.

"What the heck?" Annie quietly exclaimed as she did a double-take.

She watched the threesome descend the stairs. In the glow from the building's lights and Lucy's porch light, she could see that the little guy in front had blood on his jaw that he sporadically wiped on his pants. When she saw Lucy, she bit her hand to stifle a cry—which would have given her away. Lucy limped down the stairs with her hands tied with duct tape; her face was swollen and covered with blood; her right shoulder hung limply out of place. She glanced where Annie sat in the dark and slightly shook her head before the mountain pushed her and caused her to tumble down the last two steps only to land on her knees before she did a face plant into the concrete. Then he roughly pulled her up. Annie heard Lucy cry out, but the mountain put his massive hand over her mouth and moved her toward another spot down the way where a red Chevy Nova was parked.

Annie anxiously searched for any sign of life in the near vicinity from inside the car, but the neighborhood was so quiet not even a dog barked. She tried to turn her phone on, but there was no battery power. She watched as the two men marched Lucy to the red car and shoved her into the back seat with the little guy right behind her. At the same time, the mountain got into the driver's seat, and the car sped away. Annie tried to memorize the license plate as the car disappeared.

"Oh my gosh, oh my gosh, oh my gosh," Annie repeated aloud as she tried to figure out what to do. Should she call the police? Should she chase after them herself? What would she do once she caught up with them? All these questions were racing through her mind when she saw Lucy's phone. She'd forgotten that Lucy had left it there. She grabbed the phone and tried to open it, but she needed Lucy's fingerprint to do so. She sat in shock as her heart raced and tears came to her eyes.

Where were Lucy's keys? They weren't in the ignition. Annie desperately looked under the driver's seat, in the side pocket, under the mat. Was she stuck here? *Lucy did not plan this well at all*, Annie told herself. Nevertheless, the fear that she may have just seen her friend alive for the last time spurred her into action.

Confident the car with Lucy and the two men were gone, she tried to memorize the license plate she'd seen since she didn't have paper or pen to write it on and couldn't take a picture of it with her phone.

Desperate for some help, Annie ran to the

neighboring homes and banged on the doors one at a time if someone were around, and she could get some help, but with it being a three-day weekend. Everyone was out of town, it seemed, but Lucy, the little man, and the mountain.

Frozen in fear, Annie stood alone in her friend's yard at a loss of what to do. When she heard the beep of a text notification, she looked at Lucy's phone in time to see that the text was from Davy Jones. *How would she get in touch with this guy?* She asked herself as she watched the phone's screen return to black. Then a thought struck her; she turned towards the stairs she'd seen Lucy come down moments before. With much trepidation, Annie cautiously walked up the stairs to an already open door.

Annie could barely see into the darkened apartment where the blinds were still closed, and no lights were on inside. She only had the light from the porch until she remembered a triple light switch near the second bedroom doorway. Annie reached across and flipped the first switch; nothing happened. She flipped the second one and was instantly hit with a warm light that quickly spread, illuminating the ravaged room. Annie looked in horror at the slashed cushions from her wonderful old couch on the floor. The large, overstuffed ottoman had been sliced open, and stuffing spilled out, leaving some on the rug in front of her gas fireplace. All the pictures on her walls had been tossed on the floor, with the glass busted in each one.

"Now that's just mean," Annie said aloud when she picked up the picture of Lucy's dad from where it rested under broken glass with a boot print across it.

Upon further inspection of Lucy's place, Annie also

saw her dining table busted, her refrigerator door pulled off, and all the contents on the floor in front of it. It almost looked like her place was hit by an earthquake, but she knew it was the work of that mountain guy she'd seen. Annie stood amid the mess and tried to get her bearings. Then she remembered that Lucy had a little green book she kept all her passwords in, just in case she forgot one of them. If she could only remember where Lucy kept it— she hoped the Mountain hadn't found it to destroy.

Annie turned back towards the opened front door but went into the closed door next to it instead of walking out. *Had they only destroyed the living room?* She hoped. But upon entry into the room, she found they had done just as much damage in that room; there just wasn't as much in it to break. Annie could see under the tipped-over armoire a glimpse of fabric that looked familiar to her. She tried to lift the emptied armoire up but only lifted it enough to pull out the broken shamble of the bag Lucy took with her to work, but that was enough. She felt inside the pockets, then the main pocket, when she felt a small square object at the very bottom that had got caught under one of the bars that connected the wheels.

"Perfect," Annie said as she held the little green book in her hand. This was indeed a blessing; otherwise, how would she be able to help her friend? She removed the elastic that held it shut and turned page by page by page, hoping that Lucy had put the password to her phone in there. When she came to the last page with no writing on it, she realized she hadn't seen the password.

Annie sat on the back of the overstuffed chair Lucy had been so proud of when she purchased it as part of the deal when she bought her beloved couch. She was deep in thought when she heard another notification that Lucy had received another text. She pulled the phone out of the back pocket of her skinny jeans in time to witness a third text that came from Davy.

> *I got back early. Wanna get*
> *some tea?*

Annie stared at the text as it disappeared into the darkness of her phone again. She had to find a way to let Davy know that Lucy was in danger, but how would she unlock Lucy's phone? She opened the green book and looked at all the passwords again. There were many different ones, but there was also one that seemed to repeat more than the others. *Is that the one that will open the phone?* She wondered. She pushed the button on Lucy's phone to light up the screen, swiped up, so the request for the password appeared and punched in: D-R-8-1-M-E-R-! Annie held her breath until she saw the smiling face of Lucy's dad. It worked! She now had access to the phone.

Chapter 28

Once inside the Chevy Nova, the little guy placed a piece across her mouth. Lucy sat in the back and fought the waves of pain that passed through her body. Then, with the little guy, Johnny, seated next to her, she stared at the back of the big guy, Sal's head. He'd opened the small side window, lit a cigarette, and held it by the tip out the window.

"You better keep that stink outside," Sal warned. "I don't want my car smelling of smoke. She doesn't like it."

"I'm careful," Johnny said as he sucked another lungful of smoke, held his breath, then put his lips close to the opening of the little window and blew it out. *Does he know how silly he looks doing that?* Lucy wondered as she stifled a cough caused by the smoke that didn't escape its small confines.

As her head lolled against the window, she observed her captors. *They're so different from one another*, Lucy thought. How were they friends? Or were they just colleagues? Who was this "she" the big guy kept

335

mentioning? Whoever she was, it seemed as though the mountain and Johnny were scared of her. She studied Sal's face through the rearview mirror. He wasn't a bad-looking guy if you closed one eye and squinted with the other and liked the Peanuts cartoon. But he was just so big and mean. Lucy was sure her face was swollen from where he'd hit her. *But was it as round as his head?* She mused to herself.

"Ugh," she involuntarily expelled at the wave of pain in her face when the car bumped over a pothole. Johnny gave her a menacing look. Lucy winced as the car bumped again. She saw Sal sneer at her through the rearview mirror.

"Do you think the boss will be happy that we got his girlfriend?" Johnny asked Sal from beside Lucy in the back seat. *Whose girlfriend?* She wondered.

"If it gets his attention and we get what we paid for, I don't think she'll care," Sal snarled.

"What if it doesn't work?" Johnny asked with a frown.

"Then she becomes dead weight," Sal growled as he glared at Lucy in the mirror.

Lucy struggled to maintain consciousness as she tried to make sense of their conversation but had so many questions: *Who were they talking about? Why did they have her? Would anyone rescue her?*

"He's not gonna like that we have his girlfriend," Johnny stated.

"I don't care what he likes," Sal barked at Johnny. "I want what's ours!"

Sal and Johnny's voices began to overshadow the

thoughts in her head as she sat in the back of the car. They mentioned someone's girlfriend. *Is it me? If so, whose girlfriend am I supposed to be? If it is me, why am I just learning about him now?*

***

"What do you mean they took her?" Davy asked anxiously.

"Just what I told you. And you better come over and see what they did to Lucy's place," Annie told him. She'd never spoken with Davy before, but she could see why Lucy liked it so much. He sounded very masculine and sexy.

"Get a grip, girl," she said aloud. Now wasn't the time to follow her lust. Her friend was missing.

"Did you say something?" Davy asked.

"Uh, no." Annie fought the rush of heat that rose in her face at getting caught talking to herself.

"Don't leave until I get there," he told her.

"Okay," Annie rolled her eyes. *Where would I go?* She thought to herself. She didn't have any transportation. And she still needed to recharge her phone. "Should I call the cops?" Annie asked.

"No," Davy said definitively. "Just wait until I get there." Annie took the phone away from her ear. He'd hung up just like that. When he'd picked up, and she told him what happened, there was no mistaking the concern that emanated from his voice.

***

"They've taken her," Davy said into his phone as he threw his backpack over onto the passenger seat in his truck. He'd just exited the plane from his final flight as a FAM when he received the call from Annie. He'd been afraid this would happen but hadn't known how to stop Lucy from interfering without blowing his cover.

"Whose taken who?" Joel asked from the other end of the line.

"Sal and Johnny. They've taken a civilian," Davy told him as he started his truck and backed out of his parking spot.

"Who's the civilian?" Joel asked. Davy had wanted to avoid having this conversation because he didn't want to hear him say he told him so, but now it was unavoidable. "Who's the civilian?" Joel asked again firmly.

Davy took a deep breath a said, "My friend."

"Your friend?" Joel asked. "Oh no," he groaned, "is this THE friend?"

Davy paused for only a moment before he responded, "Yeah. Her."

Joel sighed, "I thought you were going to take care of it."

"I thought I had. But she isn't one to give up easily, I guess." Davy said as he sped down the freeway.

"What's her name?" Joel asked.

"Lucy,"

"Lucy, what?"

"Lyman, Lucy Lyman."

"How do you know the Italians have her?"

"Her friend called. Lucy hadn't taken her phone, so she found my number on there and called," Davy told Joel.

"Did she call the police?" Joel asked.

"I told her not to. I told her to wait until I got there," Davy said.

"Okay, I'll send a couple of agents over to look at her place and pull whatever evidence they can find."

"They beat her up," Davy said with an effort to keep his voice even.

"They what?" Joel asked, stunned.

"Yeah, from what her friend said. When she came out of the apartment, she looked pretty beaten up. She said they even pushed her down the stairs, those sons of—"

"They pushed her down the stairs?!" Joel interrupted in disbelief. "They must think she has something they want."

"They think something, but it won't be for long," Davy said threateningly. He knew where they'd taken her. But why had they beaten her up when it was him they were after?

"Do you think they did this under orders from their boss?" Joel asked.

"It doesn't matter. They did it, and now I have to do something back," Davy said with finality.

"We might be able to use this as a way to pull the head of the snake out of hiding," Joel said.

"I have to get Lucy."

"There are always casualties in war," Joel reminded him.

"Not this time, not Lucy."

"You're taking this personally," Joel said and waited for Davy's admission.

"I'm at her place. I'll text you her address," Davy said, abruptly ending the call.

Annie watched the black truck pull into the parking spot next to Lucy's 4Runner. *This has to be him,* she thought to herself as she watched a tall, well-built man step out of the truck and walk towards her. She stood as he approached.

"Are you Annie?" he asked. She nodded. "Thanks for calling me. How long ago was she taken?" He asked with a deathly calm to his voice.

"Uhm," Annie said, unnerved by his tone, "it's been about an hour now. I couldn't get into her phone until I found her password; she had it set up to use her finger—," Annie felt herself babbling to him from nerves. Davy nodded his head as he passed by her and proceeded up to Lucy's place.

Annie hesitantly followed Davy up the stairs and found herself wishing Lucy were there to see him in action. She'd love how he took over and was just so darn masculine. She shook her head to clear it of these lustful thoughts—it so wasn't the time.

Davy took one step into Lucy's home and stopped. He remembered how it looked when they'd watched the Italian movie. He looked at the white front door that now had a smear of blood on it. He seethed with anger but knew he had to control it to do his job.

Without looking at Annie, he asked, "The two guys were already here when Lucy got home?"

"They had to have been. I only saw them when they

walked out with her."

Davy turned towards Annie and asked, "What did they look like?"

"There were two of them: a little guy and then the other was the size of a mountain. He seemed bigger than you," Annie scrunched her face apologetically.

He nodded his head as he said, "I know who they are." Annie felt a shiver up her spine at the tone in his voice and the flatness of his eyes. "I need you to go home and don't tell anyone about this, please."

"Shouldn't I call the police and report this?" Annie asked, confused.

"No, I'll take care of this." Davy continued to walk through the mess, then squatted down to look more closely at some drops of blood on the floor.

"Lucy was my ride," Annie confessed. "My phone is dead, so I can't call anyone," she continued to tell him.

Davy looked up at her as if he'd forgotten she was there. He stood and said, "I'll get a car to take you home." Then he punched a button on his phone and proceeded to give Lucy's address and Annie's description before he hung up. "If you'll wait outside, a car will be here soon that will take you home. The driver's name is Travis."

"Oh-okay," Annie stuttered as Davy moved her towards the door.

"He'll be here in a matter of minutes if he isn't already," Davy told her before he returned his attention to the mess in Lucy's home.

As Annie slowly descended the stairs, she pondered about what Lucy had gotten herself involved in, and she feared for the worst. Would she see her friend again?

Alive?

Annie just stepped off the bottom step in time to see a black Cadillac drive up and stop just behind where Lucy and Davy's vehicles were parked. At first, she didn't register what that meant until a tall, clean-shaven, handsome man exited and approached.

"Good evening ma'am, my name is Travis. I'm here to give you a ride home," he said in a deep voice followed by a smile that could melt an iceberg. Annie nodded her acknowledgment as if in a trance, then allowed him to lead her to the rear passenger door. He opened it without Annie needing to stop for a second and wait. *Who are these guys?* She wondered as she looked into his face while she sat on the seat then swung her legs in. Without another word, Travis closed the door.

Chapter 29

Davy and Joel stood amidst the mess that used to be Lucy's home. They watched the other agents as they gathered fragments of residual objects and placed them in plastic bags. One stood at the front door and swabbed at the blood smear before she put it in a tube and sealed it closed.

"She walked out of here?" Joel asked as he picked up a torn picture from the floor and placed it on the counter nearby.

"Yes," Davy answered tersely. "Her friend said she'd seen them lead her to a car—the Chevy Nova. She was alive, badly beaten, but alive."

Joel studied Davy before he responded, "Maybe you're too close to this to be able to see this to the end." Joel had known Davy for a long time and had never seen a case affect him like this one. He was sure it was due to the girl.

"No, I have to finish this. They took Lucy because of me. I have to get her back, alive."

"I can send someone else in to finish this," Joel told him.

"No," Davy said definitively. "This is mine to finish. Now they've made it personal."

"What are you going to do?" Joel asked him warily as he watched Davy walk to her kitchen, where the refrigerator had been pushed over from the wall with the door pulled off and leaning haphazardly against the opposite counter.

Davy examined the room, then walked to where the refrigerator rested against the counter and pushed it upright into its spot against the wall, then leaned the door against it. Once he did this, he moved further into the kitchen, stepping over the food that had spilled onto the floor. Davy hated what these guys must have done to Lucy and mentally beat himself up for not being there to protect her. Why had he gotten sloppy and put her in such danger? Why did he let her get under his skin? Why did he care? Was his desire for companionship overshadowing his obligations? Joel patiently waited as he observed Davy's reaction to the situation.

"I think we need to end this thing and raid the place," Davy said with suppressed anger.

Joel stopped, surprised, "You're ready to raid the warehouse?"

"I have to save Lucy and settle a disagreement," Davy said as he adjusted the baseball cap on his head.

"You can't take this personally," Joel reminded him.

"It became personal when they took my friend," Davy stated.

"This operation is much bigger than just your

girlfriend," Joel told him.

Davy glared at Joel, "You don't think I know that? I've been working on this for two years. I let my guard down, and now my friend, someone I care about, her life is in danger."

Joel arched an eyebrow at Davy's response. He knew Davy was exhausted. He'd worked two years on this operation and before that six years in the cartel. Stress was 24/7. Joel couldn't blame him for needing some sort of release, but it was too bad it might cause the death of an innocent woman.

"I'll give the go-ahead for the flyers that are transporting drugs through LAX to be arrested at the same time we do the raid," he told Davy, who silently nodded. "Then we can set the trap to catch the snake."

"But first, I need to get Lucy out of there," Davy said as if he were thinking aloud.

Joel marveled at the coolness of his manner. He knew, from years of experience, that the wheels were turning in his head, putting together a plan of attack. Heaven help the men who crossed him, for they never made that mistake twice.

"When do you want to do the raid? Later today?" Joel asked since it was almost

Davy walked out the door and told him over his shoulder, "No. I'm not gonna leave her to suffer more than she has already. I have to get her out now."

"When do you want to move?" Joel asked as he followed Davy down the stairs holding his phone.

"Give me an hour." Davy pulled open his truck's door and stepped in. "I'll see ya there," Davy told him from inside his truck. His window was down, expelling the loud beat of AC/DC's Thunderstruck from its stereo.

"Right behind ya," Joel said as he put the phone to his ear, already making a call as he walked to his car. Then, for a moment, he turned and watched Davy speed out of Lucy's neighborhood down her street. "He better not get pulled over," he said aloud to no one.

***

"What in the heck are you doing bringing her here?" the boss yelled as Sal and Johnny leaned against an old table on its side.

"We thought she had our drugs," Johnny admitted.

"You thought she had your drugs," the boss yelled. "Why? Why would that amazon have your drugs?"

Sal looked down at the tiny but deadly bundle of fire in fear. He had seen Junie gut a man his size for no reason. She was little but dangerous.

"She's Davy's friend," Johnny offered. Junie jerked her head toward him, causing her barbie like golden ponytail to bounce and swing innocently. He immediately shrunk away from her when he saw the look on her face.

"Davy's friend?" she asked with menace in her voice, "How so?" Junie moved aggressively closer to Johnny. His eyes shifted between Sal and Junie.

"J-just friends," Johnny stuttered in response.

Sal made a motion to stand, but Junie held up her index finger and said, "Stay." Her eyes never left Johnny's face. "Why would this friend of Davy's have drugs that belong to me?" She interrogated Johnny. "Why does she even know about my drugs?" she demanded.

"We thought—," Sal started to say.

Junie spun on him, and in her eardrum splitting, Urkel voice screeched, "You thought? That is the first problem," Junie walked towards Sal and reached up and grabbed his shirt and pulled him down to the point that his nose was inches from her pert little nose. "Why didn't you tell me about this?" She asked as spit hit Sal in the face.

"Sor-sorry Junie," He started to say, "We just thought that with your mom being sick, we could take care of this and save you the trouble."

"We see how well that worked." Before he could move, she drove her Manolo Blahnik stiletto into his leg just above his knee. Time froze as a horrified look engulfed Sal's face. Unaffected, Junie pulled her foot from the shoe, then tugged on her shoe to release it from the flesh of his leg. Sal cried out in pain as the blood spurted out, covered his jeans, and fell to his knees.

Seeing that Sal's blood was now on the cute sweater she'd put on against the cold winter nights at the beach, she angrily yelled, "Oh great! Look what you've done." She glared at Sal, who sat on the table he'd previously leaned against in pain. "Get my drugs now!" She screeched as she left the room.

As Junie stormed out of the room, Johnny knelt next to Sal and tried to apply pressure to the wound, only to have Sal's hulk-like fist smash into his face from the pain Johnny's pressure on his wounded leg caused him.

Johnny reeled back in pain. "Whadya do that for?" He yelled, holding his nose as blood trailed down his arm. "Was only tryin' to stop you bleedin' to death." He stomped off to look for something to hold to his nose.

***

Lucy moaned as she began to gain consciousness. She couldn't remember where she was and why she hurt so severely through the fog of pain. Then as the fog started to clear, the memories flooded back.

She'd been so surprised to open the door to her home and find them rummaging through all her belongings.

"What are you doing?" Lucy demanded.

Sal turned toward her, holding a leg of one of her dining chairs, and stepped towards her menacingly, "Where is it?" he growled.

"Who are you? Why are you here?" Lucy asked, ignoring his question.

"Where is it?" Johnny parroted.

"Where's what?" Lucy asked as the shock turned to anger. "What have you done to my place?"

"Where is it?" Sal demanded as he moved closer to Lucy.

"You better leave. I'm calling the police," Lucy told him as she retreated and nervously searched her pockets for her phone.

"You're not calling anyone. Where is it?" Sal demanded again as he grabbed her wrist.

"I don't know what it is?" Lucy told him as she tried to pull her wrist out of his grasp.

Sal swung his left hand backward and smashed into Lucy's face; the ring on Sal's hand tore the skin on her cheek. The force of the hit propelled her into the still open front door that banged into the closet behind it. Lucy heard a crack as she crashed into the door but wasn't sure whether it was the door or her. Lucy's body crumpled to the floor as she laid there stunned. She winced as her fingers gingerly traced the open wound on her cheek. She looked at her fingers that covered with blood.

"Get 'er up," Sal told Johnny as he motioned towards Lucy on the floor.

Johnny walked over to Lucy and grabbed her arm to pull her to her feet but wrestled with Lucy's dead weight as she laid on the floor, unable to focus her eyes. "Get up!" He said as he kicked her leg. Lucy cried out in pain when Johnny pulled her hair to move her into a better position so he could lift her. When he placed his hands under her armpits and lifted, she cried out in pain and fought the blackness that tried to envelop her. As she began to drift away, Johnny slapped her face. The shock of the hit startled her, and she could feel the blood run down her chin. As Johnny leaned her against the wall, she thought she'd faint from the pain that seared through her torso. Instead, Lucy stood there, taking in shallow breaths that wouldn't cause her chest to move to avoid the excruciating waves of pain in her shoulder.

As the two monsters continued to break everything, she focused on a picture, almost torn in half, of her parents that had fallen to the floor in all the commotion. She couldn't stop the tears that sprang to her eyes at the peace the sight of them gave her.

"Mom," she mumbled in almost a whisper, "help me."

The longer she focused on the picture, the more tears

began to roll down her face releasing. Finally, Lucy was so focused on her parents that she jumped when she heard Sal speak.

"Where is it?" Sal demanded as he stood over her.

"Where is what?" Lucy forced the words through her swollen lips. "What is it you think I have?" She asked as she tried to understand what he asked through her pain.

"You know what I'm talkin' about," Sal told her as he wrenched her right shoulder down. She cried out in pain.

"I don't know what you want," she cried through swollen lips and tears.

"The package," Johnny said, still standing behind her.

"Package?" Lucy asked, confused.

"Yeah, the package," Johnny said as he put his hand on her forehead while the other circled her shoulder. Then to her horror, she felt the cold steel of a knife pressed against her neck. "Where is the package you took?"

"What package? I didn't take any package," Lucy struggled to say, afraid to move with the knife still pressed to her throat and the pain his arm around her shoulder caused her.

"She doesn't know anything. We're wasting our time," Sal told Johnny.

"I bet she does. She's just not saying. Want I should force her to say?" Johnny asked as he pressed the knife harder against her throat.

Lucy let out a cry of alarm. "I don't know what you're talking about."

"Let's go," Sal told him, "And bring her with us."

"Bring her with us?" Johnny echoed in disbelief. "Why?" He removed the knife from Lucy's throat and released her.

"I don't want to go. Just leave, and I won't say anything," Lucy said.

Sal punched her in the stomach, which caused her to double over in pain. Then he grabbed the hair at the back of her head, pulled it back until she looked in his eyes as he told her, "You'll go where I tell you to go." Lucy coughed, and blood from her split lip sprayed on his white t-shirt.

Lucy shuddered at the memory, which caused another wave of pain to course through her body. She had to get out of there, but how?

Unable to move her right arm or see out of her left eye and barely able to move her lips, she gingerly examined her face and shoulder with her good hand. She fought the waves of nausea as she imagined how they must look. She envisioned herself as the female version of Quasimodo. Luckily, she didn't have a mirror available to either confirm or deny her fears.

Slowly Lucy maneuvered herself into a sitting position so that she could better see where she was. She was on a dirty futon set up against the wall in a drab little room. If she straightened her leg, she could have rested her foot on the handle of the desk that sat against the opposite wall. But, to her surprise, on the desktop was an old traditional phone. Slowly Lucy pushed herself off the futon and hobbled over to the desk. She picked up the handset intending to call 911 but found that she couldn't do them simultaneously with only one good hand. She set the handset down and dialed 911, then picked it up and carefully placed it near her ear, expecting to hear the operator requesting what her emergency was. Instead, there was no dial tone. It was stone silent on the other end.

Lucy set the handset back on the base and looked at the phone's back to follow the cord to see if it was plugged in. But there wasn't a cord for her to follow. "No wonder this doesn't work," she mumbled through her swollen lips.

As Lucy stood near the desk, she saw a door at the end of the small office. Although her knees hurt to move from her tumble down the stairs, her desire to escape her confines was much stronger than the pain. Warily she hobbled over to the door, grasped the doorknob, and twisted. It was locked. She pulled on it as she twisted it in the hope that something would give, but it wouldn't budge.

Lucy bowed her head as she leaned against the door in disappointment. What were they going to do to her? Could she get out? The questions floated around her head through the exhaustion that enveloped her body. She turned and leaned against the door as she scanned the little room for another possibility of escape. But, the floor began to ripple. She blinked her eye a couple of times to stop it, only to have the room start to float about her, then the floor rushed up as the blackness surrounded her once more.

With his head tipped back, Johnny sat in a chair with an old towel he'd found held to his bleeding nose when he heard the thump of Lucy's body falling to the floor. He jumped up and looked out the doorway to see Sal still sitting on the floor where he'd left him, but now two other goons that worked for Junie were helping him stop the bleeding. He turned away from that scene and walked to the door of the room where they'd left Davy's friend.

Johnny tapped on the door. "Hey, you okay in there?" He asked. He waited a couple of seconds for an answer, but none came. So he tapped again and asked, "Hey! You okay?" Still no answer. He stretched his arm to reach above the door frame where Sal had set the key and unlocked the door.

Johnny partially opened the door and saw Lucy's feet nearby, then he pushed it further open and saw her passed out on the floor. "Hey you," he said, "wake up. You should be on the futon, not here." He nervously looked over his shoulder to where Sal was being helped to his feet by the two guys and slipped through the door and shut it without anyone noticing, he hoped. Johnny knelt next to her and felt for a pulse. They didn't need to deal with a body at a time like this, he reasoned to himself. He rolled Lucy onto her back and saw the dark spot on the carpet where the cut on her cheek had bled.

"Oooh," Lucy quietly moaned and began to sob quietly.

"C'mon, we need to get you off the floor," Johnny said quietly and attempted to move her, only to have Lucy cry out in pain. He tried a couple more times, but each time she'd cry. "I should just leave you here," he told her in frustration and stepped over her and moved to open the door.

"I'm sorry," she mumbled as she tried to pull herself up by holding to a corner of a small file cabinet next to the desk. Johnny continued out the door, and Lucy heard it lock behind him.

***

Sitting in the dark of his truck's cab, Davy texted Joel that he was at the warehouse and ready to go in. He knew Joel would be there soon, with other agents leading the raid. He just wanted to have Lucy out and safe before it got too bad—if she were there.

Davy exited his truck and quietly closed the door. He couldn't do anything to alert them to his presence. The nights were turning colder, but he didn't feel it as he checked his pistol to make sure that the clip was full, as well as the two extra clips he always carried. Davy's concern for Lucy's welfare propelled him on to the location of Junie and the others. He couldn't wait for Joel and leave Lucy's life in danger.

Davy walked along the shadows of the street as he progressed towards the small warehouse that he believed to be the target for the night. He could hear the ocean's roar through the early morning sounds. It was just past midnight, and a little further down the beach, he could hear the sounds of people calling one another, singing, cars honking, soft music from different bars—all oblivious to the old warehouse and what it held.

Davy approached the warehouse from the back to avoid being seen. When he turned the corner of the building, he could see that the light over the door was out, leaving the area in darkness—which worked to his benefit this time. As Davy passed by the first darkened window on his right, he stopped to look through the dirt-encrusted glass. *Everyone must be in the back or upstairs breaking down the drugs into smaller packets,* he thought to himself. He continued to the little side door.

Davy set his ear against the door and could hear the faint strains of Oingo Boingo's song *Stay.* Cautiously he looked through the dirty window at the top of the door to confirm no one was around. Guardedly he pushed the hook handle on the door down, but it didn't move. He jiggled it to see if it were caught and would open, but still, it stayed firm. He stepped away and looked at the nearby rubbish to see if he could use something to leverage the handle or bust the lock. Finally, he settled on a rusted old door hinge that had been discarded. It felt strong enough to jimmy the lock. He pushed it between the door and the frame and began to push it down on the lock. He needed to leverage to force the door to open and disengage the lock from its socket. But after multiple attempts with no luck at busting the lock, Davy reverted to the obvious. He broke the glass in the door's window. He made sure there was still no one around before he did it, then he reached his arm through the opening and unlocked the deadbolt from the inside.

Davy had never liked Oingo Boingo, but it was Junie's favorite group, and she played their songs constantly. So when he was in Junie's company, he had to suffer through the loud strains of their tunes played repeatedly. Tonight he was grateful for her music since the volume covered the noise of the glass breaking—at least he hoped it had.

The warehouse was dark, but he could hear faint

sounds of movement from overhead. After the raid, he needed to make sure those people were freed and returned to their countries since most had been kidnapped and brought here under duress.

He began to move between the car skeletons in the different stages of getting refurbished—as a front to the operation—when he felt an arm around his neck in a stranglehold. Surprised, he shoved his elbow into the assailant's ribs with all his might and felt the grasp loosen for a second. That was his cue to turn, still holding the man's arm, and maneuver it behind his back as he pushed him up against one of the cars and banged his head into the hood. As he did so, he heard a tool fall to the ground. The assailant pushed him away, freeing his arm, and stepped back. As he did so, Davy could see from the moonlight that strained through the filthy side window that it was Adam, also known as Snarky.

Snarky was a big Samoan that had recently gotten out of prison. He showed up at the warehouse one day, and Junie hired him as security for the slaves she held upstairs. Snarky swiped at Davy with a knife. Davy countered with a kick.

As Snarky lunged for Davy, his knife tip caught the bottom portion of Davy's t-shirt and tore it, so it hung precariously as Davy skipped back and lost his balance and fell to the ground. As Snarky dove for him, Davy rolled away from his attack onto the lug wrench. Snarky moved to his feet at a speed that surprised Davy for someone that carried the weight Snarky did. Snarky crouched, ready to jump when Davy stood, and with the lug wrench in hand, swung it, hitting Snarky hard on the side of his head. He swiftly dropped to the ground, out cold.

Breathing heavily from the exertion, Davy watched him for a moment to see if he would move, but when Snarky didn't move, Davy leaned against one of the cars and wiped the heel of his hand across his mouth and saw blood on it. He wiped his hand on his pants as he gained his bearings. He had to find Lucy.

Davy squinted in the dark as he wondered where they'd put Lucy. If he remembered correctly, there was an office on the main floor just off this big area where all the cars were, but he'd only seen it once since he usually headed upstairs when he was there because that was where Junie was. Slowly he moved towards the wall the furthest from him when he heard the upstairs door open, and the voices become louder. He crouched down in the dark and waited. He looked over his shoulder to make sure that Snarky was still out of commission. Someone started down the stairs.

"Lobo, get back here."

"I thought I heard something, Jing," Lobo responded.

"It was probably just her stereo," Jing said. "We've gotta get this batch done for delivery tomorrow."

Lobo sighed, "You're probably right." Then the steps retreated up the stairs, and the door closed.

Davy hadn't noticed he'd been holding his breath until he released it and moved forward. As he approached the wall, he stayed close to it as he felt for the hallway, then he found it. His hand reached into space. He turned the corner at the end and went down a small, dark hall, and at the end was a doorway.

Stealthily Davy approached the door, unsure what or who would be on the other side, but he needed to get her out of there if it were Lucy. There was no light coming from under the door, so he turned the knob. It was locked. He turned it again with all his might and heard the wood of the door split; luckily, it was a hollow door that gave way quickly. He cautiously pushed the door inward and entered the dark room. There was no sign of a window, so no chance of any light entering. He had to make sure she wasn't in there before he left. He dug in his pocket for his phone—worried he might have lost it in his fight with Snarky, but it was there. He pulled it out and saw the glass on the front was shattered, but he tapped the flashlight app and gave a sigh of relief when it came on. Slowly he scanned the room but stopped at the figure seated at the end of the futon set against the wall.

She sat with her bare feet on the stained futon with her good arm wrapped about her legs in a ball with her head resting on her knees. When the light from Davy's phone hit her, she looked up. Davy gasped at the sight of her swollen, misshapen face and hair matted with dried blood.

"Lucy?" he asked as he walked towards her. She tried to respond, but nothing came out. Upon seeing him, her feet dropped to the floor, and she moved as if to stand but groaned in pain. Davy stopped her as he sat next to her to assess her injuries. He saw the single tear that rolled down her face from her eye that wasn't swollen shut. She leaned towards him as he tenderly put his arm about her shoulders. His heart swelled with emotion when he saw her and held her in the one-arm hug longer than he should have. He knew at that moment that he loved her, and he couldn't bear the thought of losing her. So he'd do whatever it took to save her.

As he looked at her face, she had a black eye, and he thought her jaw might be broken along with her nose. His hands gently traced along her shoulders and stopped at the broken collar bone on her right side. She let out a cry of pain when he barely touched it.

"What have they done to you?" he asked. "I'm so sorry, I'm so sorry, I'm so sorry," he said as he tried to comfort her by resting his hand on the side of her face that wasn't bruised—since he thought that might be the only place that didn't hurt on her face. Next, he gently felt the back of her head for any injuries. As he did so, she leaned forward and began to whimper as she rested her head on his chest.

He gave a light kiss on her head before he realized it and said, "I'll get you out of here. I promise." The anger that welled up inside him at what they'd done to her fueled his adrenaline.

With his arm gently about her waist, he carefully helped her stand on legs that weren't stable. He could see bruises on her arms where her sleeves were torn away. Her toes and legs were bloodied from whatever torture she'd experienced that night. He held her a little tighter about the waist until she cried in pain, then reluctantly loosened his hold. He couldn't believe they'd beat an innocent person this way but wasn't surprised because of who they were. He should have never allowed their friendship to go beyond the initial hello. Lucy gave a little whimper of pain with each step as they walked to the door. Once there, Davy leaned her against the wall as he opened the door to see if the way were clear. With no one in sight, he put his arm around Lucy to help guide her out. He needed to get her out of the warehouse to safety. Then he'd go back and deal with Sal and Johnny.

Their progress was slow, but they'd just cleared the small hallway and had stepped into the main room when Davy felt excruciating pain at the back of his head.

Chapter 30

Davy fell forward onto the warehouse floor from the force of the blow. He shook his head to clear the flashing lights he saw as he tried to stand but was too dizzy and fell back down. He looked up at the dim lights now turned on in the back part of the warehouse where they were. At first, he couldn't tell who all was there because of the light beyond their heads. Then as he squinted, he could see Sal, Lobo, and Jing immediately around him. After that, he knew there were others he couldn't see.

He saw Lucy raise her one good arm to shield her eyes from the light as she struggled to stand. He reached out to help her as he tried to stand himself.

"Get her back in that room. We'll deal with her later," Davy heard Junie gruffly tell Johnny as Lucy cried out in pain when he roughly lifted her from the floor where she'd fallen.

Davy raised himself to his knees and, with a threatening look, growled, "Take it easy with her." That was all he managed to say before he felt the forceful kick from a pointed-toe cowboy boot and fell onto his side convulsed in pain.

"What do you want us to do with her?" Johnny asked as he held Lucy up.

"Kill her," Junie said without any emotion.

"Don't touch her!" Davy told them defiantly as he awkwardly got to his feet.

"But Boss——," Johnny started to say.

"Boss?" Davy asked, surprised, and looked from Junie to Sal, then Johnny.

"If you can't do it, I'll find someone to take care of both of you!" Junie told him crossly. She turned back to Davy with an innocent smile pasted to her face. A smile that didn't make it to her eyes. "So, Davy honey, where are my drugs?"

"Come on," Johnny said to Lucy as he pulled her back towards the little room.

"Ow!" Lucy weakly said as he pulled her away.

"Boss?" Davy asked Junie directly.

Junie threw her head back and cackled. "Look who figured out who runs this place?" The mugs around her all began to laugh.

"Who's Strega?" Davy asked. "I thought he was the boss."

Junie threw her head back and cackled with glee. "Me! I'm Strega Straniera," Junie said in a perfect Italian accent.

"You?" Davy asked, stunned.

"Si," Junie responded with authority. "Io mi chiamo, Strega." She looked at him with disdain.

Davy watched as Junie's countenance seemed to

changed and become darker as her eyes bored into his. Gone was the southern accent, but still, she sounded like Steve Urkel.

"Where are the drugs?" Junie demanded as she lifted his head by the chin.

Davy heard Lucy's muffled whimpers with each step. He had to hold out until Joel, and the team arrived. "What drugs?" he asked before he was hit from behind and fell back on the floor.

"Hold him up," he heard Sal say. Lobo pulled him to his feet as he tried to get some air and again shake the flashing lights in his head.

Standing with his hands held behind his back. Another set of hands patted him down, found the gun, and handed it to Sal.

"He's clean," the voice said. When Davy looked to see who it was, he saw a tattooed, muscular kid an inch taller than Sal.

"Where you recruiting from now?" Davy asked Sal. "The high schools?" The kid scowled at him.

"Where are the drugs?" Junie barked in her nasal voice, then abruptly stopped as if to calm herself.

Sal tossed Davy's gun between his hands. "You better answer her," he said.

"What if I don't?"

Sal chuckled and said, "After all you two shared? You won't answer her?" Davy groaned as pain shot through is head. *Is it the memory of pretending to love this woman or an actual headache*, he wondered to himself.

"Davy, honey." He heard Junie revert to the small, nasally voice. Her voice was like fingernails on a chalkboard. It had been tough to pretend to be in love with her and hear that voice in his ear. To think he could've cut the head off this snake at any time had he only grasped the power of this nasty cockroach. He'd already sacrificed so much for his country to fight these types of evil; cutting his lips off for having ever touched hers seemed like child's play.

"Answer her!" Sal demanded, followed by a punch in his stomach so hard Davy thought it had gone all the way to his spine. When he didn't answer, Sal backhanded him with a strength that would have spun Davy around had his arms not been held. "Answer her!" He demanded, but Davy only chuckled, then spat at Sal and watched the blood-colored liquid land on his chin, where he wiped it off. "Hold him tight," Sal said as both Jing and Lobo each took an arm. Sal pulled his arm back, coiled to strike, when Junie held up her small claw.

"That's enough for now, Sally," she purred, then turned to Davy. "You don't have them?" Junie asked and moved closer to him.

"Don't have what?" he asked without looking at her.

With a quick jerk of Junie's head in Lucy's direction and without a word said, Sal limped toward the room where Johnny had taken Lucy.

"If you do anything more to her, you'll never get your drugs. I'm warning you," Davy told her.

Snarky, now sporting a gash the length of his face where Davy had hit him with the lug wrench earlier, guffawed, "You're warning us?" He slightly winced and reached up to touch his face before he continued. "You? You ain't in a position to be warning us," Snarky threateningly moved towards him but was stopped by Junie's hand on his firm stomach.

"Ooh, you've been working out," Junie cooed.

"I have boss," he admitted bashfully.

"Pfft," Davy commented. Snarky stepped towards him with menace. Junie held him back and stepped right in front of Davy. She gazed up at him with an angelic look on her angular face.

"Oh honey," Junie said with false sympathy as she reached up to stroke his hair. Davy moved his head to avoid her touch.

Snarky's fist immediately plowed into his stomach in the guise of an uppercut that lifted Davy off his feet. Involuntarily he crunched forward but watched Sal walk into the small office. He attempted to turn in that direction, but Lobo and Jing held him in place. Snarky grabbed a fistful of his hair and yanked it back. "You don't pull away from her touch," he growled into Davy's face. Snarky released his hair when Junie pushed him aside.

"Tell me where the drugs are," Junie told him with a sadistic grin. "Tell me where the drugs are, and I'll let your little—," Junie giggled, "Oops, I almost called her your little girlfriend, but she isn't, is she? Little that is." She giggled again as she perkily stepped closer to Davy while pushing another man who'd joined the group from upstairs out of the way. She sensually ran her fingers along his cheek down to his lips as she smiled and placed her hands on either side of his face, leaned in, and gave him a long deep kiss. Davy struggled to free himself from her grasp.

She wiped Davy's blood from her mouth as she stepped back and said, "So, you tell me where the drugs are, and we will let your," she giggled again, "girlfriend go."

Davy's head jerked up at the sound of a shot. Junie's eyes widened in mock surprise. "Oops! I guess it's too late." She gave him an innocent look, shrugged her tiny shoulders, and retreated. "Get my drugs," she commanded Snarky as she walked towards the stairs where her living quarters were.

"Why's it too late? Just let her go," Davy demanded.

Junie stopped and turned towards Davy. She casually leaned her weight on one heel and rested her little claw on her hip. "You know we can't do that."

"Why not? She doesn't know anything about the drugs," Davy stated.

Junie put her hand to her lips in mock surprise. "I think it's too late. But give us the drugs and find out," she smiled big.

"You b—," Davy began to say before Snarky's fist collided once more with his face, and the force of it almost caused the two thugs to lose their grip. Junie laughed.

"Don't you love me anymore, honey?" she asked as the clank of her heels echoed around the walls on her approach to Davy again.

"Don't swear," Snarky grunted as he pointed his index finger as emphasis. As Davy coughed and blood droplets sprayed onto Junie's white top.

Junie screamed, "You've ruined my top! This is the second one today," she stopped abruptly as if to collect herself, took a couple of deep breaths and gave Davy an innocent look, shrugged her shoulders, and turned to leave. But as she passed by Snarky, she stopped, gave him a loving smile, and said. "Snarky honey, please persuade him to tell us where the drugs are." Then she turned to leave.

"Let her go," Davy called to her retreating figure. Then a second shot sounded from the small room. Davy used all his strength to break free from Lobo and Jing. He needed to get to that room and stop Sal's slaughter of Lucy.

Junie stopped mid-step and turned back around. She looked at Davy as if in contemplation. After what seemed minutes but was probably mere seconds, she walked towards him with her stiletto's clacking on the floor with each step. Her petite frame pushed Snarky out of the way so that she stood in front of Davy. With a flip of her blonde ponytail, she let her head fall back and cackled aloud before she looked at Davy and sighed, "Give us the drugs."

Junie gave him a side glance before she turned her attention to observe Sal as he emerged from the small hall that led to the little room. He casually tucked the revolver into the back of his pants and gave Davy a big grin.

"No!" Davy yelled, then charged Sal as he passed but was stopped by Snarky's fist into his stomach again as Lobo and Jing maintained their grip on him even as he fell to the ground. Within seconds they hauled him back to a standing position.

"Where's Lucy?" He demanded.

Junie looked at him curiously and said, "You seem to care about this big girl. If you give us the drugs, then maybe we won't kill her, but only maim her."

"Tsk, tsk, tsk," Sal shook his head as he passed by Davy.

"Oh dear, it may be too late," Junie said to Davy before she looked at Sal, and they both began to laugh.

"If she's dead, you're next," Davy threatened.

Sal began to laugh, then the rest of the group laughed. "Oh, am I?" Sal asked, standing in front of Davy. Davy tried to lunge for him again, Lobo and Jing struggled to hold him by his arms, and Sal hit him with a left jab, followed by an uppercut that, if he hadn't been held in place, would have flipped him over. Davy winced in pain but didn't make a sound. "Just tell us where the drugs are, and we'll let you go."

"We're not gonna let him go, are we? He knows too much," One of the younger guys said.

"Shut the frick up," Sal told him without his eyes leaving Davy's.

Davy laughed, "I see Junie still doesn't allow swearing." He laughed out loud, which angered Sal.

"Shut up," Sal said and moved towards menacingly.

"Frick you! Darn, darn, darn," Davy imitated Sal as Herman Munster and laughed. He wanted to fight Sal more than anything.

Sal's face darkened with anger. He didn't like being mocked. Because of his size, rarely did anyone have the nerve to do so, but Davy, bloodied, restrained by two men, and in no position to protect himself from incoming assaults, didn't recoil from him. Instead, he poked the bear.

Sal stood in front of Davy, at his full height of six

feet six inches, leaned in close, and in a menacing tone said, "Where are the drugs?"

"Frick you," Davy responded emotionless. Sal squinted in response, then head-butted him. Davy's head fell back as the front of his face exploded in more pain.

"Freeze! Federal Agents!" Davy heard Joel yell from somewhere in the warehouse. Immediately Lobo and Jing released Davy, who fell to his knees as blood spurted from his nose.

Instantly it sounded as though a train was roaring through as a rush of agents entered the warehouse. Agents' voices could be heard from every direction as they gave orders to the inhabitants.

"Everyone on the ground! Now!" Joel yelled, and other agents echoed the same line in other areas. Then Joel yelled, "Simpson report!"

"We got a runner," another agent called as a rush of workers tried to leave the warehouse-like cockroaches when a light comes on.

"Frank, secure it!"

Within moments, the agents began to call from all different directions. "Backroom secure!"

"Kitchen secure!"

"Upstairs secure!"

"Office secure!"

"Apartment secure!"

Joel rushed to Davy, "You look awful!"

"Thanks. What took you so long?" Davy asked.

"Logistics," Joel said.

"Did they get Sal?" Davy asked.

Joel called to the agent Simpson, "You guys secure

Sal Vortelli?" Sampson shook his head.

"That means he's hiding," Davy said.

"Any sign of Strega Straniera?" Joel asked.

"Yeah, you'll find him in the shape of a little pint-size woman that goes by Junie."

Joel looked at him in disbelief before he asked, "What? So you've been dating him this whole time?" Joel snickered at Davy's face.

Davy scowled. "Strega Straniera translates to an evil foreigner. Not whether it is a man or woman," he told them.

"I think by the name ending in an 'a', it denotes the sex—that of female in this case," Sampson interjected. Davy and Joel looked at each other.

"You didn't know that?" Joel asked Davy.

Davy shrugged and responded, "I'm not Italian. I'm Welsh."

"Hey, boss," one of the agents called as he approached Joel, having just come from the little room that Lucy had been returned to earlier, "there are two dead bodies in the room over here!"

Davy felt his heart lurch, "No!" was all he could say as he knelt on the floor.

Joel looked from Davy to the agent and asked, "Two bodies? Male or female?"

"One of each, sir," the agent told him. Joel looked at Davy with concern. *Can he handle another loss like this?* He wondered.

"Give me your gun?" Davy told him as he stood. Joel paused, concerned as to what Davy would do. "I'm not asking," he said as he grabbed it. "Sal took mine. Lucy is the female in that," he said as he pointed towards the small hall. "Make sure her body is retrieved."

Joel grabbed Davy's arm and said, "We've got everyone."

"Not Vortelli," he said.

"Maybe you should wait and have a medic look at you first," Joel suggested.

"I've got a score to settle," Davy told Joel.

"Leave it for another day. You know we'll catch him," Joel tried to placate Davy.

Davy disengaged his arm from Joel's grasp and moved towards the stairs before Joel could stop him.

Joel walked towards the small room Davy had mentioned while the other agents moved the caught gang members outside. He stepped over the lifeless body of a large Samoan with a gash down the side of his face and proceeded to the small room. Joel opened the doorway to see two bodies lying on the floor in a pool of blood. One was the lifeless body of a smaller man lying across the thighs of a tall, badly beaten woman. He could only assume it was Lucy since Davy had said she'd be in this room.

Where only the male showed signs of a broken nose, the woman was far worse. With one eye swollen shut, broken jaw and collar bone, multiple bruises, and a chest wound—it seemed as if her attack were personal. Although Davy hadn't said it, Joel could tell she had been more than just a casual interest for him. He hated that Davy would have another personal loss like this.

After he holstered his gun, he set his walkie-talkie to the side and knelt to check the pulse of the male for any sign of life, but there was none. Expecting the same outcome with the woman, he pressed his first two fingers against her neck, expecting the same response, but there was a faint beat. Surprised, he grabbed the walkie-talkie.

"Didn't you check for a pulse when you first came in here?" Joel demanded of the agent that had followed him into the room.

"I did, sir, but didn't feel anything," he responded.

"I need medics in here now!" he shouted into the radio. As he lifted the corpse of the male off Lucy, he heard a faint sigh. He stared at Lucy with alarm. "Stat! Get them in here asap!" He stood and quickly exited the room to the hallway so he could direct the medics.

"Lucy," Joel spoke softly to her as he held her good hand in his. "Can you hear me?"

Lucy gave a soft moan.

"Stay with us," Joel said.

Lucy moaned as she struggled to open her good eye. "Davy?" She muttered through swollen lips. "Davy," she said as a tear escaped her eye.

Joel gulped the emotion that rose in his throat down as he stared into the bruised and broken face, "It's not Davy, it's Agent Smith."

"Davy," she whimpered and softly sobbed.

"Lucy, we're going to get you out of here and to a hospital. Just hold on," he told her as he moved aside to make room for the two EMTs that crashed into the small office with their gear.

With relief, Joel watched as the two EMTs performed the necessary procedures to stabilize Lucy. He thought of Davy and how pleased he would be that she was still alive. Soon the EMTs had the semi-conscious Lucy on a gurney with her neck and right arm in protective wraps and an oxygen mask that lightly covered her face. When they initially rolled her out of the warehouse, she whimpered with each bump. Joel walked with the gurney and made sure they moved slowly and carefully. He didn't leave until she was inside the ambulance, the doors were closed, and he watched it speed away with lights flashing and siren blaring.

With Lucy on her way to the hospital, Joel sighed relief. He observed the organized chaos among the agents and perps they led to the waiting patrol cars that would take them to the police station for processing. Joel watched in surprise as a very tiny woman with a blonde ponytail was escorted by Fred, one of his agents. He watched as she bit Fred's hand then kicked and spewed words that he hadn't heard since his time in the Navy. Soon she'd kicked off her four-inch heels, and Fred handed her off to the female officer that put her in the waiting squad.

"Be careful with that one. She's the head of this ring," Joel informed Fred as he held his bitten hand and wrapped a handkerchief around the bite wounds.

"That little thing?" Fred asked.

"Yup. Put her into an interview room once you get her to the station. I'll deal with her personally before the FBI takes over."

"You got it," Fred told him as he stood next to Joel, holding his hurt hand.

"You better get that looked at," Joel told him. "Maybe even get a rabies shot," Joel told him.

Fred gave a slight chuckle and said, "Yeah. You might be right." Then, Fred headed to an ambulance parked to the side of all the cars.

Joel watched his agents leading the gang members from the warehouse. Then when no more people exited the warehouse's main entrance, Joel stopped Agent Simpson, who trailed out at the end, and asked, "Is it contained?"

"I believe so, sir," Agent Simpson told him.

Have you seen Jones?" Joel asked while he continued to scrutinize every section of the vicinity for any sign of Davy.

"The last I saw, he was going upstairs."

"And you haven't seen him since then?" Joel asked, concerned.

"No, sir, but I wasn't looking for him either," the agent answered as the perp he held began to struggle against his bindings. "I better get him in a car."

Joel nodded absentmindedly as he focused on the warehouse. "I'm going in. I think Jones is still in there," he told the agent. He took a couple of steps towards the warehouse when it exploded.

The force from the explosion threw everyone to the ground. They continued to shield themselves from the debris flying through the air. There were small fires sporadically throughout and around the property and on some of the cars.

As Joel rose from the ground, he saw that the perp and the agent had been blown backward onto the asphalt. The perp immediately tried to run but was tackled by the female officer who had just put Junie in one car. The officer held onto the perp until the agent took over and pulled him over to another waiting vehicle. Junie's hysterical screams could be heard as burning debris landed on her car. One of the sheriffs at the scene pulled her from the car. He began to walk her to another patrol car but was stopped by Agent Simpson.

"I'll take her. This one needs special care," Agent Simpson told the Sheriff.

"Whatever you say," the Sheriff responded as he handed Junie to Agent Simpson.

Junie began to swear at him in Italian. When that didn't work, she would spit at Agent Simpson and try to bite his hands. Calmly he leads her to a waiting car and puts her inside.

Joel looked with disbelief at the warehouse. Had Davy been inside, or did he get out? Did he just lose one of his oldest friends? It was at times like this that he hated his job.

***

Annie sat in the chair next to Lucy's bed in her hospital room, reading an e-book. She'd been there most days, not that it mattered if she were or not since Lucy was in a medically induced coma. Her trauma had been so extreme that putting her in a coma was the only way the doctors knew to let her body heal quicker.

Annie was thankful that her friend was still alive but knew she had a long road ahead. She hadn't realized just how serious the danger had been for Lucy until she received a call from the local FBI asking her to come to the hospital.

Once there, she met Agent Joel Smith. He explained that their Forensics had managed to unlock Lucy's phone for them to find the next of kin. Luckily, Lucy had listed Annie as her emergency contact, so he called her.

Annie was horrified when she first saw Lucy lying in the hospital bed with all the bruises, swelling, and tubes running out of just about every visible space. She stood there frozen in place until she felt a warm hand on the small of her back. She looked over to see a nice-looking man, about six feet tall, with a full beard and a baseball cap set on his head backward.

"I take it you're a friend of Ms. Lyman's?" He asked.

"Uh. . .yeah," Annie answered with a trembling voice.

"I called you. I'm Agent Smith," he said. Annie looked at him confused, then he continued, "I worked with Agent Jones."

Annie did a double-take then asked, "You worked with Agent Jones?" Annie couldn't hide the shock she felt at hearing him use the past tense to describe his connection to Davy. "Where is he? Why'd he let this happen?" Annie asked him with suppressed anger.

"I think we need to talk," Agent Smith said as he led her over to a couple of chairs set in Lucy's room. After they were seated in the chairs, he continued, "You were the one that called Agent Jones about your friend kidnapping, right?" He searched her face in earnestness.

Annie nodded.

"We're trying to contact Lucy's brother. But unfortunately, I can't tell you much more of what happened since you aren't the next of kin," he gently explained to her.

Annie looked at him, appalled. "You can't tell me?! I'm the one that called you guys. I saw her leave. I saw the injuries she got from those thugs, and you can't tell me?!" Annie's big blue eyes blazed at the audacity he had not to inform her of her friend's experience.

"I'm sorry, but we—," Agent Smith began only to be interrupted.

A younger agent stepped in the door frame and said, "Sir, Director Janssen is here.

Agent Smith, with a surprised look on his face, stood. "Excuse me," was all he said as he exited through the door.

"Director, I'm surprised you're here," Annie heard Agent Smith say. She stood and walked towards the door so she could listen to their conversation more clearly.

"How is she?" Director Janssen asked.

Annie peaked her head around the door, saw Agent Smith, the younger agent, and saw who she assumed must be Director Janssen standing in a small circle a couple of feet away from the door.

"She'll live, thankfully, but it's going to be a big bill the government will need to cover," Agent Smith told the Director with frankness.

The Director nodded his head as he looked down at his feet.

"Any word on Jones?" Agent Smith asked.

The Director looked at him gravely and said, "It's not good."

The group stood in silence until Agent Smith asked,

"Does his family know?"

"Not yet," Director Janssen answered crisply.

Agent Smith gave a very thick sigh, then, with a deep intake of breath, said, "We have her friend that called us about the kidnapping in her room now," Agent Smith said with a nod of his head in her direction.

"Does her family know?" Director Janssen asked.

"We're still trying to reach her brother, but it seems he's out of the country right now," Agent Barnes interjected. The other two nodded their heads in concurrence.

"I need to get back to Washington," Director Janssen informed the two agents. "I just came here to see for myself how she was doing since I have to report on it." That said, he walked toward the room entrance. Annie quickly returned to the chair she'd occupied before Agent Smith had left the room.

Director Janssen walked into the room with an air of concerned importance. He stood next to Lucy's bed and stared at the freeway of tubes going in and out of her body. Then he turned and saw Annie, for the first time.

"You're the one who called Agent Jones?" He asked in a sympathetic tone.

"Yes," Annie's answer was barely audible.

"I'm sorry for your friend. But rest assured that the government will make sure she has everything she needs to get better," He put his hand on Annie's shoulder, gave it a light squeeze, then said, "We're sorry for her loss." That said, he turned and walked out the door with Joel and Agent Barnes right behind him.

Joel and Agent Barnes watched as the Director

entered the waiting car. Then, as it drove away, they relaxed.

"Sir, why would the Director come from Washington to see Ms. Lyman?" Agent Barnes enquired.

"I'm not sure," Joel answered with puzzled concern, then turned and re-entered the hospital door.

Weeks later, as Annie sat vigil in Lucy's room, she thought back to the last conversation she'd had with Agent Smith.

"Any news on Davy?" Annie asked Joel as he sat next to her. He usually showed up once a week to check on Lucy's progress. Today, for some unknown reason, he'd chosen to hang around longer than expected.

"No," he responded without looking at her.

Annie huffed. "I can't believe he doesn't come to visit the woman he called a friend, especially when she was on the brink of death." Annie gave Joel a side glance to see his reaction.

Joel only gave a low growl. Annie looked at him in disbelief.

"What?" he asked defensively.

"What happened to Davy?" Annie asked, turning towards Joel.

Joel shook his head. "I'm not at liberty to say." Then, without another word, Joel rose from the chair and left the room. Annie stared after him, stunned at his reaction.

Annie looked at Lucy lying peacefully in her bed. The swelling in her face had gone down. Her jaw had been reconstructed, her collar bone set. When Sal had shot Johnny, the bullet had gone through him and into her thigh, then he'd followed up with shooting her in the chest. Thinking he'd killed her; he'd left her after that. Either her will to live or her guardian angel had saved her. The bullet had missed all vital organs.

"It's gonna kill Lucy to find out he's dead when she comes to," Annie said resignedly.

Chapter 31

Six Months Later

Lucy struggled to open the library door. She used her good hand while the other hand rested in a sling across her body – her collar bone was still healing. The effort it took her to open the door caused her body to scream from the pain she still felt as she recovered. *I'm way too old for this*, she told herself with a sigh.

She'd been in the hospital for months before she was allowed home. The doctors decided that she couldn't go home until she could care for herself. Once at home, she survived on pre-made protein shakes that she'd stocked in her pantry.

She'd lost so much weight in the hospital that all her clothes hung on her. She didn't care what she ate as long as she had something to take with the necessary pain meds. She was grateful that the mountain and the mole, the nicknames she and Annie had given to Sal and Johnny, hadn't ruined the things in her pantry—that was another miracle.

During surgery, the bullets in her chest and thigh had

been removed. Both had missed all vital organs. Luckily, the one in her leg had missed the main artery by a mere centimeter. Otherwise, she could have bled out before they'd have found her. So, now she walked with a slight limp since her leg was still healing after the surgery. Her doctor told her that her guardian angel must've worked overtime that night.

Her face was still a little swollen as her jaw continued to heal from the reconstruction and, her eye had only been bruised from her broken nose. The packing was taken out of her nose with the instructions that she would not bump it. Every now and then, her nose would start to bleed—so she'd gotten into the habit of having a tissue at hand to catch it before it ruined any more of her clothes. Her collar bone was so badly broken, a plate was inserted to connect the bone—just another surgery she had to live through. Her arm was still weak, thus the sling she still had to wear, but the physical therapy was helping it grow stronger.

This experience had taught her a lesson. She should have never let her curiosity get the better of her or let her heart decide what actions she needed to take. Instead, she'd stepped into something way over her head.

She had never felt such pain before—or had hoped her life would end to escape the excruciating pain. The last thing she remembered was the little guy standing in front of her as Sal punched him in the face to get him to move. When Johnny had fallen back due to the force of Sal's hit, Lucy had fallen to the floor, too weak to withstand someone's body bumping into hers, let alone giving their life for her.

"You can't kill her. She's innocent," Johnny said as he tried to reason with Sal.

"Get out of my way," Sal told him, unmoved by Johnny's plea.

"C'mon, Sal. You don't have to do this. I'll keep her quiet. The boss doesn't need to know."

"Get out of the way, Johnny. She wants her dead," Sal said determinedly.

"You don't have to do this," Johnny repeated as he stood in front of Lucy, who had collapsed to the floor.

"Move," Sal pointed Davy's Sig at Johnny, but he didn't move. *Fine time for him to grow a backbone*, Sal thought to himself.

"C'mon S—," Johnny started to say before he dropped to the floor with a bullet through the heart. Sal noticed Lucy's body jerk a second after Johnny's body fell on top of her. He limped over to where Lucy laid under Johnny and looked at her still body. She opened her good eye and looked at the huge mountain of a man with a look of sheer terror in her eye.

Sal pointed the gun at Lucy with a sneer on his face and thought how poetic for her to die by Davy's gun. "Here's a little something from your boyfriend," Sal gave a cynical chuckle as he first aimed the gun at her head. Then, without understanding why he did it, he moved his aim lower at her chest then squeezed the trigger. Again, her body bounced when the bullet hit her, but not too much since the weight of Johnny's dead body weighed it down.

Lucy shook her head as if to rid herself of that memory. Inwardly she mourned the thought that a man she didn't know or trusted, in the end, tried to save her life only to lose his. Although she'd never be able to thank him for his sacrifice—whether noble or not—it was still an act of bravery for him to try and fight Sal.

Months later, when Lucy was finally sent home from the hospital, she'd dreaded opening her door to a place that held so many painful memories now. She feared those memories would flood in when she walked in the first time. But to her surprise, her place had been remodeled in the time she'd been gone. She saw that the walls were no longer the soft grey but had been painted a cheery, sunny yellow with a feeling of relief. And all her furniture had been replaced; gone were the torn cushions or broken chairs and table or the turned over refrigerator, only to be replaced by lovely vintage furniture and a new refrigerator. She loved the look and feel of the place.

It turned out that the people from her church had heard about the incident, and, in the months she'd been hospitalized, they'd been able to repair everything—even the photos that had been ruined. In addition, someone had been kind enough to bring a picture of her parents to sit beside her bed so that when she came out of the coma, she would see their faces first.

But now, she needed to get her life back to normal—or as normal as she could until she was completely healed and could go back to work. She hadn't heard from Davy, so she didn't know if he were alive or not. Whenever she'd ask Annie or Joel, they always avoided the question. Her heart began to tell her that he'd been killed at the warehouse, but she couldn't deal with it then, so she'd put it in the back of her mind until she was out of the hospital and felt strong enough to deal with the loss. Now she was out of the hospital, and her thoughts and memories were on a continual loop of her time with Davy. She couldn't avoid the sorrow she felt at this loss any longer.

"Oh, my goodness," Mrs. Gable quietly cried as she saw Lucy enter through the door a young boy had run to open for her when he saw her struggle. "What happened to you?" Lucy could see the horror in Mrs. Gable's face.

"I had a little accident," Lucy said with a grimace. It still hurt to move her jaw too much.

"Oh dear," Mrs. Gable's voice shook with checked emotion. "Can I help you?" She asked as she hurried around from behind her desk.

Lucy slowly moved towards the table where she'd met Davy. "I would like to go sit at my table," she managed to say very slowly. Mrs. Gable walked beside her and helped her sit at the empty table. "Thank you," she told Mrs. Gable.

"You're quite alright. Now, if you need anything, please just call out." Mrs. Gable gently rubbed her hand along Lucy's shoulders. Lucy winced at the touch, although it felt good to feel the human touch that wasn't the prodding and poking touch of a doctor. Her eyes misted to know that she wasn't alone, and she could feel her body begin to relax now that she sat in her spot at their table.

"I don't want to be a problem," Lucy said as she tried to hold back the emotion she'd held inside for so long. When she was in the hospital, she refused to let her feelings get the better of her. She couldn't afford any pity parties; she had too much work to do to get better.

"Oh, pish! You are no problem," Mrs. Gable said as she began to walk away. "Just call out. I'll keep an eye on you."

"Thanks." Lucy wanted to smile, but it hurt too much.

Lucy sat at the same table she'd shared with Davy, alone, remembering the fun and scary times she'd experienced with him. She'd never expected it but should have known something like this would happen if she were involved in the life of a hero. Although, he would never admit to being a hero.

***

Because Lucy was out on sick leave, she had nowhere she needed to be and found her days were too long and tedious just sitting in her home.

"Where are you?" Lori asked.

Lucy held the phone to her ear as she cautiously sat down on the bench outside of the library double doors, "I'm at the library." Lori had moved away over a year ago—long before the real excitement began, to be able to help her mother. But when she had learned about Lucy being in the hospital, she had called regularly to check on her progress.

"Again? Weren't you there yesterday?" Lori said in a bored tone.

Lucy gave a slight chuckle, "Yeah. I'm here every day."

"Have you seen him?" Lori asked hesitantly.

"Not a sign. I don't know if I ever will," Lucy

confessed with a slight tremor in her voice.

"Why?" Lori asked, concerned. Lucy could hear Bingo barking in the background, "Hush baby," Lori told him.

"I hope that was to the dog and not me," Lucy said as she made a feeble attempt at humor. It was good to be talking to Lori after so long.

Lori laughed, "Yes, it was for the dog, not you." They sat in silence for a moment, then Lori asked again, "So, you haven't heard from him?"

"I don't even know if he's alive. Every time I try to get an answer, they change the subject."

"They? They who?" Lori asked.

"Annie and Joel," Lucy told her.

"I'm sorry if he's gone, but he was quite the mystery man. Maybe this is for the better," Lori suggested to her. She heard Lucy groan. "Are you okay?" Lori asked, alarmed.

"Yeah. I'm just too old for this kind of stuff."

"You're not too old; you're just reckless," Lori told her.

"Why couldn't I have the typical romance?" Lucy asked with a sigh.

"I'm not sure those exist," Lori answered. "Did you think that snooping around his home would make it a typical romance?" she asked.

"No, I just thought I could rescue him from his life of crime," Lucy admitted with an embarrassed laugh. "No one is an island, whether they're a hero or not, and everyone needs someone,"

"What made you think you could rescue him? You

were totally out of your element there."

"Well. . . I knew he was in trouble, and I thought I could do something. I mean, they always do something in the movies; Bruce Willis always comes out the hero at the end, maybe the worse for wear, but it always works out."

Lori began to chuckle and said, "Okay, there's your big problem; this wasn't a movie. You didn't have a stunt double."

"Tell me about it," Lucy said dryly.

"So, to change the subject, how often do you go to the library?" Lori asked, "and what do you do while you're there, besides pouring salt in your wounds."

"Ha!" Lucy responded cynically.

"Well, it is kind of sadistic to keep going back there when you know he isn't coming."

"I don't know that. Unless you know something and haven't told me," Lucy said with a tinge of hope in her voice.

"Nope, I'm sorry, sweetie, I don't know anything," Lori reassured her.

Lucy gave a sad, shaky sigh.

"You didn't answer my question, though," Lori reminded her.

"Which question was that?"

"How often are you going to the library?"

"Every day. It's free, and what else am I going to do with my time?"

"Why don't you write about your adventure?" Lori suggested.

"I'm not sure I'm ready to live through it again. Right now, it is just bits and pieces," Lucy confessed to

Lori.

"It's going on three months, and you've gone to the library every day," Lori stated.

"Yeah? So? I just feel like I should be here," Lucy confided.

"Really? When are you going back to work?"

"When the doctor releases me." Another silence crept into their conversation until Lucy said, "Well, thanks for calling. It's always good to chat with you, but I am gonna head into the library now."

"Hey, Luce?"

"Yeah?"

"Please don't make the library your crypt as you wait for a man who might never show up again," Lori said sincerely.

Lucy sighed and said, "I won't. I'm only trying to come to terms with the idea I may have had a chance with this guy. A man who I thought was perfect for me, and true to my luck, he disappeared—maybe even died." Lucy couldn't hide her disappointment.

"Hey Luce, I gotta take this call. I'll talk to ya later, k?" Lori said, then hung up.

Lucy sat on the bench for a couple of minutes, thinking about what Lori said. She knew she needed to forget about Davy and move on. She prayed there was another someone out there for her; Someone that could see her for who she really was no matter her age. Her mood began to get as dark as a cloud moved in front of the sun, but then the shadow moved past the sun, and her spirit seemed to lift as she felt its warmth on her face. The heat from the sun began to melt the aches away.

Lucy stood and walked toward the double doors of the library. No longer did she need the aid of a cane, and her arm was only encased in a light sling. She leaned against the door and let the weight of her much lighter body push the door open. Mrs. Gable smiled at her from behind her desk.

"You are looking better each day," She said to Lucy.

"Thanks, Mrs. Gable. I'm feeling better. I should be able to go back to work soon, I hope."

"That's good, but we will sure miss seeing you here each day."

Lucy gave a slight laugh and said, "Oh, I'll still be around. I love the library and all the wonderful books."

"I'm glad." Mrs. Gable said as she turned to help a young girl who had approached the desk.

Lucy walked to her regular table and looked longingly at the empty chair that Davy had once possessed. She pulled out her laptop and set it on the table but wasn't sure if she'd use it or read a book.

Yes, the dream had started up again but not as often as it had before this whole adventure had started. In the dream, she still sat at the cubicle, but now she preferred the table. She no longer let the dream run her life. She'd concluded that it was only a dream, and if there were a stranger, then he'd have to just have to guts to approach her—whether he was friend or foe. No longer would she spend her evenings reading the same page repeatedly; instead, she would either work on her computer or read a book of her choice. Besides, her heart was still healing from the loss of her hero.

"Would you like me to get you a book today," Baby

Jane asked her.

"No thanks. I think I'll get it myself. But thanks for the offer." Lucy said with a smile. Baby Jane had surprised Lucy with how kind she was to her since her hospital stay. She had turned out to be quite a sweet person, and the funny part was her name really was Jane. Lucy chuckled and wished Davy were there to share the laugh. She really did miss Davy Jones—like the Monkees.

Lucy walked over to the row she had approached so often before she'd met Davy. Even though she still sporadically had the dream, she didn't think about the stranger whose face she couldn't see. Now in the dream, it was always Davy she saw. But the dream was just that—a dream. *Did she even need a dream when she'd known a guy like Davy?*

She found the now familiar book 'The Sands of Crime' and passed it to the next one in the series and returned to the table. With her resolve to move on, she was determined to lose herself in a good cozy mystery. She wasn't a widow, and she'd be an idiot to stop living her life because of a man she'd only known for a short while.

Feeling energized, she turned to the first page of chapter one and began to read. Then she turned to the second page and had only read a couple of lines when she stopped. She couldn't deny it. She'd felt the undeniable tingle up her spine. The hairs on her arms and the tiny hairs on her neck stood up. She shivered. Gingerly her fingers tips traced the goosebumps on the back of her neck. She hadn't expected that to happen. It shouldn't happen; she was doing nothing like in the dream. Her hand that held the now turned page began to tremble—followed by the full-body shiver that started to encompass her. With her shallow breath, her only sign of life, she sat like a stone. She felt as though she would cry if this turned out to be a foe. She wasn't ready for another adventure like the last one. She had waited so long for this; she sat there in fear of what would happen next.

Slowly she looked over her shoulder down at the carpet—as in her dream—gradually, her eyes crept along the carpet, then stopped at a pair of brown shoes. Lucy took shallow breaths as her eyes slowly moved from the brown shoes up along the tan pant leg. Her mind screamed *This can't be happening! This isn't supposed to be real!* Her lungs deflated more with each breath as her eyes crawled up the leg to the knee, then to the brown belt with the silver buckle. Lucy desperately wanted to look away, but her eyes refused to shift. So, she continued onward as though she trudged through quicksand.

Her eyes moved past the silver buckle to the familiar light blue shirt. Methodically, they climbed button by button at a snail-like pace until they reached the open collar that exposed the muscular tan neck. With quivering breaths, she continued to the chin—still denied the speed she desperately desired. For the first time, she saw the lips that smiled warmly, then the nose. Finally, the glue that had held her back released her like a slingshot, and she saw the eyes—eyes that sparkled with pleasure. Her vision blurred from tears that filled her eyes as she gazed into the beautiful face of the man of her dreams.

"Davy!" she cried.

THE END

ABOUT THE AUTHOR

L. K. Lawrence is a West Coast author that has finally found a way to share her imagination with others. Her passion is to show women of substance who have a sense of humor and whom her audience can relate to, whether it is a bittersweet love story, a romance, a thriller, or a cozy mystery

Made in the USA
Columbia, SC
24 December 2021

51807035R00238